"A sweeping, majestic tale of love and bravery, evil and goodness . . . The scope and flow of [McIntosh's] writing, her meticulous research and the detailed description in this taut novel set up an excellent introduction to what will be a trilogy. A truly grand vision brought to life on the page."

—*Good Reading* (Australia)

"A magnificent setting distinguishes this first of a new fantasy trilogy . . . [S]trong characters and an enticing plot bode well for future installments."

—*Publishers Weekly*

"Two words on the cover ('Fiona McIntosh') always let me know that I'm in for a good read."

—Robin Hobb

"McIntosh's work has always been grittier than most [epic fantasy]."

—*Guardian* (London)

"South Australia's queen of fantasy."

—*Advertiser* (Adelaide)

Also by FIONA MCINTOSH

THE PERCHERON SAGA

Odalisque

THE QUICKENING TRILOGY

Myrren's Gift
Blood and Memory
Bridge of Souls

EMISSARY

Book Two
of The Percheron Saga

FIONA McINTOSH

An Imprint of HarperCollins*Publishers*

Designed by Mia Risberg
Map by Matt Whitney

Library of Congress Cataloging-in-Publication Data

McIntosh, Fiona, 1960–
    Emissary : book two of the Percheron saga / Fiona McIntosh.
        p. cm.
"Originally published in 2006 by Voyager, an imprint of HarperCollins Australia"—T.p. verso.
    ISBN: 978-0-06-089906-6 (trade pbk. : alk. paper)
    1. Kings and rulers—Succession—Fiction.   2. Harems—Fiction.
I. Title.

PR9619.4.M386E65 2007
813'.6—dc22

                                                            2007029814

07   08   09   10   11   ID/RRD   10   9   8   7   6   5   4   3   2

For Mum and Dad—50 years!
. . . amazing.

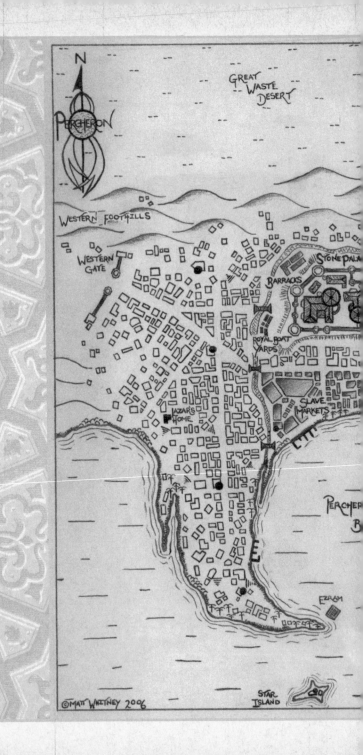

EASTERN FOOTHILLS

EASTERN GATE

TARID'S HOUSE

EX.

THE BAZAAR

BELOTH'S TABLE

SPICE MARKETS

CARAVAN DISTRICT

SEA TEMPLE OF LYANA

THE
FARANEL SEA

LEGEND
STAIRWAY
MINARET
PALM GROVE
BEACH
ROCKS
BRIDGE

ACKNOWLEDGMENTS

A trip to the Gulf this year allowed me to ride a camel into the golden sands of the desert on the outskirt of Dubai, as well as to learn more about Bedouin settlements, to experience belly dancing under the stars surrounded by the shifting dunes, and to explore a traditional spice souk, filled with sensory goodies. It was a boon for the story of Percheron.

Many people make a vital contribution to my books but suddenly there's so many of you that I'm hoping a simple list will suffice. So . . . my thanks to:

Pip Klimentou, Sonya Caddy, Gary Havelberg, Judy Downs, Matt Whitney, Trent Hayes, Apolonia Niemerowski, Bryce Courtenay, and Robin Hobb. Plus, of course, Kate Nintzel at Eos for her editing and friendship as we move through this adventure, Greg Bridges for his amazing art again, and to my agent, Chris Lotts, for his partnership and support.

My thanks to all the wonderful librarians who have involved

me in their communities this past year and encouraged their readers to give fantasy and specifically Percheron a go and the nomination for the international literary award in Dublin is a most unexpected surprise. And special thanks to the booksellers, at the coalface, who do such a terrific job of handselling sf to an eager community, especially that amazing man Steve Hubbard in Minnesota and the lovely gang at Borderlands in San Francisco that I was fortunate to meet last year.

Finally, heartfelt gratitude to Ian, Will, and Jack for their endless patience in losing me to other worlds.

EMISSARY

PROLOGUE

The slave held a painted silk parasol above the woman's head as she glided along, her face turned out toward the glistening Faranel. It was still only early spring, but the women of the harem preferred to keep their complexions pale, unblemished by the harsh Percheron sun. This woman was slim, taller than she had been when the slave first remembered seeing her and much more curvy, but her hair—loosely plaited today—remained its familiar brightly golden color. The eunuch slave had gotten to know her well this past eleven moons and could sense her wistfulness this morning.

"Are you in good health today, Odalisque Ana?"

"I am, Kett. Thank you for escorting me."

"You seem sad. Is there anything I can do for you?"

She smiled. "Dear Kett. I have always felt that is the precise question I should be asking you. After all you—"

The memory of Kett's emasculation had always hung between them, an unspoken grief of an evening in which both had shared much despair. On the night that Kett had been made a eunuch, Ana had been sold into the care of the palace; both had become instant prisoners of the harem.

"Don't, please, that was nearly a year ago. I am recovered and almost fully resigned to my situation." The slave shrugged. "It was never your fault."

She knew as much, but it didn't stop her feeling connected to him, sad for him. She stopped walking, pausing to stare out toward an island that was beyond the harbor but still under the watchful protection of the giant statues, Beloch and Ezram. "Why is my gaze always drawn there?" she wondered aloud. "What is that place?"

Kett looked out to sea. "It is a leper colony, Miss Ana, and although I have never visited it, I hear that it is very beautiful. Perhaps you are drawn to handsome, rugged, windswept things?"

In spite of her mood, she giggled soft amusement at his words, and touched his arm briefly, feeling how his skin shivered at her small show of affection. "You make me smile. I'm fortunate to have you in the harem."

"But, Odalisque Ana," he exclaimed softly, "everyone loves you. You are the most popular of all the women."

"Not so popular with the Valide and the Grand Master Eunuch I fear—although, Kett, I am really trying to keep my word and fit into the harem. I have not raised either's ire in many a moon."

"And yet you stare out across the water, Miss Ana, searching to escape—in spirit perhaps, if not in body?"

"Ah, Kett, you know me better than anyone," she said sadly.

"Only because I feel the same as you do. It is why I am only *almost* resigned to my situation. We both wish we could escape this place—am I right?"

"Yes, although I could admit that to no one else. I have given my word to those who care about me and made an oath to myself that I must not attempt to leave the harem again. I have learned that the repercussions often stretch painfully to others."

"You refer to Spur Lazar, I think?"

She flinched at the mention of his name. "The Spur is dead because of my irresponsible actions. I can never forgive myself."

"He would never blame you, Miss Ana. He wanted to protect you, that's why he claimed Protectorship, took your punishment." The story of the Spur's self-sacrificing decision had spread like fanned flames through the harem, firing the hearts of the young women hoping for romance in their lives—who, sadly, would probably go to their graves unfulfilled. Love did not often blossom in the harem.

"I know, but still my actions killed him," Ana said, unable to mask her pain. She changed the subject though the former Spur was still very much alive in her mind . . . and her heart. "And you, Kett, how do you cope with being a member of the harem? I suppose at least you have some small measure of freedom."

"I run errands for Grand Master Salmeo on occasion, yes."

"Do you ever think of running and never coming back?" she asked, a yearning in her tone.

"Always." He looked back at her, his wide-eyed gaze intense. "But on each occasion I have returned."

Ana's expression told him that she was assuming it was a lack of courage that brought him back to the palace each time. She tried to hide her disappointment by returning her wistful gaze to Star Island. "I wonder why?" Ana replied, finally continuing her journey into another part of the palace again. She did not see the look on the eunuch slave's face, did not appreciate the subtle message of loyalty and love that he had tried to pass to her. "I'm sure if I had your opportunity I might be tempted to break my word and my oath, for despite my strong words, the faith behind them is hollow, dear Kett. I think I am a liar to those around me and to myself."

Her friend frowned. "Please, Miss Ana, do not utter such harsh rebuke against yourself."

"But it is true," she returned calmly, waving to one of the girls who stared out from behind the latticed windows of the Sherbet Rooms. "I want to believe I would keep my promise—really, I do—but as I consider a whole lifetime stretching before me here in the harem, I think I would take any chance that came my way to escape."

"And risk death?"

"Yes," she answered without hesitation, then added softly, "For this is a living death for me anyway."

"There is a story amongst the Elim about an odalisque who did escape from the harem once." Kett hadn't meant to share this apparent myth, but it had spilled from his mouth in an attempt to lift his friend's spirits.

Ana turned her head to stare gravely at her companion. "You jest, surely?"

Kett shook his head. "Only yesterday I saw the Grand Master Eunuch laughing at the idea—the story is so old that no one knows if it is true anymore—that she persuaded one of the bundle women to carry her out in the bundle itself, and so escaped to freedom."

Ana stopped in her tracks. "Forever?" she asked, her expression incredulous. "But—"

"Hush," he cautioned, eyes frightened, gaze searching for eavesdroppers. "Let us continue, Miss Ana." He guided her forward once again.

Ana obediently began moving, but persisted, "Do you mean she was never returned to the harem?"

"Apparently they never found her. Salmeo said such a thing would never happen under his keep."

"How did the odalisque do it?" Ana demanded in a tight whisper. "What did she offer the woman?"

"She stole something and used it to bribe the bundle woman. The older Elim didn't say what it was." At the look in Ana's eyes, Kett wondered whether he might live to regret sharing this tale of escape. "Come, Miss Ana, you cannot be late for His Majesty."

"Forgive me for dawdling," Ana apologized immediately, "but I am intrigued by your tale, Kett."

"Not too intrigued, I hope. It's far too dangerous and I would hate to lose you," the slave said sincerely, hastily adding: "So would all the girls of the harem."

Ana smiled. "You're very kind. Here comes the Zar's men," she said, noticing the two mutes approaching. "I would be lying if I said I didn't enjoy these meetings with Zar Boaz. He is a very good conversationalist. We even talk in different languages sometimes. I test him on his Galinsean."

"Are you better than him?" Kett asked, impressed.

"A little," Ana admitted, conspiratorially. "I'm told I have a natural tongue for language, although linguistic skills are of little use to me here."

"You never know," Kett said. "I imagine the Zar will choose you soon, Miss Ana. It is obvious how fond of you he is."

"Not too soon, I pray," Ana replied, before fixing her veil across her face. "Thank you for the story of the odalisque, Kett. I know you told it to me to cheer me and it has." She smiled reassuringly at his trusting eyes before she turned to address the mutes, who were upon them now, with a gentle nod of her head.

He grinned and handed the parasol to the mute Salazin, who would now escort the odalisque into the private chambers of the Zar.

As he watched her petite figure retreat, dwarfed by the warriors who formed an elite guard for the Zar, Kett wondered when his former childhood playmate would take Ana for his Favorite. He suspected it wouldn't be long now, for the Zar was nearing seventeen and Ana had grown from a beautiful child into an exquisite woman.

He sighed as he realized he would very soon be forced to love this woman not just from afar, as he had this past year, but also as another man's wife. And he would have to continue to lie to her and at times to himself about his true feelings for Odalisque Ana.

1

Three moons later . . .

It was Pez's idea but it was Zafira who had found him, had seen the potential; still she was shocked by his skill. She feared for the young man, but his uncannily calm manner and quiet confidence convinced her that he was right for this curious role. He asked for no money, which made it harder for her to ask him to do what she did. And when she pressed him for his reason for taking on such personal risk, he had staggered her by confiding that all he wanted to do was serve the Goddess. At his tender age what could he know about Lyana? And yet he had been firm in his claim that he had been called by the Goddess to this dangerous task.

Now Pez echoed all her anxieties. She had hoped he would ooze his usual confidence—needed him to—but it seemed he was as unnerved as she was by this youngster.

They sat in a small room stirred gently by a soft breath of

wind that although it had journeyed halfway up the hillside of Percheron, still carried the scent of the sea. They could see the harbor from here. The massive giant statues of Beloch and Ezram gazed out across the Faranel, ever watchful for the long-feared raid that hadn't come in centuries.

"How does an orphanage command such a view?" Pez wondered aloud.

"I gather the palace gave it over to widowed wives of the Percherese Guard. Down the decades those families were given better care—separate housing, a stipend from the royal coffers—and this building became defunct. Then one Zar gifted it to the orphans of Percheron. It's still known as the Widow's Enclave."

"It's wonderful."

"Yes, although there's talk of that magnanimous act being revoked now."

"Surely not?" Pez frowned, unable to imagine Boaz drafting such an ungenerous decree.

"So the sisters quietly claim."

"What would the Zar want it for?"

"Not the Zar. I think his newly intimate adviser has designs on it."

Pez pulled a face of disgust. "Tariq is certainly carving a new role for himself."

"Well, his role is to advise the Zar, of course. But according to what you've told me, it sounds as though our last Zar never chose to have his close counsel."

"And who could blame Joreb? The odd thing is that Boaz always despised the man as much as his father did."

Zafira nodded. "I saw Vizier Tariq the other day—"

"That's Grand Vizier Tariq, Zafira," Pez interrupted, grimacing. "It's amazing what nearly a year's worth of constant ingratiation can achieve," he added bitterly.

"What is it, Pez?" she inquired gently. "Has Boaz cast you aside?"

The dwarf shook his great head. "No, but he doesn't look to me for all of his companionship now."

"He's coming up toward seventeen. He had to grow up sometime, my friend. You've been his confidant for many years. He's just spreading his wings a little," the priestess reasoned. "He has a man's job to do—little wonder he had to cast off childhood so fast."

"True." Pez sighed. "I just wish it hadn't been Tariq's arms he walked into," he complained, adding, with a tone of frustration, "The man's undergone some sort of metamorphosis."

"Well, how odd that you say that," Zafira said, leaning forward eagerly. "When I saw him the other day, we passed each other around the main fountain in the market and I hardly recognized him."

Pez frowned. "Curious, isn't it?"

"Am I deceiving myself?"

Pez gave a derisive smirk. "No, I've noticed it, too. Younger, straighter, more . . . what is it?" He paused, searching for the word. "More presence. The old Tariq was weak, and his greatest weakness was craving attention from the royals. This newly invented Tariq exudes absolute confidence. He needs no endorsement from anyone, it seems. I swear he all but treats the Valide Zara with disdain."

"Well, so do you," Zafira reminded him.

"But I'm supposed to be mad, remember . . . and rude to everyone—especially Herezah, whenever I can find the opportunity. Tariq has all of his faculties intact and he openly does not suffer fools gladly."

"Are you saying the Valide is a fool?"

Pez gave some semblance of a rueful grin. "Far from it, but I sense she's as baffled as I am by this relationship that seems to deepen by the day."

"And you? How does he regard you?"

"Tariq? I sense that he's suspicious of me. He watches me carefully. He thinks I don't notice, but I am aware of his constant attention."

"What is he suspicious of?"

"I don't know. He can't know the truth of my sanity, I'm sure of it, but it's as if he suspects there's more to me than meets the eye and so he keeps watching for some sign."

"Iridor?" the priestess posed, her voice a whisper.

Pez shook his head. "Why would he suspect that?"

She shrugged. "If you have magic, why not others?" she suggested, keeping her voice low. "Or perhaps it's that Tariq's jealous of your relationship with Boaz."

"It could be—that would make sense. Yet I feel as though he is searching for any slip, any small sign that I am not what everyone believes me to be. It doesn't add up, but then neither does his behavior over the past year. I need to be more attentive." Pez moved restlessly to the window to watch the children playing a boisterous game of pigball in the courtyard.

"Are you sure about him?"

"He's astounding, Pez. He can do it. But can you do it to him?"

"There are bigger things at stake than individual lives, Zafira."

"Except, if you lose enough lives individually, you can lose a nation," she counseled softly.

"Don't preach at me," Pez said mildly.

"I just need to be sure that you understand the stakes. You're gambling with his life, not yours."

"I'm aware of that, Priestess, no need to remind me," Pez replied, a spike of irritation in his voice.

Zafira responded in kind, angry that Pez wasn't helping to diminish her own guilt, and if she was honest, angry at herself for agreeing to this madness. "And I suppose I don't need to remind you that he doesn't want your money either?"

"Pardon?" Pez said, swinging around to face her. "What does he want?"

"Nothing we can give. He told me he's doing it because he serves Lyana."

Pez's expression changed from confusion to incredulity. "And you accept this?"

Zafira shrugged helplessly. "He made it clear that she had called upon him."

"Do you believe him?"

"I believe he's true, yes. He told me she first spoke to him in a dream when he was very small. She has come to him frequently since, he says. He mentioned the name Iridor but didn't seem to know what it signifies."

Pez looked deeply troubled. "I'd prefer him to accept the money," he admitted.

"I imagine it would ease your conscience."

"Zafira—" Pez began, his tone exasperated.

She interrupted him, equally frustrated. "I'm sorry, Pez, but I am fearful for this boy. What he is prepared to shoulder is frightening. We both know that should our clever plan be discovered, he will not be given an easy death."

The dwarf's irritation dissipated. His head dropped in resignation. "I know it."

The priestess heard such a depth of emotion in those three words that she hurried to soothe her friend's troubled soul. "You have equipped him well, Pez. I would be lying if I told you that he's not ready."

"I hope so." He found a sad smile. "Tell Lazar I shall visit later today. We have things to discuss. How is he?"

"Oh, angry, distant, scowling, handsome, exasperating. Need I go on?"

Pez smiled genuinely for the first time during their meeting. "That sounds promising."

She nodded, reflecting his smile. "I think he is recovered physically, yes."

"Not emotionally, though."

"Ana has scarred his heart. There are times I wish the two had never met."

"Then none of this would have happened. No, Zafira. This is Lyana's work. She is manipulating all of us. Lazar and Ana were meant to meet, though I don't understand why. What's the purpose of such a brief meeting—and one marked by such pain and suffering on both sides?"

"The Goddess works in mysterious ways, Pez. Let that be a comfort." Zafira thought briefly of the mysterious stranger Ellyana, still found it unsettling that the woman had come into their lives at a time of such high drama and then left so soon, with no warning, no farewell, and no further instructions . . . except for a caution; she had told Zafira that Iridor, the demigod in his owl form, would rise, and once that occurred, then the battle of the gods, which she had spoken about, would have begun. She had counseled that Lazar was integral to the success of the Goddess but wouldn't, or perhaps couldn't, explain why.

Zafira hadn't really understood much of it at all, but Ellyana was not one to be pressed, and then she had disappeared. They hadn't seen or heard from her in almost a year. And though Zafira had suspected who Iridor might be, she had had no idea of what his rising meant for her, or any of those who served Lyana. She was none the wiser now, although her suspicions of who the Messenger of Lyana the Goddess was had been confirmed on the night after Horz of the Elim had died. It had come as no surprise in truth, but despite her easy acceptance, she nevertheless experienced an intense feeling of awe every time she saw the beautiful snowy owl.

Pez broke into her thoughts. "It's a cold comfort but I'm glad our man is back. Now we have to discover his purpose."

"He may have already served it. He nearly died, after all."

Pez shook his head. "No. Lyana has more in store for the former Spur. We just have to be patient."

2

Maliz, the demon, comfortable in the body of the newly promoted Grand Vizier, approached the Zar confidently. The young ruler was in his private courtyard with its wide verandah overlooking the Faranel. Alongside the slim Zar stood the monstrously large form of Salmeo, Grand Master Eunuch of the harem.

Maliz smiled. Tariq, the man whose body he had stolen, had hated the black castrate and the feeling had been so intensely mutual that none of Maliz's genuine attempts at repairing past damage were welcomed with any warmth by the suspicious head of the harem. History prevailed, hate reigned. Maliz found it amusing, as much as wise, to keep trying, though.

He bowed—"Zar Boaz"—before nodding toward Salmeo in a far more polite gesture than Tariq could ever have mustered. "Grand Master Eunuch. Please forgive my interruption."

The Zar nodded. "We were just finishing, Tariq. Salmeo has

agreed to organize the boating picnic I promised the women many moons ago."

"Oh, how charming," Maliz replied, and meant it. It was obvious, however, that Salmeo thought he was being sarcastic.

"It is the Zar's desire," the black eunuch reminded him softly, the firmness of his voice a warning that he did not like to be challenged in front of the Zar.

"And it is you the women will remember for this idea, Salmeo," Maliz said in a conciliatory tone.

Salmeo blinked, slow as a lizard, as if weighing up carefully what the Vizier was saying, testing it for guile. "I shall take my leave, Majesty," he said finally without another glance to the Vizier. "I have many arrangements to make. Would you like me to inform the women of the upcoming treat, Highness?"

Maliz heard the soft lisp in the black eunuch's speech and wondered how many had assumed incorrectly that such an affectation meant the man was in some way gentle.

"By all means," Boaz said, "although I would appreciate it if you would advise the Valide first and seek her participation." He smiled hesitantly, and again Maliz noted how uncomfortable the Zar was around the massive eunuch. The royal worked hard to hide how much he disliked Salmeo, but Maliz was too sharp not to notice all the silent signs Boaz's body gave of not wanting to spend a moment more than he had to in the private company of the man.

"Thank you, my Zar," Salmeo lisped, bowing before he glided away, curiously light on his feet.

Boaz sighed. "How does such a huge man tread so softly," he mused, turning to his Vizier. "It would be so much easier if you two liked each other," he complained with irritation, returning his gaze to the glinting sea.

Maliz, unfazed by the power of the man who stood before him, gave a wry smile to the Zar's back. "I could say the same to you, Majesty."

Boaz swung around abruptly, clearly surprised by the bold comment, but Maliz remained relaxed, allowing the hint of a mischievous grin to crease the corners of Tariq's mouth. Boaz looked at his Vizier intently for a moment. "I wish my father had known the new Tariq who stands so brazenly before me. I believe he would have liked you, Vizier."

"No, Highness," Maliz continued smoothly, "I think even I might have disliked me in your father's day. It is only since you have come to power that I've realized how important my role can be. Previously I searched for gratification, reward, power . . . oh dear, the list of cringing need feels endless sometimes." He shrugged in a self-deprecating manner.

"And now?"

"A change did come over me at your father's death, Majesty. There's no denying it. I realized that as soon as you took the Crown of Percheron, you could have had me executed, Majesty. You and I were never what could have been termed friends."

"I hated you," Boaz replied candidly.

Maliz nodded. The Zar had matured much in these past few moons, growing into his role, accepting its burden. His directness was refreshing compared with the usual politicking that took place in the palace. "And I understand why. I had so little autonomy, my Zar. I could have been a good Vizier to your father—may Zarab keep him—but he was headstrong and fiercely independent. He didn't want advisers and he did not like me from the outset."

"Neither did I. I'm still not sure I do."

This surprised but privately amused the demon, who had no real interest in the Zar's success. This relationship with Boaz was simply convenient and mildly entertaining. His own agenda concerned much more than the simple politics of Percheron. If anyone knew or understood what was truly at stake . . .

Of course someone else did know. But that person remained elusive. Maliz was sure that Iridor had not only risen but was roaming these very corridors. He could feel that his ancient enemy was near—and that meant Lyana, too, was close. He must exercise patience. He would find and destroy them both. He had before in every battle, over millennia.

"I appreciate your candor, my Zar, and hope I never offend you."

"I hope so, too, Tariq," Boaz said softly, but there was a threat in his tone and Maliz realized that, for all his careful work, the Zar remained suspicious and hesitant to give his trust. Despite himself, the demon admired Boaz for his reluctance. Percheron was fortunate to have two Zars in a row who were worthy of their status.

Boaz interrupted his thoughts. "You wanted to talk with me?"

"Yes, Zar Boaz, I do."

"Walk with me, then. I was going to take some sea air on the high balcony."

"It would be a pleasure," Maliz replied, knowing that walk would take Boaz past the Sherbet Rooms, where many of the members from the harem liked to relax. It wouldn't be long now, Maliz thought, before those girls, quickly turning into young women, would be called upon to no longer just look pretty, dance sweetly, giggle coquettishly, but to offer a new, much more grown-up homage to their Zar. It was going to be fun to observe these delicious girls as they set about their single-minded business of attracting the Zar's eye. If they knew what it was like to be a young man, his wits challenged by the fierce new drive of sexuality, they would understand that they would have to do very little to win his attention. The mere suggestion of the rise of breast behind their robes, the glimpse of a nipple beneath a silken sheath, the very outline of a nubile body moving gracefully—any hint of sensuality was enough to send a hot-blooded youngster into a frenzy of desire.

He smiled slyly. "Perhaps we should send a runner ahead to let others know I accompany you, Zar Boaz."

"No need," Boaz replied nonchalantly. "That's what I was talking to Salmeo about. I'm relaxing some of the rules attached to the harem. I see no reason why the Zar—and whomever he chooses to enjoy the palace surrounds with him—should not be permitted to walk alongside certain buildings without permission."

"Indeed, Highness," Maliz said, surprised and delighted. "Is the Grand Master Eunuch comfortable with this . . . relaxing of the old rules?"

"What do you think?"

"I imagine he believes it's an encroachment," Maliz answered truthfully.

"Yes, that's precisely what he believes. But I know Salmeo considers it an encroachment on his personal status rather than on tradition. He cares not for the old ways so much as for his territory. I don't intend to stare into windows or hunt down the women. I just don't see that I must avoid them."

"It's part of your role as a ruler to modernize life," Maliz encouraged.

"Salmeo believes I'm stomping on tradition."

"That's what I'd expect him to say."

"You think it's appropriate, then." Boaz did not make it a question.

Maliz was sharp enough to realize that though the Zar was not asking his permission, the young ruler was gently searching for approval. "I think it's wise, Majesty. Each Zar will surely introduce his own modern thinking to his reign. Your father made many changes. Some were fought by the traditionalists, but had he backed down, good things such as your great education might never have happened. Your grandfather did not believe in his heirs being educated as broadly. Your father learned the art of warfare and diplomacy, for example, but taught himself how to read and write as well as he did."

"I never knew that," Boaz commented with surprise. "He was so creative, too."

"This is true, but that was your father's inherent talent. He had the soul of an artist. We can see his influence all over the city, and certainly in the palace. Just think of how much poorer the citizens would be had he not exercised his right to change things. You are not doing anything that Zars before you have not already done. It is fitting that you make subtle improvements wherever you see the need."

"It seems so archaic to separate the women to the point of imprisonment."

"Ah, now we touch on something else," Maliz warned.

"Not really. I don't see it that way."

"Others will. If you don't mind me offering humble advice, may I suggest you move slowly, my Zar. Don't try to change too much at once. Small leaps will still cover the same distance as big ones . . . it takes longer, but it makes it easier on those who feel the effects of change."

"Salmeo, you mean," Boaz qualified.

Maliz's flick of his hand was a gesture that told Boaz the Vizier could likely reel off a dozen names. "Salmeo included, definitely. The Valide might also feel that you are undermining her status if you grant too much freedom to the women. You must remember, my Zar, if I dare be so bold as to guide you here, that the harem is your mother's power base. If you implement too much change in a short time, the other women will soon be looking to you to override not only Salmeo but also the most powerful woman in the realm. Your mother sits atop a throne in the harem; I know you understand this because you were raised in it, so I don't mean to give you a lecture." The older man bowed slightly in deference.

"I understand. Please continue," Boaz commanded.

"You don't want your mother as an enemy," the Vizier said directly.

Boaz paused and Maliz wondered if he'd made an error in judgment. "What is that supposed to mean?" the Zar asked.

Maliz had said too much to pull out now. "The relationship I've noticed between you two is strained. It is none of my business, of course, and I realize it is neither the fault of your mother nor yourself. Circumstances of the harem will almost always put this sort of pressure on any slave mother who rises to this position and her precious son that claims the throne." He paused, ensuring that Boaz was not taking offense. Boaz said nothing but his stare was intense. Maliz continued: "Her future is in your hands. Whatever power you grant her is all she gets and she must feed off your status at all times. She is nothing without you."

"I have heard such advice before," Boaz replied steadily.

"Then forgive me for being repetitive. The Valide is a weapon that you can use, my Zar. I would caution against alienating her by undermining her authority over the other women. The more freedom you give them, the less mystery to her role and her access to you."

Boaz remained silent for a long moment; then, "I shall consider your advice, Vizier," was all Maliz got for his careful guidance. "As you can see," the Zar continued, waving in the direction of the pale, ornate building known as the Sherbet Rooms that they were now approaching, "Salmeo seems to have my measure anyway." He was referring to the ring of red-robed Elim guards who stood against each tall window that might give the women a chance to eye their Zar at too close range for Salmeo's comfort . . . and vice versa, of course.

Maliz permitted himself a smile. "It seems he does." It was the right thing to say. Boaz gave a grudging grin, as if acknowledging that they both shared a common dislike for the man. Maliz considered that it might be easier to maintain the mutual hatred that Tariq had begun. It seemed more useful in terms of remaining closer to the Zar, anyway.

Boaz inhaled the sudden fresh breeze blowing off the Faranel that rolled like a restless animal before them. He placed his hands on the stone balcony and raised his face to the sun to accept some of her early-season warmth. Anyone looking at the Zar could be forgiven for thinking all traces of childhood had disappeared this past year, but Maliz, now well attuned to Boaz, could still sense faint echoes of the boy.

"What did you want to speak to me about, Tariq?" Boaz asked, not opening his eyes.

"About your security, my Zar," Maliz replied, without missing a beat.

Now the Zar did open his eyes. Turning, he faced the Vizier. "That's a regular haunt for you, isn't it?"

"It is part of my greater responsibility, Zar Boaz. Did you know that less than a century ago we did not even have a Spur? The Grand Vizier was responsible for the entire realm's security."

Maliz had deliberately mentioned the Spur, knowing that his words, though softly spoken, would reopen the wound of loss that the young Zar tried to ignore. The Vizier knew this was impossible. Boaz had clearly admired Lazar, probably loved him; those wounds would never heal, especially since the Spur's death was shrouded in such mystery.

"Yes, I know that from my history lessons," Boaz said evenly, though not without a hint of sorrow.

"I just think these are more dangerous times, my Zar. The fact is if Percheron's head of security can disappear without a trace, we have a problem in our city. I accept that Lazar invoked the law of Protectorship and was punished on behalf of Oda-lisque Ana. It is also clear that his flogging was savage, mis-handled badly enough to speed him to an early death." Maliz watched with satisfaction the Zar's jaw silently working with tightly held emotion. He continued: "But to have to trust the word of an old woman that the corpse was properly dealt with according to the Spur's wishes, and so on . . ." He added a note of weariness to his tone, suggesting it sounded too far-fetched for his liking. "Well, it doesn't sit comfortably with me, High-ness. You are my responsibility, after all, and in the absence of our Spur, I feel moved to make suggestions to improve your safety. One tragedy in our palace is one too many; you must not allow our people to suffer another loss of even greater magnitude."

Boaz nodded, his expression thoughtful. "You mentioned a

change in the guard not so long ago. I presume you now have an idea to share?"

"Yes, Majesty. I am proposing an elite group of strong young men who will permanently be at your side, so to speak."

"How many?"

"At least a dozen on call so I can ensure a ring of men in and around your chambers or wherever you are, every minute of the day."

"This began as food tasters in the kitchens, Tariq. Now you're suggesting they all but live with me? I fear I will find your measures claustrophobic."

Maliz nodded, hoping to convey a tone of unfortunate resignation. "At least one will sleep near your bedside, Highness."

"No!" Boaz said. "Absolutely not. How uncomfortable will my life be if they can hear everything I say, repeat it to their companions and—"

Maliz raised a hand gently but the smile on his face had a malevolent quality to it. "Hear me out, Majesty."

Boaz's expression suggested he couldn't imagine what the Vizier could possibly say to change his mind, but he nodded for Maliz to continue.

Maliz inclined his head in gratitude. "I am proposing that this elite corps will be highly trained and very capable of killing whoever might overstep the cordon without permission." He paused dramatically. "But they will also be deaf mutes."

Now Boaz looked startled. "To a man? How do we train them? How do we instruct them? How do we find that many brilliant warriors?"

Maliz tutted, and Boaz raised his eyebrows in irritation. The demon realized he must be on guard at all times against his own impatience showing through, must constantly remember that he was still Tariq to all who met him. He bowed. "Forgive me, Zar. I did not explain this well. The men will be hand selected for their fighting prowess and ability to follow orders using signals. Once we have selected them, and trained them fully in their roles, they will be made deaf and rendered mute." He stressed the final five words.

Boaz opened his mouth, paused, and closed it again. He took a moment or two to gather himself. "You will maim healthy men for this role?"

"Yes," the Vizier said simply.

"But that's barbaric."

"I care not for how we make them, Majesty. I care only that we protect your life to the best of our ability. I know if Lazar were sharing this conversation with us now, he would agree in principle with what I'm proposing."

"Then that shows how well you did not know the man, Tariq," Boaz countered firmly. "I assure you Lazar would never condone such injury to a warrior."

"Lazar would not allow his Zar to be under any threat," Maliz replied, unfazed.

"Well, am I?"

"Pardon, Majesty?"

Boaz frowned. "Has a direct threat been detected?"

Maliz considered lying, then opted not to. "No, Highness, but these are different times from the ones your father lived through. None of your enemies could know how capable you are. They imagine a youth, vulnerable, easily killed or deposed. Perhaps spies have reported the death of your Spur. That puts you even more at risk. Furthermore, Percheron has never been more vital as a critical trading point between east and west. I suspect that if we are going to be attacked, it will happen during the early years of your reign, Highness. We must think ahead, be prepared."

"All speculation," Boaz dismissed.

"But that's my job, Zar Boaz. I must anticipate all scenarios. And without the Spur, I feel compelled to offer higher protection than we currently have." He could see Boaz tiring of the conversation, so he pushed once more. "I shall keep it to just a few men if that makes it easier on your conscience, my Zar."

"Then I insist they must take their roles willingly."

Maliz couldn't help the bemusement that spread across Tariq's face. "To be willingly made deaf and mute?"

"Or I won't allow it. Offer them and their families gold in exchange for the maiming. Be generous. If you insist upon this course, then I will set the parameters. I will also approve each man before the maiming takes place."

Maliz smiled inwardly. He had won. "As you wish, my Zar," he said obediently, and bowed his head. He could now have the Zar constantly observed—and, perhaps more importantly, he could keep an eye on the dwarf, whom he firmly suspected to be an enemy of Zarab.

3

The Valide sipped the fruit infusion she took each morning, maintaining it kept her complexion unlined and unblemished. "And what did he want to see him about?" she asked her guest as she put the porcelain cup down beside her. She was simply making conversation, for she couldn't trouble herself with every discussion that her son had with the reinvented Tariq.

"I don't know, Valide," Salmeo admitted. "I thought you might."

"Boaz doesn't include me in his decisions anymore—certainly not in recent times. As he looks like a man now, he thinks like one, too," she said, and he heard the not-so-well disguised sorrow in her voice.

"Then he'll be acting like one soon," Salmeo replied, knowing the Valide would understand his innuendo.

"He'll choose her first," she warned.

It was not something the Grand Master Eunuch needed to be told. "We can't stop that."

"She's dangerous, Salmeo. I made a mistake in choosing Ana. I should have let Lazar have his little girl."

"I'm not sure anything used to simmer in Lazar for anyone," he commented, always glad to be reminded of the Spur's demise.

"If you were a woman you'd understand," Herezah replied caustically. "He didn't just simmer for her; he was feverish. But he arrogantly thought he hid it. From me!" She shook her mane of hair, which had lost none of its black glossiness even though she was now past her third decade. "I'll never understand why he even brought her through those palace gates if he was so infatuated with the child."

Salmeo understood instantly that none of the Valide's own fiery infatuation with the long-dead Spur had cooled.

It surprised him that even after all this time she burned so fiercely for the soldier, or at least the memory of him. She had not mentioned Lazar's name to him since the day his "murderer," Horz, had been executed—after being accused of poisoning the whip used to flog and ultimately kill the Spur. Horz was dead and forgotten, but not so Spur Lazar—it seemed his memory would never die, and certainly not for the Valide. He stored the thought away.

The Valide was not an enemy but she could be. That accepted, Salmeo had long ago realized that his fate was tied up with the Valide. There would never be any opportunity to ingratiate himself with the new Zar—it was all too obvious what the young ruler felt toward his keeper of the harem—but Salmeo did have a chance with Herezah. As distant as Boaz might have made himself from his mother, he was still of her blood and would see no wrong done to her.

If I can remain her ally, Salmeo thought, *I might buy my own protection should the truth of my involvement in Lazar's death come out.* He didn't think it would. Having successfully blackmailed Horz into taking the blame, Salmeo felt his secret was safe, once Horz's corpse had been left to rot on the impaling post outside the palace. But he also knew in his heart that the Zar believed he was at the root of the Spur's mysterious death. Boaz would be looking for anything that might connect Salmeo with wrongdoing; staying close to the Valide, pandering to her needs and making himself indispensable to her machinations, might be that extra insurance the eunuch needed.

He deeply regretted that rare moment of spite in which he had impulsively allowed his anger to overtake his common sense. Poisoning the whip that would ultimately flog the Spur had been effective but ultimately perilous. Yes, it killed the proud, arrogant soldier who had become such an impediment to Salmeo's plans to dominate Odalisque Ana—but was his death really necessary? No, he thought, it was stupidly reckless, and although blame had been laid elsewhere through some swift manipulations, it had almost found him and wrapped itself about his own shoulders. Salmeo suddenly realized the Valide had been watching him whilst he mused, no doubt waiting for a response to her grumbling over Ana.

"I could just have her killed, Valide. She could accidentally slip or mysteriously drown—the boating excursion provides a marvelous opportunity. I could even manufacture a culprit if you deemed it necessary." He did not look her in the eye, but simply waited patiently for her response. He guessed his suggestion sent a flare of hope torching through Herezah's body.

The thought of the young odalisque who was rapidly shaping herself as the Zar's Favorite disappearing from the harem was a daydream he suspected the Valide permitted herself. Ana was a threat to her. The Valide had not anticipated Boaz taking on the challenge of being a Zar quite so swiftly; she had hoped he would accept the role in title only and then return to his more studious pursuits, giving her free rein to essentially run the realm. Salmeo suspected that her intention had always been to involve her son, probably holding meetings over supper each evening to discuss the day's affairs as though she was consulting with him. Herezah was too clever not to factor in male pride and Salmeo knew she would be more than happy to continue the pretense that a new Zar was confidently on his throne whilst she herself pulled all the strings of the puppet ruler.

But it was not to be. For all her cunning and clever ways, Herezah simply hadn't counted on her once shy, slightly withdrawn son first embracing his new role and then shouldering it with dignity, and now living it with a real sense of purpose. Now she was paying the price of raising a well-educated son who had never been allowed to shirk a sense of duty.

Herezah could live with this mature Boaz. She could carve out new powers for herself. But what she couldn't abide, Salmeo knew, was the profound effect Ana was having on her son. Ana and her speedy rise in the Zar's estimation threatened to kill off any aspirations that the Valide still held for herself.

Nothing had occurred sexually between Ana and the Zar yet, Salmeo knew, but they had a bond, for certain. It had formed when the girl had first been brought to the palace—she had been lonely and vulnerable, whilst Boaz was uncertain and fearful of his new role as Zar. Herezah had only herself to blame for not having paid sufficient attention to her son's emotions at that time.

Boaz had genuinely grieved for the loss of his father, whilst Herezah had expected him to get over the death quickly and find an excitement similar to hers at their new status—Valide and Zar.

Of course her mistake had been in imagining that ambition would somehow naturally override Boaz's love and grief for his father, and her expectations of her son had been interpreted by him as heartlessness, Salmeo deduced. The eunuch appreciated that Herezah was right to expect Boaz to show no weakness, to pick up his father's mantle—overnight—in order to establish his rule. But from what he could tell, it remained an unspoken rift between the Zar and his mother.

Salmeo slipped one of the violet tablets he habitually sucked into his mouth and raised his eyebrows at the Valide, awaiting her answer to his offer.

"Too risky," she said finally. "Any number of things could go wrong. No, Ana needs to be entrapped by her own doing."

"I don't follow, Valide," he said, intrigued, lacing his fat, bejeweled fingers together.

She picked up her cup again and sipped slowly. "Ana is by far the smartest odalisque in the harem, wouldn't you agree?"

"I would. Most of the others seem to look to her for leadership, I note."

Herezah frowned. "Hmm. You see, that in itself is a declaration of her intentions."

Salmeo disagreed. "To be honest, Valide, I think Ana would be happier if she had less attention. She's a strange sort of a girl—very contained, seems to need no one, and yet she's the very person most of them look to for friendship or comfort."

"Is it just the younger ones?"

He shook his head. "I'm afraid not. She's a natural leader. I would be lying if I didn't admit that the entire harem adores her."

Herezah smirked. "That will change."

Salmeo's mind moved quickly with the Valide's. "When Boaz begins choosing his sexual partners, you mean?"

"The moment my son starts singling out girls for his romantic attention, those chosen will be the target of hate from all the others."

"Then Ana will be despised, for I have no doubt that she will be Absolute Favorite."

Herezah slammed down her cup and Salmeo wondered if he didn't hear it crack with protest at such treatment. "That is my very point! She must be undone before she attains such a position."

Salmeo stifled the smile he was privately enjoying at the Valide's insecurity. Herezah might consider herself powerful, but she was clearly not feeling terribly powerful right now, with her son so independent and a slip of a girl about to claim the single most prized position in the harem for an odalisque, and one that would ultimately threaten the Valide's future. "You were telling me how we might undo such aspirations," he said, calming her.

Herezah took a deep breath. "We agree she's clever, so we must use that intelligence against her. I'll wager she is bored?"

"Senseless," he confirmed. "She hates the harem, as you would guess. She is not interested in anything it offers, from its decadence to its pampering or its riches. She couldn't be less interested in any of it."

"Good. Let's keep her bored and frustrated." The Valide sipped her drink, taking a few moments to organize her thoughts. Salmeo knew to remain quiet during her pause.

"This boat trip you want my involvement with, when is it planned for?"

"Soon—in several days, I imagine."

"Even better. That will give her a taste of freedom. And her imprisonment back in the harem afterward will feel all the more smothering. Let's plan some tedious training in the meantime, shall we?"

"Embroidery?"

She groaned, presumably remembering her own hours of soul-destroying boredom spent with needle and silk. "Precisely, and letters. No swimming or outside walks. Keep it all indoors, especially now whilst the sun is shining with its promise of summer."

"And?" He knew the crux of her plan was yet to be revealed.

"We'll make it easy for her to try an escape."

Salmeo made a soft sound of disbelief. "Do you really think she'd disobey the most important rule of the harem?"

"She did it once before," Herezah replied, tapping her teeth with a bloodred painted fingernail . . . a habit Salmeo knew she couldn't help when in deep thought.

Salmeo wasn't convinced. "She had hardly arrived then and we'd just inflicted the Test of Virtue on her."

"She's a year older, a year bolder, and a year more bored with her life. She's ripe to make another attempt. She just needs a push."

"You speak with knowledge, Valide," Salmeo commented.

"I fought the urge every day of my life, eunuch; I sometimes think I still do," Herezah said, unable to disguise a slightly wistful note in her tone. "But Ana believes she has the ear of the Zar and his indulgence. She'll risk it, I promise . . . and just in case, I might sow the right seeds in her mind."

"Oh?"

"Send her to me today. I think I'll be giving her some responsibility in the harem. It's time anyway that the girls take on some special roles, but I'll endow Ana with the most trust . . . confide a few things in her."

"Let her think you might be friends?"

Herezah shrugged. "I wouldn't go that far. Ana's too much of an island, but perhaps some fragile bridges might be built."

"And then what, Valide?"

"I'll tear them down and expose her. What is the harshest punishment for leaving the harem?"

"Lashes . . . you'd remember that from Ana's previous attempt at escape. But this time there'll be no Spur Lazar to twist the rules and take the strokes on her behalf."

"Is that the best we can do?"

"Well, being caught unveiled, perhaps in the company of a man, would certainly increase the punishment," he considered, enjoying where this conversation was headed.

"To what?"

"Death." He said it coldly, without hesitation, and saw how the word appealed to her by the involuntary twitch at the corner of her mouth. He loved it.

"Mandatory?"

He nodded confidently. "Drowning in the Daramo is the easiest escape. I'm not sure anyone could save her then, bar an extraordinary set of circumstances."

"Such as?" Herezah demanded.

Salmeo shrugged his huge shoulders as he considered. Then he held his great hands out, his palms shockingly pale pink against his black skin. "I simply can't imagine what, Valide."

Herezah smiled. "Excellent. That's what I want you to arrange, Salmeo."

"You want me to bring about her death, Valide?" he queried

innocently, making it unequivocally clear between them what was being planned and who was giving the orders.

The Valide held his gaze and spoke slowly, directly. "I want you to ensure she is somehow found in that unforgivable position you suggested and cannot be saved from the consequences. The rest is up to the laws of our harem."

"And the Zar, Valide, what of his interests?"

She frowned, not understanding. "What do you mean, Salmeo?"

"Only that if he were on our side it would be easier to manipulate the law in our favor," he said gently, his eyes heavy-lidded, spicing his tone with intrigue.

Herezah sighed. "Boaz, unfortunately, will not be our pawn. As I have said, he has become a man these past thirteen or so moons and he will not be manipulated easily."

"He need not know, Valide," Salmeo said, softly breaking eye contact and looking down at his fingernails.

"You want to use my son without his knowledge?" she asked, all innuendo gone from her voice.

Salmeo nodded but still kept his gaze trained down. "He need not be in on our plan."

THE WORD *OUR* WAS not lost on her. She knew from this moment on her future was tied to that of Salmeo's. Her grand notion to align herself with Tariq, keeping Salmeo at a more subservient distance, had not unfolded as she had hoped. The Vizier was now Grand Vizier and far more powerful, and he had so cleverly ingratiated himself with her son, it was sickening. Even now she couldn't quite grasp how it had happened under her nose and with such speed. At the time of the old Zar's death he had been a sniveling, obsequious adviser with no one's respect and only her lukewarm patronage to save him. But within weeks of the new Zar being crowned, Tariq had become a changed man who was suddenly interesting, pithy, dry-witted, and downright clever—qualities she had not once previously appreciated in the Vizier. And, damn him, he looked different. Gone was the stooped carriage and all the vulgar adornments he had so favored—jewels in his beard and on his sandals. Now she couldn't spot a single item that sparkled on his person, and his clothes were no longer ostentatious. He was wearing subtle colors and simple lines, more befitting a man of his status as Grand Vizier. Herezah could swear he now had a roving eye for women, too, something that had never occurred to her before. Tariq had seemed almost sexless in the years gone by and she knew he lived alone, took no women casually, and certainly had no longtime lovers. This much Zar Joreb had confirmed explicitly with her on one of their cozy nights together. But this new Tariq all but flirted with her, winked at some of the serving girls, and, in the rare company of the veiled members of the harem, gave them lingering appreciation.

It was Tariq who was now seemingly closest to the Zar—him and the despised dwarf, of course; how could she overlook Pez? She realized Salmeo was watching her and drew herself back from those thoughts that irritated her so much.

With her next words she knew she was not just aligning herself with Salmeo, but also risking her fragile relationship with her son. "Please explain to me how we shall be able to use my son without his consent," she said. "But first, I need a fresh brew of my tea. Would you organize it, please, whilst I change out of my silk robe."

Salmeo gave instructions to a eunuch servant as Herezah disappeared into her sleeping chamber, which led into her dressing rooms. She emerged as Salmeo was dismissing the servant who had laid out fresh crockery.

"You look very lovely, Valide," the chief eunuch commented.

She nodded, not really needing to be told. It was obvious from her proud bearing that she knew how splendid she appeared today. There was work to do and she needed to be her dazzling best.

"May I pour for you?" Salmeo added.

"Please," she replied, settling herself by the window, and as she stared into the gardens, she contemplated, not for the first time, how often she stared at the gardens or the sea, as all in the harem did, with inextinguishable longing to be elsewhere.

"We're all prisoners of this beautiful place," she said, speaking her thoughts aloud.

"Privileged prisoners, Valide," Salmeo commented from behind. He lightly stepped toward Herezah and delicately handed her the tall, exquisite cup, filled with the steaming citrus brew, that stood on an equally beautiful saucer. It was her own design, commissioned by Joreb when she was pronounced wife and Absolute Favorite. Its colors were bold and daring, reflecting Herezah's personality, Joreb had told her.

She sipped, making a soft sound of pleasure at the warmth. "All servants dismissed?" she checked.

"We are alone, Valide."

"Then I am all ears, Grand Master Eunuch. Tell me your cunning plan."

4

The man, hunched like a sack of grain in the chair, stared intently out to sea. Hair, once black as the famous velvet from Shagaire, now curiously golden, blew across his face, unnoticed.

The wind was refreshing rather than cold, for summer had begun to lay its new warmth over the land. Nevertheless the man's bones seemed to rattle from a constant shivering that had nothing to do with any chill. The goat's-wool blanket hung loosely from his hollow frame, ignored and as unwanted by the wearer as any other form of comfort that tried its healing qualities but failed. This one wanted to suffer, for in suffering there was life.

The day itself had been sublime, its brightness almost painful on the eyes, but the man's gaze was distracted neither by the sparkle of the first season's sun nor the glistening Faranel Sea it lit and ultimately warmed. Instead all focus was riveted on the far distance and the glowing outline of the city of Percheron, blushing fiercely in the late afternoon sunlight. High on the hill that overlooked the magnificent horseshoe-shaped bay was the Stone Palace, and it was to these quiet hallways and chambers that his thoughts fled. And although the twin giants who kept guard over Percheron captured his attention from time to time, as though trying to distract him from the lonely vigil, that gaze was always quickly drawn back to the dominating presence of the Zar's palace.

"You should move inside now," the old woman who had limped up urged gently. "And it's time for your medicine."

"For whatever good it will do me," he replied.

Her tone was bitter, though he knew she didn't mean for it to be. "It's no good staring toward the palace, Lazar. She cannot see you. She is safe. Let that be enough."

They both knew that this was simply her opening gambit in an old argument. He bit. "Don't lecture me, Priestess. At least you can go into the city freely. I am stuck here, as much a prisoner of this leper colony as Ana is of the harem."

"Well, blame yourself! You took too big a risk and set yourself back moons with a journey you were not well enough to make." She made a sound of disgust. "Attending Horz's execution was madness."

"I needed to get the note to Pez," he replied, his anger stoking.

"I could have taken the note to Pez. You wanted to see Ana again. What good are you to us if you insist on speeding your own death?"

"My life is my own," Lazar growled. "It does not belong to you, or anyone!"

"Is that so?" she said haughtily. "You can try to fool us, but I suspect you can't fool yourself with such hollow words. Your life is already given—she owns it," she stated, her crooked finger pointing angrily toward the palace in which Ana lived.

Lazar remained silent until Zafira sighed, an action he unconsciously repeated. He knew what she said was true, but he also knew, as well as she, that the stakes of this strange battle they were now engaged in were high, and in truth, risks were all they had to choose from.

"I shall be in shortly," he finally replied.

"Let me help you."

"No. I will manage."

"Lazar, you must forget her," she cautioned softly. "I suspect—"

"Just a few more minutes, Zafira," he said, cutting off her words.

He didn't deny that it was the sad memory of the loss of a woman that was so destructive to his healing, and yet he knew that it was because of that very woman that Lazar still lived, still bothered to wake each day and breathe, to eat, to hobble around keeping his limbs supple, if not strong. It was so ironic. Opposing emotions pulling him apart, both good and bad for his health.

He had pretended—even to himself—that the perilous trip into the city was to let Pez know that he lived and to summon the dwarf to come to Star Island immediately. This was his pretext for slipping away from Zafira, risking his life just hours after being revived from the unconsciousness that had followed the flogging and poison. He and the priestess had argued bitterly over it because it was true, he was not nearly strong enough to make the journey across the water. His true motive, of course, was to have that one final glimpse of the Odalisque Ana. And that effort had nearly taken what little life he had had left.

He had barely clung to existence after the poisoning from the whip that opened his back so badly. Blood loss, drezden poison, and a deep sorrow all conspired to kill him. But love had sustained him. He had held on to life because it might mean he would see her once more. And so he had fought death these past eleven moons, fought it so hard he was left a living wreck—but a wreck with a legacy.

Lazar now understood that the drezden brought with all its evil intention a dark gift—it tried to kill him but it was also the one thing that could continue to save him . . . but at a price. The curious woman known as Ellyana had warned him that the legacy would exact its debt.

"It will stay with you forever," she had counseled when he was sufficiently recovered to focus on words, and on living. "It will lie dormant within you and then like a sickness curse you all over again on a whim."

"What is my warning? How will I know when it comes?" he had asked, when he was strong enough, his throat raspy from having gone so long without speaking.

"You won't. It simply attacks when it chooses."

"And how can Lazar protect himself then?" Zafira had asked on his behalf.

"With the drezden itself. You must always carry a vial of it with you. Put a drop of the concentrated poison on your finger—no more than a single drop, mind—and put that on your tongue. It will take some hours, but it will restore you."

"But it hasn't restored me on this occasion."

"Lazar, you were as good as dead from the whipping alone. I defy any physician to have brought you back from the brink of the abyss with their modern potions and notions. Trust me. If you were at the palace or under the care of the male doctors, you would have been given up to your god. Drezden saved you. It will again, and much faster now that your body can cope with it, but only—" She stopped, shrugged.

"For a while," Lazar finished what Ellyana had not said.

The woman had simply nodded. Not long after, she had disappeared.

Lazar returned his thoughts to the present, realizing that the priestess had remained standing beside him. He needed a few more minutes alone. "Please, Zafira."

His plea must have reminded her that he needed encouragement, not recrimination, because she sighed again. "You are mending, Spur. I have been hard on you, perhaps not as honest as I should be. I know you feel weak but your back is healed and I've watched you exercising. I see you have some strength back." He nodded, remained silent. "Allow yourself to be well. The medicine can only do so much. Now it's up to you."

"I realize this. Now please, just a few more moments."

Even he heard the plaintive note in his voice. The old woman shook her head. She turned to hobble away toward the small hut that served as home nowadays and Lazar noticed how she winced. He suspected it was the same snag of pain in her hip that she'd mentioned occasionally but no doubt constantly reminded her she was well past her best years. He wondered if any of them was up to whatever this challenge was that lay ahead—a dwarf, an imprisoned odalisque, a wizened priestess, and him, not much better than a cripple himself.

ANA BOWED LOW AND gracefully. "You wished to see me, Valide?"

"I did, child. Come, walk with me in the courtyard. This mild weather is too delicious to waste," Herezah replied, noting with surprise how different Ana appeared since she had last paid her any close scrutiny. Herezah detested the girl so much she had deliberately ignored her, had in fact had so little to do with the girls these most recent moons that she had allowed Ana—and no doubt some of the older odalisques—to suddenly blossom into womanhood without her noticing. That was a mistake and most unlike her, but she had been strongly affected by Lazar's death and hadn't taken much interest in much at all these last ten moons. For all her outward goading of the Spur, her public rebukes, and the hardships she could force upon him, he had been the one man over her lonely lifetime who had made made her otherwise cold heart burn. She had never loved Zar Joreb, but she had admired and enjoyed him—and without his favor she shuddered to imagine what would have become of her. In truth, love was something she had never experienced, so whether she loved Lazar she could not say. But did her lust overflow for him? Yes! She had never wanted any other man with that kind of intense passion, but he had ignored her advances, denied her even simple pleasures—a kind word, a smile. And since Ana had arrived in their lives, his polite shunning of Herezah had crystallized into hatred, she was sure of it. He despised her for denying him access to Ana. And still, after all this time, Herezah's heart could jump at the mention of his name, could ache when she allowed herself space and time to think about his loss. And so, very unwisely, amidst her most private sorrow and her desire to improve her relationship with her son, she had permitted the harem, her seat of power, to essentially function without her closest supervision. As she watched Ana approach she realized the price of her error. It wasn't too late, though: striking woman or not, Ana was still just an odalisque and very much under the Valide's law.

"And how are you, my dear?" Herezah asked, not at all interested but keen to appear as friendly as possible.

"I am well, Valide, thank you," Ana answered as she followed Herezah into the small, private garden.

"Come and stand in the light, Ana, so that I may look at you," Herezah suggested. She watched the girl glide toward the column of sunlight that cut through the cypress pines and warmed the stone flagstones beneath her sandals. She felt instant envy at the way the girl's hair blazed brightly beneath the golden rays, glinting as she moved her head, clearly ignorant of the effect it had on an onlooker, particularly a male one. "You have changed, Ana."

"How so, Valide?" Ana asked politely.

Herezah considered. "You are taller, you have a good eye for costume, I see, and you are fuller of figure, too—which is a good thing, for you were on the narrow side."

"I try not to eat too many of the sweet dishes that the kitchens tempt us with, Valide," Ana replied.

"I don't think you have to worry too much, my dear. At your age I could eat a camel for a snack and not put on so much as a sheld. It's after childbirth that you have to observe new eating habits. You wouldn't have been acquainted with the old Zar's harem."

"It was disbanded just prior to my arrival."

"Well, you'd have seen a line of fat women waddling out of the palace, I assure you," Herezah said, more viciously than she had intended.

Ana remained frustratingly serene under Herezah's gaze. "I was once told that roundness of body meant prosperity, Valide."

Herezah blinked in irritation. The girl was far too forward

in presenting her own thoughts. "That may well be, Ana," she said sharply, "but no Zar is going to choose a corpulent woman over one whose body is voluptuous but still trim."

It was as if Ana ignored the Valide's comment. "I was also told that beauty is in the eye of the beholder, Valide. Perhaps each Zar has different ideas of what is attractive in a woman. Zar Boaz may find a woman's mind beautiful and not lay so much store by her figure."

Herezah couldn't stifle the gasp of indignation that escaped her.

Ana realized her error. "Forgive me, Valide. I meant no offense. I am merely posing an idea."

"You offer your private thoughts too easily, Ana, for one so young."

"I apologize, Valide Herezah," Ana tried again, this time going to her knees. "I am trying to teach myself not to."

Herezah looked at the kneeling figure and it was as though she were looking at herself fifteen years earlier. Elegant, headstrong, beautiful on the outside, and a sharp intelligence held within. Herezah remembered how the fire of ambition had burned so brightly inwardly—that was all that had gotten her through the years of destructive boredom. But ambition did not burn in this girl, she deduced. It was something completely different and yet still it gave off the similar heat, simmering constantly but invisibly.

"What is it that you want?" Herezah said, the words slipping out before she could stop them.

Ana looked up in surprise. "I want nothing, Valide. I just want to be," she answered.

Herezah again felt the twitch of exasperation. "To be? Whatever does that mean?"

Ana shrugged. "Pardon me, but I'm just not sure how to put my feelings into words."

"You say you want nothing," Herezah repeated, clutching at the only thing Ana had said that made sense, "and yet you have all the girls in the harem eating out of your palm."

Again Ana looked down and Herezah knew the girl understood. "It is not from choice, Valide. I do not encourage it."

"And still it happens, Ana. Are you dangerous for the harem? You may stand."

Ana rose in a fluid movement and once again Herezah was struck by the golden beauty and grace of this young woman. She looked ripe for the plucking, as the Grand Master Eunuch had observed. He was right; Boaz could be unwittingly used to bring this threat to Herezah's status to an end.

"Dangerous?" Ana repeated.

"Your innocence is always convincing, Ana, but it does not fool me," Herezah commented, carefully covering her rancor with a soft tone, as though she were merely making an observation rather than an accusation. "It will serve you well. I'm sure the Zar will love it."

Now Ana dared to raise her depthless green eyes and regard the Valide, her gaze serious. Herezah felt impaled by the stare.

She affected a coy laugh as if embarrassed. "Oh, surely you realize that my son will want to bed you soon, Ana?" Not all of the mockery in her tone was disguised. She wanted Ana to hear it. "And I for one will be delighted when he takes his first virgin between his sheets," she continued.

Ana opened her mouth, then closed it again, clearly at a loss for words. Herezah smiled inwardly. This was where she wanted the girl—unsure, hesitant.

"Anyway, let's not talk about that," she said in a more

friendly manner, waving away the previous conversation. "I brought you here today to discuss Zar Boaz's picnic for the harem."

"Oh?"

"Yes, you see, I imagine some of the younger girls are going to be a little fearful of being taken out of the harem. They've been here now for a year, so this is where they feel secure."

Ana had regained her composure to some degree and answered quickly. "No, Valide, I think everyone in the harem is very excited. I sense no fear."

Herezah blinked slowly, as if talking to someone too dull to understand. "Nevertheless, while you may think most are looking forward to it, I assure you some will be reluctant."

Ana nodded, understanding her lack of tact.

Once again Herezah found and fixed a friendly smile to her face. "I am hopeful, Ana, that you will counsel the youngsters, dissuade any hesitation, and especially show them not to fear their Zar."

"How do you mean, Valide?" Ana asked, frowning.

"Let's take a tour of the garden," Herezah suggested, even linking arms with the girl, though she despised the feel of her young and unblemished silken flesh next to her own. The Valide understood that she, too, had once enjoyed similar qualities, but that freshness and vitality was gone now. Oh yes, she remained beautiful, but she was an older woman now, a Valide, no less. No man was going to come looking for her these days—no man would dare—but she missed being able to use her body to render a man helpless. It was such a powerful feeling, one Ana had not yet known . . . or had she? Lazar had been totally in Ana's thrall; Herezah had seen it in his hungry, desperate gaze as he lied through his teeth to save the girl from the harem's imprisonment. During the Choosing Ceremony, when all the purchased girls were first presented to the Valide, he had argued persuasively for access to Ana. Herezah suspected it was a lie that the mother in the foothills had demanded as part of the sale that Lazar act as some sort of ongoing mentor—though he had made it sound credible—but nevertheless, adroit though the Spur was, he could not hide . . . not from her anyway . . . the helpless ardor he felt for Ana. Her hackles rose just thinking of it. Not only did Ana seem to have Boaz focused on her, but the girl had somehow managed to win the heart of the only man Herezah had ever desired and yet never so much as touched.

She remembered now Lazar half-naked, standing tall at first against the whipping post in the Courtyard of Sorrows. It hadn't taken too many bites from the Viper's Nest to savagely open up his back and for precious blood to flow all too freely out of Lazar's hard, proud body, to leave it slumped and lifeless by the end of the twenty strokes. She felt a keen pain as she allowed the frustration and anger she normally kept so securely buried to have free rein.

What she would have given for one night with Lazar. She knew he paid prostitutes for their services and that riled her. She would have given him all of herself for free, risked everything for a single night. And Ana had had several nights with Lazar at Herezah's expense, from traveling with him from her home in the foothills to a carefree evening the girl had spent with him in Percheron prior to Lazar's presenting her at the palace. Herezah had discovered this on that final night of Ana's freedom; she and the Spur had wandered the bazaar—hand in hand, no less!—had shared a meal and sat close together beside a fountain. Her spies reported laughter, tenderness, and even sorrow when the time came to leave the alley of gold—where he had bought her a present—their last call prior to wending their way to the palace. Her fury, a year on, still burned.

Herezah had only two men in her life, two men on her mind, and Ana laid claim to both of them. It hurt like a savage wound and it took all of the Valide's willpower not to pull her arm from the young woman walking carefully beside her.

The silence between them had lengthened. Herezah pointed to a bench seat beneath a fig tree. She swallowed her anger and her voice came out bright and steady. "Let's sit, shall we?"

Ana did as asked, maintaining her silence, unsure of what was coming.

"Do you ever think of Spur Lazar, Ana?" The Valide felt the involuntary movement next to her, knew she had hit a nerve.

"I do, from time to time, with sorrow that he is no longer striding around the city."

"Is that how you remember him?"

Ana began to shrug, then caught herself. "I don't really know how I remember him. My time with him was limited," she said noncomittally.

"But you admired him?" Herezah prompted, unable to help herself.

"Yes, I did. I thought he was a fine man and a loyal one to Percheron. It was not right, what happened on account of my indiscretion."

Herezah heard the pain in the girl's voice. She sensed that the odalisque was trying to mask her true feeling as she tried to shape carefully chosen words into a polite response, but the girl's body language alone revealed to the Valide the depth of her feeling for the Spur. "No one could know that Lazar would be quite as gallant as he was, child. He was very protective of the youngsters he brought in. It was a terrible thing, I agree, but it was no one's fault."

"It was someone's fault that the whip was tipped with poison, Valide, surely?"

Again Herezah felt the breath catch in her throat at Ana's audaciousness. "And he paid the price."

"My uncle Horz would never do such a thing, Valide. I did not know him as well as you, perhaps, but I knew him to be a faithful and proud servant of the harem. We were distant relatives—I'd met him only twice in my life before I was brought to the palace and it is merely coincidence that two of the same family lived here. He never treated me any differently from the other odalisques and he was loyal to the Elim. He was no murderer."

"And still coincidence that you both became embroiled in the drama that led to Lazar's death?"

The Valide watched Ana nod unhappily.

"Then who, Ana?" Herezah asked innocently, interested to hear what the girl might say. "Who poisoned the whip?"

Ana turned now and leveled a long glance at the Valide.

Zarab save us, Herezah thought, *she thinks I contrived it!* "What does that look mean?"

Ana instantly dropped her gaze. "I . . . I mean nothing by it, Valide, my apologies. I just thought you might know something more than has been explained."

You lie well, Herezah thought, *but not well enough to dupe me.* "I know only what you do, odalisque," the Valide replied in a rare moment of honesty. "He cannot be brought back no matter what the truth is."

"He should never have gone, though, Valide. It is my fault and I can never forgive myself."

"Perhaps you have learned your lesson, then?" Herezah asked, pleased that Ana had led herself to exactly this point.

"Definitely," Ana replied unequivocally.

Herezah was not yet satisfied. She would remind Ana of this conversation in time to come. "So nothing could persuade you to escape again?"

Ana looked pained but she held the Valide's gaze. "Nothing."

Herezah smiled. "Thank you, Ana. I appreciate this. You know I chose you as the finest odalisque of the exquisite selection of girls on offer those many moons ago. I have high hopes for you. Perhaps you see yourself as a Favorite? Possibly Absolute Favorite, as I was?"

"No, Valide," Ana answered gravely. "I have never thought about such things."

"Well, you should, my girl. You have the right intelligence and there is no doubting your suitability as a mate for the Zar. Doesn't producing heirs to the throne of Percheron excite you?"

Ana shivered, despite the warmth, and shook her head. "I know what happens to spare heirs, Valide. No, I would not wish that on any mother. I will happily remain barren to avoid such trauma."

Now Herezah did gasp. "You must not talk like that, Ana. You have a role now in the harem. Even if you can't see it, we can. You are the most likely first choice of the Zar. I can't speak for him but I can see what he sees."

"Beauty is not everything," Ana whispered.

"So you've said, but it is vital as an odalisque. You have little else to recommend yourself to the Zar."

"It will not matter to me if he does not choose me, Valide.

If you'll forgive my candidness, I think this is where you and I differ."

The courage of the girl to speak so forthrightly to the most powerful woman in the palace had to be admired, and Herezah forgave her the couched insult—for Herezah had never made any secret of her own ambition—and secretly admired Ana her spine. It reminded her painfully of her own determination, even though they seemed to want different things. Herezah still had not clarified what it was Ana wanted. Freedom, probably—what every odalisque would take over all the riches and pampering.

With a small smile, Herezah returned to their earlier conversation. "I'm pleased, Ana, that you will stay faithful to the harem and not test us again with any further escape attempts from the palace. Your dash for freedom from the harem after the Choosing Ceremony was gravely ill advised, as you've now discovered in the harshest possible way. Though I put it down to a fearless nature combined with your immaturity, it must never happen again. Let that fearlessness manifest itself in positive ways—in your duties as odalisque. You have led a blemish-free existence these past thirteen moons, as I understand it." Ana nodded, staring at the ground. "This is wise," Herezah reiterated. "Which is why I am asking you to take charge of the picnic next full moon. The girls are still very frightened of me, so they will find it far easier to follow your lead."

"I understand," Ana replied.

"And, as a reward for your help, I am recommending that you be allowed to visit the Grand Bazaar."

Ana looked up sharply, her eyes wide. "Leave the palace?" she asked, her tone filled with disbelief.

Herezah smiled again, indulgently. "Fully veiled, and with Elim escorts, of course."

"Valide . . . I . . . I . . ."

"It's all right, Ana. I know what you're trying to say. I think you forget that I, too, was a prisoner of the harem as a young woman and wanted nothing but to escape its smothering ways. I still am a prisoner. I still yearn for freedom but I have learned to accept my place, as you will. But I don't want you to suffer as I did. If I can allow you to enjoy some rare moments of independence—the boat picnic or this trip into the city—then I will allow it. I feel the freedom will keep you less . . . troubled, shall we say."

"I really don't know what to say, or how to thank you," Ana stammered, shock written on her face.

"Thank me by being true. Keep your promise not to try anything silly and help me to give these girls a good time out on the water. Help me in the harem itself by being cooperative, less sullen, not so withdrawn. This is your life now. I want to try to make it easier to live, but I can't save you completely. You must accept it, as I did, embrace your role as odalisque and do the very best you can. You're so bright; I'd like to see you studying more. Is there anything you really enjoy?"

"Well," Ana began, "I believe I'm good at language, Valide. Perhaps I can concentrate fully on that."

"And not embroidery?"

Ana actually smiled and Herezah saw how any man would be instantly captivated by the way her eyes sparked when she was happy. "I don't care much for sewing," she admitted wryly.

"And who could blame you," Herezah replied, arching her eyebrows, feeling the fragile bond forming between them. "All right, I think focusing on language is an excellent idea. We always have a need for translators. Any particular one?"

"Galinsean," Ana gushed, then reined in her enthusiasm. "And of course, Merlinean."

Herezah really was amused now. "Galinsean! It's an impossible tongue, child! And we don't need Galinsean."

"Since losing the Spur, I would suggest that we do, Valide. He was the only person who spoke Galinsean fluently, as I understand it. And although I know he was Percheron's army head—and I'm merely a slave—it may be handy to have someone other than the Zar who understands the language. I must admit to you that I've actually been teaching myself the language for the past year. But I'd like to devote more time to it—perhaps a tutor can help with my accent?"

The Valide gave a sound of surprise at the girl's claim. "Taught yourself?"

Ana nodded, embarrassed.

"How?"

"The library, Valide."

Ana failed to mention that Pez had guided her in this, found all the right books and secretly aided her learning, even introduced her to a shy slave—an old man who had suffered the misfortune of being captured by slavers twice in his life. He was originally from the north, where Lazar's great friend, Jumo, hailed from. Jumo had disappeared since Lazar's death, but he had known the slave in the library and had suggested him to Pez as a tutor for Ana's learning of the tough language from the west. After his second capture by the Galinseans, the slave was sold to the aristocracy because of his skills in painting portraits. The librarian had learned both the language of the streets and the higher language of the wealthy. Finally taking his chance to flee from slavery, he had risked an escape with a caravan across the Great Desert in an effort to reach his homeland but had been captured by Percherese slavers and sold to the palace, where he now worked in the library assembling a contemporary history of Percheron in pictures. He had taught Ana well.

"And how fluently do you speak Galinsean now, Ana?" Herezah asked, unable to hide her shock.

"You are right, it is a difficult language," came the diplomatic reply.

Herezah had to admit that talking with Ana felt like she was conversing with a peer. The girl still looked too young to have anything much in her head save expensive gowns and glittering jewels, but it was obvious that all the perfectly normal traits of being young and female and spoiled were completely absent from this one. Even her manner of speaking was mature. "Not even Boaz can master Galinsean and he has been studying it most of his life."

"I would like to try, Valide, if you'll permit it."

"I'll permit it, Ana, but I see no use in it. I'll recommend to Salmeo that you be given tutoring but I would like you to learn Akresh as well, which is far more useful for visiting dignitaries and the like."

"I'm happy to do so."

"Good. So, it is agreed—we'll both help each other. You have only days to get the girls prepared for their boating picnic. I will recommend the trip into the city to pick out some fabrics and some jewels for you. It's time we started dressing you to show off your lovely figure and to present you as a potential Favorite for the Zar."

At this, Ana's eyes clouded again, but she maintained her eager expression. It was obvious to Herezah that all mentions of bedding the Zar were scaring Ana. Well, like most things, after the first time, it all got easier. Ana would survive, as every fearful odalisque down the centuries had done. "I shall start helping to plan the picnic festivities now, Valide."

"Excellent. And I'll inform Salmeo of our bargain."

Ana excused herself and in her hurry to depart missed the sly smile of the Valide, well pleased with how adroitly she had manipulated the young woman. Herezah reached for her bell to summon a runner. Salmeo must hear that their plan was now in play.

5

Pez found Ana sitting with most of the other odalisques in the divan suite. Here couches were laid out around the walls and across the room at well-spaced intervals so the young women could lounge, relax, take some iced tea or sweet pastries if they chose, but, most importantly, this was where most could inhale the fumes of the burning garammala.

This oil, yielded by squeezing the leaves of a tree that grew only on the fringe of the desert, was headily expensive, yet most of the rich of Percheron enjoyed it occasionally. Pez had tried it only twice and both times had been violently ill, so he had never grasped the attraction, although watching others, he realized it usually had a completely different effect. It appeared to relax users to a state of calm whilst somehow keeping them alert, as if all their senses were heightened. Unlike other relaxants, garammala did not make users slur, drowse, or hallucinate. It simply put them into a gentle, happy mood, bordering on mildly euphoric. It apparently made the inhaler feel almost instantly erotic, too, for Pez remembered wandering into this room when the previous harem had made good use of the pipes and noting that all inhibitions were dropped. It seemed the women were quite happy to spend their newfound erotic currency with anyone who'd pay attention, including the eunuchs. Knowing how they were left long and lonely and sexually frustrated for years, Pez could feel only pity for the women who escaped their demons through garammala.

Only Herezah, he recalled, never took the oil, and just as the Valide had resisted it all those years ago, now sat Ana, contriving similar symptoms of joyful mood but ignoring the pipe by her side, knowing no one would notice . . . no one except him, of course. He winked at Ana and she gave him a soft smile as she swung her legs down and stood to greet him.

"I've missed you," she said, hugging her friend. "Where have you been?"

Pez gave her an equally gentle smile, but one tinged with regret. "I'm sorry," was all he said, pulling at his hair as if it were crawling with nits. A couple of girls nearby laughed. "What have you been up to in my absence?" he added more brightly in a whisper.

She took a breath and arched her eyebrows as if to say plenty had occurred. "The Valide requested a meeting with me today."

Pez expressed his surprise while performing foolish little hops and jumps. He burped. More of the girls giggled. "And?"

"Shall we walk?" she asked.

"Cartwheel for us, Pez," one of the youngsters beseeched.

He did so, happily spinning around the room and expertly avoiding collisions with furniture and beautifully attired women. He enjoyed warranted applause before pretending to be dizzy and staggering onto the pathways outside the room. Ana duly followed; no one took much note of her departure. Pez carefully sat on a small wall and studiously picked his nose, staring at the sky as if uninterested in the person who had followed him. Ana spoke in a low voice as she strolled by him very slowly, pretending to enjoy some sun on her face.

"She made a bargain with me."

"Tell me," he whispered.

"I'm to co-operate, help her with the others girls, especially on this boating trip."

"And?"

"And if I promise not to try anything that breaks the harem rules, she's going to let me out for a few hours of freedom."

"What's that supposed to mean?"

"I'm to be permitted into the city. Alone, save an Elim escort."

Pez stopped picking his nose and resisted the urge to stare at Ana in his anxiety. "She's up to something." He watched the beautiful odalisque do an unhurried circumference of a pond.

"Such as?" she asked as she returned to pass by him.

"I don't know," he answered, worried. "What else?"

"I'm to be given a tutor to study Galinsean."

"You didn't tell her you were fluent, did you?"

"Hardly," Ana replied, once again returning and passing him. "I didn't give away much at all other than that I've been teaching myself."

Pez leaped down from the wall and took her hand, pretending to walk alongside her like one of the strange monkeys from the Zar's zoo. "Ana, you have a gift of tongues."

"Like you."

"No, better than me," he whispered, pausing briefly to stare at the sky and hoot loudly. "You speak Galinsean already better than any tutor—I hope you can lie your way through the lessons."

She sighed. "I will. It makes me feel closer to him."

Now Pez stopped, both from sorrow and the guilt of knowledge he did not share with her. He knew precisely to whom she referred. "This does not do you any good, Ana."

"Keep lurching beside me, Pez. Everyone is watching us and enjoying your antics," she cautioned. As he turned a somersault, she continued. "Galinsean could be useful anyway," she continued.

He snorted. "What possible use could it be?"

Ana shook her head in gentle capitulation. "None, I suppose. She wants me to learn Akresh as well."

"Now that is a practical suggestion."

"I wonder why she's being nice."

"Herezah always has a reason for everything she does. Be suspicious at every turn, Ana. She fears you."

"Why?"

Pez made a clicking sound of exasperation with his tongue. "Because Boaz adores you. Isn't that obvious? The two of you meet often enough. You forget I'm usually there and hear you laughing with him."

"I have asked him not to single me out," she countered.

Pez decided it was time to career around the courtyard like an angry monkey. When he charged nearby her, his back to the divan suite, he replied, "But still he does, whether you like it or not. His admiration is obvious . . . and he's seventeen, Ana. Old enough. You must be ready for where his thoughts head now."

She scowled. "I love another," she said, truly shocking him

now into stillness, his expression betraying his complete understanding.

He waddled over to where Ana stood and took her hand,
heedless of any eyes watching, although grateful that they were
too far away to be overheard. "This is not about love, child.
This is about duty. An odalisque's duty. As for the person you
refer to, it is hopeless." That was all he could say without revealing the terrible secret.

"He's dead, I know, but that doesn't stop my heart aching
for him, my mind remembering every single little item it can
about him, my conscience reminding me that I am the reason he
is no longer alive."

"Ana, stop!" Pez said, knowing tears were next and then
raised eyebrows, should anyone notice. The other girls would
then have to come outside to find out why she was crying. He
dropped his voice. "This is foolhardy." Pez cartwheeled away
and then, back on his feet, he ran from the suite.

"ARE YOU ALL RIGHT, Ana?" someone asked. "Did Pez upset
you?"

Ana turned. It was an exquisite girl called Sascha from the
region of Akresh, a hilly realm to the east of Percheron famed
for its sapphires. Her hair was the color of burnished copper
and she had become something of a friend these past moons.
Ana knew Sascha could see the tears in her eyes. It was best to
go along with the idea that Pez ultimately upset everyone for
one reason or another. "Yes, he was threatening to stone the
monkeys in the zoo."

Sascha gave a pained expression. "Don't believe him. You
know he says stupid things all day long."

"He sounded so determined, I feel as though he's rushed off to do the stoning now."

Sascha took Ana's arm. "Pez is mad, Ana. Everyone knows that. He says anything and everything that comes into his head. Most of the time he's amusing, I'll admit, but sometimes he can be quite vicious . . . but I don't think he even knows it himself."

Ana found a watery smile. "You're right," she said, squeezing the girl's arm. "I shall ignore him."

"That's the right way to treat him. Pez hates to be ignored and I'm sure to be ignored by you will wound him terribly."

"Why do you say that?"

Sascha gave her a soft look of exasperation. "Everyone can see how he loves you. You're definitely his favorite."

Ana was tired of hearing that word. "Come on, we have to make preparations for our boat excursion," she said, determined to keep her promise to the Valide.

IRIDOR FLEW. PEZ WAS risking much in this flight, having received a request from the Zar to meet with him for the midday meal. Boaz was used to Pez's unreliability, but as they hadn't seen each other in several days now, a delay might make the Zar suspicious and Pez didn't want him mentioning anything to the nosy Vizier.

But he had to speak with Lazar. This was becoming a detestable situation. It was not so bad for Zafira—she did not have daily contact with Odalisque Ana. But Pez did, his blatant lying to the girl was well past the point of discomfort.

He also needed time to think about Herezah's latest move. What was she up to?

He found Lazar in the small copse behind the cottage.

"There you are," he said, in his dwarf shape once again.

"Greetings, Pez. Zafira said you planned to visit. Join me on my walk."

"Is that what you call it?" Pez asked, and grinned at the crease of confusion on Lazar's forehead. "More like lurching." It wasn't true, of course; he was genuinely thrilled to see his friend moving so easily once again.

"Be quiet, dwarf. You can hardly make fun with that strange waddle of yours," Lazar replied. It was the first time in a year that Pez had heard Lazar say anything that was even remotely lighthearted. Considering that even as recently as three moons ago, the man had not been able to concentrate for any length of time, other than when gazing forlornly across the water, this was stunning progress. "You'll take into account I don't use sticks anymore," he added, a note of triumph in his voice.

"I do. I'm impressed, Lazar, truly," Pez said.

"One day I shall run again. I'll even be able to overtake you," Lazar said, warming to his subject now. The hint of amusement in his tone made Pez's heart soar.

"You fail to appreciate, friend cripple, that I fly with such grace I would leave you in my wake."

They both grinned. It felt to Pez as though they were crawling out of a dark tunnel. Because Lazar had been so ill, they hadn't even had the opportunity on the two brief occasions they'd seen each other to talk about all that had occurred. Perhaps today was the day to have that discussion.

"It's good to have you back, Lazar," he said.

The former Spur sighed. "I made a decision last moon that I either give in to this affliction and hope the next attack kills me, or I fight back to complete health. I'm almost there."

"But you're still in danger from unexpected attacks, right?" Pez asked.

"According to Ellyana, I am. But the drezden will have to attack a fit body rather than a frail one. That's my only defense."

Pez nodded, moved by the change in his friend's mind-set He had always assumed it would arrive but as the year had drawn on, the dwarf had begun to question his faith in Lazar's resilience. "That's the spirit. And your hair is now its true color, I presume?"

"Yes, just as yours is," Lazar replied tartly, referring to the strange line of white hair that ran down one side of Pez's head.

"Ah, but my change makes me look even more odd than I ever did. But you, my friend, you look more handsome than ever."

Lazar gave a soft self-deprecating snort.

Pez continued, waving his arms theatrically. "Now you look truly like a Galinsean Prince."

Lazar impaled him with those light eyes that gave him away as a foreigner. "It's a relief not to have to color it anymore," he said, and the sigh that followed was rich with secrets and family, pain and grief.

"Such lengths to hide an identity." Pez gave a sound of admonishment.

"We are not so different, you and I," Lazar reminded Pez. "You've feigned madness for decades to hide yours."

"Not to hide my identity," Pez corrected.

"Just your sanity, right?"

Pez nodded. "And something else." Despite his need to be back at the palace swiftly, he had promised himself that today he would at last share all his secrets with Lazar.

His ambiguous statement captured Lazar's attention. "Oh? What else have you been hiding from me?"

Pez took a deep breath. "I have the Lore." Lazar froze, his easy posture immediately tensing. Silently he stared at Pez for what felt like an eternity to Pez. "Say something," the dwarf added, uncomfortable in the silence.

His friend shook his head in wonder. "I thought I had you worked out, but you are full of surprises. I also thought the Lore was make-believe."

"It's not."

"What does it mean for you?"

"It means secrets, Lazar. It means hiding and constant anxiety about being found out. It means denying the call of the magic that is at my fingertips, which I refuse—most of the time, anyway—to even acknowledge."

Lazar moved to a nearby tree stump and sat down slowly. "Most of the time?"

"I relented and used it twice recently. Before those two moments, I had resisted its call all my years in the palace."

"What happened?" Lazar asked.

This was going to be the hardest bit, Pez knew. "Remember Kett?"

Lazar's eyes narrowed. "How can I forget?"

"I was there. I was in the corridor with him when he was captured."

"What?"

Pez nodded. He hesitated, then added, "So was Boaz."

Lazar stood and Pez could see the effort it took. He watched Lazar move awkwardly to lean against a nearby tree. "Tell me." It was an order—just like the old Lazar.

"I needed to divert Boaz's attention. It was an impulsive decision. I thought he might like to see the girls being chosen for him."

"Wait," Lazar interrupted. "Pez, I've known you a long time and I know you do nothing on a whim. Tell me the truth, all of it."

Pez sighed. Lazar was right. He should hear everything. "I can't explain it, Lazar, and I know you won't want to hear this, but I felt a calling toward Ana. I'd never met her, I didn't know of her existence. But from the moment she entered the palace, I became aware of her, sensed the arrival of some sort of force or power."

Lazar looked bewildered. "Ana is enchanted?"

"No," Pez replied emphatically. Then he half smiled and shook his head. "Well, in truth, I don't know. I *sensed* her. I needed to know what was calling to me so strongly. Until I saw Ana I had no idea it was a young woman. Anyway, I did need to divert Boaz, so I killed two birds with one stone, you could say. Sadly, we stumbled upon Kett, and without going into the details, suddenly all three of us were in the forbidden area. But if Kett hadn't sneezed we'd have been safe."

"And when he did?"

"I could only shepherd Boaz and myself."

"Shepherd?"

"I made us invisible," Pez explained sheepishly.

Lazar said nothing. He stared at Pez openmouthed. Finally he said: "And the next time?"

"To aid Boaz in facing Horz's death. I simply channeled some strength to him."

"Strength?"

Pez shrugged. "Courage. He was nervous, terrified that he would let us all down. Terrified that he wouldn't be able to face the execution."

"I hear Horz was incredibly brave. Zafira tells me the city was abuzz with the news that he died without murmuring so much as a sound."

"He was a good man. He did not deserve to die badly, especially for a crime we both know he did not commit."

Lazar paused, and Pez could see the pieces of the jigsaw puzzle slotting into place. "And so you helped him, too," the Spur said slowly.

"Not using magic. I used the Lore on Boaz only." Pez looked at his friend, uncomfortable and uncertain of Lazar's reaction. "Do you believe me?"

Lazar clamped his jaw shut and studied Pez for a long moment before answering. "Of course I believe you." He laughed humorlessly. "You can change yourself into a bird, why not become invisible?"

Pez didn't react to the familiar bite of sarcasm. "The bird business is something entirely different—that has nothing to do with the Lore," he assured Lazar.

"I'm not sure I believe that, Pez. It's probably because of the Lore, or because of what you possess, that you have been chosen to be Iridor. I can't believe I say that so blithely. Iridor! Messenger to Lyana!" Lazar shook his head. "And your connection to Ana *is* real—we know that now. It can't be coincidence." He made a sound of disgust as he banged the tree trunk with his open hand. "I feel as though we're pieces in some grand game, being manipulated toward some final goal."

Pez nodded. "I feel the same way, Lazar. I used to think I had complete control of myself and my life; the deception of madness was all part of that control. But ever since Ellyana appeared to me and saw through my clever disguise, I've felt as though someone else is orchestrating things."

It was Lazar's turn to nod. "Ellyana knows," he said sagely. "She just didn't bother telling us before she vanished." He sat down again. "What news from the city?"

"Plenty. It's why I'm here unexpectedly."

"So, tell me."

"Who first?"

"Ana."

No surprises with that answer. Pez had promised himself he would be honest. "She's more beautiful and graceful than ever. She's also still filled with sorrow. She can't move past the notion that she is to blame for your death. It's getting worse rather than better. It is unbearable to be around her, I have to tell you. A year on and none of her grief has eased."

Lazar looked at Pez sharply. "You did not—"

"No, I didn't!" Pez replied. "Though I have to say: one moment I wonder why we are keeping this charade going, and the next agonizing over what it will do to her to discover that you aren't dead."

Lazar looked pained and Pez could tell the former Spur was as uncertain about this decision as he himself felt. "Hopefully she will never learn the truth. Ellyana wanted to preserve the secret."

"Ellyana wanted a lot of things but she gave us no reasons for any of it," Pez returned caustically. "Why is Ellyana in charge of us? Why does she still orchestrate us? She's not even here."

"Pez, you yourself admit that she was touched by a powerful magic. Don't you remember saying that to me?" The dwarf grimaced and kept a grumpy silence. "Well, do you?" Lazar prompted.

Pez relented. "I do."

"Then you and she are inextricably tied—you both possess enchantment. I've seen her abilities with my own eyes. She was definitely the same woman that Ana and I met in the market that first night in Percheron. And I maintain that my eyes did not deceive me: I bought Ana a simple gold chain. But when Ellyana handed it to Ana it had turned into an image of Iridor. You tell us she visited you in the harem, one moment an old crone, the next a fresh-faced young woman."

"All true."

"And now you have a new and happy knack of transforming yourself into an owl and I believe it as though it's the most normal thing in my day."

"Magnificent, aren't I," Pez said.

"Annoying as well," Lazar said.

"There's nothing normal about your days," Pez retaliated sulkily.

Lazar ignored Pez's gripe. "As I was saying, I have no doubt that you and she are linked. And then Zafira and myself are linked through both of you. We're the pieces in Ellyana's game, you might say."

Pez nodded in agreement, his heavy brow creased in thought. "There is another."

"Another pawn?" Lazar asked, and Pez nodded. "Who?"

"I don't know, but I feel him. I also feel that he's more than a mere pawn."

"Him?"

Pez shrugged. He wasn't ready to discuss this. "I think it's a him. When I was talking with Boaz after Kett's unfortunate capture, I felt a disruption in the Lore. Someone was eavesdropping on our conversation and that person was not around in the flesh."

"More magic?" Lazar asked, gawping.

Pez nodded. "I believe so."

"What did you do?"

"Took instant precaution. Fortunately my 'madness' is my best protection and of course Boaz is used to me suddenly acting the lunatic. I wrote him a note telling him to hold his tongue, that we were being listened to."

Lazar's eyes widened as he made the leap. "You told Boaz about the Lore."

"I had to—he wasn't going to let me get away with the shepherding trick without an explanation. But although he might have forgotten my caution over the eavesdropper, I haven't."

Lazar sighed. "Who do you think it was? Is there someone else in the palace with the Lore, or some sort of power? Either be direct or stop alluding to a threat I don't understand."

"I'll stop, then," Pez said, frowning. "I'm not ready to say more until I myself understand more." He gave Lazar a look begging for his trust. "Suffice to say, his name is Maliz."

Now Lazar looked incredulous. "From the ancient myths? The one who turned Beloch and Ezram to stone? Lyana's nemesis?"

The dwarf nodded unhappily.

"You think *he* was watching you?"

"I told you, I don't know!"

Lazar shook his head, obviously confused. "All the more reason to trust Ellyana perhaps," he said slowly. "She seems to be the only one who can see the whole picture. She was firm about not letting Ana know that I was still alive. She obviously thought even Jumo couldn't know about any of this, which probably explains his disappearance," he said, scratching his newly golden hair.

Time for truth, Pez reminded himself. "Lazar, I do know something about Jumo," he said, feeling awkward, but at the look of hope on Lazar's face he decided to wait till the end of the conversation to say anything. Lazar probably wouldn't speak to him once he found out what Pez knew. "But let's finish my report first."

Lazar looked anxious to hear about his former manservant but nodded. "I will remind you of Jumo, though."

"I'm sure you will. Ana has had a meeting with the Valide."

At this, the former Spur looked back at his short friend sharply.

Pez told him everything that Ana had told him.

"Herezah's plotting something," Lazar stated firmly.

"My thoughts exactly."

"You have to find out what."

"I intend to."

"How?"

"That's my concern. I came here today to tell you that Ana is vulnerable and her weakness for you is not helping her be strong when she needs to be. I'm sure I don't have to remind you what an odalisque is required to do should the Zar's eyes fall favorably upon her?"

Lazar scowled. "No, you certainly don't."

"Well, that time is rapidly approaching, Lazar. And I can't change that—Lore or not."

"I don't expect you to."

"Oh no? Well, why do you lose hours staring at the palace, or—"

"Don't, Pez," Lazar warned.

The dwarf heeded the warning. "Lazar, you know Boaz is going to choose her!"

"And there's nothing I can do about it," Lazar roared, "so why keep rubbing it in my face!"

Pez opened his mouth to protest that this was the first time he had mentioned it. But he knew full well that Lazar probably thought about little else. "Forgive me," he said instead.

Lazar stood and walked away a few paces, his emotions visibly raw. "She was his from the moment I paid forty karels to her grasping mother," he groaned. "She was always going to be his," he added softly.

"But she is also part of this 'game.'"

"Because Ellyana singled her out with the owl statue."

"That as well, but I think it was the other way around, actually, I can't shake the knowledge that I was drawn to the power that Ana gives off long before I even knew of her existence. And now that I do know her, I can feel it emanating from her when I'm around her. I believe Ana chose Ellyana; Ana is the power, not Ellyana."

"What makes you think that?"

"Because whenever I hold Ana's hand or inadvertently touch her, I feel a thrum of some sort of powerful force pass through me. I don't think she's aware of it. She recognizes nothing in me as far as I can tell, so it appears we are not sharing our secrets."

"But it's not the Lore that she has?"

"Definitely not. I wouldn't even term it magic. It is a force all of its own and I can't access it. I've tried. All I can do is sense its presence."

"A bit like you sense the 'him' you spoke of?" Lazar reminded him.

At his friend's words Pez suddenly realized the link he had been missing. "Of course! I'm so stupid," he exclaimed, hopping around with excitement. "That's it, that's precisely it, Lazar!"

The former Spur had to smile at his friend's antics. "Nice jig, Pez. Are you going to explain?"

"I'm not sure I can. But I'll try."

But before he could speak further, Zafira hobbled out of the shadows.

"Forgive me, gentlemen. I came to offer quishtar."

At the intrusion of the priestess, Pez remembered the urgency of his return to the palace. "I don't have time, Zafira, but thank you. The Zar has not seen me in many days and he will begin to question my absence. Although it is very hard to refuse your quishtar." She smiled and nodded.

"What about Jumo?" Lazar asked.

"We have much to discuss. I will do my best to visit often now that I know you are well enough to see me at length, but for now I must go." He grinned apologetically, but his mind had already fled to the danger waiting for him. "Forgive me," he murmured distractedly to them both.

6

The Zar had invited the Valide to meet the young men being presented. He explained, "They are primarily for my protection, Mother, but I would like to put them at your service as well."

Herezah felt a stab of joy. So her son hadn't forgotten her. "Me?" she said, infusing her voice with innocence.

"Of course. Mother to the Zar? I cannot have you under any threat."

Now the Valide smiled at her son. "Thank you, Boaz, although I cannot imagine any danger to me within the harem."

"It's Tariq to whom we owe gratitude," Boaz admitted, and Herezah's joy turned sour.

"Oh?"

"This is his idea. He wants all-day, all-night protection for me. He suggested this morning that you should be included in this special ring of security."

"I see," Herezah said, trying to disguise the chill in her tone with a forced smile. "I must thank him. Is there a threat we should be concerned about?"

Boaz reached for one of the huge redberries piled on a silver platter. He dipped it into the glistening bowl of honey nearby before putting the fruit into his mouth. Finally he answered. "No, I don't believe so. Tariq just wants to ensure that we tighten up our security in general."

"Why? What does he fear?"

"Well," Boaz began, licking his lips free of the sticky honey, "he feels that the Crown of Percheron has never been more vulnerable. Our enemies might think now is a good time to take advantage of a new Zar, a young one."

"He is right in principle. But who does he believe might make such a move?"

"The Galinseans, I suspect, although he's not coming out and saying as much."

Herezah arched her eyebrows. "Perhaps Ana is right," she murmured.

"Pardon?"

"Oh, nothing, my beloved. One of our odalisques wants to learn Galinsean. I was surprised to hear it but perhaps she has a point. A translator—now that Lazar is no longer with us—may be valuable."

Boaz gave a snort. "Are you talking about Ana?"

Herezah bristled at the familiarity. "The odalisque known as Ana, yes."

Her son laughed again. "She speaks Galinsean with ease. Her command of it is amazing, and what she speaks sounds very different from the Galinsean I know. She says it is more a pidgin version used by foreigners, but I suspect she's being diplomatic."

Herezah pursed her lips before replying, calming her rising irritation, knowing that time with the Zar was precious and should not be spent in snarls. She felt as though she were living her early life all over again, waiting for the Zar's favor to fall upon her. Except this time it was wrong. This Zar was her son! She was the Valide, the most powerful woman in Percheron. She should be ruling, not discussing boating trips for the harem! Forcing herself to maintain her serene expression, Herezah said merely, "She did say she had begun to teach herself."

The Zar was eating another redberry. He chuckled as he chewed, irritating her still more. "Well, I'm hazarding she speaks courtly Galinsean as though it's her mother tongue, and now she's moved on to mastering it at the colloquial level."

"Has she indeed? And how do you know this, Boaz?"

"I've spoken to her about it. She used to practice now and then with me, but, as I say, I became useless to her after a while. She has found a new teacher, one of the slaves, a Merlinean."

"You seem on very friendly terms with Odalisque Ana?" Herezah probed. "I should tell you that I approve. I met with Ana yesterday to discuss her taking a more leading role in harem life. She has a fine mind and an innate knack for leadership. I shall reward her if she rewards me with honesty and trust," Herezah added, keen to ensure he understood that the harem was her seat of power.

She could tell Boaz hadn't expected her to take such a forceful position, could see by his hesitation that he wasn't sure how to respond. "I intend to be on very friendly terms with all in the harem, Mother. You know I am relaxing some of the more archaic rules."

"I'd heard."

Boaz gave a sly sneer. "I imagine Salmeo shares everything."

Herezah felt her back stiffen. She would not to be treated with disdain by her own child. "Need I remind you that that's his role, my son? He and I run the harem."

"No, you don't need to remind me," Boaz replied, glowering now. "But perhaps I should remind you that he is the same man who taunted and persecuted you for a great deal of your life. And as you've told me often enough, the same man—if you can call him that—who tested your virginity at eight years old and then viciously destroyed it at barely thirteen, no doubt smiling that gap-toothed grin of his the whole time. Perhaps I don't understand women well enough yet, but it strikes me that all of this might leave a lasting memory on someone like you, who bears grudges."

Herezah's fury had gathered during this tirade. She knew her son hated Salmeo, having lived under his rule for so many years of his childhood, and she knew that Boaz would not forget her own endless nights of weeping at Salmeo's harshness. But she would not let him turn his years of hate for the eunuch on her, use it as weapon against her. She had worked too hard for Boaz to have this position and status, which he now enjoyed because of her alone.

Her voice, when it came, was icy. "Salmeo did for your father, Boaz, precisely what he will do for you. And I am the one thing standing between his sharp fingernail and Odalisque Ana's virginity. When the time comes—and it will, my son, trust me—and I see in your eyes that she will be your first choice—when that time comes, it will be only because of me that Salmeo will be forced to be gentle. I would counsel you on taking a less disdainful approach with the chief eunuch and a less authoritarian approach with me. I am your mother. I demand respect."

At this Herezah rose, bowed low and elegantly to her Zar, and took her leave.

BOAZ WAS STILL STUNNED by the reprimand. It made him feel like a child again, and reminded him that when his mother was cornered she was at her most dangerous. He had to admit she was dazzling, and he could once again appreciate why his father had been so smitten by her.

He was intrigued by her bringing up Ana; obviously something was playing on her mind. Her suggestion that Ana would make a good Favorite made him smile inwardly. Having seen his mother's reaction to Ana from the moment she met her, it was obvious to Boaz that Ana was—and always had been—a prime choice in her mind. In truth this pleased him. He had even gone so far as to inquire of Ana whether his mother had had much to do with her, and Ana had surprised him with the news that she had barely glimpsed the Valide in the past few moons. He had expected Ana to be under his mother's watchful eye constantly.

However, the Valide's distance didn't necessarily mean that Ana was not being observed. Herezah and Salmeo were more than capable of subtly and effortlessly spying on someone as naive as Ana. And yet his mother's surprise at Ana's education in Galinsean was genuine. The Valide's offer to reward Ana in return for her loyalty was also suspect, for Herezah's motivations were never so simple. There would be more to this move of his mother's, he was sure. And yet . . . Herezah's praise of

Ana was reassuring. Boaz wanted his mother to get on well with her. They'd had a rocky start with Ana's escape from the harem—and then all the business with Lazar! But that seemed to be behind them, Boaz decided. If his mother was making an attempt to forge a relationship with Ana, that could only be a good thing . . . for the harem, for himself, and indeed for the Crown. Boaz had every intention of making Ana his Favorite. Every time he saw her, each opportunity he had to talk with her, and whenever he dined with the girls, as he tried to at least each new moon, his interest in her grew.

She was always courteous and gracious around the other girls, making sure as many as she could involve were brought into their discussions. But on the rare occasions that he could speak with her privately, Ana impressed him even more. She was a marvelous mimic and could impersonate the voices and mannerisms of Salmeo—and even more dangerously the Valide—with hilarious precision. That she would risk sharing this with him warmed him.

He was glad that she seemed to adore Pez. The other girls, especially the younger ones, were a bit scared of the dwarf and his unusual looks. They laughed at him rather than with him, but Boaz could see that Ana, in contrast, cherished Pez. It occurred to him now, as he sat waiting for Tariq to appear, that Pez might have shared his secret of sanity with Ana. Boaz suddenly straightened, his brow creasing in thought. That was it! Of course! Ana surely had such a deep relationship with Pez because he'd shared his great jest with her. The Zar felt a prick of intense jealousy, but it subsided as he continued to think through the situation. If Pez had shared his secret, Boaz had all the more reason to get closer to Ana. Pez trusted her as much as he trusted the Zar. That had to be worth something, Boaz reasoned.

And now that he was thinking of Pez: Where was the dwarf? Boaz had invited him to dine with him because it had been too many days since they'd seen each other. More importantly, he wished he was here now. Boaz summoned Bin, his personal assistant, to give instructions to find the dwarf. He knew Pez was used to disregarding official protocol, but this was unacceptable.

After nodding that he would find Pez immediately, Bin delivered his own message. "Zar Boaz, Grand Vizier Tariq has conveyed that he is ready to escort you to the Making of the Mutes."

Boaz felt his belly twist, answering the nagging fear that had been with him all morning and probably had been the reason for his baiting of his mother. His natural inclination was to avoid what was obviously going to be a horrific ordeal. And it would be so easy to just say no; he wouldn't even have to give a reason. But Tariq and then Bin and undoubtedly the rest of the palace would hear about his cowardice. And that would not do. He could all but hear his mother telling him he must attend.

Suddenly he wondered whether his mother would care to attend such a ghoulish event. Although he'd invited her to meet the men being presented, he hadn't anticipated that she would want to be present for the actual ritual itself. But then again; her inclination was always toward the cruel—she would no doubt accept whether she was still seething or not. And with the invitation he could make amends for mocking her slightly today.

"Inform the Valide that a special event, the Making of the Mutes, is imminent, Bin," he said, glad to note his voice was steady. "Invite her to join me if she cares to, but be sure she knows that the Zar will not be offended in the slightest if she chooses to decline. And find Pez."

Bin bowed. "I shall deliver the message before I find Pez, my Zar. The Elim will escort you to the chamber."

"Which chamber?"

"Grand Vizier Tariq has chosen the Chamber of Silence, Majesty."

"Appropriate," Boaz murmured.

"Yes, he thought so too, Highness." Bin bowed. "May I tell the Elim you are ready, my Zar?"

"I shall be ready when I'm ready," Boaz replied sharply, unnerved by the threat of the upcoming blood and shrieks of Tariq's showpiece. He could use some of Pez's strengthening Lore magic right now. Where was the dwarf? And furthermore, did he detect a high-handed tone in Bin's voice? "They can wait."

"My Zar, forgive me but—"

Boaz glared at the servant. "Begone, Bin. I'm not sure why you're still here when I expressly asked you to deliver a message to the Valide."

"I am gone, my Zar," Bin said, very humbly. He bowed deeply as he withdrew.

As the door closed on Bin, the sound of clapping broke out behind Boaz. "All hail the Zar and his mighty power."

"Pez!" Boaz's relief at seeing the dwarf was countered by his surging emotions. "Were you hiding?"

The palace clown leaped nimbly down from the sill of the open window. "Absolutely not," he said, sounding indignant.

"That's a mighty fall beneath the window. What are you doing here?"

"I've come to see you." Pez's voice was mild.

"I realize that," Boaz said more pointedly. "But where were you that you could appear at my window so many shevels from the ground? Where were you that you could sneak up on me and eavesdrop on my private conversations?" Though his words were sharp, Boaz couldn't stop picturing proud young men waiting to have their tongues torn out. And for some reason all he could think of was Lazar and hear his old friend sighing with regret that Boaz was maiming healthy Percherese in the archaic manner of the Zar's forebears.

"Well, I can see I'm not welcome," Pez grumbled, still not outwardly offended. "And there I was thinking you might have missed me."

"Stop it, Pez. Were you using your Lore skills?"

Pez hesitated. His large forehead creased. "Are you upset about something, Boaz?"

The dwarf's tone wasn't patronizing, but the Zar chose to take it that way. "Don't take that attitude with me, Pez. Remember your place. You may have the ear of the Zar, but you remain his servant, and servants should not miss luncheons with their royal."

Pez looked at him with an expression Boaz struggled to read; it seemed to be a mixture of deep disappointment and shock. He watched with private regret as the small man gathered himself, cleared his throat. "My manner of arrival was just a jest, my Zar. A surprise," he said, bowing, his hand touching his heart in the formal manner used for everything from salutations to apology in Percheron. "I've missed you," he added with a slight tone of injury that sounded genuine to Boaz—as genuine as the swift attack that followed. "You don't seem to really need my company these days, Highness, not now that you have your groveling Grand Vizier to play with."

Boaz bristled. "You know he's not groveling. Quite the opposite, in fact."

"I don't know anything anymore, Highness, because you

don't include me. I deeply regret missing breaking bread with you. I'm sure the Vizier kept you company, though."

"You're not jealous, are you, Pez?" Boaz couldn't help himself; his voice dripped sarcasm.

"Of Tariq?" Pez asked, sounding incredulous. "Now you jest, my Zar." The dwarf's obvious hurt cut like a blade, and Boaz guiltily rushed to reassure his friend.

"I didn't think so. There's nothing to envy. He intrigues me, that's all."

"Is it?"

"Well, surely his chameleonlike changes fascinate you?"

"In a different way from you, perhaps, my Zar," Pez said, his expression still pained.

"How so?"

"You say you find him intriguing. Personally, I find him dangerous."

Boaz gave a snort of disbelief. "Dangerous? Tariq?"

Pez grew grave. He did not say anything but simply stared hard at the Zar.

Boaz filled the awkward silence. "But that's ridiculous. Dangerous to whom?"

"I'm not sure . . . not yet."

"You're being paranoid. Who could Tariq endanger?"

"You, me, the Valide, your harem . . . do you want me to go on?"

Boaz shook his head. Where did Pez get such nonsense? Annoyed, he filled his voice with sarcasm again. "He's dangerous to my mother? Do explain."

Pez didn't hesitate. "Prior to your father's death, who would you say aligned himself most closely with Herezah the Absolute Favorite?"

Boaz looked away momentarily, irritated to have led himself to this point.

"You asked me to explain, so I'm trying," Pez said, his tone friendly as ever now.

Boaz sighed. "All right, it was Tariq."

"Indeed. I think now the Valide would have to all but make an appointment to meet him face-to-face."

"She's in the harem. He can't—"

"Don't make excuses, my Zar. You know I'm right. And while he's been curiously withdrawing from the Valide, he has invested that time ingratiating himself with you."

"It is his task, his duty as Vizier." Boaz heard the defensiveness in his tone and felt his temper stoke.

Pez shrugged. "I suppose so," he said, and began humming to himself.

"You're infuriating, Pez."

"Oh, but that's my task, my duty as your royal buffoon, my Zar," Pez replied humorlessly, echoing the Zar's earlier words.

Boaz helplessly heard his voice rise. "I won't have you treat me like a child."

Pez rounded on him. "Then don't act like one!"

It was the first time in his life that Boaz had been scolded in such stern fashion by his friend. "How dare you," he said, a voice as wintry as though it were coming from the Shagaire ice caps.

Whether Pez had intended such provocation or not, it seemed he wasn't going to retract his insult. "I dare, my Zar, because I care about you."

"Is this how you spoke to my father?" Boaz snarled.

"I had no need to."

"And you will never have an opportunity to address me so again."

Pez nodded sadly. "Then Tariq has won, my Zar. Your father despised the Vizier . . . and for good reason."

"Give me that reason!" Boaz bellowed.

Pez would not give him the satisfaction. "I shouldn't have to. You should feel it as I do," the dwarf accused.

Boaz pulled back as if stung. "Begone, dwarf. I'll choose to surround myself with whomever I want."

But Pez wasn't quite finished. "Yes, that's why I fear for you, my Zar. You should dismiss him as your father always wanted to. You can, you know, because your reign is still young. Mark my words, Zar Boaz, you will regret it if you don't. And now I am gone, Majesty." Despite his awkward gait, the dwarf managed a noble air as he walked toward the door.

Boaz spoke to his childhood friend's back. "I shall summon you should I ever want to see you again, Pez. Don't visit me without invitation."

Pez turned and their gazes met, then locked, before Pez dipped his glance in required deference to the Zar and removed himself fully from the chamber.

Boaz sat down heavily as the door closed. His heart was racing. He had never felt as lonely as he did just then with Pez's words echoing in his mind.

PEZ FELT HOLLOW. THAT conversation certainly hadn't gone according to plan. He had hoped to use the element of his surprise arrival to bluff his way through any question of his absence. But the Zar had seemed agitated when he arrived and Pez suspected his timing had been ill chosen. And now he no longer had the ear of the Zar—or his indulgence. For the first time in over two decades, he was vulnerable. And it was his own fault; he had brought it all upon himself.

He had traveled blindly since leaving Boaz's chambers, his legs moving as if by memory rather than by present attention, but Pez found himself crossing the threshold of the harem and knew he would find comfort here.

She was sewing, a look of disgust on her face as she poked the tiny needle through her silk.

"Pez!" one of the other girls cried with delight, and it was obvious they were all looking for a distraction.

The tutor's pinched expression turned even more sour as Pez scratched at his crotch and belched. The class disintegrated into laughter, and the helpless tutor, unable by palace law to banish the clown, took her leave with a promise to return after the midday meal for more of the same.

"Let's swim with the fishes," Pez suggested, pretending to glide through make-believe water.

"We're not allowed outside, Pez," someone told him.

He looked to Ana, who was sucking at a finger she had pricked upon seeing him, and smiled. "We have to sew adequately first," she agreed, sighing.

But already the class had broken up and girls were moving into groups, munching on the platters of fruit and confections a host of servants had delivered. Pez knew the garammala pipes would inevitably follow.

Pez glanced toward the food and back to Ana. It was an invitation she declined with a soft shake of her head. "You're looking thin," he whispered.

"And you're looking miserable. What's happened?"

He told her very briefly and watched as something akin to his own pain settled across her face. "With Boaz in this mood he might permit anything," he concluded.

"Are you sure he has banished you?" she asked, referring to the Zar's dismissal and warning.

"Quite. I could hardly mistake the finality of his words. I can only show my face if and when he summons me. Our friendship is over."

"I don't think so. Even the little I know of our Zar suggests he will think it through and regret the way the discussion went."

"You may be right," he whispered, moving to stand on his head and act out his part.

"Salmeo for sure will take every advantage of this new turn of events," Ana said softly, frowning.

"And the Valide will relish any opportunity to return years of frustrating harassment with cruel interest," he asserted, carefully watching that no one was paying them any attention.

"Oh, Pez. What are we going to do to help you?"

"I must lay low for a while, not be seen around too much. Forgive me if I disappear."

"You can't leave me."

"I won't, I promise. I'd better go now, but I'll come tonight. Leave your window open."

"My window?" she queried, watching him roll back to his feet and pull an ugly face at a girl passing by, who giggled. "I'm on the top floor."

"Just do as I ask," he said, winking before skipping out of the room.

THE VALIDE SMILED AS she took her seat in the Chamber of Silence. It had been so many years since she had been in this area of the palace that she had forgotten it existed. This was the chamber where she had been first presented as a newly purchased slave to the Valide Zara of the day, a stern, seemingly permanently scowling woman, who had fortunately lost her position soon after. Herezah pursed her lips as she recalled what had happened. The scowling Valide's son, Zar Koriz, had died suddenly and with his death claimed his mother's long-sought and powerful position. He had fallen prey to the feared bloatfish, which earned its name from the fact that it swelled grotesquely as it died in the fishing nets. Though it was considered a delicacy in Pecheron, it required very special handling to ensure that the liver was fully removed, for that organ contained some of the most powerful toxins known, and eating even the tiniest morsel of it meant certain death. Zar Koriz was a fine cook, and had prided himself on being skilled at cleaning and gutting this favorite fish with precision. He did just that after one of his regular fishing expeditions. These were days when no one dared even offer advice to the Zar unless asked, and although one of Koriz's newest aides found the courage to suggest that it would be best to take the fish back to the palace, the Zar scoffed. He wanted to cook the fish on the banks of the Daramo, the swift-moving river that flowed into the Faranel. It was on these same shores that the aide lost his tongue for his trouble and the Zar lost his life. The poison was swift but not fast enough to prevent immense suffering as the vicious toxin gradually claimed every inch of his body with paralysis. By the time his shocked party got the Zar back into the city, all of his major organs had burst and he was bleeding from his nostrils, ears, mouth. He was dead before he could even be laid in his chamber.

This story had always stayed with Herezah, not so much because of its colorful details but because of this particular Zar.

It amazed her that, despite this Zar's predisposition to punish his servants mercilessly for something so innocent as trying to offer him protection, he nonetheless had a deep soft spot for his half brothers and had refused his mother's pleas to execute them when he took the throne. Zar Koriz's compassion for his siblings had worked in her favor, for his favorite brother was Joreb and it was Joreb who took the throne after Koriz's death, his eyes still wet from weeping over his lost brother. Joreb's mother had insisted upon tradition and the remaining half brothers had been swiftly dealt with.

The new Valide, however, chose not to dismantle the harem, for the girls were still young and new. Joreb inherited his brother's harem and with it came a precocious girl called Herezah.

She hadn't been in this chamber since that fateful day when the old Valide's stern gaze had fallen upon her. She had been chosen within seconds of that first glance, her fate sealed, although her destiny—like any woman of the harem—was her own to carve.

And carve it I did, she thought now, pride catching in her throat as she saw her son enter the room. He looked taller, more imposing, and there was more color in his cheeks. He also looked miserable, which Herezah presumed was fear of what he was about to witness. *He was always a squeamish one,* she thought as he bent to take her hand.

"Mother," he acknowledged, kissing her hand.

She felt a shiver of delight. He was certainly making a show of affection. And to be invited to this private event! She was going to put this morning's pointed discussion behind them. She had overreacted, she was sure. "Darling, I'm sorry about my mood earlier. Forgive me. And thank you for sharing this with me," she said smoothly.

To her surprise, he waved away her apology as if it had not troubled him. "I can't promise a fun afternoon, I'm afraid," he said, falling heavily into his chair beside her. "This is duty, not my idea of entertainment."

Herezah was secretly pleased to know he continued to put duty ahead of his fears, but she knew better than to mention it. "Then where is your clingy clown? Surely your court jester should be here to provide that entertainment," she replied lightly, and then, contriving concern, she looked to where the Grand Vizier stood patiently. "Tariq, where is the dwarf?"

The Vizier glided toward the royal couple and bowed. She hadn't seen him in several weeks, and although she knew he was in his senior years, he looked more dashing than ever. His beard was neatly groomed, not oiled, and shorter now—no longer demanding to be noticed. It was also no longer the rich glossy black that the Tariq of old had insisted on achieving through dye. He had allowed the peppery gray to emerge, and to Herezah's expert eye it looked far more distinguished. His neatly kempt hair was also now the same color. She approved.

He answered Boaz, not her. "I was told he left your chambers not so long ago, my Zar. Perhaps you know better than I do of his whereabouts," he suggested, frowning.

Again Boaz waved away the concern as if it did not trouble him. "I know not of his location, Vizier. Carry on," he ordered.

Tariq bowed again and withdrew. A signal was given, and as a tray of refreshments was brought in for the royals, a small line of young men was led in through another door.

"Is something wrong, son?" Herezah inquired, distracted from the Vizier and intrigued by her child's mood. Following her instincts, she continued. "Are you upset about Pez?" Boaz turned to her, and by the surprise she could see in his eyes, she knew she was right with her wild stab in the dark. "Has something happened to him?" She knew how much he cared for the dwarf. This would be the right initial question to pose—it showed the right element of care.

"No, he is well. He has drawn my ire, that's all," her son said casually.

"Oh?"

"That's all," he repeated, and she could tell from his tone that he would not be giving her any more on this subject. That didn't mean she wouldn't make it her business to learn more, but she had subtle methods for achieving that. The notion that Pez had finally displeased a Zar was too delicious a prospect; this day was certainly turning out well. Herezah patted her son's arm, smiling inwardly, but deliberately and deftly changed the subject as she reached for a glass of bloodred pomegranate juice. Quite fitting a choice of beverage considering what was about to occur, she noted. "I haven't been in this chamber since I was chosen for the Zar's harem."

Boaz sipped the drink in his hand. He was clearly distracted, showed no interest in her comment. She tried again. "So tell me more about the mute guard, Boaz."

He sat up straighter, presumably understanding now that he must appear more interested. "These men you see here," he said, motioning with his goblet across her line of vision, "have been selected as my new private bodyguard."

"Selected?"

"Volunteered first, then culled for suitability and finally interviewed by me as the final seal of approval."

"And these fine young bloods are going to watch over you

day and night? You mentioned that the Vizier was worried about some sort of attack."

Boaz nodded. "These men are all trained in the fighting arts and can protect me. They have committed to memory a series of signals so we can communicate—they are all in perfect health."

"I can see," she said approvingly as the men stripped down to plain white baggy pants, revealing hardened, sculpted bodies, and knelt before the Zar. Herezah was reminded of the Spur in a similar stage of undress just a year ago. How that sight had brought a rush of blood to her cheeks . . .

Tariq cleared his throat and Herezah gave him her attention. "My Zar, Valide Zara," he said, bowing graciously, "these men will protect you with their lives. And though they will always be close to you, my Zar, what they see will never be revealed."

Boaz nodded. "Do you men all freely volunteer for this role?"

Each man, with one exception, stood, bowed, and said the formal words "I do, my Zar. I give all of me."

Boaz frowned at the last man, who, at a signal from the Grand Vizier, simply bowed and put his hand over his heart. Boaz glanced toward Tariq, who gave a smug, almost imperceptible nod.

The Zar took a slow deep breath before he gave the next command. "Let it be so," he finally said. "Proceed."

Boaz and Herezah watched as each man's head was shaved in ritual fashion while the Elim who were present chanted a song of farewell, similar to that sung prior to the eunuchs' cutting.

Each was then given a tiny glass of a dark liquid to drink.

Tariq whispered nearby, "We wait a short while for that to take effect."

"What is it?" Boaz asked.

"The dulling potion," Herezah answered for Tariq. "It doesn't prevent pain, but it puts the victim into an introverted mood, I'm told."

Tariq nodded. "The Valide is absolutely correct. It takes the men within themselves. The physic who prepared this potion says it makes them feel safe, at peace."

"That is considerate of you, Tariq," Boaz commented, unused to any pity being shown during the more barbaric practices of Percheron.

Herezah's and Tariq's gazes met, sympathetic amusement in that shared glance.

It was Herezah who responded. "This is not done out of kindness, son," she whispered. "It is given to these men to keep them still. A struggling man is a difficult one to control. Putting your volunteers into the soft stupor we speak of will ensure an easier time of it for the administrators."

"I see," Boaz replied, showing none of the disappointment he felt. "Mother, do you enjoy witnessing events such as this?"

"No," came the reply. "But I will never shirk my duty."

"This is not your duty. I gave you the choice to attend or not attend. The decision was yours."

Herezah placed her manicured hand lightly against his arm. "I understood the nature of your invitation. I do not feel compelled to be part of the grisly process of making a team of mutes. I do, however, see it as my duty to stand by my Zar, to support him in all of his endeavors, to help bear the burden of some of the less pleasant tasks, and to share his pleasure at his successes. What you do today is unpleasant but important, Boaz. I know that you like beauty—in this you are your father all over again," she said, smiling softly, "and that is why I'm here, to be at your side through the uglier challenges of your role."

Boaz was once again struck by his mother's strength. And now she was using it to help him instead of herself. All of his life his mother had used him to elevate herself, but perhaps now that she'd attained the role of Valide—something she had dreamed of since arriving at the palace, probably—she could give her attentions for selfless reasons. He wondered what Pez would say about that. Their final conversation stabbed constantly like a knife in his back.

"Thank you, Mother," he said. And meant it.

The Grand Vizier spoke up. "My Zar, Valide, we will now begin the Making of the Mutes. May I proceed? I must warn it is . . . messy."

"Proceed," Boaz said, knowing there was no way back now.

They watched as the physic in charge of proceedings, who was one of the Elim, blindfolded each of the men, except the last one, the man who had not sworn his life to the Zar.

"Who is that fellow?" Boaz inquired of Tariq. "I have not met him."

"No, Majesty, you have not. But I will explain him shortly. Right now the men are being blindfolded because it is believed that the Elim performing the maiming must not see the suffering in the eyes of each victim. It is considered bad luck."

"Such a superstitious lot, the Elim," Herezah interjected. "They don't seem too worried by what is perpetrated on the women of the harem."

Tariq ignored that comment, nodding at the Elim, who caught his gaze.

The first man was held, his arms pinned from behind.

"I can see now how the potion makes them compliant," Boaz whispered to his mother.

He watched as the Elim physic encouraged the man to open his mouth. Pincers pulled at the victim's tongue and within a heartbeat the bulk of the tongue had been cut off with a single slice of a keen blade. To prevent fatal blood loss the stump was immediately cauterized with a glowing brand. The man fainted, groaning, but to Boaz's relief there was no screaming or struggle.

"They will wait for him to recover before performing the deafening," Tariq explained.

"Surely it would be more merciful to do it whilst he is unconscious?" Boaz inquired.

"But it would be considered cowardly," Tariq followed up quickly. "This is about bravery and duty, Majesty. I know you wish for this to be easy on the men who give themselves so freely. But the maiming is all part of the test of their commitment. That's why they do not scream."

The blindfold was removed and a cold linen was placed on the man's face to revive him. As soon as his eyes fluttered open, though he was clearly dazed by the pain, he was quickly restored to his knees and once again held securely, this time by two strong Elim. The physic reached for a vicious-looking needle and Boaz prayed to Zarab that he would not let himself down by looking away. He fixed his gaze somewhere slightly beyond the action whilst not giving away that he wasn't actually looking and then he told himself to think of something beautiful.

Ana came to mind—no surprise there. He saw the stabbing movement and resisted the urge to gag as a small, sharp spume of blood hit the physic's belly. Instead he thought only of Ana's face, Ana's hair, Ana's newly voluptuous body. And as the physic pierced the other eardrum of the brave warrior, this time to the sound of a guttural growl of pain, Boaz turned himself over fully to the daydream of how it might be to lie with Ana, naked.

He imagined caressing her body, taking his own pleasure from it. He saw himself lying back, lifting her onto his hips, urging her despite her shyness to lower herself so he could slide deep within her. Ignoring the fact that he, too, was a virgin, Boaz envisaged himself as a skilled but gentle lover. As Ana instinctively began to rotate her pelvis, Boaz closed his eyes to enjoy the dream's climax. Suddenly his mother's voice disturbed him.

"Darling?"

It sounded to Boaz from the slightly strained tone that this was not the first time she had said the word.

"Yes," he said, grudgingly releasing himself from Ana's spell. As he refocused he saw that all the men bar one had ruined, bloodied mouths and running ears. Most were slumped on the floor, propped against the legs of an Elim so that they might retain a modicum of dignity after their trauma.

"Where were you, my love?" Herezah asked.

The smell of blood was thick in the room. Boaz suspected she knew he had somehow vanished in spirit, if not in body, from the terrible maiming ritual. "I was thinking," he said curtly. "We are done, Grand Vizier?"

One fellow began to wail. The Vizier cleared his throat. "That one might not turn out to be as suitable as we'd hoped. Yes, we have completed the maiming, Majesty."

THE MAIMED WARRIORS WERE helped away, leaving one whole man in the room.

"And this last warrior?" Boaz asked.

"My great pride, Highness," the Vizier replied, unable to disguise the smug tone. He snapped his fingers and one of the Elim brought over the young warrior, whose gaze was fixed on the intricately patterned tiled floor. The slave knelt.

Maliz looked at the young man with pride. It was all about this one youth, the reason for the whole campaign to install a ring of guardians around the Zar.

"This is Salazin, my Zar. He is the inspiration for this new personal protectorate you now have. I discovered him not so long ago. He is an orphan who learned to tough things out the hardest possible way, Majesty, for Salazin was made deaf and dumb from an early age by an unfortunate illness."

"Ah," Boaz said, nodding. "He needs no maiming."

"He is perfect, Majesty, for Zarab made him this way."

"And Zarab led you to him, Tariq?" Herezah asked, with a note of irony not missed by the Vizier.

"I like to think so, Valide," he said, and smiled privately at how close to the truth he spoke. Zarab had surely led him to Salazin, for Salazin, he hoped, would lead him to Iridor.

"How did you come across him?" Boaz asked.

"I was giving alms to some of the orphanages, my Zar, as you have requested. He was from one of the city establishments."

"Not the one you aim to close?" Boaz asked mildly.

"As a matter of fact, yes, Majesty. I paid the orphanage a visit to consider how we would dismantle it, find new housing for its"—he searched for the word, found it—"guests. I needed to consider what would happen to the sisterhood who cares for these youngsters."

"Where is this place we speak of?" Herezah inquired.

Boaz looked at his mother, his glare defying her to make a fuss. "I have promised the Grand Vizier his own villa overlooking the Faranel. He has taken a liking to an orphanage, and although I'm yet to make a final decision, I have given him permission to consider how he will rehouse the present occupants."

"Are you talking about the Widows' Enclave?" Herezah asked, frowning.

"I think it used to go by that name, yes, Valide," Maliz answered without hesitation.

"But that's for army families," Herezah protested.

"Originally, yes," Maliz said patiently. "But we have not had war in living memory and so now only a few families of the unlucky injured or killed army members live there. The building no longer serves its original purpose, Valide. It's a huge place for so few people."

"But not so huge for one, presumably," Herezah replied tartly. "My Zar, with your indulgence, I might return to my chambers now. Again, my thanks for including me in this special ritual." She bowed, then glanced somewhat angrily toward Maliz before turning back to her son. "Perhaps you'll take supper with me sometime soon."

Boaz stood and helped the Valide to do the same. "I shall look forward to it, Mother," he said.

Maliz signaled and two of the Elim were instantly at Herezah's side to escort her back to the harem. She rehooked her veil across her face dutifully, as she was now leaving the company of the Zar, and elegantly glided out of the room between her burly companions.

Boaz sighed. "The Valide does not approve of your plan, clearly."

Maliz kept his counsel on that subject, schooling Tariq's features so the Zar could not gauge just how much he wanted that villa. He smoothly changed the subject, gilding the truth as he did so. "Salazin was one of the oldest in the orphanage. I gather from the sisterhood that he has no known living relatives. He has only known silence since an illness claimed his hearing during childhood, I'm told. He makes no sound at all, my Zar. His deafness is profound."

"No sound at all?" Boaz repeated, incredulous. "You have tested him?"

A sly smile crept across the Vizier's mouth. "I had to, to be sure. I will not go into the detail of it, Majesty, but rest assured that this young man cannot hear and he cannot talk," He gestured at Salazin. "He will see but he cannot listen in to anything you say, nor can he repeat what his eyes show him."

"So he cannot write what he sees either?" Boaz inquired.

Maliz nodded, reinforcing his lie. "The sisterhood confirms he is illiterate, which is understandable considering his afflictions."

"The perfect mute, in other words," Boaz commented, returning his attention to the bent head of his new protector.

Maliz nodded. "Indeed, Highness. He is also the strongest of the warriors here, by far the most adept with weapons and with fists."

"His age?"

"From what I can tell, he is around nineteen summers."

"Let him stand," Boaz commanded. An Elim raised the

young man to his feet. Boaz reached to lift the man's chin and looked into his clear gray eyes. "How will he know what is wanted of him?"

"The sisterhood have their own methods of communicating with him," Maliz said. "I have been taught its use." He smiled. "They had no choice but to teach me and now I have schooled all these young men. You, too, can learn it, Majesty. As for this one, he fully understands his role to protect you with his life, my Zar."

"If he has no family to give money to, what is his reward for offering his life to me?" Boaz queried. "The others are presumably volunteering because they can offer their families security through the generous gold I presume you have offered."

Maliz bowed his head gently. "I did as instructed, my Zar. Each man has been so handsomely rewarded that his family is now well set up for the future. As for Salazin, I cannot say what motivates this one," he lied. "Except to say that he wishes to serve the Zar. As you sit on your throne by Zarab's design, Highness. He sees you as our god's mortal incarnation."

"Really? But he was raised by the priestesses—I would have thought—"

"No, Highness. He despises them, I gather. They are as glad to get him off their hands as he is to leave their care."

"But without them surely he would have perished as a child?"

"I imagine so," Maliz said airily, as if this were a trivial matter. "It doesn't make him like them. He is a man of Zarab through and through. That is why he leaped at the opportunity to serve you."

"He is that committed?"

"Oh yes," Maliz replied, serious now. "But he is not the only one. I must admit I believe Zarab's hand guided your father in his choice of heir. Most Percherese would feel the same."

"I understand tradition, Tariq. I just find it hard to believe that today's thinking still holds true to this belief."

Maliz was astounded. He had not taken into account how protected and thus ignorant the royals had become. "My Zar, with your indulgence, I might suggest that your life is too sheltered. We must rectify this."

"Oh?"

"Yes, Majesty. We should let you meet some more of your people so that you may know how close to Zarab they truly believe you are. You are answerable only to our god—surely you know that?"

Boaz nodded. "King of Kings, Mightiest of the Mighties," he said wearily.

"Salazin has been raised in a cloistered environment, so his faith is strong. To him you are the embodiment of Zarab himself."

"It strikes me as odd, Tariq, that the sisterhood would raise a child to believe so strongly in Zarab, when they themselves worship Lyana."

Maliz quickly stifled the anger the mention of her name roused in him.

"I mean," Boaz continued thoughtfully, "the Goddess is everything to them, even though her time is long past."

"Majesty," Maliz began carefully. "The sisterhood knows that the very existence of the orphanage is due to the indulgence of the Zar. Their time is long gone. They may not subscribe to the belief, but they certainly understand that, outside of their few remaining numbers, Percheron worships Zarab. They would have no housing, no sustenance for themselves or the families they care for, if not for the Zar's benevolence. They appreciate that these children need to be raised in the Percherese manner, despite the faith they privately practice."

"You're saying this is their work, nothing to do with faith."

Maliz nodded. "That's a reasonable way of putting it, Majesty, although I might term it as their vocation. Their faith is sadly misplaced but it is also private. We tolerate their silent beliefs and they are allowed to pursue their vocation in caring for the sick, the lonely, the needy, the desperate, the orphaned, and so on, which the royal coffers make possible."

"And I am very happy to continue providing," Boaz replied firmly. "I gave a promise to a sister once that I would care for the temple and I have no intention of breaking my word."

Maliz bristled beneath the calm exterior of Grand Vizier Tariq. It galled him that any Zar would offer any form of protection to the hateful sisters of the Goddess. "Nor would any of us expect you to, Majesty," he said, affecting a soft tone of injury. "All I am saying is that their beliefs remain private. They are not in a position to convert disciples to their broken faith, Majesty. They serve Percheron by caring for those in need."

Boaz looked again at the still figure of Salazin. The man had not moved, not so much as blinked, in the time they had talked over and around him, and about him. "Your plan for Salazin?"

"He is the most complete of all the warriors we have chosen, Majesty. I would make him your most personal of all the servants. My desire is that he protect you every hour, every minute, of the day. Whilst you go about your day, he will be your shadow. And at night, my Zar, whilst you sleep, he will watch over you."

"When does he sleep?" Boaz asked facetiously. "And when I wish to have time alone?"

"I would not advise it, Highness."

"Is that so?" Boaz asked, amusement in his voice as he stepped down from his podium and stretched. "Well, Tariq, I can assure you that there will be occasions when I demand privacy that not even a deaf and dumb man can provide. As you've rightly pointed out, he still sees."

Maliz caught on swiftly. "Of course," he said, bowing his tall frame in gentle apology. "In which case, my Zar, Salazin will be directed to search the chamber first before waiting just outside."

Boaz nodded. "Let him rest, get acquainted with the palace. When does this begin?"

"Immediately, my Zar. The others will need to heal, but Salazin will take up his duties from this evening, with your permission."

"As you choose, Vizier," Boaz said. "And now I need to take some air . . . alone."

Maliz bowed, as did the mute warrior, remaining prostrate until the Zar had departed. When the two men were alone Maliz beckoned to Salazin, who followed him to a small room attached to the main chamber.

The demon signed: *I lied about your ability to read and write.*

The mute nodded.

Maliz continued: *The game has begun. You report to me on everything. Everything! His moods, who he sees, whatever he does, I want to know about it.*

Salazin smiled.

More importantly—far more important than the Zar, in fact—I want to know everything about the dwarf named Pez.

Salazin answered: *It will be done, master.*

Maliz nodded slowly. The mute would, he was sure, deliver

Iridor. He was convinced he could sense the aura of Iridor hovering nearby the Zar. He had no idea yet who it could be, but he could not dismiss it. His instincts kept bringing him back to the dwarf. Maliz knew Iridor was far too wily to be the half-wit he knew Pez to be and yet . . . once, during his freedom—before he had cast out Tariq's soul— he had felt Iridor's presence strongly, and to his greater shock, he thought he had also felt the presence of the Lore. He had tried to lock onto it but it had disappeared instantly and he had not been able to trace it back to the person wielding it. And Pez had acted strangely in Boaz's presence when both Maliz and Tariq had been watching the young Zar. Yet Maliz knew this theory had no real substance. Well, now Salazin would spy constantly, and if Pez was indeed Iridor, the demon could destroy him—and by turn the Goddess, whoever she was—before she had even the chance to rise again.

Maliz's smile turned nasty. He patted Salazin on the arm and signed: *Tonight you begin your life's most important task for Zarab.*

7

Ana now shared a sleeping chamber with only one other girl. History had shown that youngsters put into one main chamber tended to achieve nothing other than a lack of sleep. And although tradition had it that older women preferred congregating together for sleeping, many of the odalisques in this harem were still children. Even most of the older ones remained immature and giggly, with years of growing up to do before they could be considered sedate members of the harem.

Ana and her chamber companion and only friend, Sascha, were the most composed girls and Salmeo hoped they would lead the other odalisques by example. Sascha, a shy, intelligent young woman, was not well this evening. Ana had guided Sascha, who had been bent double with an ache in her belly, to find one of the Elim to take her to the harem's infirmary. The strong Elim carried the ailing girl away and Ana conveniently found herself alone this night.

She toyed with the idea of going for a stroll—now that almost a year had passed, the girls were free to move around certain areas of the harem without censure—but couldn't risk not being in her chamber when Pez came as promised, so she remained in her chamber, staring out of the open shutters at the bright moonlight. Her lids grew heavy, though, and ultimately she drifted off.

Ana's peaceful slumber was disturbed by what sounded, to her drowsy mind, like flapping. When she rubbed some of the sleep from her eyes, she realized she was staring at a magnificent snow owl, who was regarding her intently from her window sill.

She was surprised into silence, and awed by the majesty of the creature. Moving as slowly as she dared, Ana brought her feet to rest on the floor and then gradually stood, her gaze never leaving the owl, who remained so still it could have been a statue.

It was that notion that startled her and made her whisper a single word. "Iridor," she breathed dreamily.

Before she could approach the owl, it changed before her sleepy eyes. She blinked, confused. Standing before her was Pez.

Rubbing her eyes agin, Ana laughed softly as she yawned. "I . . . I was dreaming, Pez. I thought you were an owl. You were so beautiful."

"Was I? Good evening, Ana."

"You were Iridor—do you know who he is?"

"He is the messenger of Lyana, the loyal companion of the Goddess."

"That's right. You know your folklore."

"It's not folklore."

"That makes it truth," she said jauntily, as though this was going to be one of their fun conversations.

Pez was in a more somber frame of mind. "That's right. It's why I'm here tonight. We have things to discuss, child."

She grew more serious, sensing his mood. She reached for a gown to throw over her bare shoulders. "You left abruptly today. How are you feeling, Pez?"

He shook his head. "I'm feeling sad. I made an error today with the Zar and we can't afford to do that."

"We?"

"Ana . . . what you saw just now . . ." His voice trailed off.

"The owl?"

"Iridor," he confirmed. "That *was* me. I am him."

Ana stared at the dwarf, her eyes huge in the moonlit darkness. For a long time she remained silent, her thoughts racing. Finally she responded. "And Ellyana the crone?"

Before Pez could speak, she answered her own question, the words coming from her mouth before she knew what she was going to say. "The crone forewarns the coming of the Goddess. But it begins with the rising of Iridor. The owl aligns himself with the woman who will be Lyana's incarnation for the next battle . . ." She trailed off, looking fearfully at Pez.

"How do you know that, Ana?" her friend asked gently, a shade of—was it fear?—in his voice.

"I don't know how," she replied slowly. "I just know it. Like I know other things."

"Such as?"

"Such as the names of the stone statues of Percheron. All of them."

"They all originally served Lyana—do you know that?"

She nodded slowly. Feeling a tightness in her belly. Deep inside, she had known her knowledge made her different. She had tried to put it aside, deny it. Numbly, she listened as Pez began a story she already knew.

"They were real once, Ana. Beloch and Ezram once roamed Percheron. Likewise the winged lions, Crendel and Darso, as well as the mightiest of them all, Shakar, the dragon. They all loved and served the Goddess."

"They were turned to stone by Zarab. She had no magic to counter his spell. He used a special magic, not of the gods."

Pez nodded, excitement on his face. "That's right. Someone helped him. A mortal."

"Maliz," she answered instantly, looking directly at Pez. "He made a deal with the god: if he was granted immortality, he would deliver Lyana."

"Go on," her friend urged.

"The bargain was struck," she continued. "Maliz, a sorcerer, was given everlasting life in order that he might rise each time the Goddess tries to reclaim her mortal following. Maliz returns time and again and each time he has won . . . but this time it may be different."

"Why is this time different?" Pez's words were gentle, hushed, as though he did not want to disturb her momentum. He couldn't have; Ana herself could barely stem the flow of words.

"The factors are the same. The crone identifies the new Iridor long before he rises. Maliz, who slumbers in any body he can claim, reawakens with the freedom as a spirit to roam until he senses where Iridor will rise. He never knows who will take Iridor's form—nor does Iridor know Maliz. They have to find each other. Maliz chooses his next mortal body with care. It is the one he must live in and use to destroy Lyana." She paused but at Pez's silent nodding carried on with her story. "When

Iridor finally assumes his role, it triggers the rising of Lyana, whose spirit emerges through a mortal."

"And so the principal players are complete," Pez said in conclusion.

"Not this time," she stated. "For this battle there is a newcomer."

"Who?" Pez asked eagerly.

She shivered. "I don't know. I have no sense of name, or whether it is a woman or a man. I don't even know their purpose—only that their role will immeasurably change the fabric of the struggle."

Pez nodded slowly. "And so we know that Ellyana is the crone who began all of this. She recognized me. She came into the harem, masquerading as a bundle woman, some time ago, Ana. She told me to work out who I was. And then at the temple I had a vision— Zafira saw my hair turn white. It was an omen of who I was to become."

Ana bit her lip. "I should have guessed."

Pez smiled at her kindly. "Looking back now, there were many clues," he began.

Ana interrupted him. "Beginning with Ellyana seeking me out in the bazaar." She shook her head, her expression rueful. "I thought I was noticing her, but she already knew me. She was selling a gold chain. Lazar saw it, too." Mentioning his name, she faltered briefly, then continued: "When we stepped in to save her from a poor bargain with one of the alley cats, she gave me the piece in her hand. It had turned into a gold owl. I recognized Iridor."

Pez sighed. He dug into his pocket and pulled out a small gold statue. "It found its way to me, Ana."

She looked at him, surprised. "How? I gave that to—"

"Lazar, I know. He sent it to me."

"Before he died? How could he?"

Pez simply shook his head. "I don't know. Another secret of the cycle of the war between the gods, I suppose."

Thinking of Lazar, Ana said softly, "Lazar was surprised that I knew the names of the statues."

"He was surprised by everything about you, Ana."

"Nothing surprised me about him. I loved him, Pez."

"I know." Pez hesitated, then gravely began, "Ana . . ."

Ana knew what he was going to say, and she felt her blood turn to ice. Terrified, she held up a hand. "It can't be so."

"What can't be so?"

"You're . . . you're going to name Lyana," Ana hedged.

"Then you do it," he urged. "You tell me her mortal incarnation."

Ana dropped her face to her hands but she did not cry. She shook her head. "It cannot be."

"It is. You feel it. You know it. Ana, every time I have touched you I've felt the tingle of your magical being. I didn't understand it at first. But when I became Iridor I realized it was not a magic so much as a force—a bond between us. I guessed who you were becoming. This is why we're together. This is why I will give my life, as I always have before, to protect you. This time, Ana, my beloved Lyana . . . we will win."

Ana fled to Pez's arms. Despite the shortness of his limbs, he comforted her with a partial embrace, stroking her back as best he could.

Finally Ana pulled away. Taking a deep breath, she shakily admitted, "I don't know what I'm supposed to do."

"What we have always done down the ages," Pez comforted. "We go on instinct now."

Ana wiped her eyes. "Who else is on our side?"

"No one in the palace," he warned her. "I've cautioned you before and I hope you'll heed these words. No one in the palace is your friend except me."

"Not even Boaz?"

He grimaced. "He certainly does not want my friendship anymore. No, not even Boaz, because he is being influenced, and until the Zar begins to make all his own decisions, I can't trust him . . . and you definitely must not trust anyone."

"So we have no allies?"

"Well . . . Zafira," Pez offered.

"And Jumo," she suggested. "Wherever that poor man is."

"Ellyana, if she ever returns," he added.

"Kett," she concluded.

"Ah?" Pez said, sounding surprised. "What makes you say that?"

Ana shrugged "I feel connected to him."

"The Raven," Pez said thoughtfully. "That's what he called himself when he was barely conscious after his ordeal of being made a eunuch. The Raven is always amongst us."

"But he's the bringer of bad tidings," Ana added fearfully.

"Not always. My memories tell me he can simply be used to deliver sage advice. We must work out how to bring Kett closer to us."

"Well, without Boaz you have no pull in the palace anymore. I must speak with the Zar. And perhaps I can help to mend this broken bond? It's not right, Pez. He knows your secret. It's dangerous."

"I know this," he said. "But I have taken some steps."

"Steps? What do you mean?"

He smiled at her with an effort. "Ask me no more right now. Just trust me."

Ana tried to tamp down her frustration. "So what must I do?"

"Live. Be Ana. That's who you are. Continue life in the harem as it must be lived and the eternal struggle will take care of itself. I don't know how this is going to unfold, child. Each time I am reborn I have only a vague memory of the struggle taking place. Each cycle is different in complexity, even though the outcome has been the same for so many battles."

"When was the last one?"

"Centuries ago. So many in fact that it is no more than myth in the minds of most."

Ana sighed, forcing her thoughts back to the present. "So I go on our boating trip . . ."

"And you stay out of the eagle eyes of Salmeo and the Valide as best you can."

"That won't be easy. Everyone seems to think the Zar is going to choose me."

"He will. Regardless of your true reason for being, Ana, that's why you are here in the harem."

"I feel like I'm just a vessel, with various uses," Ana said in a small voice. She looked at Pez beseechingly. "I just want to be myself. To discover things, to learn, to not be someone's slave."

"I understand."

"Do you?"

"You forget, I've been a slave to the palace for most of my life."

"But, Pez, you have freedom. You can leave if you want. And now . . . now you can fly. Where do you fly to?"

She expected a dramatic answer. Instead Pez said mildly, "I just fly."

She sighed but then was taken by a new thought. "What about Maliz? If we know who we are, then surely he has known for some time that Iridor has risen."

Pez looked surprised by the turn in conversation but nodded gravely. "Correct. And he's looking for us. He'll begin by focusing on Iridor. Fortunately my magic is not soul sucking, as his is. The magic of Lyana is cleaner, kinder. We choose when to use our magic. My understanding of Maliz is that once he has taken his form and claimed someone's body, that's where he must remain . . . unless he wants to have a lesser hold on that body and simply hover within it."

"What do you mean?' she frowned.

"He can freely inhabit another person—they usually have to be weak of mind—without committing himself to them fully. In doing so, he can just take over their lives, but he is vulnerable. He has very little magical energy to call upon, which is why he usually chooses someone who is aged, infirm, fragile in some way. He exists until he chooses whose body he will claim for each battle. Then he is committed to that body for the cycle. He cannot flit between it and another. He must leave it behind if he chooses to move and he must do so by death."

"But you can shape-shift at will, unlike him."

"Yes, I can change between being myself or shifting into Iridor, but only once the cycle actually begins."

"But then that means you are always Iridor. You were born Iridor and Iridor actually takes your shape rather than the other way around. Iridor was just waiting to be called upon before he showed himself."

He nodded sadly. "I suppose you are right."

"And me?"

"My magic is more obvious, you are shielded."

"I am? Why?"

He shook his head. "You are; that's how it is. I will reveal you," he said sadly. "I am traditionally the cause of our demise. It has always been me who is discovered first."

"Are you frightened?" she asked, curious.

He lifted his chin, folded his arms. "Not at all."

At his show of determination, Ana smiled. "Why not?"

"Because you assure me that this time it's different . . . and I intend to find out why and because of whom."

8

After leaving Ana, Pez had flown to Star Island, where he suspected he would find a ready companion in Lazar. With the newfound freedom of his wings and the fact that he was clearly not required by the Zar, there was no need to remain at the palace that night. He understood he wouldn't be able to sleep anyway with his mind racing from his conversation with Ana, particularly the discussion about Kett.

Pez knew that the Raven always appeared after Iridor and before Lyana. Another servant of the Goddess, he was often referred to as the black bird of omen, but Pez hadn't wanted to say too much that might frighten Ana. As it was, her acceptance of the potential mantle of Lyana's incarnation felt so calm it was remarkable. But Kett was definitely someone that Pez would have to watch and somehow find a way to bring closer to Ana. If what he suspected was right and Ana was the reemerging Goddess, then she would need to receive whatever message Lyana had passed on through the Raven for her.

"Couldn't sleep?" Pez asked softly, approaching the hut and not surprised to see a familiar figure leaning up against the outside wall.

Lazar shook his head. "And it's such a beautiful night anyway."

"I forgot to mention last time that the beard is interesting," Pez commented.

"It occurred to me I may need a new disguise," Lazar said, scratching at his chin. "Horrible things. I've been growing this for months and hate it."

"How are you feeling?"

"Stronger. Much stronger, in fact."

"You look it—even in the moonlight." Pez grinned at his friend's sneer. "Truly. You appear almost your grumpy self again."

"I feel like myself again," Lazar admitted. "The improvement is suddenly vigorous."

"Weren't you warned it would be like this?"

Lazar nodded, pushed his large hand through his hair. "Zafira was told that. My strength would return rapidly once my body had learned how to manage alongside the poison. Presumably it has done that."

"So what now?"

Lazar's voice hardened. "Well, first you're going to tell me about Jumo—don't think I'm going to let you off the hook after your cryptic comment of last time."

Pez felt a chill crawl up his spine. There was no point in avoiding this conversation any longer, though. He hadn't meant to the last time but events got in the way.

"Where is Jumo, Pez?" Lazar demanded.

"By now I imagine he's roaming around Galinsea," Pez said, blurting out the words, not giving himself any further time to think.

He expected a roar of anger, but it didn't come. Instead he had to stand beneath Lazar's simmering glare, trying not to squirm amidst the thick, uncomfortable silence that now wrapped itself about him.

Finally Lazar spoke, all good humor evaporated from his voice. "Galinsea." It wasn't a question. "Who sent him?"

"He was determined to find your family, tell them of your demise."

"I repeat, who sent him there? Only two of us know my background."

"Then why are you asking?" Pez said, disgusted by his sense of helpless inadequacy.

"You told Jumo who I was?" There was threat in Lazar's tone. Pez could see the former Spur visibly shaking with anger.

Pez had never been scared by Lazar, but for the first time he understood what it might be like to be this man's adversary. "Yes. That was our agreement, remember? I would tell Jumo should anything fatal occur to you. And because of Ellyana's bullheaded ways and your determination to follow them, you kept me in the dark about your survival for just long enough for me to make an error. It is your fault that Jumo knows."

"Does anyone else know?"

"No."

Lazar pushed away from the wall of the hut and strode toward the cliff edge. Pez had no choice but to follow like a shamed dog.

"Where's Zafira?" he asked, desperate for conversation that might rescue the grim mood.

"At her temple," Lazar growled. "I'm well enough to care for myself now."

"Lazar, I—"

"How long have I protected that secret, Pez?" the former Spur said, staring angrily at the twinkling lights of the city across the bay.

"I couldn't have Jumo rushing off blindly in such a bereft state with no idea of who to look for regarding your kin. I hope—"

"Sixteen years," Lazar said with feeling, swinging back to glower at Pez. "Painful, all of them."

"Were you not ever happy amongst us in Percheron?"

Lazar waved away Pez's question as if it had no relevance. "Do you have any idea what it takes to renounce one's heritage? Lineage? Realm? Crown?"

"No, Lazar. But that was your decision."

"That's right. It was also my decision to keep it a secret."

"You shared it with me."

Lazar intensified his glare, exasperation flooding through the fury he was barely controlling. "I see I have learned a lesson tonight. A secret is no longer a secret once it is shared."

"How true!" Pez snapped, his own anger, fueled by the frustrations of the day, also spilling over. "Why tell anyone anything if you don't anticipate that you are empowering someone with that knowledge, Lazar? Jumo deserved to know the truth, and you and I had an agreement. I followed it to the letter. You were dead, as far as we knew. He was heartbroken—can you imagine how it felt to hear that the man he called his master and friend had died? And that his body had already been disposed of? And him not much more than a bystander to your suffering?"

"I have some idea," Lazar replied, effort in his voice. "I'm allowed this anger. I was not privy to this decision to appear dead. It was made for me."

"And I made another one for you. I told your closest and most loyal friend the truth. No one deserved it more than Jumo, not even Ana."

At the mention of her name, Lazar's head snapped back as though slapped. "And you will tell her nothing!" he commanded.

"There is always danger in knowledge, Lazar, but be careful your precautions don't drift into cowardice."

Pez's spoke kindly, trying to take away his friend's rage. Lazar's head dropped, his chin almost touching his broad chest. "When did Jumo leave?"

"The morning after the night of your purported death."

"I am no coward, Pez. I have kept that secret to protect those I care about. You were already well protected by your madness—and Zar Joreb proclaiming you above almost all palace law. But Jumo is in danger."

"From your family?"

"Possibly. I can't be sure, but now I know where I must go."

"You're going back to Galinsea?" Pez stated his own shock so baldly that Lazar flinched. "You're leaving her?"

When the former Spur turned his gaze this time on Pez, there was only grief in his eyes. "I am no good to her anymore. She is the Zar's woman."

Pez could not bear the disguised self-pity in that statement, nor could he tolerate Lazar's denial of Ana for a moment longer. It was time to tell the whole story. "She is so much more than that. Ana only masquerades as an odalisque. She was never a goatherd's daughter in anything more than accidental name."

Genuine pain claimed Lazar's expression, stunning Pez. He had known this man since his arrival in Percheron and had watched his subsequent rise from prisoner to the city's top security position. Lazar was so self-contained that no one, not even Pez, could successfully guess what thoughts were going on behind those intelligent eyes. But the very mention of Ana could shatter the invisible yet seemingly implacable fortress that Lazar had built around himself. Her very name seemed to have a magical quality, as if it were some sort of touchstone that opened the gates of the fortress, allowing the tightly imprisoned emotions to rush out.

Pez understood suddenly: it wasn't the drezden that would be Lazar's weakness in life. It was Ana. Since he had first laid his love-starved eyes on that young woman, she had become both his salvation and his potential destruction. Only time would tell which.

Lazar bridled at Pez's challenge. "What do you mean she is so much more? I know Ana as well as anyone else—better, in fact. I found her. I know who she is."

"You know nothing, Lazar," Pez said, and watched a shiver pass through his friend as if he were cold. But Pez knew he wasn't trembling from a chill; Lazar was finding the courage to ask his next question and Pez was ready for it.

"Who is she?" the former Spur demanded.

"I believe she is Lyana, the Mother Goddess, incarnated in the flesh."

A silence stretched between both men. Pez knew Lazar would neither ridicule nor try to counter his claim; probably he knew his friend felt the truth of those words strike like a knife in his heart.

It was a long time before either spoke. Lazar broke the silence. "How can you be sure?" he finally whispered.

"Who can ever be sure about the gods, Lazar? But I feel it. I can't deny it any longer. I'm Iridor and she's Lyana. That's why we're together in the palace. You know the old story, I presume?"

Lazar nodded, still seemingly choked with emotion. "But that's all it's been to me. A story. The foundation of my faith, the tale that was too seductive to ignore, passed down through centuries. Although the story tells us that Lyana was vanquished by Zarab, a few of us still believe she will rise again and prevail. I certainly felt a kinship when I saw her likeness in Zafira's temple. Galinsea has no specific deities. It worships the land and the sea, the sky and its firmament . . ." Lazar shrugged. "I feel I belong in Percheron, where some still cling to the faith of the Goddess."

Peg smiled gently. "But Nature is what Lyana stands for, of course, so Galinsea, although it thinks it has moved on, is still true to her in its way. Lyana is about the land and the forces that impact on it—sea, sun, desert, storm. She does not put herself above the natural forces of our existence as Zarab does. He claims godliness over everything, power over the land and its forces, its—"

"But Lyana is not real . . . not in the flesh, anyway. She is part of our shared history; she is myth." Lazar's final words sounded like a plea. He continued: "No one knows if Zarab is real but most Percherese pray to him. In this, neither Lyana nor Zarab is any different. They could both be myth."

Pez's passion evaporated as he turned grave. "The story that founded your original faith is true. But there is also a cyclical aspect to that story—every few centuries, when Lyana feels strong enough, she rises again to fight the demon who serves Zarab . . . to claim back her rightful place."

"Yes, I know the tale. And you think that Ana . . . ?"

"She is part of the new cycle. I believe that, for the coming battle, Ana is the mortal reincarnation of Lyana."

"And what if you're wrong?" Lazar demanded. "What if Ana is no more than a young woman trying to survive in the Zar's harem?"

"No newborn, left alone in the desert, survives the much-feared Samazen windstorm, Lazar," Pez reminded softly. "No young woman can communicate the force of power that I sense in Ana unless she is truly enchanted by something greater than any of us. Even you would have to be surprised by her knowledge of the Stones of Percheron. She knows every statue and its history . . . tell me how a goatherd's daughter could have learned this? And what about her ability with language? Perhaps you don't know how talented she is with tongues—why should you, you hardly know her? But it's extraordinary. And her composure, in one so young? Ana is an ancient soul, Lazar. You must accept it."

"I won't," Lazar growled at the dwarf. "You've given me nothing but conjecture." He ran both hands through his golden hair in a rare show of anxiety. "I want fact, Pez. Give me something real, something that is unequivocal."

"That's easy, Lazar," Pez said, mindful of the pain he was inflicting. He wondered fleetingly whether this conversation might set Lazar back in his recovery—or act as a catalyst. This could galvanize him into action, and though Pez wasn't sure what that action might be, he'd had a quiet feeling of dread ever since Ana had said that this time Lyana's battle would be different. What if the difference was the Prince of Galinsea? If that were true, he needed Lazar strong. "It is easy," he repeated. "Here's an undeniable fact. I can suddenly change at will into a white owl. Lyana's messenger of old has always been a white owl. The owl is called Iridor. He rises before she does. He is the trigger that the demon senses, the sign that it is time to begin his grim work for his god. You speak with Iridor regularly; you have witnessed his transformation. You know who I am. You have heard of the black bird of omen?"

"The Raven. I knew him as the bird of sorrows."

"That's right, he is known as that, too. He is drawn to her as well."

"And he's shown himself, I suppose you're going to tell me."

"Kett is the Raven. He said as much to me."

Lazar looked as though he had been slapped even harder this time. "He told you he was the Raven?" His words came out strained.

"To my face he called himself the black bird. Do you still think this is all a coincidence? Or will you believe, as I suspect Ellyana and Zafira do, that Ana is the Goddess? Why else did she run to the statue of Lyana at the temple when she escaped the harem? Admit the facts, as I have had to. Ana is the Lyana incarnate . . . even her name suggests as much."

Pez stopped talking, watching Lazar carefully. The former Spur lifted his chin, his eyes raised to the heavens, and let loose a groan of such torment it tore at Pez's heart. When he had exhausted his emotion, Lazar slumped to the ground, burying his golden-haired head in his knees and wrapping his long arms around them. From between his knees Lazar croaked one word. "Maliz?"

Pez sighed privately, pleased to move on. "He, too, has . . . become. I know he is searching for me."

Lazar uncrossed his arms and raised his head to turn and face his friend. His expression was naked; there was a mixture of fear and alarm spreading across his face, frightening Pez. "You know that for sure?"

The dwarf shrugged mirthlessly. "I feel him, too. He is amongst us at the palace."

Now the soldier looked horrified. "That close! Ana's that close to danger?"

"He has no idea of her existence yet," Pez assured him, but he could see his words had little impact. "What I mean is, he may have seen Ana but he hasn't connected her to the Goddess. We still have some time." He sighed. "Ana knows who she is. We talked about it this evening."

Grief flickered across Lazar's already hurt expression. "Had she any idea previous to tonight?"

Pez shook his head. "I don't believe so. That said, Ana is very perceptive. But if she did have any notion, she wasn't letting on. She accepted it more calmly than you have. She knew I spoke the truth . . . as do you."

"How do I protect her?" Lazar asked, standing.

Pez didn't want to destroy what heart his friend had left. He needed him to remain courageous, so he chose the words of his response with care. "You can't, Lazar. This is a much bigger game we now play. It's no longer palace politicking; there's no enemy you can brandish a sword at. We have no idea from where the fight will come, or in what form. We are all somehow players on the board, as you described, and we need to work out our roles. We must simply trust one another to do our duty as it unfolds and as our duties reveal themselves."

"I'm involved?" Lazar asked, aghast.

Pez frowned. "You must be. Or why would you be linked with us?"

"Chance, surely."

"No, no, no," Pez said, pacing now, warming to his own thoughts. "Ellyana's interest in you was far too keen for you to be a chance or innocent bystander. She orchestrated the whole situation surrounding your apparent death. It's baffling."

"She wants the palace to believe me dead, you mean?"

"Yes, except I don't understand why. I don't understand why Ana must be kept in the dark either, especially if she is Lyana."

"There is only one reason for that kind of secrecy," Lazar replied, "and that's protection."

Pez nodded. "Who is she protecting Ana from, though, by keeping you secret, unless it's Maliz? But what does Maliz fear from you?"

"Death?"

"You can't kill him, Lazar. You'll need magic to do that, and even though you've all but risen from the dead, I know you possess no enchantments. You are merely mortal, my friend. No, Maliz does not fear you."

"But Maliz does not know me either, presumably. Perhaps it's the secret of my being alive that is important."

"Perhaps. I shall think on it further. But I would say this is all the more reason for you to remain in Percheron. Rushing off after Jumo into Galinsea is unwise. Whatever has happened, has happened."

"Is that more of your twisted dwarf logic?" Lazar asked, scowling.

Pez was pleased by the scowl. He needed Lazar angry, with all of his sarcasm and arrogance—and above all, courage—intact. "Well, what I mean is that what's done is done. Jumo left almost a year ago to cross the ocean. If he has made it to the Galinsean royal family, they already know of your death."

"Pez, you're missing the point. I may have walked away from my crown, and my parents may well have considered me dead for all of these many years. But Jumo's revelation will tell them I have been alive serving the Percherese Crown and that that same crown has just put me to death. I'll give you one guess what comes next."

"War," Pez said in a whisper, horrible understanding dawning now.

Lazar nodded grimly. "And swiftly. Beloved or not, my family will not sit idly by if the Percherese Zar has slain their son and heir. We know the Zar didn't have much involvement, but that's not how they'll view it. Believe me, retribution will be sought. Revenge will be taken. I would suggest time is short. Jumo left a year ago, near enough . . . two moons to sail, perhaps another moon or more to get an audience."

"Weeks of arguing," Pez said grimly.

"They'll need time to assemble their army."

"And two moons to sail back."

Lazar grimaced. "They are upon us within weeks at best calculations."

"They will send diplomatic messengers, surely?" Pez reasoned.

Lazar nodded. "Probably. And if we follow that reasoning, then those people will be entering the city at any moment."

"What can be done? We cannot fight both mortal and godly wars."

Lazar frowned in thought. "Against Ellyana's advice I think I must declare myself." He strode up to the edge of the cliff, speaking quickly. "It is fortunate I am well enough to travel. I must show myself to Boaz—he must understand what we face now from Galinsea. I shall have to dream up an excuse for my long absence."

"Stick with the truth of how sick you've been," Pez suggested.

"Yes, but Zafira claimed me dead, given to the seas. I need to counter that."

"Zafira expects no quarter. Let her take the blame. You can say she said what she did of her own accord. That you gave no approval for such actions and you're only now well enough to present yourself. We shall give her warning for escape. I will go to the temple now."

"Yes, but what could be the reason for her deceit? Boaz is too bright not to ask for that reason."

"Make one up. It doesn't matter. I leave to warn Zafira."

Lazar nodded.

Pez felt obliged to ask the obvious. "Ana?"

Now Lazar scowled. "I can't help her finding out."

"It will break her heart."

"You can't have it both ways, Pez. Just moments ago you were arguing her case for knowledge. You can't protect her from the injury of that knowledge." Pez nodded sadly as Lazar continued: "More importantly, if Maliz has yet not recognized his nemesis, then I have some time. You must see to it that you are not found out, so that I can make the journey to Galinsea the fastest way and prove that I am alive . . . hopefully avert war."

"The fastest way?"

"Across the desert."

"In early summer? Do you have a death wish?"

Lazar gave a derisive snort. "I've stared at death's hungry eyes, Pez. It doesn't scare me."

"Did it ever?" Pez asked, but didn't expect a response; nor did he get one. He carried on his previous line of thought. "Jumo could be back any day now."

Lazar shook his head. "He has no reason to return to Percheron now. He will likely head north . . . home. In the meantime we must prepare. Expect me in Percheron in two days. Warn Boaz."

"I can't."

"Why not?"

Pez swallowed, feeling his stomach tighten. "We've had a falling out."

"What happened?"

Pez explained briefly.

Lazar scratched his head. "I didn't think you two could ever fall out. Still, I shall be the gift you bring back to him to appease his anger. Boaz listens to me."

Pez shook his head. "You can't be sure that he will listen. He takes new counsel these days."

Lazar nodded slowly. "You mentioned that Tariq has ingratiated himself."

"Oh, it's much worse, Lazar. Grand Vizier Tariq now all but controls the Zar's waking thoughts."

"You're overreacting, Pez. Like a jealous woman." Lazar found a grin, much to the surprise of them both.

"I wish I were. Tariq is dangerous."

"Tariq is a sop. I've known that man—"

"You don't know this one." Pez cut off his friend. He gave a painful frown. "Tariq has changed, Lazar. He is so different you would hardly recognize him now."

"No man changes that much."

"This one has. It's remarkable. He even looks different. He certainly sounds different—not in his voice but how he voices his thoughts. They're intelligent, inspired, clever. There's new cunning in those eyes now, Lazar, that has nothing to do with the stupid self-importance and social climbing that the Tariq of old was known for. This Tariq is totally self-possessed. He requires no one's sanction . . . nor does he look for it."

Lazar shook his head. "I can't imagine you're speaking about the same man."

The dwarf threw up his hands in disgust. "It is as though someone has possessed Tariq," he claimed angrily. At those words he felt his blood turn to ice. He looked at Lazar, seeing his thoughts reflected in his friend's ashen face.

"Is it possible?" Lazar finally whispered, disbelief in his eyes.

Pez could hardly answer. Overwhelmed by an onslaught of a fury he had never felt before, he covered his eyes with his deformed hands, as if to cover himself from the vision of Maliz smiling from behind Tariq's dark eyes. "Of course it's possible," he croaked. "More than possible. In fact, that's precisely what's occurred. Iridor rose. So did Maliz. And he chose Tariq as his vessel. It's so obvious now that I can't believe I missed it. Maliz the warlock was as vain as the summer day is long. He is using his magic to improve the body in which he is imprisoned now until his next death."

"His destruction, you mean," Lazar said, something cruel and hard in his tone.

Pez stared at his friend. "I'll warn you again and you must pay this the attention it deserves, Lazar. Maliz cannot be killed by conventional means. You have to trust me on this. I can see where your thoughts are running, but if you think you can protect Ana by killing Tariq, you are tragically mistaken. All you will do is declare yourself to the demon. He will kill you, more like, using his magics and then come after anyone who is close to you."

"Then, *what*?" Lazar demanded, clearly frustrated—and shocked by the fear in the dwarf's voice.

"We move far more carefully. I think it's a good idea for you to return to the palace now. Yes, come back, Lazar, and let's see how the Vizier reacts to you. Are you prepared to risk it?"

"Risk it? I want his death, Pez. Of course I'll risk it. In spite of you and the Zar being at odds, find a way to let Boaz know you have a special surprise being delivered."

IT WAS ALREADY LATE; Pez decided to tell Zafira the new developments at daybreak. Telling her now would allow her to do nothing right except spend a few sleepless hours before sunrise.

But he had one more errand to run this night. As the first tentative lightening of dawn threatened, he alighted on one of the minarets that framed the palace. Anyone looking up would have seen a large bird dropping silently through the air and disappearing beneath the rooftops. The man waiting for him saw only the familiar shape of the dwarf, dangling awkwardly before clambering uneasily onto a balcony.

"Are we safe?" Pez whispered.

The man nodded.

"Anything?"

His companion shook his head. "Nothing out of the ordinary."

"Tariq?"

"I have not seen him since the Zar retired and that was early."

"Did the Zar say anything about me?"

"He asked his secretary where you were, but the servant said he didn't know. The Zar said no more. He sent a note to the harem. He is bringing the boating trip forward. He asked Salmeo to make preparations. They include you."

"I see. Very good, Razeen. Be careful."

"You must not worry about me."

Pez nodded unhappily, unbalanced by the young man's confidence. "Focus on the Grand Vizier. I want everything you can tell me about him."

"That will be easy."

Pez found an uneasy yet soft smile. "Take no unnecessary risk."

"I must go," Razeen replied. "I might be missed."

Pez nodded again. "Lyana watch over you."

Razeen grinned in the cocksure way of those possessed with a youthful sense of invincibility. Pez felt the fragility of such delusion and shivered. He promised himself to take even more precaution with these meetings as he watched Razeen step through the doors leading back into the suite of chambers that belonged to the Zar.

9

It was no good. Despite her best efforts, Ana could not contain the general excitement within the harem spilling into screeches and raised voices that were not considered appropriate for any of the odalisques. And she could not blame a single one of her companions, for she, too, had felt her heart swell this morning at the news that their boat picnic had been brought forward—they were going out today.

For almost two weeks they had been trapped inside doing tedious needlework and tirelessly rehearsing court etiquette—how to behave when addressed by the Valide, how to behave in front of the Zar, his guests, visiting dignitaries. There were endless lessons, and although most of the young women took to these studies with enthusiasm—for they were eager to succeed in the harem—the bright days outside served only to make Ana feel listless and downright resentful at times. It felt like punishment on these sparkling spring mornings to be cooped up inside. Even her pleasure at language studies had been sorely tested.

When Ana had awoken this morning she hadn't thought she could bear another day like the previous one. Even though some good sense had discouraged her from doing anything unwise, Ana couldn't help her mind wandering off. Physical freedom called to her softly like the breeze off the Faranel, but emotional freedom . . . perhaps that could never be attained, even in her daydreams. The pain of losing Lazar was her closest companion, a dull, soft ache, one she knew she would have to learn to live alongside for as long as she breathed.

The Valide's threat that the Zar would choose her in the near future had rattled her as well. Ana wasn't naive; she understood her role in the harem and she would have to have the brain of a bird not to realize that Boaz was already showing a hunger for her. But she hadn't thought it would happen so soon.

Frowning, she turned her thoughts to the chilling conversation she had had with Pez the previous night. What he had said didn't scare her. If anything, it made her feel empowered, as if suddenly everything around her was trite and pointless. Well . . . perhaps everything but Spur Lazar. Ana wanted nothing to do with life in the harem, but it had given her Lazar and for that she felt a modicum of gratitude. If the old Zar had not died, if the palace had not needed to assemble a new harem, if Herezah had not wanted to punish Lazar by sending him on the girl-hunting task that he found so distasteful, if her stepmother had not been so ready to sell her into slavery, ridding herself of the orphaned child she detested, then Ana might never have known such love in her life as she felt for the Spur.

They had taken his body from her but they would never be able to take away her feelings for him or her brief but vivid memory of touching him, looking into his eyes and recognizing the sorrow deep within, sensing his secrets and, yes, his startled desire for her. She had understood how he struggled against the tide of his emotions. But there was nothing wrong in loving each other; Ana knew their love was pure and would always remain that way, for it had never moved beyond the unspoken pain of forbidden yearning.

So felt no fear this morning. Not even after Salmeo's unsettling news, when he had announced to the general harem that the boating trip would be moved forward. The subsequent squeals of anticipation and unrestrained joy from the girls had brought a smile to the Grand Master Eunuch's thick lips.

"We do our best," he had said to Ana, his tongue darting out to moisten those fat lips.

She had apologized several times for the girls' lack of composure, even struggling to contain her own pleasure, but his huge hand had waved away her softly spoken requests for forgiveness. "They are still children, Ana, I understand."

She had known this to be a lie—Salmeo would never understand childhood needs—but she had schooled her expression to remain contrite. "I promised the Valide that I would teach them to comport themselves properly, Grand Master Eunuch," she tried to explain.

He had smiled indulgently, confusing her. "Fret not. The Valide places much faith in you, Odalisque Ana, and I'm sure your skills in leadership will be a great help in preparing the girls for this outing." He had paused momentarily. The smell of violets had assaulted her as he spoke and, combined with Salmeo's cloying sweetness, had set her nerves jangling. The Grand Master Eunuch had continued: "Which is why it is a little sad that you cannot join the rest of the harem on this trip."

Ana had thought she had heard him wrong. She had stared at him, frowning in confusion.

"Oh dear," he had sighed softly, "perhaps the Valide has not already mentioned this. She requires your company today." He had given a moue of sympathy. "She should be here any moment and will no doubt explain."

"Remain behind?" Ana had asked, unable to hide her distress. "But I've been looking forward to this outing as much as the others," she had gabbled, only quieting herself with force of willpower.

"I appreciate the fact that the timing is not ideal," Salmeo had replied, his light voice all the more irritating for its contrived tone of sorrow on her behalf, "but I am led to believe that you and the Valide have a special understanding. Is that right?" Ana stared at him, baffled, so Salmeo filled the awkward silence. "Apparently you are to assist the Valide in all her needs. You've agreed to be reliable and trustworthy . . . no rebelliousness."

Ana had shaken her head, clearing the cobwebs of disbelief. "I have agreed to that but—"

"Ah," he had interrupted, smiling as if everything was settled.

"But I never—"

"Hush, Ana. No rebellion, remember?" Salmeo had said lightly, giggling behind the chubby, bejeweled finger he had held to his lips to silence her.

Ana had steeled herself to remain composed. "As the Valide chooses," she had managed to grind out politely, even bowing with some semblance of courtesy, but as she had straightened she could see only delight in the eunuch's eyes. They had planned this. This had been deliberately done to build up her hopes and then dash them. Was Boaz in on the plot? She didn't think so, but she also could not understand why the Valide would provoke her. When they had met, Herezah had appeared—to all intents—to genuinely want the two of them to be more companionable.

Of course, Herezah knew that in order to remain close to her son she would also need to accept his women, especially his wives. While the Valide had chosen all the girls in the harem herself, it was up to Boaz to select which of them would fill the premium positions.

Ana understood that she and the Valide had gotten off to a very poor start. Her escape had humiliated the harem. But Herezah's cares were not really centered on the harem, were they? The harem was her seat of power, the realm over which she presided with her fat partner in cunning, but it was not where her heart lay. Her heart was with a much larger power—with the Zar, and in ensuring those ties were never fractured. Was this all about preventing Boaz from spending time with the odalisque he seemed to be favoring?

Now the Valide swept into the room, gorgeously attired in tightly bound dark silks. She was certainly not going on any boat outing, judging by such sumptuous robes. Ana's heart sank as she watched Herezah glide effortlessly toward her, without even sparing a glance toward Salmeo.

Ana bowed as graciously as she could. "Valide," was all she would trust herself to say.

"I see there's an air of hysteria in the harem this morning."

Ana nodded. "The girls have just found out that the Zar's boating trip is taking place today. They've been looking forward to this since joining the harem."

"I don't doubt it," Herezah answered in her smoky voice. "And you, Ana, you don't echo their joy." Her smile was bright.

"Not since hearing that I will not be joining them on this outing, Valide. I understand that you need my services."

"I do."

Ana nodded. She dared not say more, she was busy fighting back tears.

"Why so sad, Ana? Does a day with me sound so disappointing?"

"Forgive me, Valide," Ana replied, bobbing a small curtsy. "I allowed myself to anticipate a day out on the water. I am struggling a little, I'll admit, to resign myself to the idea that I will not be enjoying this freedom."

"Ah, freedom," Herezah echoed. "A powerful notion, eh?" Ana nodded, desperately trying to hide her misery. "But what makes you think that freedom has been denied?"

Ana watched as the now fully veiled girls were being herded out of the chamber. She could see beyond to where Salmeo's army had trunks of provisions to take with them, no doubt filled with everything from fresh clothes to drying linens, should the girls decide to swim. And from the kitchens Ana imagined another army was steadily marching with an endless array of baskets carrying sumptuous food worthy of the Zar's special picnic for his women. She sighed. "I understand you have some work for me to do, Valide," she replied.

Herezah's eyebrow lifted sardonically. "If you call a shopping expedition into the city work, then so be it."

Ana couldn't help her display of surprise. One hand covered her mouth just in time to stop the shriek.

Herezah smiled. "I can't imagine what Salmeo led you to believe, my girl, but we are not working on a fine day like this. I promised you an escorted trip into the city, did I not?"

Ana nodded dumbly.

"Well, hurry up and get ready, girl."

"We're going together?"

"Who else did you think would have the right taste and experience to choose fabrics and jewelery for a Zar's wife?" Herezah commented archly, and at Ana's disbelieving expression, she laughed, not unkindly. "I shall give you until the next bell or I leave without you. Fully veiled, remember."

"I'll be ready in moments," Ana replied eagerly. Perhaps it would be a day of freedom after all?

BOAZ WAS NOT SHARING the same pleasure. He had welcomed the girls of his harem theatrically and with a certain dashing charm that had them giggling beneath their veils, but it was hard to pick who each might be and his first hungry stare had not picked her out.

He watched them now excitedly clambering aboard the royal barges that, according to the Grand Vizier, had not felt the water for years.

"Are you sure you won't be coming with us today, Grand Vizier?" he offered again, not really interested but needing something to say as he searched for Ana.

"No, my Zar. There is plenty of dull paperwork for me to plow through, and as boring as it is compared to a day on the river in your fine company and amongst these bright young things, I do think I must remain dutiful."

"Your self-sacrifice is impressive, Tariq," Boaz quipped.

His high-ranking servant grinned back and shrugged. "I shall take much pleasure in hearing about the expedition tonight."

"You will take supper with me, Tariq."

"Very good, Highness. An opportune time to run through

some important items. I shall take my leave, my Zar, and wish you a wonderfully uplifting day enjoying the natural wonders of Percheron." His dark eyes slid over the boats filled with young women and both of them knew he wasn't referring to the river or the scenery.

Boaz nodded and then shook his head ruefully. Tariq had taken to making clever jests, smacking of a wit the Zar had never once witnessed in the Vizier during his time as heir. Tariq had always seemed so self-obsessed and sexless that it had not once occurred to Boaz to imagine that the Vizier was interested in women, and yet recently Boaz had seen the Grand Vizier pay an appreciative roving glance to the palace's female servants.

He beckoned to Salmeo, who lightly hurried toward him. "Majesty?"

"Where is Pez?"

Salmeo looked at him blankly. "I have not seen him, my Zar."

"I specifically asked Bin to ensure he was here today to entertain the girls."

The Vizier, seeming to overhear their conversation, stepped close to the Zar. "If I may, Majesty?" Salmeo scowled but Boaz nodded. "Bin did mention that he hadn't been able to locate the dwarf."

"I see. So he will not be with us today." When both his senior servants remained silent Boaz exploded angrily. "This is not acceptable! The Zar's clown—who enjoys significant indulgence, I might add—should at least be present when the Zar wants him."

"I couldn't agree more, my Zar," Salmeo replied.

The Grand Vizier nodded in agreement. "Highness, let me

see if we can find him now. You will still be a little while loading the boats. May I try for you?"

Salmeo's scowl darkened. "Zar Boaz, if the Vizier cannot locate your jester, perhaps I can have him hunted down in your absence?"

"He's not an animal, Grand Master Eunuch," Boaz snapped. "You make it sound as if you'd enjoy the chase. Would you beat him with a stick when you caught him?" Turning back to the Grand Vizier, the Zar continued more calmly: "Thank you, Tariq. If you can locate him easily, I think the young ladies would benefit from his sense of fun today."

"And if not, my Zar?"

"Inform him of my displeasure," came the curt reply.

The Grand Vizier bowed and took his leave. Salmeo remained, his bulk overwhelming the trim figure of the Zar. "I did not mean any insult, Highness," Salmeo said humbly.

Boaz turned to stare up into the eunuch's hooded gaze, his eyes buried deeply amongst the folds of flesh. The man never failed to revolt him. "You have never found Pez amusing."

"But I know you do, Highness, and your father before you. I would not let anything bad happen to someone so important to our Crown."

Boaz smelled the violets on the man's breath and was again reminded of his slippery ways. His mother had warned him often enough that he knew Salmeo was saying what he imagined the Zar wanted to hear. He felt a sense of anger drop like stone in his stomach at the eunuch's honeyed words, at odds with how he was feeling about Pez right now.

"The dwarf is not my favorite person just at present, Salmeo: it is true he has displeased me. But don't imagine that gives anyone the right to treat Pez in any way other than has always been demanded in this palace. That said, you would all do well to know that I will not tolerate any form of insubordination, not even from him."

Salmeo blinked slowly, his tongue flicking out to lick his lips in a ritual that Boaz thought made him look like a reptile. "Of course, Highness. Are you sure there is nothing I can do to help with the dwarf?"

"No; Tariq can handle it," Boaz snapped again, frustrated further now that he'd revealed to this cunning man his displeasure with Pez. He had not intended to, but not sighting Ana and the disappointment of his run-in with Pez had left him feeling hollow on a day that was meant to be all about fun. And lately he felt as though he was no longer in control of his moods. The smallest things seemed to darken his humor. He needed to talk to Pez just when he had banished him in anger. Noticing that Salmeo was still regarding him intently, Boaz pulled himself sharply from his thoughts. "Where is Odalisque Ana, by the way?" he demanded, hoping to distract the eunuch from his falling-out with the dwarf.

He watched the eunuch's expression rearrange itself from intrigue to a carefully contrived look of sympathy. "Odalisque Ana will not be joining us today, Highness."

Even though discontent had knifed through him at not spotting her easily, it had not occurred to Boaz that she wouldn't be present at all. He struggled to keep the disappointment from his voice. "Why ever not? Is she unwell?"

"She is in fine health, Majesty."

"Then where is she?"

"She is with the Valide today, Highness."

Boaz frowned, totally confused. "My mother? What is this about?"

The huge man shrugged but kept it courteous. "She did not share that with me, Your Highness. I was simply told that the Valide wished the Odalisque Ana to accompany her today on a trip into the city."

"To do what?"

"I don't know, Majesty. Womanly things, presumably." Now Salmeo smiled, showing the gap between his teeth. "The Valide is looking for new fabrics and she prefers to choose them herself. I imagine she sees taking Ana along with her a special honor to confer on an odalisque."

Boaz thought differently but this time he resisted sharing what was on his mind. "Are they still in the palace?"

"Sadly not," Salmeo replied. "They left early."

A new swell of fury rose within Boaz now. He was certain he was being manipulated. This would put everyone back on notice about who was in charge in the palace. "I see." Before he could help himself, he ordered, "Have Odalisque Ana fully prepared for me this evening."

The word *prepared* had special meaning to the keeper of the harem and its effect was immediate and dramatic. "Prepared, Highness? Do I understand you correctly?" Salmeo blustered, clearly caught off guard.

Before Boaz could respond, the mute, Salazin, ran up to him, bowing low before the Zar. When the man straightened to eye level, Boaz fixed an angry look of inquiry on his face, hugely irritated at the interruption.

One of the Elim spoke up. "He needs to run back to your chambers, Majesty. We have forgotten—"

"Yes, yes, don't trouble me with these trivialities!" Boaz admonished. The Elim and the mute retreated, Salazin running at full speed to retrieve whatever had been left behind.

"Apologies," Salmeo said, "I believe the Grand Vizier has instructed the mutes never to leave your side without royal sanction."

More irritation flickered in the Zar's darkening eyes. He ignored the man's explanation and returned to their original conversation. "You asked whether you understand me. We both speak Percherese perfectly well, Grand Master Eunuch. I think my plain wording should have made it precisely clear for you. Tell me what you understand by my order." Though he deliberately kept his voice low, the threat was still evident.

Salmeo actually took a step back. Boaz liked that he'd shocked the fat eunuch.

"My understanding, Highness, is that you wish Odalisque Ana to be readied for bedding by her Zar. That you choose to claim her virginity this night."

The Zar beamed, not prepared to show even a slight clue of how much that statement petrified him. "Good, I'm glad I made myself perfectly plain," he replied condescendingly. "Don't make any excuses for disappointing my wishes this time, Grand Master Eunuch. I shall expect to see her." He added as a vicious parting shot: "After my supper, which I'm taking with the Grand Vizier."

Turning, he stalked away to the boats.

10

Salmeo knew he had to catch the Valide before she and Ana left the palace. It appeared as though their crafty plan was to be outwitted by the Zar and his helpless infatuation for the girl. He found the Valide draping herself with the dark veil that would cover her tight silks from head to toe for her excursion.

She looked at him, surprised. "I permitted you only because my servants said you were breathless. So presumably this is important?"

"Highly," he said, sucking in air.

"Zarab save us! That run has cost you, eunuch. More than important, then . . . dangerous, even?"

"Very," he managed to say, bending over slightly to help himself breathe.

"Well, get on with it, Salmeo. I'm about to depart the palace. The karaks have arrived and I don't want to linger long enough for the sun to warm them too much."

"Valide," he began, wondering how best to deliver this news. She glowered at him. "It's about Odalisque Ana."

"What of her?" she demanded, irritated.

"The Zar has chosen her. Just now," he said, not sure how to read the mask that was her expression.

Silence engulfed Herezah and he watched her complexion blanch as she struggled to absorb his words. He couldn't even enjoy her shock because this turn of events had implications for him as much as the Valide. "I have just been ordered by the Zar to prepare her for tonight."

"Already? Are you absolutely sure?" she croaked, her full attention given to him now.

He nodded grimly. "There is no mistake. Your son made it embarrassingly clear what he intends for the girl. We are too late, Valide."

"Nonsense!" Herezah admonished, rapidly gathering up her wits and regaining her composure. "We just have to put our plan into action faster."

"It's impossible," Salmeo said, shaking his head in surprise. "The Zar means this night."

"And she will be gone by tonight!" Herezah snarled at him in a low, angry voice. "See to it. Make all the preparations that we've discussed. The girls will return tired but happy, presumably—we might as well keep that mood going with a little surprise of our own. Not only Boaz can offer them treats."

Salmeo nodded slowly. "Perhaps it can be achieved," he said, thinking it through.

"It will be, Grand Master Eunuch. Make it happen. I am going out now with Ana. We will not be long. Her taste of freedom will be brief and I'm sure will put her into the right frame of mind . . . especially after I allude to what's in store for her tonight."

The slyness of Salmeo's grin spread across his face until it danced in his dark eyes. "Clever, my Valide. Oh, and I have more news that will please you."

"Oh yes?"

"The dwarf has done something to displease your son. The Zar is so displeased, in fact, that he admitted it to me himself in a state of high temper."

"You jest."

The huge black man shook his head. "Told me himself that he would not tolerate such insubordination from his servants. He tried to steer it into more general terms, but he was clearly referring to Pez."

"Was Pez present?" Herezah asked enthusiastically, hungry for the details.

"He's gone missing," Salmeo replied, fueling her hunger. "But no one knows where or why."

Herezah clapped her hands. "Excellent," she purred. "This could be a special day for us. Where is the Vizier?"

"He is remaining at the palace, says he is very busy with work."

Herezah made a disparaging sound at this. "Busy spying, perhaps. I'm going now; you will put into action all that is necessary. Keep an eye on the Vizier; I'm interested to know what he does when he is not answerable to the Zar."

Salmeo nodded. "Enjoy your shopping expedition."

She smiled cruelly. "You know I will."

HEREZAH FOUND ANA VEILED, flanked by two Elim, and patiently awaiting her high-ranking companion. The Valide saw the smile in the girl's eyes as she approached, escorted by her own Elim.

The odalisque bowed. "Valide."

"Valide, I shall see to your instructions."

Herezah nodded an acknowledgment of the greeting. The women were guided out of the cool shadows of the palace's interior and into the sharp sunlight of the day.

Ana squinted. "This is very exciting for me, Valide," she gushed helplessly, allowing one of the Elim to assist her into the karak.

Herezah was being given similar assistance into her karak. "I hope you have a wonderful time, Ana. This freedom is my gift to you," she said, smirking beneath her veil.

Herezah gave the signal and the bearers lifted the two karaks, easily bearing them down the palace pathways toward the main gates. Herezah could see Ana's almost palpable sense of excitement; in her own karak, she plotted precisely what she was going to say to her naive companion in order to provoke her into making the biggest mistake of her short life.

PEZ ARRIVED BACK AT his small chamber to find a note. He recognized instantly that it was from Razeen, and its hastily scribbled scrawl clearly reflected the urgency of the contents.

Apparently he was in further trouble with the Zar, having failed to present himself for the boating trip. Pez cursed himself for the oversight—he'd forgotten in his rush to warn Zafira. No one had told him it was leaving this morning. He shook away his concern. There was nothing to be done until the Zar returned and summoned him. More frightening was the news that Boaz had chosen Ana and instructed the Grand Master Eunuch to prepare her for tonight.

Unsure of what to do but knowing he had to do something, Pez changed into more formal dress for the court and waddled out of his room, only to be assailed by two massive Elim. He began to dance, gabbling a stream of gibberish. The guards guided him, gently but firmly, beyond the halls of the harem and into the palace proper.

"Where go we?" he sang.

"We have orders to bring you to the Grand Vizier," one of the eunuchs answered patiently.

Pez felt his throat clamp with fear.

"Vizier, Vizier," he sang, thinking fast.

"The Zar asked him to find you," the other Elim said.

"I don't want to see a snake," Pez whined, childlike.

"But you must," the first said softly, smiling, probably because Pez's madness was making odd sense. "It is what Zar Boaz wishes," he added.

This news was disturbing. Had Boaz given the Vizier permission to do more than simply find the court jester—perhaps police him, or even punish him? He took the last remaining moments he had, no longer struggling but centering himself to bring all of his Lore skills to the fore. He forced all that was Iridor deep within himself, hiding it from Maliz, burying it so far away that the demon would not be able to find it even if he looked for magic. He wondered if Maliz already suspected him of being Iridor. It certainly seemed as if Maliz was not just suspicious but now searching for evidence.

Make my madness my armor, O Mother. Encase me in your love, protect me from evil, let my Lore confuse him and keep me safe, Pez whispered, his lips barely moving.

He would need to give his best performance ever and somehow throw the Vizier off his scent.

There was still so much to achieve before Maliz killed him.

ANA SIGHED WITH A sense of restless wonder as the karak moved beyond the Moon Courtyard and through the palace gates. As the Stone Palace was perched on a hill, she knew she must hold on for safety now as the Elim adjusted their grip and began the descent. The sense of freedom she felt was so strong she was sure the air smelled sweeter, and the colors were brighter. All the darkness that she had been carrying the past year dissipated to leave her lighthearted. Her emotions were clashing into one another; Ana felt at once elated and teary. Forcing herself under control, she knew that her tears came from her understanding that this was only temporary, and that sadness made the joy of being out amongst the people even more poignant.

The karak was no longer traveling at an angle; the road had begun to straighten out and Ana risked a peep through the curtains, wrapping her arms around herself with pleasure to see the masses of people going about their midmorning business. Women chatted to one another, children clasped tightly on their hips or holding their hands. Men rolled carts laden with goods. She even spotted a few of the soldiers mingling with the general population, reminding her of Lazar. A fresh gust of grief swept through her mind. It was always there, always ready to poison her day, but she chastised herself that she must not let Lazar's shadow fall too fully across this day. This was one day she was keeping as shiny and free from darkness as she could, no matter how hard it would be to return to the palace at the end.

The voices grew louder and Ana again peeped between the silks to see that they were entering the narrow streets that she knew led down to the bazaar. She heard the Elim giving orders, clearing the crowd from around the karaks, and she imagined the fascinated stares of people curious to know who from the palace had come into their midst.

Suddenly Herezah was leaning into her karak. "Come, Ana," she said conversationally, and then the Elim were helping Ana to alight. She noticed more Elim had trailed them in order that someone would remain with the transport until the women returned.

Flanked once again by her red-robed guards, but this time with her arm encircled affectionately by Herezah's, Ana stepped into the slow-moving stream of people and felt the lightness that had imbued her heart instantly turn to a weightlessness. She felt as though her sandals were no longer touching the ground.

"I can hardly breathe for excitement," she whispered to her companion. "It's been so long since I was amongst real people."

Herezah gurgled with seductive laughter. She didn't seem to take offense at Ana's innocent gibe. "It always feels like that the first time," she replied. "Enjoy yourself. I cannot promise when we might do this again, so make the very best of the short time we have."

"Oh, I will, Valide . . . and thank you. Thank you for spoiling me. I'm not sure I deserve your faith."

"I trust you, Ana," Herezah soothed. "Just don't get too seduced by freedom," she cautioned and laughed again as they were swallowed up into the first dome of the great bazaar.

"AH, PEZ," THE GRAND Vizier said, smiling, but Pez noted not even a tiny flicker of warmth touched those cold, dark eyes.

"I was promised flowers," he stated angrily.

"Oh, and you shall have them, Pez," the Vizier said, his smile not faltering.

"And cherry juice."

"Of course."

Pez burped and shook himself free from the Elim's hold.

"You may leave us," Maliz said to the men in red. At the men's hesitation, he added, a tinge of impatience in his voice, "Fret not, I shall not harm him."

Their grave expressions reminded Pez that the Elim had not forgotten Tariq's behavior at the flogging of Spur Lazar, when he had dared to kick at the dwarf, who had, to all intents, accidentally rolled across the foot of the Vizier during one of his usual acrobatic maneuvers. Pez knew better, of course.

One of the Elim bowed and stepped forward. "Grand Vizier, we are never permitted to leave the dwarf unattended in the company of someone outside of the harem."

"Is that so?" Maliz replied, sarcastically sneering.

The man nodded solemnly. "He has the full protection of the harem and the Zar, as you know. Forgive us, but we are not allowed to let him out of our sight."

Pez began to sing, covering the smile he felt tugging at his mouth. Perhaps he would be safe after all. He suddenly worshipped the Elim for being so rigid in adhering to their rules.

"But he comes and goes as he chooses—or so I understand," Maliz replied, working to hide his irritation, Pez noted.

The man nodded again. "That is true, Grand Vizier. Pez is permitted complete freedom within the harem. Beyond its boundaries he is always escorted—as is anyone from the harem."

"I'm assured the Zar's clown travels way beyond the boundaries of the palace and into the city!" Maliz grumbled, no longer able to disguise his discontent.

Now the man shrugged. "He is disobedient," was the only reply he gave.

Pez began to dance, singing loudly at the top of his voice. It was his intention to frustrate the demon as fast as possible.

"Can you quiet him?" Maliz asked of the guards over the racket.

The Elim leaned forward and touched Pez gently on the shoulder. He didn't fall silent but he stopped dancing and murmured softly to himself, picking his nose and wiping whatever he could find in it on the furniture. Stealing a glance at Maliz, he took pride in the disgust he now saw in the Grand Vizier's expression. He farted for good measure just as the official opened his mouth to speak. It closed again.

"Is this the best we can do with him?" Maliz inquired of the Elim.

The more senior one of the guards gave a soft shrug of helplessness. "He is contrary, Grand Vizier. No one controls him."

"Pez." Maliz finally addressed him directly.

Pez stopped all activity and gave the man a beatific smile.

"Good. The Zar is very unhappy with you, Pez."

Pez gave a sulky look and then bent down to grab the turned up toes of his ridiculous court shoes. Both Zars loved them for their comical effect and had many pairs made up in various fabrics. They were deliberately too large for his feet and Pez had even attached bells to this pair for added humor. He shook them now.

"Look at me, please."

As Pez complied he felt the first tentative grope of magic

pull at the protective shield of the Lore and saw recognition burn in the formerly dead-looking eyes of the Vizier. He had anticipated as much. But finding a shield meant nothing; it could be interpreted many ways. His insanity could be seen as that shield and he used his disguise to full effect now, screaming and screaming straight into the Grand Vizier's horrified stare.

Pez's screams were legendary and to be avoided at all cost. The Elim grabbed for him and covered his mouth. He continued to struggle despite their strength, as it disguised the shudder he felt at the insistent probing.

Desperate to break the link with the demon, Pez allowed his body to become peaceful as he began to count backward in Derranese, loudly, each number interspersed with spitting gobs of whatever he could muster directly at the Grand Vizier's beautifully crafted darkwood table. He hadn't been in the Vizier's chambers before, but Lazar had told him how vulgar and ostentatious the whole setup had been under Tariq. Well, there was no sign of Tariq here, Pez thought, spitting forcefully at the exquisite table, just one of several simple, priceless, and supremely elegant pieces that sparsely furnished the huge chamber.

"Stop that!" Maliz yelled, and Pez finally sensed that the probing magic's link had been broken. He silently sighed his relief as he continued to count and spit.

"Grand Vizier. Pez must not be shouted at."

"Can you not stop him behaving so?" Maliz demanded, impotent fury evident in his tone.

"We could remove him."

Pez suddenly stopped counting, issuing a soft sound of remorse instead. Everyone's glances were drawn helplessly to where he sat staring at the widening puddle around his satin trousers.

"Oh, Zarab save me!" Maliz exclaimed, both astonished and angered. "Get him out of here and have that filthy mess cleaned up."

"Yes, Grand Vizier," both Elim murmured, stifling their amusement.

"I want to stay here!" Pez screamed as the men bent to lift him. "I haven't finished yet."

"Get him out!" the Grand Vizier roared, his thunderous expression exclaiming that he was determined nothing further was going to be released from the dwarf's body into his chamber.

The men rushed Pez from the scene of his crime, dangling him between them in their haste to get him clear of the Grand Vizier's wrath. After closing the door, they put him back onto his own short legs and gave rueful glances at the damp trousers he stood in.

"I'm uncomfortable," he complained.

"That wasn't wise, Pez," one continued.

"I had plans to leave something bigger behind," the dwarf said before gently shaking himself clear of his escorts' hands and fleeing down the corridor. There was no time to even think about what had just occurred or the hideously precarious situation in which he now found himself. It was Ana who was in danger now and he'd already lost too much time with the Vizier.

There was only one person he could turn to. He needed to warn Lazar.

"LOOK HOW IT SPARKLES, Ana," Herezah breathed into her ear. "Imagine yourself naked and wearing only that emerald." Ana's eyes widened in shock at the suggestion and Herezah laughed softly. "Don't be shy, Ana. I know a beautiful body hides beneath all of these robes. You've just got to be taught how to show it off to its best glory. Your first lesson: Nothing complements bare skin better than a precious jewel."

Even veiled, Ana looked baffled. "Valide, I . . ."

Herezah kept her voice firm. "You must accept. And you must learn to use your body in ways you've never dreamed to excite, entice, and above all, keep the Zar enamored with you."

Ana shook her head softly, gaze returning to the emerald. "It's beautiful but gems have never fascinated me the way they do other women."

Now Herezah clicked her tongue with exasperation. "It matters not whether you appreciate them, Ana. This is about pleasing your Zar! Boaz loves emeralds. It is the stone of his birth. But I think tonight you should be dressed in blue, which will set off your golden hair beautifully. So perhaps a sapphire?"

The jeweler nodded and disappeared to the back of his store, returning almost immediately to reverently polish and place an exquisite jewel pendant into Herezah's waiting hands.

"This is perfect! You must please him by wearing it . . . perhaps dangling between your bare breasts, or across your naked hips . . . wherever he thinks it suits you best." She laughed again but kept it light, almost conveying a feeling of fondness.

"I shall consider it," Ana replied neutrally.

Herezah rounded on her, shooing the jeweler away. "You don't understand anything, do you?"

Ana shook her head, confused, frowning. "I don't know what you mean."

"I think you're being deliberately obtuse, Ana." Herezah was, again, careful to keep her voice friendly as if they were familiar companions, used to this sort of banter. "I have already warned you of what my son will require from you." She laughed lightly behind her veil. "After all, you are from the harem."

"Yes, you did, Valide. I don't mean to be evasive, I'm just getting myself prepared—"

"But there is no more time, Ana," Herezah said, reaching for the girl's arm and squeezing it as a friend might. "He has decided."

"Decided?" Ana repeated.

Herezah tinkled another laugh, her eyes sparkling at Ana's innocence. "We'll take this," she called to the jeweler, who nodded and reached to take the large light-colored sapphire pendant. "Match up a gold chain with it and have it delivered to the palace for tonight. The Grand Master Eunuch will settle with you."

The man bowed and disappeared behind the silk curtain that divided the shop from his back rooms.

Herezah watched the shock deepen in the girl's eyes. She elegantly sipped from the raspberry-colored glass of apple cinnamon tea the jeweler had served her earlier. "What are you thinking, Ana?" she inquired after a long pause. "I don't understand your hesitation."

"I just didn't imagine this would happen so soon, Valide." Ana's eyes were full of pleading now.

Herezah was privately amused that the girl hoped for her help. "I was barely thirteen when Joreb chose me."

As Ana's hand flew to her mouth, Herezah nodded reassuringly. "He was gentle the first time—I was but a child." She noticed Ana move to say something but quietly continued: "He took me five times that night. My virginity was well and truly paid to my master by the following morning." She smiled at the horror reflected in the girl's eyes, staring back at her. "He called for me six nights in a row and only left me on the seventh because he was tired from his hunting that day. Not a part of me didn't ache. Not an inch of my body wasn't bruised, bitten, scratched, pinched—all out of affection, of course. Not a single bit of me minded. I was the winner."

"Thirteen," Ana repeated.

Herezah shrugged, wondering if the girl understood now what might have shaped her, why the Valide had arrived in this position with such a hard attitude. "I learned fast—as you will. And you are nearly sixteen, Ana. A woman by anyone's standards."

"When, Valide?" Ana begged.

There was no point in lying. "Tonight."

Ana gasped.

Herezah knew it was time to be matter-of-fact. "He announced it this morning to Salmeo. You have been chosen. You are to be"—she hesitated, trying not to let the cruel grin behind the veil touch her eyes, which were showing only sympathy—"prepared," she finished.

"Prepared?"

"Bathed, oiled, smoothed. Every hair from your body must be waxed and plucked. Every hair on your head must be polished until it reflects the light of the moon. Your teeth must gleam, your breath must be sweetened, your nipples must be painted to excite the Zar. You will be given the varada leaf to chew to stimulate your own desires—it works faster than the smoke. It also widens your pupils to make you more alluring. You will be powdered and perfumed and finally you will be draped in a silken gauze, and then you will crawl to his bedside on your knees before opening yourself up to the Zar and doing whatever he asks of you."

"How long have you known?" Ana asked, seemingly stunned.

"I was told just moments before we left. It was all the more reason to ensure you had a wonderful time in the bazaar—this is, after all, your last chance at freedom. I never had a day such as you have had today. But as I said earlier, this is my gift to you. So come on, let us go now and look for fabrics and a beautiful present that you might bring to your Zar this evening." She paused deliberately, gave her tinkling laugh. "Actually, he needs no gift beyond your body, Ana. It will be enough, I'm sure."

OVER THE NEXT COUPLE of hours Ana was ushered from shop to shop. Herezah made all the purchases; Ana was barely more than an observer, unaware of the Valide's insistence that every item must reflect Ana's new status as First Chosen, incapable of responding to her queries on this fabric or that. The Valide chattered on, seemingly oblivious to the dread quiet at her side.

"Perhaps you may be Favorite by tomorrow morning," Herezah whispered conspiratorially. "Joreb made me Favorite on that first night."

Ana was past tearfulness. Now she was simply fearful, and fright was turning to something hard and obstinate. As Herezah spoke by her side about glassware and beautiful silver, magnificent rich fabrics and the ideas for the design of her own porcelain, Ana stared at the wondrous roof of the bazaar. There, in its beautiful blue-and-white painted tiles, she found calm. From this distance the intricate pattern of flowers and birds appeared merely as a complex design, and in taking her gaze around the ceiling, Ana felt her mind escaping.

She didn't even notice the icy sensation coursing through her body.

And then she heard the voice in her mind. *Who is this?* It sounded both hesitant to speak and yet terrified not to. She recognized it instantly.

It's me, was all she could say, shocked at being able to communicate this.

Ana?

She could feel his relief washing through her own mind. *How are we doing this?* she asked.

No idea. But it confirms that you are who I assumed.

I know I accepted it when we spoke—but it suddenly frightens me. Are you so sure this goatherd's daughter is who you think she is?

Yes. Why else are we linked? How is it that we can now talk to each other simply using our minds?

I don't know.

I am Iridor and you are Lyana. I have learned to accept it—now you must. When she didn't reply, he filled the silence. *Where are you? I hear a lot of noise.*

In the bazaar with the Valide. I know where you are—you're flying.

How do you know that?

I can hear the wind rushing by, she said wistfully.

Have you heard about Boaz and what he did this morning?

A moment ago. I can't think straight.

Don't be scared.

Why not? I can't escape this time.

I'm working on it.

What do you mean?

He suddenly sounded evasive. *Now that we can do this—we'll talk again in the same manner soon.*

Don't go, Pez!

I have to . . . er, Ana, forgive me, I am just joining someone—

Pez cut the link but not before she heard someone's voice—a voice she had not thought she would ever hear again. Surely it couldn't be? Was she imagining it because she was so distraught?

No. She had heard the man say "Hello, Pez" as clearly as if he were standing by her side.

"Well." A new voice interrupted her reverie. "I think we're done, Ana. You're going to look stunning tonight, I promise."

Disconcerted, Ana tried to refocus her gaze. The Valide's sharp eyes regarded her intently from behind her dark veil.

"Are you feeling unwell?" Herezah inquired.

Ana felt the Valide touch her arm and realized she was shaking her shoulder. Her thoughts swiftly snapped back to the moment. "I think a ghost just passed by me," she stammered, forcing out an old Percherese saying.

"Ooh." Herezah shivered. "A ghost walking by signifies that death is beckoning."

Ana shook her head. "This one meant life."

Herezah frowned, shaking her head. "We leave now. I hope you've enjoyed your excursion, Ana. Though it is your last as a virgin, it need not to be your last time roaming from the palace. If you stick to your bargain, you can do this again sometime."

"Thank you, Valide," Ana replied politely, hardly listening to the woman, her thoughts already teasing at the problem of where Lazar might be. The thrill of imagining him alive had already passed and was rapidly being replaced with shaking anger. The man she loved had tricked her in the worst possible manner . . . and, just as devastating, her only true friend was in on the duplicity. Pez was visiting Lazar now. She felt a sharp sting of betrayal. Lazar couldn't possibly have deliberately set out to hurt her. And certainly not Pez, not after this morning's conversation. But why? Why would Lazar fake his own death? Why would her uncle admit to the crime? She knew there had to be reasonable explanations, but Ana could find none, returning with sorrow to the notion that this was an act of treachery against her.

Her shaking became visible.

"Zarab save us! What's come over you, girl?" Herezah exclaimed.

And then Ana knew nothing more. She was not aware of slumping to the floor, her fall only barely broken by Herezah's quick action. She was heedless of the people rushing around her, of a strong Elim guard lifting her easily and carrying her all the way back to the palace.

She only knew who she was again when she woke to find herself draped on her own bed, pungent-smelling salts erupting through the cloudy fog to bring her back from the darkness.

And she returned to her full senses, enraged.

11

Eyes normally light in color were now darkened by news that hurt him to his soul. He worked hard to keep his expression neutral even as the fresh information was delivered, but his brow creased and then dipped, hooding his haunted face still further. His lips were pressed together as though determined to deny escape to any words that might betray their owner.

Finally Lazar let go of the breath he hadn't realized he'd held so tightly in his chest. "Boaz said it this morning?" he repeated, demanding confirmation that he did not need.

"That is what I have discovered."

"From whom? You were not there, I take it?"

"From a reliable witness."

"Why are you being evasive?"

"To protect you."

"From what?" Lazar sneered, slamming his hand down on the cottage's scrubbed table.

Pez remained patient. "From information that can incriminate. Trust me, Lazar, you do not want to hear this."

Lazar did but he didn't have time to fret over Pez's secrets right now. Ana's life was about to change once again. "And she's with Herezah, you say?"

"Apparently the Valide has taken her shopping."

Lazar shook his head. "In all my years at the palace, Herezah has never once gone shopping. She has the sellers drag their goods up to the palace for a private showing."

Pez nodded. "And if she doesn't like anything, she makes them keep repeating the process until she does."

"That's right. She enjoys their frustration. She can't have changed her ways."

"Well, perhaps because she's getting Ana ready for her son . . ." Lazar scowled and Pez quickly added, "And Ana did say that Herezah had made a bargain with her and this was the first part of their deal."

Lazar snorted. "And you believe it?"

"No," Pez admitted.

"She's up to something."

"Lazar, whatever the Valide's intentions might be with this trip into the city, they are negated by what Ana faces later."

The former Spur stomped out of the cottage, grumbling under his breath that he didn't need to be reminded of what Ana would face later. Pez caught up with him. "You're walking freely now, Lazar; your large stride has returned fully. Your stoop is gone, along with the sallow look that made me think it would be kinder to help you to an easy death. Anger is not helpful," he counseled.

"It is to me. Don't lecture me."

The dwarf pulled a contrite expression. "I have to tell you

something else. Something extraordinary." Lazar turned his angry glare on his friend, as if denying his companion from giving any more surprises. Pez continued anyway: "Ana spoke to me when I was flying. She was in the bazaar. That's how I know she was shopping."

"What do you mean?"

At Lazar's question Pez looked exasperated. "Don't be dim, Lazar. She spoke to me. We can talk across distance, using our minds . . . and our magics." Lazar grimaced, his heart constricting still further. The grief etched on his face said far more than words could.

Pez hesitated. "I'm sorry," he said. "I thought to enlighten you."

"Oh, I'm enlightened all right, Pez. According to you, she's Lyana, Mother Goddess!" Lazar roared, no longer able to contain his fury. "But it still doesn't save her a rutting at the end of Boaz's newfound manhood, does it?"

The dwarf stared at Lazar, clearly shocked. But then his expression tightened, and he said quietly, "And can you blame him?"

"What?" Lazar felt a tide of fresh fury rise uncontrollably within him.

"Can you honestly deny that you harbor similar desires?"

Pez didn't see it coming, but in his defense, neither did Lazar. He swung a strong backhander that connected perfectly with the dwarf's jaw, sending Pez to his back.

Moments later Lazar watched as his old friend blinked slowly, dully, as realization hit that he was staring up at the bright sky over Star Island. He was filled with remorse and concern as he bent over the little man, tenderly bathing his knotted features with a cool, damp linen.

"What happened?" Pez mumbled, and then moaned. "I'm seeing sparkles."

"I hit you," Lazar confessed, a deep sense of shame overriding his anger. "I had no right to," he groaned.

"I deserved it," Pez said, holding his jaw and not speaking very clearly. "Help me up."

Lazar gave an anguished sound. "No, Pez, don't forgive me so easily. I deserved your criticism. My feelings toward Ana are inappropriate and you've seen through me, as did Herezah."

Pez managed a tiny shrug. "As I say, can you blame him?" he ground out.

"No."

"Envy is a terrible thing," Pez added. "I think my jaw's broken."

"I don't know how to apologize enough."

"I can fix it. The Lore has many skills and I think healing cracked bones is not beyond it. Even though your sickness was."

Lazar hung his head. "I'm so ashamed, Pez. I pride myself on always being in control of myself and my actions."

"The heart is a law unto itself, Lazar. You have no control over it."

"Nevetheless, I—"

"Stop, please. I know you're sorry—I can see it on your face, hear it in your voice. I, too, am sorry, for goading you so ruthlessly. So we're both sorry and I can fix my jaw, although I refuse to mend your aching hand. Let it hurt for a while," Pez jested gently, his tone now kindly. "Let's get on with the important matter at hand."

Lazar nodded, contrite. He rubbed the back of the hand that had connected with Pez's large jaw. "What do you suggest?"

"Get to the temple. I need you in the city faster than we planned. Perhaps with Zafira we can think this through."

"But Ana?"

Pez looked directly at Lazar. "Ana is not yours, Lazar. She belongs to the Zar. She is only a vessel for something far more important to all of us. And furthermore, she is sixteen. She is a woman and ready to face the hurdles of her sex. Harem women pleasure the Zar; that is his right. We must not do anything reckless to unsettle the balance of the palace, Lazar. We have far higher things at stake."

"What about what Ana wants?"

"It doesn't matter what Ana wants. You bought her as a slave. She is expendable in all of this. This is about destroying Maliz—that's what we're here for." He coughed painfully.

Lazar's expression grew stormy again. "That might be what you're here for, Pez—or Iridor, whatever you prefer to be called these days—but I am not a slave of Lyana. I will not be manipulated. I accept that Ana has a role, one I purchased her for. That's something I have to live with. But I don't have to forget who I am and what I feel simply because some age-old crone demands it. You dance to Ellyana's tune too readily, dwarf."

Pez shook his head sadly. "You are fooling yourself, Lazar. You're in this struggle up to your neck, as am I. We may not know why but your role will become clearer."

"So be it," Lazar said with resignation, and then his tone softened. "Again, forgive my assault. I will find a way to repay the debt I now feel I owe you."

Pez sighed. "As you wish."

"I shall see you in the city," Lazar said as farewell.

He watched the snow-white owl take off gingerly from the cliff edge. Then he returned to the hut to pack a small sack of items, none of which, save a small bottle of liquid, were important to him. He had to get himself off the island and back onto the mainland quickly. And he would need a disguise and a way to sneak into the palace. As he moved around, plotting and planning, he firmly kept his thoughts away from the final imprisonment—being Chosen—of the woman who owned his heart.

SALMEO HAD BEEN SUMMONED to Herezah's salon. Now seated, he was delighted at being served the bright red pomegranate tea by her own hand.

"Did your excursion go well, Valide?" he lisped as she settled herself back into a divan plumped with thickly feathered cushions.

"Oh, very well," she answered, amusement in her voice. "Ana fainted."

"At the news?"

Herezah smiled. "It was a slow buildup. She thought she had her emotions under control, but it was rather fascinating to watch her gradually disintegrating over our shopping expedition. Rather naive of her to think Boaz at seventeen isn't going to want to bed her—or, indeed, a dozen women."

"She's a strange one. I think Ana is beyond the other girls."

"What do you mean, Salmeo?" Herezah queried.

"Oh, it's fanciful, Valide, I know, but it's as if she knows something important the rest of us don't. And that knowledge gives her the immense aloofness and courage she has demonstrated."

"Not so courageous today," Herezah remarked with a sneer. "But I take your point. She certainly doesn't lack for spine. In fact, she doesn't stop surprising me with her insight and forth-right attitude."

"Presumably that will be her undoing, Valide," Salmeo said, daintily placing his teacup on the table between them. "It's that sense of herself that will push her over the edge into taking risks."

Herezah nodded. "Precisely, and I'll walk naked through the bazaar if I'm wrong that she doesn't take that risk tonight."

"She'll take the bait, you think?"

"I have no doubt in my mind. You're ready?"

"Completely. We'll let her think she's got away with it for a while."

"Which will make her hunting down and ultimate capture all the more sweet." Salmeo paused, considering. "Actually, my Valide, I think the Zar's decision works in our favor."

"It's not like you to take so long," Herezah teased. "Boaz did us a favor. His announcement forces not only her hand but it also makes her now answerable to him rather than to the harem."

"Yes, his punishment rather than ours."

"And he will be worked up, I'm sure. I know Boaz and how high his passions can run. He is such an intense boy, really. Ana's actions will provoke a violent response, I imagine."

"I think we can count on it, Valide."

ANA WAS LED TO the magnificent domed building attached to the harem through a tiled walkway that housed the bathing chambers.

As all members of the harem were currently enjoying the boating picnic, Ana was the only odalisque present. Everyone else was a servant or attendant and each had been charged with the information that this girl had been formally chosen by the Zar.

Each new young woman to be called to the Zar's bedroom to relinquish her maidenhood held special significance. But the First Chosen for a new Zar was traditionally symbolic of the success of the man's rule and the prestige of his harem.

In this instance it was even more dramatic. This was a virgin Zar choosing his first virgin. Ana's head attendant, Elza, was impressing upon the silent Ana the enormous responsibility she now carried.

"Everyone will be looking to you to make this go smoothly. You must please the Zar more than any who might follow in your footsteps. And you must remember, this is also his first time. You will be guiding each other. His pleasure is paramount. Yours is a gift from him should he so choose."

"And if he chooses to hurt me?"

Elza did not hesitate. "That's his wish," she replied firmly as she slipped the robe off Ana's naked shoulders.

Kett knelt before Ana, gently helping her to pull her feet from the tall wooden pattens that the girls wore into the bathing chamber to lift them away from the constant water that flowed across the marble.

"A soak first," Elza said, guiding Ana into the vast pool. Ana had not yet experienced the full bathing process. It hadn't been necessary until now for any of the girls to do much more than simple soaping and rinsing, although they had been learning about the long and tedious hours that they would spend in preparation each day for the Zar once he became sexually active.

Kett walked her into the pool and she noticed that, undressed, his body and face had lost the pudginess of childhood. His cheeks were lean and his big dark eyes regarded her with concern. He was naked save a for linen around his waist that protected his modesty.

"Relax, Miss Ana, the warmth will soothe," he comforted.

Ana slid into the pool, allowing the water to cover her head. When she emerged, Kett was still standing chest deep watching her, and Elza had left the chamber.

She decided to be candid. "I feel very awkward about you seeing me naked."

"I've seen you before in this state and it was my undoing," he said gravely. "Please don't be embarrassed on my behalf. All that makes me a man has gone, Miss Ana."

She didn't believe him. "No . . . um?" She struggled to find the right words.

He shook his shaved head. "No feelings at all. I'm told they got me early enough to take away the manly urges."

She swam over and touched his hand beneath the fizzing waters.

He shrugged gently. "I have been rewarded by being made your servant."

"My servant?"

"You have not been told? The Grand Master Eunuch Salmeo himself has appointed me to you."

Ana was instantly suspicious. "But why?"

"I gather it was originally intended as a special gift for today, but from what I have been hearing, it may be more permanent."

Elza bustled back with pots of various descriptions. "No more time wasting now, Kett," she chastised without feeling.

Kett nodded acknowledgment. "May I wash your hair for you?" he asked Ana.

"Thank you, Kett," she murmured. "You look so strong,"

she added, noticing his sculpted body as he helped her up and led her to a separate pool.

He gave a soft sigh. "I always wanted to be a warrior. The Elim have taught me that I am one, even though . . . " His voice trailed off.

Ana felt his pain and filled the awkward moment with light conversation. "So you've been training hard obviously?"

He began to lather her hair from behind. "Yes I have almost completed my Elim training. I will be given my full-time role soon. I hope it's to protect you."

She found a smile. "What do I need protection from?"

"Who knows? I shall do whatever is asked—I belong to the harem."

"Just as I do," she reassured him, hoping to alleviate the wistfulness he clearly couldn't shake. "We are kindred spirits, Kett."

Kett worked in silence for several minutes, carefully soaping Ana's hair with a mix of suds and egg yolk to make her hair shine before rinsing it, then beginning again, each time massaging her scalp until it tingled.

"It's a shame to waste all those egg whites," she commented sarcastically.

He giggled, whispering, "When you're older we use them to smear around your eyes to help with wrinkles, but for now I'm sure we can send them off to the Valide."

They both shared a conspiratorial laugh; then Kett grew serious.

"Are you scared, Miss Ana?" he dared.

"Yes," she replied candidly. "But I am like you. Others decide my fate for me."

She heard him pause before he replied. "It need not be that

way," he said, tipping a bucket of clean, cooler water over her head.

"What do you mean?"

He came around to face her, looking abashed. "Now we must wash your body," Kett said, his eyes glancing away from hers.

Ana turned to see Elza approaching.

"Come, Odalisque Ana, Kett will now soap your body."

Ana felt instantly coy. "Can I not do it, Elza?"

The senior attendant laughed, her bare breasts over the top of her loose pants wobbling with the mirth. "You have to get used to the touch of a man, although Kett here is hardly that." She laughed again, not unkindly. "You must also get used to this routine. If not Kett, then another of the youngest eunuchs will attend to your bathing."

"Why not you?" Ana persisted.

"I am senior, Miss Ana," Elza said archly. "I have more important roles."

Ana felt sorry for the woman. They were both slaves, both prisoners of the harem. The only thing that separated them was age and desirability in terms of the Zar's needs, and yet Elza was left to take solace from the fact that her slaving duties were more important than Kett's. She sighed. Status existed everywhere, even amongst the downtrodden.

Elza and Kett sat Ana down on a stool near a fountain of running water.

"Just let him do what he must," Elza said. "Get used to it. He's been practicing. He knows what to do for you." She left them both, although Ana knew the slave woman would not go far, as her role was presumably to supervise.

Ana didn't want to make trouble for Kett. She looked toward his downcast gaze and knew he felt as awkward about this as she did. Once again, neither of them had a choice.

"It's not your fault, Kett," she assured him. "I suppose we'd better get over the discomfort of our situation and get on with it."

He looked up and she knew he fought his treacherous eyes and his gaze that moved unhappily toward her breasts. She liked Kett—had always somehow felt responsible for his sorrowful situation, even though she knew in her heart that her circumstances that night had been equally helpless.

Ana reassured herself that Kett would get used to the sight of her body and she would get used to his ministrations. They just had to overcome this delicate beginning.

"Right," she said brightly. "Do I need to do anything?"

"No, Miss Ana," Kett said. He reached for a soft sea sponge and dipped it into a bucket filled with perfumed suds. He gently lifted Ana's long, slim arm, proceeding to soap it from fingertip to shoulder. She had to admit it felt good, and before long she relieved Kett's embarrassment and her own by closing her eyes and losing herself as best she could in her own thoughts. It was the invigorating surprise of being doused with cool water that brought her out of her musings. She opened her eyes to see Elza in front of her.

"Come, Odalisque Ana, now for the massage," the senior servant said.

Ana had never experienced the massage but she had heard plenty about it this past year in her training. It was unique to the Percherese and apparently one of the few true pleasures found in the harem.

"You must lie on the marble floor over here," Elza said, pointing to a large raised area. Ana noticed holes in the marble, through which fizzed warm water. She couldn't imagine how that happened and she wasn't given time to consider the ingenuity of the men who had designed the system. Dutifully she lay down, no longer bothered by her nakedness in front of Kett, his black skin gleaming from his exertions and a contrast to the bright red loincloth of the Elim that hooked around his waist and saved her the sight of his wound.

"Kett has strong fingers," Elza said. "He will make your body feel loose and pliant."

The water bubbling through the holes made the marble slippery and Kett was able to spin Ana into any position he needed. She laughed, delighted by the unexpected movement when he took her leg and pulled her around so he could work on her shoulders first.

"Behave," Elza warned.

"I was told the women use this time to entertain one another, Elza," Ana countered.

"This is different, Odalisque Ana. There is no one here but ourselves and this is no ordinary day of bathing," the servant reminded her, her expression stern.

Ana fell silent, knowing it wasn't worth the breath arguing the point with Elza. She watched the slave walk away as Kett dragged her into the middle of the marble. The water was hotter here; Ana sighed as the heat melted through her body and Kett's fingers busily worked down her back.

"What did you mean earlier?" she said softly.

"Pardon, Miss Ana?"

"You suggested that others need not decide my fate."

Kett didn't answer immediately, although she felt his telltale pause as he massaged her. He resumed, his fingers working harder. "I spoke out of turn, Miss Ana," he finally said.

"She's not here, Kett. Tell me what you meant." Ana could sense him checking for Elza's whereabouts. "Please."

He spun her around again to face away from him but this time knelt close to her head as he pretended to work on her neck and shoulders. He whispered, "I overheard Salmeo organizing for the bundle women to come up tonight. It's a treat for the girls."

"Another one? We are spoiled," Ana commented tartly.

"I think he said the Valide wanted to add something to their exciting day on the water—something she can share with them."

"Doesn't sound like the Valide."

He hissed softly to stop her saying anything more. "Be careful, Miss Ana."

"Why? A Zar wants my body. They can hardly hurt me."

"They can afterward," he counseled.

Ana knew he was right. "Go on," she urged.

"It's just that I know one of the women. She can be bribed."

Both fell silent as the implications of this hung between them.

Ana broke the tension, her breathing suddenly shallow. "How well do you know her?"

"Not well. I've gotten to know her through my work for the harem. Salmeo uses me for errands and I come across her from time to time. I know she is corrupt. I know she can be bought."

"What's her name?"

"Sheffa. She usually brings the cheap shawls."

"Can word be gotten to her?"

"Possibly, I'm not sure."

Ana could hear the pain in his voice and she spun herself around now on the fizzing water fountain. They both looked for Elza before she spoke. "You did the right thing in telling me, Kett," she assured him. "Can you get word to her? Please, I'm begging you. Tell her I will give her something of immense value tonight if she will carry me out."

Kett looked forlorn, terrified. "I wish I'd never mentioned—"

"But you did. And I haven't forgotten that day on the terraces when you first shared the tale of the odalisque who escaped in the bundle woman's wares, and I know you told me because you want me to escape."

"I can't bear the thought of you going to the Zar unwillingly," he said.

Ana sensed that he was skirting the truth of what he truly meant but she no longer cared. "Neither can I. But escape is my risk alone and I'm prepared to take it. How can we contact her?"

"I can probably do it myself. I'm frightened, though, Miss Ana. It was wrong of me to put this thought into your mind, but no one understands better how it feels to be trapped. I can't escape but perhaps you can." He was babbling, and she could tell that Kett was torn between her safety and his desire to free her from the Zar's claim.

"Please do it, Kett. But keep yourself safe. The danger must be mine alone."

Elza entered the bathing chamber and they both grew quiet. "I take over from here now, Miss Ana," she said.

"What's next?" Ana asked too brightly, covering their sudden hush in conversation.

Elza looked at her, raising an eyebrow. "You seem very alert."

"That's not a bad thing, is it? I found the waters refreshing," Ana replied, feeling the excitement and tension of her small escape plan shaping.

"No, but the waters are meant to relax, not make you too jumpy."

"I'm not jumpy, Elza."

"Well, don't try to convince me you're excited," the slave said, a hint of sarcasm icing her words.

Elza knew her too well. Ana attempted a rueful smile. "I just want to get it all over and done with, to be honest."

"That's fair enough, too, Miss Ana. I understand." Elza returned the smile before continuing briskly: "Next we have to remove your body hair."

Ana had heard that highborn females and those who married above themselves strove to keep their bodies free of all hair save what flowed from their heads. Her stepmother had scoffed at the notion, claiming it was an idle pastime for idle women. No one Ana had ever met had the time or inclination to follow this practice.

"Now don't look at me like that, Miss Ana. This is the way of the harem."

"How is it done?"

"With paste," the woman replied simply. "Come and lie here on these warmed towels."

Ana did as she was told, watching, somewhat fascinated, as Elza lifted the lid on one of her many pots before beginning to smear the pungent paste onto Ana's shins.

"Quicklime and orpiment—crystals of arsenic," she explained as she worked deftly with her ivory spatula. As she finished attending to the second leg with the paste, she reached for a small gray implement.

"What's that?" Ana said, sitting up.

"A mussel shell that's been sharpened. Watch," Elza replied as she used the fine edge of the shell like a razor to lift away the paste and with it the fine golden hair on Ana's legs. She repeated the process on Ana's arms, her underarms, and then removed the modesty sheet covering her middle. "Now for the important bit," she said, grinning, "so our young stallion can see you in all your glory." Lightly, she slapped Ana's thigh.

Ana groaned. "I don't—"

"Don't start," Elza warned. "I told you this is the important part. You'll need to raise your legs, girl, and open those knees."

Ana balled her fists with a mixture of anger and resentment as the slave woman forced her knees apart and she began to feel the acidic paste stinging between her legs. She refused to voice her rage by crying out, although the desire to do so was great.

"We cannot leave this on for too long or the arsenic will corrode your flesh," Elza said, not unkindly but too matter-of-fact to sound mindful of the younger woman's discomfort.

"It's burning me now."

"It will," Elza said coolly, before warning, "I must use it on all your orifices, Miss Ana—nose, ears—"

"Say no more," Ana warned, cutting off what Elza was going to list next and feeling sickened as the slave turned her over and pushed her legs apart once again.

"On your knees, girl, make it easier for me."

Ana gave in to her rising tide of emotion, felt her eyes water with the humiliation of this activity, and Kett, standing nearby, hung his head hung with his own sense of shame on her behalf. She thought of her father and his simple life, simple needs. She thought of her brother and sisters and how she would give anything to be living with them again, and she thought of the statue of Lyana whom Pez believed Ana now represented. And then she considered this pampered prisoner life she was now being committed to and her mind snapped itself into a stony decision.

Escape, be it out of Percheron or by death, was her only option. She would take her chance tonight, no matter what happened.

When Elza was satisfied, after an embarrassingly long and close scrutiny, that Ana was free of all superfluous hair, she pulled a small rough burlap bag on over each hand.

"Now what?" Ana asked testily.

"I must polish your body. Turn over and be quiet, child."

Elza began to rub every inch of her charge with the rough bags whilst Kett scrubbed the soles of Ana's feet with rasps. Ana no longer found any of it diverting. The humiliation she still felt fired her imagination further, and she reveled in the notion that she could cheat Salmeo and Herezah. She didn't enjoy the idea of snubbing Boaz, who had in all truth been nothing but a friend to her, but even that relationship had this dark side to it, where she was expected to give her body for his use.

In her frustration she remembered hearing Lazar's voice coming through Pez, and it made her feel hot where she shouldn't and this angered her even more. How could they have lied to her, allowed her to grieve and feel guilty as she had done the past year?

She flicked her hair angrily. "Are we finished?"

Elza had finished, apparently, because she turned to Kett, ignoring Ana. "Bathe her again before she is oiled."

Ana grimaced but said nothing, obeying the woman who was in charge of her preparation. After another dip in the heated waters, Kett smoothed warmed perfumed oil from her neck to the tips of her toes, rubbing it in gently. It was a marvelous sensation, and beneath the strong-fingered ministrations of Kett, Ana genuinely did feel every inch of herself relax, for perhaps the first time since entering the palace.

Warmed pouches of wheat were placed on her eyelids whilst

Kett finished smoothing the oil into the front of her body and Ana felt herself drifting into a light doze.

"Almost ready?" a familiar voice lisped. Ana felt her momentarty sense of peacefulness evaporate as her stomach clenched.

"Just her hair to be dried, brushed, and dressed," Elza said softly.

"Kett, you've done well," said the voice. "She looks calm— just how we need her."

Kett did not respond and Ana felt frozen to the marble-surfaced table on which she lay, naked and vulnerable.

"Ana," Salmeo said firmly. "You are almost ready in your preparations." He removed the wheat bags and she managed to muster a small amount of defiance to load into her stare. "Just hair and clothes to go," he continued, hardly noticing her glower but looking up and down her body, making soft noises of appreciation.

"I don't need your help to get dressed, Grand Master Salmeo," she replied, aware that her words were impertinent but carefully tempering her voice.

He stroked her belly, and his gap-toothed smile was prompted by her flinch. "No, but I am required to perform one final act upon you before I hand you over to our Zar for his pleasure."

She sat up, fearful, and Elza made a hushing sound. "Now, Miss Ana, this is the usual practice, the way of the harem."

"Don't touch me," she warned Salmeo.

He sighed theatrically. "Pity. I thought we could make this easy on you, Ana." He clapped and four grave-looking Elim entered. "Do I need to ask these men to assist?" He held his sharp-pointed fingernail in the air, freshly painted red for the occasion. "Make a decision, Ana. It can be a crowd or it can be intimate—just the two of us . . . again."

She knew she had lost her small fight and nodded, fighting back the tears at her hopeless rebellion.

A signal from Salmeo dismissed the Elim. Ana stole a desperate glance at a frightened-looking Kett and nodded, begging him to understand the intent of her message. Slowly he nodded back.

"Go about your other business, Kett. I've left a list of errands—they require you to go to the bazaar." Kett bowed and hurried away.

Ana could hardly dare to believe that he had been ordered to go precisely where she wanted him to visit. "Can Elza stay?" she begged Salmeo.

"Leave us, woman," Salmeo said cruelly in answer. "She cannot save you this, Ana. Now, where is the emollient?" He directed his question at the male slave who dutifully held out a pot of the paste. Ana recognized him from her first night in the palace, the night she had taken her Test of Virtue. Elza, no longer permitted to stay, patted Ana on the leg and left her to Salmeo. The male slave followed.

Ana and Salmeo were alone. She closed her eyes to shut him out.

"As I told you once before, Ana, you can make this easy, or if you fight me, you can make it hurt."

"Just do it!" she growled, tears flowing freely now, even through her tightly clenched eyelids.

She missed his lascivious smile as he first caressed her between the legs then plunged his fingers into her body once again, taking his time, massaging her so she would open more willingly. He moved his fingers into and out of her, lingering, knowing just where to touch to win an uncontrolled gasp from her.

"Feels nice, doesn't it?" he said. "Don't clench against my fingers, Ana. Relax yourself. It's good practice for Zar Boaz."

She refused to say anything, hating herself for responding physically. Although his touch made bile rise to her throat, it seemed the effect it had on her traitorous body was the opposite. She fought her instinct to move with the soft throb his pudgy fingers had won from her.

"Now, Ana," he said, his voice thick with his own lust, "I can see you'll be very responsive to our Zar. Right here," he said, teasing and rubbing harder, "is where he needs to touch you to make you slippery and ready for him. If he doesn't do it, do it to yourself, girl, or what he does do will hurt you badly. He will have little idea of this, I'm guessing; he'll be all clumsy thrusts and eagerness, I'm sure, not precise and soft . . . and knowledgeable like Salmeo," he lisped in a lover's voice. He tantalizied her further with his oiled fingers until she groaned, confused by her conflicting emotions. She tried to push his hand away but he slapped her hard.

"Don't, Ana. This is my time with you and I'm giving you a very good lesson. Without my advice it will go badly for you tonight. Remember what I've said, what I've shown you today." Ana felt her whole body trembling, privately begging him to finish what he'd begun, but still she resisted the call of his insistent fingers.

Suddenly he stopped and she all but shrieked, not sure whether it was from disappointment or relief.

"No finishing for you, Ana. We want you swollen and eager like this. You must remember this feeling. This is the point you must reach tonight before he enters you and then you will be ready and you will satisfy him because your own urges will be in concert with his. Oh, and do not try to take your own pleasures either, my girl." He ignored her soft panting. "The Valide will give you strict counsel before you are led into the Zar's chambers but heed my own warning: You are there purely to satisfy Zar Boaz, not the other way around. You will do everything he requests, perform any act he requires. Do you understand?"

She nodded bleakly, hating the unsated feeling that her body was experiencing as it slid from the delicate ecstasy the eunuch had so cunningly achieved. Salmeo's little finger slipped back into her and she gasped again.

"Relax, Ana," he said, and she saw his smile this time as his tongue flicked out to moisten his lips. "Now to the true purpose of my visit."

And Salmeo put his stained red nail to its ugly purpose as Ana arched her back and cried out her pain and her resentment.

She bled, proving once again that Lazar had delivered the perfect prize to the harem.

12

Pez's plans to see Zafira had unraveled. He had not been able to find her in the morning as he'd intended and now it was getting late in the day after his run-in with Lazar. He had tried to find Ana but had learned through one of the Elim that she was being prepared for the Zar. He made use of the quiet to wield the Lore to help mend the crack that Lazar's fist had inflicted on his jaw, but it didn't do much to lessen the pain. That would be with him until it fully healed.

He decided that flying to the temple was just too risky—he had been flying too much lately, and a snowy-white owl, if spotted, would be considered a prize acquisition for a wily hunter. Instead he slipped away from the palace in the late afternoon and took a stroll down to the temple. As always when passing through the grand bazaar, Pez got lost in his own thoughts. He loved this bustling, thriving city within the city, but because there were so many people around him, and Pez had allowed his concentration to lapse, he did not notice the figure that followed him down the hill from the palace, blending into the moving mass of humanity.

Pez was instantly recognizable to most in the bazaar, but unless he was actually performing for them, they tended to leave him to himself. Frankly, many were scared of the contrary dwarf. Pez did nothing to alleviate this vague sense of disquiet in passersby, keeping up a mindless stream of gibberish interspersed with humming. It took little effort on his part and allowed him to drift in his thoughts until he arrived at the temple, where he did find Zafira, laying out some sea daisies before the statue of Lyana.

He cartwheeled around the temple, inwardly begging the Goddess to forgive him his silly antics in her place of quiet worship, knowing in his heart she would likely find it amusing.

"Ah, Pez, I wondered when I'd see you."

"I want some fruit," he called aggressively, rubbing his jaw gingerly from the pain of talking. He grabbed her arm, listing all the names of the fruits he loved, and dragged her into the far corner, checking surreptitiously that there were no other people in the temple.

"I came earlier," he whispered.

As usual, Zafira seemed to take his erratic behavior—even when they were alone—in her stride. "I had things to do."

"Well, I have more important things for you to do. I told you, I need some fruit!" Pez couldn't hide his worry from her.

"Oh?"

"Take me to your kitchen, flitchen, gitchen, ditchen."

Zafira beckoned. "Come, Pez, I have some fruit upstairs," she said, openly playing along. Then whispered: "Let us take a final cup of quishtar together."

"My face hurts," he mumbled.

But she had turned away. He followed her now in silence, dragging his knuckles on the ground as he had seen the monkeys in the zoo move, slowly ascending the stairs.

Once upstairs, he moved to the window, staring out wistfully.

"We are alone," she confirmed. Pez knew she sensed his anxiety, was trying to assure him that he could drop his act.

He didn't turn from the window but spoke softly. "You must leave Percheron today . . . now."

She smiled gently. "Leave?"

"It's time," he said, more kindly. He glanced around, ensuring that no one else could possibly eavesdrop, and as an extra measure reached out with the Lore. He felt nothing. "I know who Maliz is."

Zafira took her time answering. Fear was etched clearly on her face. "Already?"

He nodded, shouted out the names of more fruit in a demanding voice this time before dropping almost to a whisper again. "It can be no one else. He sensed my presence at the palace and knows Lyana will be close, but then you already know who she is." He didn't mean for it to sound quite like the accusation it did. "I want pomegranates!" he yelled, and then fell quiet, staring out from her window at Beloch as Zafira maintained her own dread silence whilst she brewed quishtar.

He tested his surroundings once again with the Lore and finally permitted himself to feel safe. "Is it my imagination or does Beloch have cracks in his stone that were not there before?"

Zafira joined him at the small window, handing him a steaming bowl of quishtar. "I've never seen that before and I look at Beloch every day. How odd."

"His brother's too far away for me to note if he's cracking, too," Pez said, wincing as he took a sip of the hot liquid that sent a fresh scream of pain through his jaw.

"They are crumbling like us," she said sadly.

"We've never been stronger, Zafira. We have to believe that."

"Who is it?" she asked, an edge in her voice.

"Can you not guess?" Pez didn't mean to be mischievous. He wanted to see if the clues had been strong enough for Zafira to work out.

She frowned and sipped her brew. "I obviously know him for you to suggest I guess."

He nodded gravely and she held his stare.

She puzzled at it for a few moments before saying: "The Vizier?"

Pez closed his eyes momentarily in silent despair. Maliz had been under their noses for perhaps a year and they hadn't noticed. Yet the clues had been there—Zafira's guess confirmed it.

"Am I right?" She sounded incredulous.

He nodded somberly. "I believe Maliz has taken over Tariq, yes."

She turned away from the window, distracted but not disbelieving him. "How can it be? How did we miss it?" she hissed.

Pez had had longer to get used to the notion, longer to temper his frustration. He needed to reassure her. "It is the way he works, Zafira. We are not meant to know. That's his disguise, but it works in our favor, too. He doesn't know who we are either."

"But the changes—they're so obvious," she countered, angry as she put her bowl down. "We should have been more focused. We should have been looking for him."

"And we would not have arrived at this conclusion any earlier, I'm sure of it."

"What makes you sure of his identity?"

"Something Lazar said triggered the thought and then it was so obvious I've hated myself since," he said, touching his jaw.

"Ana!" Zafia exclaimed, clutching a hand to her chest. Just as suddenly, she glanced at Pez, awareness of what she'd accidentally let slip in her eyes.

Pez nodded. "You could have told me what you suspected and not left me to work it out for myself," he admonished softly.

"Ellyana insisted we say nothing to anyone about Ana."

Pez frowned. So Ellyana had deliberately kept them in the dark, blundering around, not trusting anyone but themselves. He forced himself to move on. "Well, Lazar and I agree that Ana is safer at the palace than anywhere else. She has certain protections that the harem gives her. Maliz has little access to her physically."

Zafira sneered. "Protection of sorts. If Maliz suspects who Ana is, he would already be making moves to destroy her."

"Well, he obviously doesn't suspect yet, but we have to be very careful. That's why I think you should leave the temple, leave Percheron."

"What prompted this? Your discovering his identity?"

"Everything! Tariq, Lazar deciding to return to the city, which will reveal you as a liar. And, I discovered that Ana's been formally chosen by Boaz. She will be presented tonight. There's so much to discuss but no time."

The priestess did not seem perturbed by any of this news. "Does Ana know about her role in all of this?"

"Yes. I spoke to her. She accepts it."

"She has known all along. She just had to find the truth deep within. She was drawn to Lyana's statue, the temple; she knew."

Pez sighed, frustrated. "I wish I knew what happens next. I hate all this waiting."

"None of us ever knows, Pez. That's how it always is. We fight when required."

"Fight? How?" He aired his thoughts aloud only through frustration. Pez knew Zafira had no answers.

She shook her head helplessly. "I really don't know. That's why I won't leave."

"You have to leave," he insisted. "You are in danger here."

"More danger than you or Ana?" Pez remained silent and she continued. "Don't be naive, Pez. I felt the danger before you did. You may recall our conversation here thirteen moons ago or so when I mentioned that I felt I was part of something but didn't know what. I was frightened, you may also remember."

"I do."

"Well, I'm still frightened, but now I know what I'm part of and I won't run from it. Lazar's return is the least of my worries. This is my calling. This is why I'm here. I just wish I wasn't so old and useless to her cause, but still Lyana has chosen me as she has chosen you and Ana."

"For what?"

"I don't know. Perhaps I've already played my part. Perhaps in having conversations with you and Lazar on the evening of the choosing, and then Ana that same night, my role is already done. The temple is where we have all met. It might be that I bind us through the temple, which is the focus of Lyana in Percheron—all that is left of her."

"Not all," Pez countered. "The stone creatures echo her rule."

"What use are they to her now?" she asked, hopelessness in her voice.

"Who knows? When we were moving Lazar from the temple on the day of his flogging to Star Island for secrecy, Ellyana made us row her up to Beloch so she could touch him—perhaps we should read something into that gesture?"

"Bah, that was out of respect."

"No, Zafira. I paid attention. She spoke to him. It was a chant or a prayer or maybe just words of encouragement. I couldn't hear what she said but I understood its intent. She was communicating with the giant."

The priestess appeared skeptical. "What's your point?"

Pez shook his head ruefully. "I have no point. I feel like I'm plowing through a swamp in my thoughts. I have only seemingly meaningless observations to offer."

"You think the stone creatures of Percheron are somehow involved in our struggle?" Zafira persisted incredulously.

He knew it sounded ridiculous. "As you say, none of us knows much at all. We fight when required."

The thought of the giant being somehow alive lingered between them, though, and they both glanced again at the impressive crack down his near side.

"You don't think he's crumbling, do you?" she said flatly. "You have a different idea of what's occurring here." It sounded like an accusation.

Pez looked at her and his dark eyes gleamed. He shrugged. "He could be emerging."

Zafira laughed, startled. "Well, for all the fear you've brought with you today, Pez, I'm pleased you haven't lost your whimsical style. A giant emerging from stone?"

"He was entrapped in stone. He was real once."

"We're talking centuries and centuries ago. You think he lives?"

Pez grinned and there was mischief in it. "I don't know, I'm simply airing random thoughts."

"There's nothing random about you, Pez. We should heed your words." She looked again at Beloch. "Why now?"

Pez became serious again. "Ana said something intriguing. She mentioned that this time, this battle, it would be different. I don't know what she means by that—I don't even know if *she* does, but she seemed determined that the struggle would be different."

"And you think the difference could be Beloch and Ezram?"

"Zafira, my mind is wandering everywhere," he admitted wearily. "Yesterday I was convinced it was something else, today I'm thinking it's the stone creatures."

"The stone creatures? All of them? Crendel, Darso?"

He nodded. "If the giants, why not the others?"

The priestess shook her head, disbelieving. "Who did you imagine it was yesterday?"

Pez hesitated. "I don't know if I should share my thoughts, Zafira. You don't share what you know."

He could see that the accusation hit home by the hurt expression that darkened her face. "No more secrets between us, Pez, I promise."

He regarded her for a long time, decided she meant it. "I thought it was Lazar."

"Why?"

"Because I know he's not random either. He is involved for a reason. Ellyana's loyalty to him suggests that. She wanted him to live but she wanted no one to know the fact. She has been waiting for something . . . something to occur or some secret signal to be given." He shook his head. "I hate all this guessing."

"Well, if it's any consolation, although I can't confirm if he's the difference, I do know Lazar is involved."

Pez swung around and faced her expectantly, annoyed by her continuing secrets.

She spread her hands, palms up. "Ellyana admits she doesn't know what his part in this cycle is, but she did tell me that he is involved and will play a critical role. She said, as we were fighting for his life, that Lazar was a new player in the game of gods. That this time it was to be different."

"That's how Ana feels but she didn't pinpoint Lazar. How could she? She thinks he's dead!"

"I promise that's as much as I know," Zafira soothed. "I can't tell you if he makes the difference. Ellyana *was* determined to save his life. Although I think there were moments there when she, too, felt we had lost him."

"Why the secrecy, though? Why so much pain for those who care for Lazar?"

"Secrets can protect. I have to presume that she is deliberately keeping Ana and Lazar apart, deliberately keeping him away from the palace. Jumo's pain cannot be helped. And now that you've discovered the Vizier for who he truly is, I can only say she was right in doing so. If all of Lyana's warriors were instantly recognizable and in one spot, it would give Ana away immediately."

"Well, it won't last, Zafira. As I said, Lazar's returning to the city."

"Why? What does he hope to accomplish?"

"Anything's better than wasting away on Star Island. How long did you think you could keep that man trapped there?"

She pursed her lips. "Not much longer. That's why I wasn't here when you came earlier."

Pez nodded, slowly understanding. "Ellyana?"

"She needs to know his condition. Perhaps she suspected he was ready to make his move."

"And you went to meet her."

"No," she said, sitting down heavily. "I go to a particular spot and tie a message to a homing pigeon. I don't know where it goes, but this morning's message was that I didn't think Lazar could be contained for much longer."

Pez grimaced at the secrecy, at Ellyana's manipulative ways. "He'll be back in Percheron tonight."

"What is he going to do?"

"Present himself to Boaz, as far as I know. Lazar has nothing to hide. But blame will be accorded to you, when they realize you lied. That's why I want you to go."

She began to shake her head but Pez persisted. "You are more use to Lyana alive, Zafira. The Zar will not spare you once he knows you lied to him—and that's how Lazar will have to tell it. And let's be truthful here, he had no hand in the decisions and terrible manipulations anyway."

Zafira hesitated, biting her lip.

Pez pressed harder. "You can't help us if you're dead."

She nodded, agreeing. "Where shall I go?"

"Anywhere but here. Go to Z'alotny—to the burial ground of the priestesses."

She looked at him ruefully. "Appropriate—at least when the Zar finds and executes me I'll be in the right spot."

He ignored her comment. "It's safe, private, no one goes there. Give me two days and then I shall either come to you or

get word to you and we'll work out what to do from there. But
you have to leave here now."

She nodded. "I shall go."

"Make haste, Zafira. I don't trust anyone at the palace."

"I shall be gone within the hour."

He reached around her tiny figure and hugged her. "Go
sooner if you can."

MALIZ TWIRLED THE STEM of a goblet of pale wine between
Tariq's thumb and forefinger as he considered what he'd just
heard. "You're quite sure."

The man nodded.

"And he didn't stay very long, you say."

Now the man shook his head.

"Did he bow in the temple to Lyana?"

"No, Grand Vizier. I watched carefully. He did no such
thing. He arrived doing acrobatics, and continued through the
temple. There was no respect for the place he was in. He spoke
briefly to the priestess—well, screamed to tell the truth—about
wanting some fruit and she seemed familiar with him—she
acted kindly toward him. He dragged her to the back of the
temple and I could hear him still yelling about fruit and listing all of their names. Finally, she took him upstairs to give
him some. I could hear him demanding a pomegranate. That's
when I left, for fear of being seen. I waited and he came out
not long afterward clutching an orange. He kept smelling the
orange—"

"Yes, yes, I understand. He didn't touch the sculpture of
Lyana?" the Grand Vizier persisted, determined to connect Pez
with the Goddess.

"He paid her no heed whatsoever," the man confirmed, bowing. "He was as annoying and silly as he usually is."

"Keep shadowing the dwarf whenever he leaves the palace. I will pay you well." He tossed a small pouch at the man's feet. It landed with a solid thump.

"Thank you, Grand Vizier."

"I pay for your secrecy, too, Elaz. Don't speak out of turn to anyone or I shall close your lips forever."

The man nodded. Maliz waved him away and considered what he had discovered. There was no proof. The dwarf behaved true to form. Perhaps the priestess simply took pity on the idiot, someone the dwarf, in his delusions, considered a friend. But why go to the temple? The coincidence of the temple being the sacred place of Lyana was irresistible to Maliz. He would have to learn more.

He would begin with the priestess.

13

Ana had never looked more stunning. Even she was surprised by the solemn yet dazzling person staring back at her from the glass.

"He will adore you," Elza whispered, praying to Zarab that the girl would put behind her the episode with the Grand Master Eunuch that had left her trembling, bleeding, and puffy-eyed from weeping. When she had tried to comfort the young woman, Ana had exclaimed that she was crying not from grief, but from anger.

"I don't care," Ana replied stiffly, her rouged lips making her scowl seem alluring rather than how she intended it to be.

"Miss Ana, please. Let this go well for you. To be First Chosen is one of the highest prizes. Look how the harem honors you with its finest jewels. I hear the Valide herself chose and bought them for you. The Grand Master Eunuch put them around your neck himself to honor you."

Ana's voice was waspish when it came. "For your sake alone, Elza, I am not ripping these jewels from my neck and wrists and ankles."

The slave gasped. "They are worth more than ten of me, child."

"And I hate them. I don't want them."

"What do you want, Miss Ana?"

"Freedom. Leave me, Elza."

"I cannot. I have promised to escort you into the divan suite. Grand Master Salmeo says the other girls must see you in all your finery before you are taken to the Zar's chambers."

"So he can make the other girls jealous, so they will hate me?"

Elza shrugged, embarrassed. "I must do as I'm told, Miss Ana."

"Let us go now, then, for I cannot stand the sight of myself a moment longer. I am like the jewels—pretty but dead."

Elza shook her head, worried, but gestured for Ana to follow her.

THE GRAND VIZIER ARRIVED at the Sea Temple as the sun was dipping low behind the statue of Ezram. The giant looked to be framed by a halo of fire as the sky had blistered to a burning orange as if in final salutation to the day. Its farewell cast a bright glow onto the waters, making the bay appear like a cauldron of molten gold, but the Vizier did not appreciate Percheron's theater of natural beauty. Maliz was entirely distracted, grimacing at being so close to the worshipping place of Lyana. His revulsion only intensified when he stepped into the temple's cool shadows and saw the sculpture of the woman he reviled.

Lyana looked back at him, her expression as hard and unyielding as the stone from which she was formed. Maliz felt his bile rise at being in her presence. As he approached Lyana he could no longer control his repulsion and he spat at her. His spittle slid down her chin to land on her left breast, and whether it was a trick of the eye or simply the way the slit of dying golden sunlight made a last effort to light her, the liquid seemed to stain the pale stone.

Maliz sneered. "I will destroy you again and again, Lyana," he said softly, cruelly. "The faithful will never worship a woman."

He was disturbed by the arrival of a tiny person, an old priestess who had descended the stairs with a small sack. At first she covered her surprise at his presence with a quick smile—the sort she kept for someone come to pay quiet homage, he guessed, but Maliz noticed how the smile died fast on her wrinkled face. She tried to disguise her alarm but he saw it clearly.

"Grand Vizier Tariq?" she asked, overbrightly, he thought. "What a surprise. How can I help you?"

"Perhaps you can," he replied smoothly. "I am looking for Pez."

She frowned. "The Zar's buffoon?"

"That's the only Pez I know of in Percheron," Maliz said drily.

The priestess shook her head. "Pez is not here, Grand Vizier. I'm sorry your journey has been wasted."

"He has been, though, hasn't he, Priestess?"

To her credit, Zafira didn't so much as blink at his trap. "Earlier today, yes. Silly fellow was looking for fruit, of all things. He can be quite contrary—as I'm sure you must know—but I feel sorry for him." He noticed how she wrung the corners of the sack ends in her hands. Another clue. The priestess was nervous.

"I'm sorry, you know me but I don't have your name?"

"I am Zafira." She put the sack down and pushed her hands into the pockets of her aquamarine robes to appear relaxed. He thought it was more likely an attempt to steady them.

He pressed on, keeping his voice friendly. "So Pez visits regularly, Zafira?"

"I wouldn't say regularly," she replied, smiling tensely. "He finds kindness here, Grand Vizier. He calls whenever his odd mood swings bring him; I never have any warning before he arrives. If I can help him to calm, I usually do. Sometimes all the troubled soul needs is some time."

"Does he communicate with you?"

She gave an expression of disdain. "As well as he communicates with anyone. He speaks gibberish most of the time." Now she looked quizzical. "I'm sure I'm not telling you anything you don't already know, Grand Vizier, as you are around him in the palace and see him much more than I."

"I have very little to do with him."

"I find myself in the same position. Pez is welcome here, as anyone is welcome. No one is turned away. But his trips are rare, and although he did stop by today in a fractious mood that was soothed with an orange, he's not here at present. Now, if you've finished with your questions, I'm actually in a hurry." She bent to pick up the sack again.

"Are you going somewhere, Zafira?" As Maliz stepped forward, the priestess shrank back. It was his best clue yet. She had no reason to be fearful of him and yet it was obvious she was entirely disturbed by his presence. "Do not be scared of me."

"I'm not," she said too quickly.

"Your voice shakes. Is something wrong?" He took another step toward her.

She retreated again and now he was sure. "No. You just surprised me and I have to be somewhere."

"Where?"

The priestess made a poor attempt at indigntion. "Somewhere private, sir."

"Away from here."

"Yes."

"Why the hurry?"

"I'm late."

"Can I escort you there?"

"No, Grand Vizier. I'm capable of finding my own way. Frankly, I'm surprised that you can be bothered with one of Lyana's servants."

Her words gave Maliz the opening he needed.

"What makes you think I would make such a distinction?" He could see the fear taking hold of her now, see it in her startled eyes. There was only one reason his question would have caused such fear. She must know that inside Tariq's body walked a demon.

He laughed aloud, deep and menacing. He had found one of Lyana's disciples. It was a start.

The battle had begun.

ANA ENTERED THE DIVAN suite to the sounds of rapturous welcome as the other odalisques rushed to touch her gown, her precious jewels, her polished skin that was dusted with a powder that made it glow, and her shining golden hair. She was dressed in a shimmering pale blue outfit that was little more than gauze, just as Herezah had envisaged. It was edged with silver and dusted with diamond glitter, so that her every movement, however slight, made her entire body sparkle. Her hair was worked up in a delicately wrought silver clasp, studded with diamonds, and after Salmeo had finished with her, he had ordered further piercings for her ears. These were now hung with diamond drops and sapphires. Her nose had also been pierced twice and the curiously slight injuries—for all that pain—were now covered by diamond studs. Ana took grim amusement in the thought that had this been the middle of the day and not early evening, no one would have been able to look at her for fear of being blinded by her dazzling presence.

Ana knew that the girls would need a few moments to express their wonder, but the sounds of appreciation continued to escalate rather than lessen and so she begged them to stop. She did not enjoy this celebrity and her mind was again filled with the notion of escape. Ana knew the risk was huge; knew it was going against the promises she had made to Lazar, to Pez, even to the Valide. To fail in her bid this time would mean death, but the prize for success would be freedom, and after her meeting with Salmeo earlier, death did not frighten her. If she made it out she had already decided that she wouldn't go home. There would be no point. The palace would hunt her down and Salmeo would likely have her family killed out of spite. No, she had no home anymore. Instead, she would head west—perhaps to Merlinea where she had been told Lazar came from. The west still respected Lyana and perhaps she could find a convent or temple to take her in for a while. If they would have her, she might live the life of a priestess.

She came out of her musings as a youngster called Prem grabbed her arm, gushing, "The bundle women are coming soon as a special treat for us."

"I know, I'm looking forward to it, too," Ana said, trying not to show just how earnestly she meant it. "Did you all have a wonderful day on the water?"

That set off a chorus of conversation that Ana was pleased to lose herself in whilst she nervously awaited the arrival of the bundle women. One of the Elim, a man called Olam, whom she liked, sidled up to her.

"Miss Ana."

"Yes?"

"We are to escort you to the Zar's chambers at nightfall."

"I will see the bundle women with the rest of the girls, won't I?" she asked, feigning anxiety about her harem companions. "It's just, I missed out on the river barging with them." Ana's only thought now was for the arrival of the bundle women and not missing them.

He nodded reassuringly. "Yes, Miss Ana. I will collect you as soon as the bundle women have departed. You will miss your evening meal, but the Grand Master Eunuch felt it was best you go to the Zar empty rather than full."

Ana smiled wanly and nodded, covering her lap with her folded hands—the only modesty she could provide for herself. Olam's eyes, however, did not waver from her own.

"Can I organize something light for you before the bundle women come, Miss Ana?"

"I'm not hungry, Olam."

"I understand," he said, backing away after a short bow.

"Not hungry? I'm starving," Prem groaned.

Sascha, sitting nearby, laughed. "You've been eating all day, Prem. You'd better watch yourself or you'll get fat and the Zar will never want to lie with you like he does with Ana. Then you'll never have a chance at being a wife, or giving him an heir."

Prem looked mortified by the threat, and Ana felt equally embarrassed, but for other reasons. The girls were taking this all so lightly. Was she the only one who feared the Zar's touch? No, she knew that wasn't true. They would all be as frightened as she their first time with a man, but her feelings went deeper; Ana did not want to be bedded by Boaz, whereas they all apparently did. She had listened to them talk about his handsome looks and wonder at what it would be like to be alone with him. They had all accepted their roles as odalisques and were planning ahead to their own special first nights with the Zar. As Sascha's comment attested, some of the older ones were already thinking about children—about trying to give him an heir quickly.

But she was revolted by the thought. And it was not because she was too young, too frigid, or too uninterested in sexual liaison. None of that was relevant. There was only one obstacle, and its name was Lazar. Lazar was the only man she wanted to touch her—the only man she wanted to touch tenderly in return. Although, she thought wryly, if it were true that Lazar was alive, any chance she had to touch him might be squandered in the form of a punch. She had put the simmering thought of his lies about his death to the back of her mind for the past few hours but now it had erupted to wound her again. And Pez was in on the lie, and that meant Zafira was, too . . . and Jumo? Had Jumo rushed off to Merlinea to find Lazar's kin, as Boaz had explained, or was that all part of the elaborate ruse? She blinked back a tear of self-pity and forced a bright smile onto her face.

"Well, at least you'll have the benefit of my experience with the Zar," she said amiably to the small crowd that had gathered around the conversation. "I can tell you what he likes."

Over the sound of laughter, Prem's voice suddenly rang

out. "The Elim are arriving! The bundle women must be here."

Squeals of childish joy exploded from the younger girls, while the older odalisques, more demure, stood, gathering close to Ana, to await at a polite distance. All the girls had veiled themselves without having to be asked. Though it was not strictly necessary, the Valide had insisted they get into the habit so that it became instinctive.

Right enough, behind the first four Elim came a motley assortment of brightly dressed women, all veiled—as was traditionally expected within the palace confines—and carrying the enormous bundles they were famous for.

"The Grand Master Eunuch said we can have whatever we want. The palace will settle the bill," Sascha whispered.

"Very generous," Ana replied tartly, inwardly sighing at how easily Salmeo manipulated the harem. But her only concern now was finding the right woman. She bit her lip in consternation at the worrying thought that she and Kett had not even planned how the woman would recognize her. Ana had to presume that Kett would have given a detailed enough description that the woman would be able to pick her out, and for the first time that evening she was grateful for the sheerness of the garments she was draped in. Her face, along with the rest of her body, was clearly visible.

She watched the girls peeling off from the main group to look at the various trinkets, fabrics, scarves, even some wooden toys for the youngest in the harem. The Elim had departed but would wait just outside the divan suite, leaving the various eunuch servants to watch from a discreet distance.

Ana saw a woman dressed in darker robes approach, her face fully veiled save for a tiny slit for her eyes. She held her breath. This was it. She had no idea how they were going to do this or even if it could be pulled off, but she cast a prayer to Lyana to guide her in this daring move. She nodded carefully at the woman.

The woman nodded back and surreptitiously pointed to an area in the suite that had a number of marble pillars. Ana understood. She beckoned to the woman to lay out her wares in and around the pillars. "I believe it's less crowded over here," she said aloud for good measure.

The stranger hefted the huge bundle from her back to the floor and Ana noticed her black hands, her fingers shaking as she untied the knot that held all the goods within. Finally they spilled out.

"Ribbons," Ana commented nervously, for want of anything better to say.

The woman looked up, regarded her from behind the veil. "No one else but you wants them," said a voice she recognized.

Taken aback, Ana stared into the dark eyes she could just see behind the veil. "Kett?"

The figure nodded. "I'll explain later. Now just do as I tell you."

Ana was too flustered to think straight, but hope surged. She had been worrying that the woman would not be able to carry her, but Kett was easily strong enough.

She watched him spread out his dozens of ribbons, stealing a glance around the room. Everyone was occupied; even the servants were distracted. She wondered why the Elim had so curiously left the room but could only thank Lyana that they had. "Kett," she whispered, "no one is paying me any attention."

"Yes, we are fortunate. But there's going to be a distraction as we draw close to the end of the session. I suggest you go and look at the other wares—make yourself noticed."

Ana did so, strolling around behind the other girls, who were fingering the trinkets. She took her time, finally arriving behind Sascha, who was intrigued by a tiny red bean that one of the sellers was showing her. Ana moved closer to look. The bean was no larger than her own small fingernail and a tiny part of its top had been cut away and replaced by a beautifully shaped lid of ivory that fit snugly into the gap. She couldn't imagine anyone carving anything so small. The woman now expertly removed the lid and tipped the contents from the bean into Sascha's palm.

Both girls gasped with pleasure to see at least a dozen or more fragile, exquisitely carved elephants. They were so tiny that Ana had to squint to make them out.

Sascha was kneeling and now turned to look at Ana. "Aren't they breathtaking?"

"How does one work on anything that small? They must carve looking through a magnifying glass."

The woman nodded and Ana could see her grinning toothlessly through her soft veil.

"Very good price for you," she encouraged, holding one of the beans out to Ana.

"Take one," Sascha urged. "We both will."

"Yes, why don't you have one of those lovely items," Salmeo suddenly said from behind her, the waft of violets sickening as it enveloped her.

Ana froze. How could she not have heard him arriving behind her? Why was he here? Surely it was not yet time! She forced herself not to look toward Kett for fear of giving him away. Instead she took a steadying breath and turned to face her nemesis.

"I have nowhere to put it, Grand Master Salmeo, as you

can see," she said, defying him to stare at her painted nipples, clearly visible through her gauzy gown.

But Salmeo accepted her challenge and proudly swept his gaze appreciatively across her body. "My dear, fret not, I shall have it sent to your chamber immediately. Does anything else take your fancy?" His lisp was worst when he was in his flirtatious mood.

"I have not finished looking yet, Grand Master Eunuch."

"Carry on, then," he replied sweetly, his tongue flicking out between the gap in his teeth as he smiled fondly at her. "Take all you want, Ana. Tonight is yours, but be ready, for Olam will come for you shortly." He made to leave and then turned back for a parting shot. "I hope you're not too sore from our intimate time together this afternoon," and gave her no chance to respond.

Seething, she watched the huge man lightly glide away. A nagging thought flickered in the back of her mind, but she was distracted by a beckoning sign from Kett. The best way to hurt Salmeo was to beat him at his own game of cunning.

She held up her bean at the bundle woman. "May I?"

The woman nodded enthusiastically and immediately Sascha and several other girls began clamoring for some of the bright red beans. Ana took her chance and the added precaution of tapping Sascha on the shoulder and saying over the cacophony, "Excuse me a moment, I must relieve myself."

"Hurry," Sascha replied. "There isn't much longer before they leave, you'll miss everything," and turned back to the trinkets, saying, "Oh, look at this!" as she found another interesting item.

Ana returned to Kett. "I'm not sure we can risk you in this," she warned. Her voice shook. "Not now that Salmeo—"

"Forget about me, Miss Ana." He cut across her words. "I am here now and no one suspects. If you wish to go, let us do it. If you have second thoughts, or are scared, I can leave with the other women and no one will be any the wiser."

"I'm not scared for me," she admonished in a whisper. "I'm worried for you."

"Don't be. This is my path. The path of sorrows."

Caught off guard by his comment, Ana opened her mouth to question it just as a squeal went up behind them. Ana swung around to see that a bundle woman had brought in a basketload of kittens. A veritable army of tiny cats was scattering in all directions and the girls as well as bundle women and servants were giving chase.

"Now!" Kett demanded, pushing her toward the huge square of cloth. "Curl up tight!"

Ana had no time to reconsider. She leaped into the middle of Kett's bundle and within moments found herself encased in the gloom of his musty-smelling wares. She was careful to ensure that no elbow or toes pointed anywhere and held herself as small and as round as she could. She knew she was very supple; it was a game she'd played with her father—she never thought of him as a stepfather, even though he had found her as an orphan—he'd roll her around their hut just like a ball. She used that talent now to make herself invisible in the bundle.

She could hear the commotion around her as the cats were noisily rounded up. Above her she could sense Kett fiddling with the bundle and securing the knot that would keep her from falling out. She guessed his activity also made him look less conspicuous.

A gong sounded and signaled the end of the bundle women's visit. Soft sighs of disappointment greeted the gong and then she could hear men's voices as the Elim began to hurry the bundle women out of the divan suite.

"Where is Odalisque Ana?" she heard one ask. It was Olam.

Ana held her breath. This was it. Both she and Kett would be impaled as a result of another of her reckless, selfish acts.

But then she heard Sascha's voice. "Ana went to relieve herself. She came and told me just a few moments ago, so she shouldn't be long."

"I shall be back to fetch her. There are some traditional rituals we must adhere to for the First Virgin before we take her to the Zar. Please tell her . . ."

Ana never heard what she was supposed to be told by Sascha, for Olam's voice faded into the distance as Kett hurried away and she settled in as best she could for the bumpy ride.

ZAFIRA FLED, DOING HER best to escape up the stairs from the advancing Grand Vizier, but at her age and with her knees no longer capable of such punishment, she gave way after about six steps, all but collapsing under her own weight.

Maliz was in no hurry. As he strolled up the stairs to where she lay, he made a tut-tutting sound of exasperation that he had had to go through this drama. There was no longer any need for pretense on his part. "Where did you think you might run to, old woman?" He grabbed her bony ankle and ruthlessly pulled her backward down the stairs, her chin, ribs, and elbows smashing savagely against the stone. He smiled to hear her shrieks of pain.

At the bottom he flipped her over, took a fistful of her robe, and pulled her up to face him, deriving pleasure from her ragged breathing.

Zafira found the courage to open her eyes, and Maliz was surprised to see nothing but defiance in those rheumy orbs. Gone was the fear, and definitely gone was the pretense. His prisoner moved her head to stare at the statue of the Goddess behind him and she began murmuring a prayer to Lyana.

He shook her as a hunting dog might shake its quarry once it is caught, but she ignored him, continued with her prayer, finally finishing with a beatific smile.

"I am done, Maliz. Do what you will." Her voice was as cold as the pillar he had shoved her up against.

Maliz snarled and pushed her harder against the pale stone. "You name me, Priestess. I'm impressed. I thought your lips might burn to say it."

She snarled back through her agony, "Enjoy your small victory, demon. It is pathetic and will be your last."

He laughed, and threw her down to the floor, hearing a brittle bone somewhere in her body protest with a snap. He kicked her viciously, that same shard of bone now puncturing through her skin, obviously slashing through a lung as well, going by the gush of blood from her mouth. She shrieked once and then wept silently, her mouth opened in a silent scream as blood and spittle continued to puddle on the floor beneath her.

"Your end is close, Priestess. Just listen to your breathing. Why don't you make it easy on yourself?"

"How?"

"Tell me who she is."

"And then what?" She sneered through the pain, her voice gurgling with the liquid in her throat.

"I shall snap your neck in an instant and you will suffer no more."

"And if I keep my secret?"

"You will die in agony."

"And you think that scares me?"

"It should."

Maliz was impressed by her courage when she spoke again through her pain. "She has spoken to me, comforted me with the knowledge that she will prevail this time. You are as good as dead, Maliz, so enjoy your last conquest. My death is meaningless, for my work is already done. You are too late."

Maliz knew he was being baited, but still he couldn't ignore her derision. He kicked her as hard as he could, relishing the cracking sound as more ribs gave way beneath his foot.

"How does that feel, Priestess?"

Unbelievably to his ears, she laughed, although blood flew from her mouth. "Each blow speeds me closer to my Goddess. Lyana is mocking you, Maliz."

"Who are your companions?"

Her scorn came out as a gurgle of blood that rattled in her throat and spilled from her nose as well as her mouth. "All of Percheron."

This time Maliz picked her up and threw her against a pillar with a sickening crunch. He knew it was idiotic to kill the only link he had to Iridor and Lyana, but his need for bloodletting and venting his anger had to be answered. She looked to be dead—was certainly almost gone to her god.

"Is the dwarf Iridor?" he demanded, leaning close to her bloodied face.

"No," she croaked, her tone filled with derision. "The dwarf is an idiot, as you well know. I will never tell you who Iridor is, but he is hunting you as we speak, Maliz, and more's the pity I won't live long enough to tell him who you are." She rattled a cough that sounded like death arriving.

A new thought struck Maliz, and as distasteful as it was, the destruction of Lyana overrode everything. "Zafira, before you leave this plane, I'm thinking I should send you to the bitch goddess with my seed running down your thighs. An intriguing irony for a virginal priestess of Lyana, don't you think?"

At this, her eyes flew open and he knew he had hit on the right threat. He reached for her robes and began lifting them. "No one comes here, Priestess. No one will rescue you from this. No one but me, that is."

Her robes were already pulled above her knees, revealing her withered thighs. Distasteful as Maliz found her body, he knew this threat was the one thing that might loosen her tongue. "I know you wanted to go to your goddess the virgin you were when you gave yourself to her. But I'm afraid I've got a rush of blood at having roughed you up, Zafira. I feel a strong desire to release that pent-up lust . . . and sadly for both of us, you're the closest thing."

He pressed his point by climbing on top of her, Zafira's weak attempts to push him off laughable. He ripped open her robes to reveal her wrinkled and naked body.

"Not very attractive, Zafira, but it will have to do," he said, reaching to loosen the top of his trousers.

"No," she begged. "Do not desecrate me or her temple."

"One word will do it, Priestess."

"I do not know who she is," she pleaded now, terror in her voice. "I promise you, I know not who is Lyana's vessel."

He believed her. In his experience it was too early for Lyana to have fully come into her new incarnation. "One word, Zafira," he repeated.

"What word?"

"Who is Iridor? Speak his name and I will finish you off quickly."

"No rape?"

He shook his head. "A single word."

She nodded, closed her eyes, and he watched her breathe a short prayer begging forgiveness. Then she opened her eyes and said the name he had been waiting to hear.

It did not surprise him. But it did enrage him.

14

Ana had lost sense of time and place. She had heard some voices—men's voices—and presumed the guards were moving them through the various gates, although she had no idea which. All she knew was the swaying rhythm of Kett's hurried movements, and just moments ago she'd felt herself tip dangerously forward, but her heart had leaped at this sudden movement—first in fear and then in hope. Surely this meant they were free of the palace, moving downhill toward the bazaar. Still, she didn't dare make any sound . . . not yet.

Kett had broken into a jog. She presumed she must be feeling unbearably heavy and he must see his destination, she thought, for him to be risking breaking into a run. Within moments she felt herself dropping and then hitting the ground hard. Fortunately the fabrics in the bundle around her cushioned her fall.

Ana could hear Kett's labored breathing. Still she waited until he opened the bundle before she said anything, for she couldn't be sure he hadn't simply dropped her from exhaustion.

"Miss Ana!" he hissed. "Are you hurt?" The familiar eyes behind the dark veils were filled with concern.

"Are we safe?" she risked asking.

He nodded. "For a short while. Did I hurt you?"

"No, Kett. You've saved my life." She sprang to her feet and hugged him, ripping off his veil so she could look upon his sweet, trusting face. "Such a risk you took." She shook her head and began kissing his cheeks.

He was still breathing hard but managed to laugh. "Hush, Miss Ana. We're not that safe!"

"I've got to get out of these clothes, Kett. Have you got anything? Where are we?"

"I have everything already arranged. Behind those big olive jars are some ordinary street clothes. Make sure you are fully veiled or that hair will give you away, Miss Ana."

They had shared too much nakedness already for her to fret about her lack of modesty; and she quickly ripped off her silken blue robes. After undoing the jewelery about her neck, she held it out to Kett. "You take this and my bracelets."

"I don't want—"

She ignored his protests. "Don't sell it here. They're too recognizable. And I can't have them about me." When he still looked doubtful, she added: "Give them away if you want, but not here." He nodded. She piled the jewelery into his cupped hands. "Use the gold to pay off whomever you have to."

"I don't have to pay anyone."

She frowned as she pulled on the street clothes. "What do you mean?"

"I couldn't tell you in the palace. But when I came to the bazaar looking for that friend I told you about, I was stopped by a woman. She was very young and beautiful. She asked me not to use the corrupt bundle woman but to go in disguise myself."

"And you did, just like that?"

Kett smiled. "She was very persuasive. She named me—knew who I was, and who I represent."

"Who you represent?"

"I am the Raven, Miss Ana. The black bird of sorrows."

"You said something similar earlier. What does that mean?" she asked as she smoothed down her clothes. Reaching for the veil, she held the thin fabric between her fingers.

He shrugged, began pulling off his skirts until he stood naked save for his loincloth. "I don't know, to be honest. All I know is that I serve her. Lyana will guide me."

Ana looked up sharply. "Lyana?"

"You, Miss Ana. I serve Lyana through serving you." The slave smiled.

"Kett, I—"

"No. Let's not talk about it. We both serve Lyana, we each have our role to play. I don't know what being the black bird means, although the lady seemed to look sad for me as we spoke. Perhaps that's why I'm the bird of sorrows."

Ana shook her head, still bafffled. "What was this woman's name? Did she tell you?"

"She called herself Ellyana. And I could refuse her nothing. We must hide all the clothes," he warned.

She nodded, understanding now. "I'm still frightened by the risk you took," Ana persisted. "Promise me you will leave the city tonight, Kett, as I must."

"It's a pity we can't leave together."

"I know, but it's too dangerous. And if I get caught I don't want you caught with me."

"You won't get caught, Miss Ana. Where are you going?"

"Get dressed, Kett. I'm going west, getting as far away from Percheron as I can. What about you? Any ideas?"

He was pulling his trousers on. "No plan. Like you, as far away from here as possible. My mother has people in the desert caravans—perhaps I can join them."

She shook her head. "No, Kett! You cannot turn to anyone who knows you or your family. Do you hear me? Salmeo will find you and he will kill everyone you love. Go in the opposite direction. Go east. Get on a ship and sail away from here. You have a fortune in jewelry. Sell it wisely and you will be a made man." She stumbled over the last two words, embarrassed by her verbal clumsiness.

Kett graciously let it pass, looking down as he reached for his shirt. "And so we shall never see each other again."

She shook her head, a sad smile on her mouth. Before she put her veil on and before he could pull his shirt on, she reached up to take his face, and putting her lips against his, she kissed him long and softly. There was no desire in it, only sincere friendship and gratitude.

At a noise behind them, they pulled apart. Ana felt as though her insides had turned instantly to water. Standing in the space where a curtain had only moments ago kept their secret stood Salmeo, surrounded by his Elim, and a horrified-looking Valide.

"Get them," was all Salmeo said. Herezah said nothing, but her look of pure hatred spoke volumes.

PEZ WAS ARGUING WITH Bin.

"Must see my Zar!" he said, stamping his foot. "He has my butterflies."

"Pez," Bin said calmly. "I've explained that he does not want to see you. He will call you when he does. He is preparing to meet with Odalisque—"

Bin was unable to say any more. Pez had begun one of his infamous screaming sessions.

Bin backed away, unsure of what to do. Pez fell to the ground, writhing, the intensity of his shrieks becoming increasingly piercing. One of the mutes happened to look outside the door to summon Bin and frowned when he saw the dwarf on the ground.

"I wish I were deaf like you, Salazin," Bin murmured to himself, nodding expectantly at the mute. Salazin signaled that the Zar wished to see him.

"Thank you," Bin gestured, then shrugged his shoulders toward Pez, suggesting that he was lost as to what to do with the dwarf.

Salazin came into the vestibule where the Zar's secretary worked and walked toward the writhing creature on the floor. He pinned the dwarf's short arms behind him and lifted him easily, shaking him like a doll to be quiet.

Pez stopped his noise and Bin sighed, relieved. "Thank you again, Salazin," he said again using the practiced sign language to say he didn't know how he was going to stop Pez.

Salazin pointed to the Zar's chambers questioningly.

Bin shook his head quickly. "No."

The mute put the dwarf down, and Pez remained mercifully

silent as the mute signed with his fingers that it would be a good thing for the Zar and his pet to be friends again.

Bin sighed. Gave a look of resignation. He signed: *It's your throat. I'll deny I had anything to do with this.*

Salazin grinned. He picked Pez up again, as if he weighed nothing, and strode into the room, Bin running behind and making merry protest for the Zar's benefit.

BOAZ WAS IN HIS dressing chamber. One other mute was in attendance whilst the Zar's dresser fussed over the outfit that had been chosen for the Zar to greet his First Virgin in.

At the interruption, the Zar glared at Bin and then at Pez, who again stayed silent. Bin bowed, as did Salazin.

"I couldn't stop him, Majesty. Pez arrived and was making a dreadful noise outside—only Salazin was spared the blood curdling shrieks— and although I said you did not wish to see Pez, Salazin believed you might."

"It's important," Pez whined, picking his nose. He was also tapping his foot. Despite his annoyance, Boaz couldn't ignore the sign. Long ago the two of them had worked out a code using physical signals to communicate simple messages. They'd employed it throughout Boaz's childhood, and although it hadn't been used in over a year, Boaz felt the sentimental pull at his heartstrings and his instant response to Pez's tension—he could not ignore the urgent plea, no matter how angry he still was at Pez. Boaz maintained his stony silence until everyone felt the discomfort. Finally he slapped away the dresser's hand. "I'm ready," he said. The man bowed, knowing he had just been dismissed.

Bin continued his lament. "Forgive me, Zar Boaz. Salazin just picked up the dwarf and brought him in."

Boaz signed a query to Salazin. He, Bin, and the Vizier were the only people permitted to know the secret signing language and each was proficient in it now, although Boaz was by far the most adept at using this challenging form of communication. Sometimes the mutes themselves didn't know what he was asking when the speed of his hands became too quick for them to follow—all but one, that is.

Salazin answered, his fingers moving as fast as Boaz's. *Because, Majesty, this is your great friend, as I understand it, and I think he will die of heartbreak soon if he can't be with you.*

I said not until I summoned him. Do you defy me, Salazin?

No, High One. I care deeply for your happiness and I know Pez makes you smile. Even a dog could be forgiven an indiscretion by its master, Majesty. This is a special night for you. Let it be a happy one.

Salazin is a clever one, Boaz thought wryly to himself. *Tariq picked wisely.* The truth was, Boaz really liked having Salazin around. The young man's presence was always comforting and indeed calming. He never communicated unless spoken to and had a knack for disappearing into the room they were in. There were times when Boaz could forget the warrior was nearby and yet the mute was always alert, always ready to leap to the Zar's needs. Yes, he liked Salazin immensely.

Forgiving the mute the interruption, he nodded decisively. "Leave us," he finally said. "I will speak with Pez."

Salazin nodded, understanding the response even without hearing the words. Bin bowed, obviously relieved.

The Zar spoke directly to his mutes now through sign language. *I want privacy with Pez. You can wait outside.*

The men nodded, bowed, and left.

"Thank you," Pez said tentatively into the silence after the door closed.

"I suppose you put on one of your shows out there?" Boaz said absently, looking at himself in the tall glass.

"The best," Pez agreed.

"I told you to wait until I wished to see you."

"That might have been never, my Zar."

"And so what if it was?" Boaz replied, determined not to let Pez have his clever way and quickly ingratiate himself. He was still furious with the dwarf for challenging him.

"Well, then, I would not be able to give you the important news I have discovered."

"Which is?" Boaz said, yawning in feigned boredom.

"Lazar is alive," Pez said flatly.

Boaz swung around to face the dwarf. Disbelief, anger, and hope warred within him.

Pez hurried to explain. "It has all been a ruse, Highness . . . but not of Lazar's doing and not of mine. Lazar nearly died, it's true. But I've found him. I've been looking for him on your behalf since I first heard the unbelievable news of his death."

"You've been looking for him?" Boaz's voice was soft, uncertain, almost apologetic.

"It's why I kept leaving the palace, my Zar. I never trusted the information we were told, even though the priestess is a friend of mine. Lazar might well have perished—but he would not have had his body committed to the sea. He was a man of the desert. That's where he would wish to lie, not on the bottom of the Faranel."

Boaz felt shaken, knew he must look unsteady. "Why didn't you share your mistrust?"

"You've never really given me a chance. We rarely get time alone anymore, Highness, and it is not something I could just drop into casual conversation. I needed to be sure."

"What about Jumo?"

Pez shrugged. "Another victim of the lie."

"Where have you found Lazar?"

"He has been recuperating on Star Island."

Boaz's eyes widened in shock. "How did you know?"

"A wild guess, Zar Boaz. None of us truly believed he might be there, but, yes, perhaps we should have checked. In the end I did, on your behalf."

"Well . . ." Boaz spluttered, unsure of what to say. He had a hundred questions, Pez could see.

The dwarf held up his gnarled hand. "He has been very sick. Deathly sick, unable to fend for himself. That's why it's taken so long for us to learn the truth. It took weeks for him to find full consciousness again, months to move without help. A year before he could walk unaided. That's how the priestess was able to spin her terrible tale. Lazar was unable to defend himself."

"But why did Zafira lie?" Boaz asked, aghast. He had trusted the old priestess, liked her.

"You will have to ask her that, my Zar. I am as injured as you by her lies."

Boaz felt utterly confused. "But with all her efforts she saved his life, didn't she?"

"She did. Why she would tell you he was dead when she alone nursed him back to health, I cannot say, although I have my suspicions."

"Which are?"

"Well, there is no doubt someone wanted Lazar dead—that someone tried to poison him. I'm guessing Zafira went down this extraordinarily mysterious path in order to protect him. She let the murderer believe that he had succeeded, and this gave her time to nurse him back to full health."

"But if she'd come to me—"

"Ah, but there was, to all intents, a murderer on the loose, Majesty—in the palace, no less, and she wasn't prepared to risk another attempt once he discovered he had not fully succeeded in killing the Spur. I suspect she simply didn't believe you could protect him."

Boaz bristled. "Get the priestess here. I have to talk to her directly."

"We cannot, Majesty."

"Why?" he demanded.

"She has disappeared."

The Zar snapped his displeasure, feeling his emotions spiraling. "Disappeared?"

Pez nodded gravely. "I went to see her at the Sea Temple today and she was gone."

"Well, that sounds suspicious?" Boaz replied, beginning to pace his chamber. Lazar alive! He didn't know whether to be excited at the news or appalled that it had taken so long for him to discover it. "And Lazar?"

"Is coming to you tonight. He wishes to present himself. I thought it only fair to warn you, High One. It was a shock for me when I found him and I didn't want you to be placed in an awkward position."

Boaz looked gently at his friend. He felt suddenly sickened to have misjudged his oldest, greatest friend. He wondered what his father might think of his behavior toward one of Joreb's favorite people. "I have wronged you, Pez. I was angry at your accusations but I should have listened to you, trusted you. You are the true friend in my life."

"I would never do anything to hurt you, my Zar, and I'm

sorry I made you so angry. I have been . . . well, shall we say, preoccupied."

"It is forgotten," Boaz said, waving their differences aside. "My concern is about how this is going to look."

"What does it matter how it looks? You have your Spur back. You had no part in the ruse. Let's be honest, my Zar, the city folk of Percheron will care only that he lives. They will welcome the opportunity to celebrate his return."

"That's right," Boaz agreed, thinking it through. "We are innocent in this. We believed what we were told by someone we thought we could trust. And a crime was still perpetrated against Lazar, and someone took responsibility for it."

"Whether he was guilty or not," Pez finished the unspoken words that Boaz could not.

The Zar continued, ignoring the interruption and the pain its words provoked. "The Crown has nothing to feel guilty about."

"Nothing at all, Majesty. Just welcome your Spur back with open arms."

Boaz nodded. "How can I ensure that this is kept secret for now?"

"Why would you want it to be kept quiet?"

"Just for now. I would like to speak with Lazar before his return becomes public knowledge."

"I can't wait to see Salmeo's face when he claps eyes on Lazar," Pez said knowingly.

"My mother's face is going to be a picture, too," Boaz offered sourly.

"I shall go, Highness," Pez said.

"To Lazar?"

At the dwarf's nod, Boaz instructed, "Tell him to come in the early hours, and hooded. Tell him to bring this." He bent over a piece of parchment and quickly dribbled some green wax on it from a special candle that burned only in his own rooms. Then, using the great seal he wore around his neck on a beautifully wrought chain, he imprinted his personal mark in the soft wax. "This will gain him instant access to the palace. I will send one of my mutes to escort him. He is not to be recognized."

"Why the early hour?"

"I have a meeting with Ana."

Pez nodded knowingly and then muttered a phrase in a language the Zar did not recognize. At Boaz's questioning look, the dwarf smiled sadly. "Roughly translated it means 'take a wife tonight.'"

The Zar looked suddenly coy. "It is my intention."

"That is good. I go now," Pez said hurriedly. "I'm glad we're friends again, Boaz."

Boaz grinned wryly at him. "Of course, no one but yourself and myself will celebrate."

"I don't doubt it," Pez replied. "I shall return," he added, leaving the Zar's chambers in a series of somersaults, before cavorting down the hallway.

"Ah, and so the world rights itself," Bin said wearily, no doubt more to himself than anyone else, for he had only mutes for company.

PEZ FLEW SILENTLY THROUGH the warm air, his spirits feeling lighter for having restored the balance of friendship between himself and Boaz. He had begun to worry about being alienated in the palace. It had occurred to him that Boaz, in his anger—if it persisted, and Boaz could always be so single-minded—might even ban him from being able to roam wherever he wanted.

He scanned the bay from his high vantage, hoping to see Lazar being rowed back to the mainland—although he suspected Lazar would doggedly row himself back. There was little movement on the water this night, though. His gaze alighting on Beloch, he scrutinized the giant. It was not Pez's imagination; distinct cracks had appeared up and down the stone of the giant's body. From afar, as most people viewed them, they were noticeable, although not especially eye-catching. But close up the cracks looked serious—it was as if Beloch were simply falling apart, crumbling to the floor. Pez couldn't shake the notion that the giant was not dying but being reborn.

"Are you, Beloch? Are you rising, as I have and Lyana must, to fight the coming battle?"

If he expected an answer, he didn't get one. The only sound was the distant rumble of the city and the lapping of the water around Beloch's feet. Not even the lonely cry of a seabird broke the silence, and the ships were still, anchored for the night. Lazar was not here, not yet anyway.

Pez sighed and in his owl guise turned to face Star Island. He felt he should go there and catch the former Spur before he left. His gaze was distracted momentarily, from the dark mound in the distance where a few torches burned to guide any night travelers to an unfamiliar shadow on the Sea Temple. It instantly struck him as odd that the new spire, which a donation from Boaz had paid for, looked misshapen. He concentrated, and as his sharp owl eyesight focused carefully, any lightness of heart, however vague fled in that instant of anguish. And with a heart growing heavier by the second, he found the courage to lift from Beloch's head and fly straight toward certain despair.

ANA AND KETT STOOD in Salmeo's salon, trembling with fear in the warm night air. The Grand Master Eunuch and the Valide hadn't allowed Kett to finish dressing, so he remained half naked. Thrown at Ana's feet was her pale blue First Virgin outfit, stained and torn. Her jewelery was laid at Kett's feet, a chilling glimpse of what the Grand Master Eunuch planned to accuse him of.

Ana was in a state of deep shock. That she was destined to die was obvious, and in her mind her life was not worth fretting over—other than to hope it was quick, for the notion of prolonged suffering made her fearful. But Kett was a different matter altogether. Kett, her friend who had risked so much— he would die, too, and she was sure that Salmeo and Herezah would show no mercy and not permit his end to be anything but truly ghoulish.

She was ashamed of herself for being so gullible. From the moment she had seen Salmeo licking his lips in that doorway of the bazaar, she had understood with a vicious clarity that she had never escaped at all. For all her ingenuity and daring, she had been permitted to leave the harem; it was another of Salmeo's and no doubt Herezah's cunning manipulations. They had wanted her to try another escape and so they had done everything they could to encourage her in this attempt.

She went over it in her mind now. The supposedly surprise trip to the bazaar had given Herezah the perfect opportunity to initiate the carefully, almost beautifully constructed conversation that had pushed Ana into making a rash decision. And then, of course, Salmeo's revolting touch. She felt sure when Sascha's turn came—as beautiful as the girl was—Salmeo would break her hymen swiftly and coolly. He had lingered with Ana, aroused her, and driven her into such a state of revulsion and passion that she would do anything to distance herself from his repulsive being . . . even attempt escape. She let out a laugh, although it came out as a dry sob; Salmeo had even urged Kett on his errand to the market—it had all been so deliberately and exquisitely constructed. Salmeo and Herezah had known everything she and Kett would do before they had even attempted it. How naive they had been to think they could fool the palace's most cruelly manipulative pair with their pathetic escapade.

Even the Elim, she realized now, had been specifically ordered to stand outside the divan suite so that she could feel safe in making her escape attempt. How stupid she had been not to ignore the nagging voice inside. It had been trying to tell her that the Elim *never* left the girls entirely alone or unsupervised. That ruse alone should have set off every alarm in her head.

Ana now realized that the whole business of the bundle women and the treat for the girls had been a sham, too. Salmeo had set it up to make it as easy as possible for Ana to make this audacious attempt—just so that he could entrap her. How low would the Valide and Grand Master Eunuch stoop to ensure that she never got close to Boaz? She smirked inwardly with wry pity for herself—they wanted nothing less than her execution and she had blindly walked down their pathway as purposefully as if they had put a ring through her nose and led her by a rope as one would a dull beast. Salmeo had probably planted the idea of escape in Kett's head. She felt ill inside thinking how excited he had been to tell her of the brave odalisque who had risked everything to escape the prison of the harem and had succeeded by hiding herself in one of the bundles. She had believed it because she wanted to, because she was so desperate to get away from Salmeo and the threat of Boaz's bed. And she had acted as only a fool would.

"Kneel in the presence of your Zar, slut!" Herezah commanded, and Ana was dragged from her miserable thoughts to realize that Boaz, flanked by Salazin, had entered, his face a mask of misery.

The Elim pushed her to her knees, although she needed no help. She was ready to collapse from shame and despair at her own stupidity.

A terrible silence descended.

"Tell me," she heard the Zar say.

She heard the rustle of silk as Salmeo bowed and began constructing his sordid story.

"Odalisque Ana had been prepared for you, my Zar, as you requested this morning. We had seen to it that she enjoyed a special day that marked her new status as First Chosen Virgin. In fact, the Valide took her alone, save a few Elim, into the grand bazaar to personally select her jewelery and other accoutrements for the occasion. It was a high honor given to one so young."

Ana heard Boaz sigh. Perhaps he, too, had already accepted the fact that Salmeo's truth would be spun with dark threads of lies.

The Zar addressed them. "Ana, Kett, you may remain kneeling, but I would prefer you faced your accusers."

Ana reluctantly lifted her head, although she could not bring herself to meet the Zar's pained gaze.

Salmeo continued: "Odalisque Ana was told that you had made your choice and had given your command concerning her. She was prepared in the ritual fashion, Majesty—"

"Which you no doubt played your critical part in, Grand Master Salmeo?"

"Of course, Highness. That is one of my duties," the eunuch said with no aggression. His voice was gentle, his lisp pronounced. And now, as he began to wave his arms, warming to the tale, the fragrance of violets assaulted Ana. "The Valide granted the odalisques a special treat in the shape of a visit from the bundle women. In fact—"

"Why?" Boaz asked, turning to his mother. "The girls had already enjoyed a long day on the water. Why was more of a treat necessary?"

"My Zar, I did not realize one could ever have too many treats," Herezah replied, lacing her tone with hurt indignation. "I grew up in the harem. I know how few and far between the moments of fun can be. I was hoping, as Valide, to change that for your odalisques. They are still so young. I may be old, but I am not so old that I can't recall the dullness forced on youth in this place. Perhaps wrongly, I thought if I personally gave them a special treat, it might encourage the younger ones to feel less daunted by me."

Ana watched Herezah finish her explanation with a plaintive shrug. The Valide was a true master of role playing; she ought to be admired for her chameleonlike ability to be anything to anyone that she chose to be. Ana despised her.

"I see," Boaz said noncommittally, although Ana sensed he saw straight through the veneer of his mother's tale. "Continue," he said to Salmeo.

"Well, Majesty, we allowed Ana to enjoy some time with the other odalisques. She had, after all, missed out on the boating trip with her Zar and so we decided to let her share the treat of the bundle women."

"That's very generous of you, Grand Master Eunuch," Boaz said. "Ana, did you select anything from all the wares on offer?"

Ana was forced to confront Boaz's pained expression and was about to shake her head when she remembered the bean. Truth was best. "Yes, Zar Boaz. At Grand Master Salmeo's insistence I felt obliged to accept this." She dug into her pocket and pulled out the tiny bean of elephants. She uncapped it and tipped the contents into her palm. "They are ivory, Majesty."

"How intriguing," Boaz said, leaning down to stare at them with fascination. She could smell his freshly bathed hair. Bathed for her. "And you say the chief eunuch encouraged you?"

She nodded. "There is nothing I want for, Majesty—"

"Except your freedom, obviously," he replied sharply.

Ana felt the stab of guilt but he was right—she could hardly deny it. "Yes, Highness. I have made a habit of proving that, haven't I?" She caught the look of anger from her accusers at her familiarity with him but ignored it. "I have no defense, Highness. An opportunity presented itself and I took it."

"May I?" Salmeo cut in.

Boaz nodded, his expression unhappy.

"My Zar, this is not a simple case of Odalisque Ana seizing a rare chance for freedom. I think a year ago we were able to make that argument on her behalf because of her age, her newness to the palace, and, through my fault, genuine opportunity that was taken on the whim of a moment."

"And this time?" the Zar queried.

"Well, this time it was premeditated, my Zar," Salmeo exclaimed, his voice filled with well-practiced indignation. "Odalisque Ana could not have escaped the palace without carefully setting up her plan first. She and the eunuch, Kett, were in this together from the start. They had ample chance during the whole of today in each other's almost exclusive company to hatch and test their plan. Forgive me my directness, Highness, but there was absolutely nothing spontaneous this time about Odalisque Ana's decision."

"And why would Kett aid Odalisque Ana? Do you see it as revenge for the justice meted out to him for his error more than a year ago?"

At Boaz's question Ana could see see Herezah's shoulders relax and Salmeo's eyelids narrow a fraction and she knew the Zar had walked into a trap. Glancing at Kett, she saw him slump still further and she closed her eyes in resignation.

"Kett is an enigma, my Zar," Salmeo began, his voice soft, almost tender now. "He has loved Odalisque Ana since the day he saw her naked and frightened in the Choosing Room. They shared a deeply emotional experience when he was cut, Majesty, and from there on, I think, in Kett's disturbed, fevered mind he and she were meant to be together. I think he now believes, in his twisted logic, that he's in love with one of your prized women, my Zar."

"That's a lie!" Ana yelled, disgusted by both the inflammatory words and how well Salmeo was playing the situation to provoke the Zar.

Herezah gasped and Salmeo pursed his fat lips. Both looked to Boaz to censure her.

Boaz did not like what he was hearing, as was clear from his darkened expression. "Ana, let the Grand Master Eunuch finish. You will have your chance to speak, for this is the most serious of accusations. Continue," he ordered Salmeo.

"I was going to say, my Zar, that no man would risk so much for a woman unless he had a special devotion to her. We found all of Ana's precious jewels with his belongings, but I don't believe Kett did this for wealth. He could hardly sell any of these jewels locally. No, Highness, Kett had more 'spiritual' reasons,

232 • Fiona McIntosh

you could say, for aiding Odalisque Ana in her misguided plan."

Ana opened her mouth to protest and shut it again at Boaz's glare.

"Finish your sorry tale, Grand Master Eunuch. I find it distressing to drag it out any longer."

Salmeo bowed his head. "Of course, Highness. We found the pair of them in a grubby backstreet of the bazaar in what could only be described as a . . . well, shall we say, regrettable position."

"Be specific, Salmeo. I want all the facts, not innuendo."

"As you wish, Highness. Odalisque Ana was discovered unveiled, her palace clothes thrown behind an olive jar, whilst her companion was all but naked. This in itself is a damning set of circumstances that demands the most stringent of punishments, Majesty. However, that is not the full extent of your odalisque's treachery. She was also found in the arms of her eunuch companion, their lips in warm embrace."

Boaz shot Ana a glare of such rage, she had no doubt that he was ready to pronounce the death sentence.

"I'm sorry, son," Herezah said softly from the background. "She is a vixen and a user of men."

Boaz did not reply to his mother. Instead his blistering gaze was fixed on Ana. "It is your turn, Ana. Can you refute any of what is leveled against you?"

Ana knew it was hopeless. Boaz's eyes were glazed with jealousy. She doubted he would see much reason now that Salmeo had primed him so skillfully. Furthermore, Boaz could not, would not, overturn certain fundamental harem rules. She had been caught with another man—she had for all intents and purposes cuckolded the Zar. Her next decision was made to deliberately inflame her accusers still further. She had nothing to lose and only pleasure to gain from watching Herezah's gathering fury as she switched into the Galinsean language. "I prefer not to debase myself further with trying to justify my actions, which Grand Master Salmeo has related with such creative embellishments, Zar Boaz. May I suggest you do the honorable thing by your crown, Majesty. Although I beg you to spare Kett. He is an innocent and was driven by a desire to serve, Highness, which I would imagine you might consider an attribute in any slave."

Herezah's expression of deep hatred seared Ana as effectively as if she had thrown a lamp of burning oil at her. Salmeo simply looked amused by her eloquent soliloquy, even though he had understood not a word. The Zar blinked several times as he first struggled to understand and then digest her cutting words.

"You wish to die?" he asked, aghast

Again she replied in Galinsean. "It is where this is all headed, Zar Boaz. It would be naive for us to think otherwise. Let us make it easier for everyone and prevent a late night of recriminations and tears." She switched back agilely to Percherese. "I am guilty, yes. I have made my second attempt at escape from the harem and I fully understood the consequences when I made that decision. My only regret is that I roped an innocent into my plan. I will add that I did not kiss Kett out of lust, as suggested, but purely in thanks for his unselfish risk taking."

"Zar Boaz, this is all very noble," Herezah cut in, exasperated. "The fact of the matter is, an odalisque has been found unveiled in the presence of a man—a half-naked man at that. In this there is no argument."

"If you can call Kett a man, Highness," Ana said calmly. "The harem took that status away from him in all but title."

"We had no choice, Highness," Salmeo lisped. "Kett broke a sacred rule. And now he has done it again. I cannot see why any mercy should—or indeed can—be shown to a person who has already been given a second chance for redemption. He has snubbed that opportunity."

"I agree," Boaz said. "Kett, I have no choice in this but to get my palace in order. I will not brook this sort of disobedience. I demand loyalty. You understood the consequences, I'm sure, of your actions."

"I did, Highness, and the truth is I would do it again for Miss Ana," Kett replied, the brave words belying his stricken expression.

Boaz nodded. "I admire your courage, Kett. You will be ganched tomorrow at noon, your body tossed onto the death hooks to squirm and die. May the hooks find their mark and kill you swiftly."

"No, Boaz!" Ana begged.

He ignored her. "Take him away," he commanded the Elim standing nearby.

Without farther ceremony, the young eunuch was pulled to his feet and hurried from the room, without so much as a chance to say farewell to Ana, although his sorrowful gaze over his shoulder said enough.

Ana felt the hot tears sliding down her face. "You brute! You are callous like your mother, Zar Boaz. I can only pity you and the people of Percheron."

Without warning Herezah stepped up and slapped the kneeling odalisque with such force that Ana toppled sideways. "Don't you dare take his or my name in vain. You are nothing!" she spat, in a rare emotional outburst. "You are not worthy so much as to look upon him again. Slut!"

"Mother," Boaz warned. "Step back or return to your chambers."

"My son, I will no longer listen to these filthy words from this girl. You have heard what she has done this day and let me add that I, too, witnessed her kissing the half-naked black eunuch. All our sacred rules have been flouted by this one girl since her arrival. You have no choice but to take punitive measures, as your father before you would have done. I shall take my leave," she finished, breathing hard, eyes glittering furiously as she took a lingering look at her son before formally dropping a low curtsy. She straightened, shot a final scathing glance at Ana, and left without another word.

Ana was initially surprised that the Valide did not want to witness Boaz's declaration as to his odalisque's fate. But then she realized that this was Herezah's great strength. She understood restraint—she grasped the intimate complexity of situations and how to play people off against one another. Leaving as she had done—as much as it would have galled her—still gave her an air of nobility; washing her hands of the wretched girl who had brought the harem into disrepute and washing her hands of the whole sorry situation, as though she was no party to it. Herezah was too clever. Ana should have spent more time learning from her rather than clashing with her.

It was too late now. In the silence, Ana pushed Boaz still further. She would not live again under the harem rules and, true to herself, would rather die than be returned to Salmeo and Herezah's care. "You should listen to your mother, Boaz. Haven't you always? You probably always will."

Salmeo looked set to explode into laughter. It was obvious he had never heard anyone speak to a Zar with the disdain that this slip of a girl was allowing herself this evening.

Seething beneath the huge eunuch's not-very-well-disguised mirth, Boaz snapped, "It seems you have a death wish, Odalisque Ana, that you would provoke me so."

"Pronounce sentence, Zar Boaz, I tire of this audience."

Boaz swallowed. She knew she left him no choice and Salmeo's delight in his Zar's discomfort was all too plain to read on the eunuch's face. Ana had played the Zar better, though; the future security of the royals was doomed if a mere odalisque could influence a Zar to back down. She held her breath as he took a steadying one and found his voice.

"Odalisque Ana, it is my painful task to advise that you will be escorted from here to the palace pits. Tomorrow at dawn you will be taken from there, secured in a weighted velvet bag, rowed out on one of the barges to a private spot on the river, and drowned." He paused and Ana understood that even in his anger he had chosen the least painful death he could contrive . . . but it was still execution that he was obliged to order. "And there at the bottom of the royal river I hope you find peace and the people you have lost."

Ana nodded. Those were the first meaningful words she had heard during this meeting. "Thank you, Zar Boaz. I shall be reunited with my uncle Horz and Kett—all of us executed on your order. I shall be candid with you. I am not afraid to die. I am more afraid to live."

Boaz turned to the eunuch. "Salmeo, leave us. I wish to say something to Ana in private. Make arrangements to have her taken to the pits in a few moments."

Salmeo's tongue flicked out between the gap in his teeth to wet his lips and then say something, but then he obviously changed his mind. "At once, Highness," he lisped.

When the huge man had departed, Boaz offered Ana his hand to help her to her feet.

She took his gracious offer silently. "I want you to know that I am deeply sorry, Zar Boaz, for all the displeasure I have caused you personally. I meant you no insult. You have been nothing but generous to me."

He regarded her through angry, wounded eyes. "Odalisque Ana, I cannot accept that apology. And I must tell you this before you go. No one else knows of this yet. You could say it is my parting gift to you on a night when I aimed to make you my wife." She bit her lip, unsure of what was coming. "You may well be reunited with Horz of the Elim, as you say. I hope so. Kett will join you later, of course. But in case you were hoping, you will not find Lazar anywhere near your watery grave, Ana, no matter how hard you search."

"What do you mean?" she asked, the hairs on the back of her neck lifting with dread anticipation, somehow knowing she was receiving the confirmation of what she believed to be true.

"I mean that he is alive. I am seeing him in a few hours."

"Alive?" she whispered.

Boaz nodded. "Pez found him." Ana found she could not speak as the truth of her fears of betrayal by two of her few allies settled like lead weights around her. "I'm sure Lazar will be devastated to learn that all his efforts to preserve your life with his own were in vain. Guard!"

"No, wait!"

"Too late, Ana. I have adored you since I first saw you and I would have treated you with kindness and tenderness all of your life. Your disdain for me and my position wounds me deeply; I suppose now I must learn to heal."

The door opened and the Elim moved in, ready to escort Ana to the palace pits.

IRIDOR ALIGHTED ON THE spire above the grisly scene and he changed instantly to Pez so the tears could spill. He wept for his friend, he wept for her suffering, and he wept for all the supporters of Lyana.

Zafira's life was the first to be lost in the battle. Though he knew it would not be the last, this was cold comfort as he looked down upon the tiny figure, broken, bloodied, and impaled upon her own temple's new spire.

As if in respect for his grief, a cloud scudded across the sky and blocked the moonlight, casting the owl and the body into darkness. Pez gingerly moved down beside Zafira. He kissed her cool cheek and was alarmed when she gasped.

"Zafira!"

"Ah, Pez," she whispered. "He came for me."

"Don't talk, I'll—"

"Listen!" she croaked, coughing blood in her struggle. He held her head, as she no longer had the strength to do anything but remain slumped until she died. It was a wonder she had survived as long as she had. "He asked a lot of questions about you." Her breath was ragged. "I put him off your scent as best I could."

"How?"

"By letting him hurt me and then making him think I was begging to tell him who Iridor is."

Pez felt his tears begin to flow again as she somehow, unbelievably, gave a pained burst of a laugh. "Who did you accuse?"

"Salmeo," she whispered. She took one last, shuddering breath and then was still, a smile on her face.

"Lyana speed you to her," Pez said reverently, and then set about his ghoulish task of lifting Zafira's near weightless body off the sharp spire.

Pez gave Zafira's body to the sea, near the temple to which she had dedicated her life. When it was done he climbed back up the stairs to sit out on the roof, where he said another prayer for her soul and her sacrifice before once again returning to his owl shape.

Perched on the spire that had finally taken his friend's life, he could see a small boat being rowed across by a single man.

ANA SAT ON THE cold ground of the area of the palace known as the pits and trembled. She groaned, wished Lazar had never come to her home in the foothills. Wished he had never come into her life.

He was alive. She hugged her knees tighter and allowed herself the luxury of self-pity. With only this night left in her life, what did it matter if she filled the hours with tears. She had no reason to be strong, no one to be strong for anymore. She welcome death, for everyone she had trusted since leaving her home had betrayed her—both the man she loved and the dwarf she had considered her closest friend. She hated them both in that moment, even more than Herezah or Salmeo. At least she had always known the propensity of the latter two for treachery. But Lazar and Pez! She wept harder and prayed that dawn would come fast and finish the misery.

Lyana indeed! If she was Lyana, where was the magic that might take her away from all this?

"DEAD?"

Pez nodded. He was back in his dwarf form, having flown

down to the boat. Lazar had not been surprised to see him, but Pez's news had stopped his friend from rowing any farther. They drifted for the moment as the former Spur digested the tidings. "I've just given her corpse to the sea. I thought it was fitting," Pez added.

"So he's declaring himself," Lazar mused, his voice morose.

"Not really. Maliz believes no one will ever know about Zafira and presumably he took steps to hide his actions. Certainly the temple's the loneliest of places—no one would have disturbed them."

"But we have the truth."

"Yes, he doesn't know this, of course. He thinks Salmeo is Iridor." He laughed bitterly. "Of course, the Grand Master Eunuch would make an incredibly big owl."

"Cunning Zafira," Lazar said. "Courageous to the last."

"True. If you saw what a mess her body was, you'd understand just how brave she was."

"So this is the beginning?"

"Yes. First blood to the demon. Not the last, I'm sure."

Lazar didn't respond to this comment. "You've spoken to Boaz?"

"We've put our differences behind us, or so he believes. He thinks I'm suffering jealousy over his 'friendship' with Tariq, or Maliz, I should say. Poor Boaz, if only he knew."

"Would it make any difference?"

Pez frowned. "You're right, probably not—how can we expect him to understand that Lyana is rising to battle it out with Maliz again. He is dealing with Tariq the Grand Vizier and obviously responding well to the man's counsel, whilst we now see him only for the snake he is . . . the demon in disguise."

"We have to be careful that the counsel he gives is not detrimental to you or Ana."

"Or you."

Lazar looked up from the oar he had been gently maneuvering to prevent them from turning in circles as they drifted.

"I've told you, you are as much a target as I am."

"I don't think so, Pez."

"Still believe you're a coincidence, eh?"

Lazar nodded, although he didn't look completely confident.

"We'll see. In the meantime, your Zar was shocked at my news of your being very alive, of course, but he was also thrilled. He wants to see you in secret in a few hours. You must arrive hooded."

Lazar nodded again. "And Ana?"

"I have not seen her," Pez said, and offered no more. "Are you all right to keep rowing?"

"I'm not an invalid!"

Pez bristled at Lazar's angry mood. "Good, because once Herezah learns the truth, she'll start warming her bed for you," he replied.

15

The Grand Vizier sipped the sweetened wine and eyed his Zar, who seemed restless, distracted. "Yes, as I was saying, I had some business to attend to in the city. And I gather there's been some excitement in my absence."

Boaz turned from the window, tearing his gaze from the Sea Temple. "Excitement? I suppose you could call sentencing two people I like to hideous deaths exciting."

"I'm sorry, my Zar, that was tactless of me. This task seems to be a habit for you."

"Odalisque Ana is my First Chosen. I had hoped to make her a Favorite; more, perhaps."

"You are that fond of her? Already?"

"She is my equal," he replied softly. And when the Vizier raised his eyebrows at the comment, Boaz explained, "Not in status, obviously. But her mind is sharp and agile. She is mysterious. Her peers are like open books that are read without much interest, whilst Ana is closed, fascinating. The others are also vain, already scheming for my attention, whilst Ana—easily the most beautiful—is hardly aware of the effect she has on me. I could never be bored around her."

"My, my, that sounds like a woman to hang on to."

"Except she's determined to shun this role in the harem. I simply can't save her from herself."

Maliz realized which woman he was talking about. Although he hadn't met her, Tariq's memories gave him the knowledge he needed. He remembered now talking to Tariq during the preparations for the Spur's flogging—which had come about because of this same woman. An intensely exquisite-looking woman, he recalled. "What happened?"

"She attempted another escape." Boaz smiled in spite of his mood, sounded almost proud to the Vizier. "Truly audacious this time. She could have gotten away with it if not . . ."

"If not for?"

"Salmeo. My mother, too, I suspect."

Maliz's inward sneer at the mention of the fat eunuch nearly showed itself, but he reined in his reaction. "Why would the Valide have any interest in the girl?"

"She has every interest in who I might eventually take for a wife. I think she might have feared this was happening too early."

"Zars far younger than you have taken wives, Majesty."

"But they didn't have Herezah for a mother, Tariq. I could be wrong but I imagine my mother sees every potential lover of mine as a wife and thus a threat to her own power. It has only been a year since I took the throne. I would hazard she had hoped for a little longer to build her own empire."

"Your choosing Favorites, wives, even siring heirs, is not something your mother can avoid for long."

Boaz looked awkward at the thought of children so soon. "No, but with Ana it was probably happening too fast. It's true I would have elevated her quickly."

"And death is unavoidable?"

"You know the rules, Tariq."

"Not of the harem necessarily."

"Attempted escape is one of the worst sins, but the worst—in the eyes of the harem down the ages—is commiting adultery, cuckolding the Zar."

"She didn't!" Maliz exclaimed, outwardly sympathetic but privately delighted by the tale.

"No, I don't believe she did, but she refuses to defend herself against the claim, and both Salmeo and the Valide unfortunately discovered her in a very compromising position. What they saw can't be argued unless Ana herself can prove otherwise."

"A very twisted web. And so she and the person who helped her escape must die, I'm presuming."

Boaz's expression melted from suppressed to open pain. "Correct. I have no choice, much in the same way as I had little choice with Horz. Ana has broken ancient, sacred rules not once but twice . . . and, indeed, so has Kett."

"Kett?"

"The black eunuch. We grew up together, can you believe. We were playmates until my position in my father's reckoning became all too obvious and my mother did not want us remaining close." Boaz smiled sadly. "It's strange, you know, when we were little I had this whimsical notion that Kett reminded me of a bird. He used to flit around, always busy, always industrious . . . usually dreaming up games for us to play. My sorrowful little black bird."

Something ticked in the back of Maliz's mind but he was exhausted from his exertions at the temple, as well as mellowed from the wine coursing through his veins. He was already pouring a third cup, and he was having such fun with this tale of woe that he paid scant attention to the nudge of familiarity. "So, deaths at dawn, I'm guessing?" When his Zar gave him another look of exasperation at the heavy wit, he put up a hand to ward off the reprimand. "Forgive me, Highness, I don't mean to be insensitive. But if I can help you look at this objectively, please permit me to say that this woman could have made a mockery of you. This cannot be tolerated. Your father ruled with a tough fist, my Zar, and you could do a lot worse than follow in those footsteps. Too much leeway in a place like the harem—a place that exists only because of a very rigid structure, an adherence to ritual and ancient rules—can bring down a dynasty if unchecked." He saw Boaz's skeptical look and shook his head. "No, hear me out. If the people sense that their Zar can't control his own women, what respect do you think they'll give the Crown? Your manner of ruling must begin with the harem.

"In truth, I like the way you're creating your own traditions, but it would be dangerous, my Zar, to allow anyone—and I include Salmeo and the Valide in this respectfully—too much familiarity with you. The harem is the true seat of your power. It's the secretiveness of it all that adds the luster to the names of the Zars of Percheron down the ages. The traditions, the structure, they must be protected at all costs, otherwise I feel you could be toppled from within." He could tell Boaz was paying attention now. "At least no real harm has been done and you have an entire harem of no doubt unbelievably beautiful girls to work your way through. I saw them as youngsters but the older ones would have matured this past year. Truly, such incredible choice. It is far better to spread your seed amongst them than to become too devoted to one so early, especially one so headstrong, my Zar."

Boaz looked crestfallen. "My father once said something quite similar to that. He said a wise Zar lay with as many in his harem as he could, and should have many, many sons so he could choose the perfect apprentice and the most suitable heir."

"The advice is sound. Lots of sons, Majesty. It not only keeps the women on their toes but the obvious advantage is that you can select the ideal candidate to give your precious crown to."

Boaz sighed. "Ana's execution is at dawn—it will be a private drowning, the harem way. I refuse to be present. Kett's will be at noon—a public ganching."

"That should bring a crowd running—we haven't had one of those in a while."

Boaz looked aggrieved. "Forgive me, Tariq, I have an appointment to keep," the Zar said abruptly, putting down his own goblet to end their meeting.

Maliz was surprised. "So late?"

"Er, yes."

"Must be someone important to keep a Zar from his bed," Maliz prodded

"I won't be doing much sleeping tonight, Tariq. I might as well keep working."

"Of course, of course. I did have a few things to discuss with you, my Zar, but all can wait for the morning."

"Good. Until then. Salazin will see you out." He gave the signal.

Outside the door Maliz signed to his spy: *I must know who he is seeing.*

Salazin nodded, signing urgently: *What about the priestess? You said you were going to see her.*

She will trouble me no more, the demon signed back.

And Salazin smiled tightly.

ON HIS RETURN TO Boaz's chambers, the Zar sent Salazin to the main gate.

"There should be a hooded figure waiting for you," was all the Zar signed "and he will be carrying a parchment with my seal that permits him entry up to my chambers."

He found the visitor as his Zar had instructed, but despite all the royal arrangements, four of the Elim searched the man before escorting him to the Zar's wing of the palace. Outside his suite, the Elim broke away and left Lazar with the four fearsome-looking mutes.

Pez came skipping down the corridor to meet him.

"These are interesting fellows," Lazar murmured.

"Vizier's orders," Pez muttered back before breaking into a song about crocodiles eating the royal barges.

Bin met them. He bowed as he did to all visitors. "The Zar has asked me to admit you upon presentation of his seal"—he eyed the hooded figure with unabashed curiosity—"although this is most unusual."

Lazar said nothing, held out the small piece of thick parchment that carried the Zar's seal, the uniqueness of the wax indisputable.

"Thank you. Please wait a moment." Bin knocked before disappearing into the room, with Salazin hot on his heels. Pez was flapping his arms as if trying to fly and spouting a new rhyme about elephant droppings.

Bin emerged and gestured to Lazar to come forward. "You may enter." At Pez's movement to also join the visitor, Bin objected. "Er, Pez, don't you think . . ."

"No, no, don't touch me," Pez shrieked. "The Zar is my friend. I need pomegranates, and he's got them all!"

Bin stepped back. He didn't want to provoke a repeat of Pez's last screaming performance. He looked at the visitor, embarrassed. Lazar shrugged as if to say it mattered not to him, and so Pez, clutching the stranger's robes, danced into the Zar's chambers, sticking out his tongue at the astonished secretary.

Inside, Bin apologized to his Zar as Pez hopped around the room, sniffing loudly and calling for hidden pomegranates.

"He can stay," Boaz said, his eyes on the bowing visitor, who was hidden from head to toe by the jamoosh.

"Can I serve refreshments, Majesty?"

"No. I want privacy now. We require nothing farther."

The servant looked disappointed. "Thank you, Highness," Bin said, bowing and backing out of the chamber.

There was a moment's awkward pause after the door closed. Pez damped down his noise to a soft humming.

The hooded figure inclined his head toward Salazin. "A new friend, my Zar?"

Boaz smiled slightly. It felt like a comforting warmth to hear that familiar, albeit sarcastic voice again. "This is Salazin; he's a mute. One of the new retinue of bodyguards the Grand Vizier insists upon. He can neither speak nor hear. We three are alone, in effect."

Lazar pulled off the jamoosh and Boaz, preparing to embrace the man, stepped back, shocked. "Your hair!" was all he could stammer.

"After all that's happened, my Zar, I thought I should be completely honest with you."

"What does this mean?"

"This is my true coloring."

"And the beard?"

Lazar shrugged. "In case I needed a disguise."

"I see. Anything else I should know?" Boaz asked, still stunned both by having Lazar before him and by Lazar's dramatic appearance.

"One more thing. I am not from Merlinea. I am a Galinsean."

Another shock. "Galinsean! But—"

Lazar, ever impatient, interrupted. "Everything I apparently stand against, yes, Majesty. Forgive me and my past deception. It is a long story and the lie I told so many years ago was for protection—both Percheron's and mine. I was young, cautious. And then after your father's generosity, I didn't want to let him down, and because I gave my heart to Percheron, the lie never felt dangerous. I have never been a threat to this realm—never once since stepping foot into your city have I given anything but profound loyalty to the Percherese Crown. Nothing has changed since the attempt on my life . . . other than my hair color."

Boaz stared at the proud golden-haired man who stood before him—Lazar, yes, but not Lazar. This man looked older, leaner. His eyebrows were lighter and he had allowed a soft beard to grow; and the hair color, once so at odds with his light eyes, now fit perfectly.

"I am no enemy, Highness." Lazar bent to one knee, pressing his point.

Boaz was moved. "I will hear that long story from you one day, Lazar, but right now let us drop the formality. You have been returned from the dead and I am grateful to Zarab for granting such a gift."

He didn't notice Pez wince. Lazar stood and Boaz moved forward, gripping him at the top of each arm. "I can't believe it's you, Lazar," he said, beaming. "Welcome back." And then the Zar of Percheron hugged his old friend briefly before adding, "My mother will be delighted."

Lazar shot him a look before all three men in the room, bar the mute, laughed. "Amazing what a year does," Lazar said. "You are a composed young man, Boaz. Boyhood has left you and you have your father's wit."

"I'll accept that as a compliment. You will, of course, accept back your old position as Spur? I never filled it, you know . . . something beyond grief prevented me from doing so."

Lazar glanced toward Pez. "I wouldn't presume—" he began.

Boaz waved away Lazar's humility. "Nonsense! Galinsean or not, I have no doubt of your loyalty. Although perhaps you should dye your hair again, especially as you're the one who has helped put the fear of the Galinseans amongst us." He grinned at Lazar.

Lazar considered, then smiled back. "I accept."

"You had no choice," Boaz said. Though he spoke lightly, no one in the room disbelieved him.

"I think Galinsea and possible invasion is something we must now really fear, Boaz," Lazar said, dropping all formality and amusement, a new edge to his tone.

Boaz looked momentarily quizzical and then he understood, his quick mind grasping what had upset the balance. "Jumo?"

Lazar nodded.

"But surely your family, however distressed or enraged by the news, cannot move the whole of Galinsea to war?" There was a thick silence as Boaz looked from Lazar and then to Pez but received no answer. "Or maybe they can," he finally said, unable to hide his surprise.

"I'm afraid so," Lazar replied sheepishly. "You could say they are influential."

Pez cleared his throat and Boaz caught the look he threw Lazar.

Lazar ignored the gesture. "The point is, we need to be very cautious. We have to step up training for the Shield and I believe we need to put it on alert. All the plans we've had in place are no longer hypothetical. This is serious. The Shield needs to understand that war could be imminent."

Boaz raised his eyebrows, astounded. "Lazar, who in Zarab's name are your parents?"

Lazar hesitated. "I am of noble birth, Highness. Suffice to say they have the ear of the king."

"And he's looking for an excuse to come against Percheron," Boaz muttered. He sighed. "All the more reason for you to take up your role as Spur again as quickly as possible."

"Can we keep my reemergence quiet for the time being?"

"Hardly," Boaz said, and meant it.

"A few hours perhaps?" Pez offered.

The Zar considered the compromise and nodded. "At most. Let's use that time to hear about everything that's happened since the last moment I saw you." He saw the swift pain cross Lazar's face and added softly, earnestly, "Lazar, if I'd known the trouble you were in, I would have put the whole medical fraternity at your feet. You were hidden very effectively from us and then I was informed—reliably, I thought—that you were dead and already given to the sea. It was all so convincing, so hopeless. I wouldn't wish the torture you endured on anyone." He paused. "You understand, of course, Ana's punishment could not be escaped."

"You know I do." Lazar's eyes narrowed. "I am informed you have formally chosen Ana." He said it flatly. It was not a question, simply a statement, and it held neither censure nor approval.

Boaz gave a wry shrug. "For whatever good that has done me," he answered, trying to keep the hurt from his voice. "Yes, I have formally chosen her. She is not just the most exquisite woman in the harem but also the most engaging to me personally. The other girls are too giggly, too excitable for my taste—they are still young, I suppose, and nervous. Ana is different. She has the ability to make me feel every inch the Zar whilst somehow never being subservient . . . not even when she's prostrate, giving her obeisance." He shook his head in bewilderment and then grinned sadly as he made an attempt to lighten his speech. "A skill she has no doubt learned from you, Lazar." It won him no amusement. "I want to be in her company all the time but it seems I am to be denied."

He shook his head with wonder, imagined what his father might have visited on a woman who spoke to him the way Ana had. Although he had many of his father's characteristics, he had refused to reduce himself by striking her, even if she had deserved another blow for her insolence, even if he hated her for forcing him into that position. But he had also had to quell the equally strong feeling of sickness he felt at losing her.

Through it all he admired her. Admired her dauntless attitude and her ability to trust the spirit of her own convictions. She was a match for him all right, but perhaps too much of one? Now he would never know. He had taken it for granted that Ana would be his wife, his Favorite; he had envisaged many nights of pleasure as well as stimulating conversation stretching before him. He could never have foreseen that he would be required to sentence her to death.

Boaz swallowed—he had had absolutely no choice, had been forced to exert his status. He had never felt this empty and he knew now he would never love another woman as he had this one, nor permit himself to.

He saw the lips of the Spur thin as an expression of anger—or was it fear?—took hold. "Why are you to be denied, my Zar?" Lazar asked evenly.

"I'm sorry for both of you that you have to hear this now when we should be celebrating your return to the palace," Boaz said. He eyed them both before continuing. "Odalisque Ana is to be executed in a few hours."

16

The ship had glided near the twin giants, announcing itself with torches rather than horns. Had Lazar and Pez been rowing from Star Island just a little later, they would have seen her. She was now anchored at the mouth of the Bay of Percheron, her timbers creaking as they gently rocked on the calm waters lapping at Ezram's feet. The night itself was no longer calm, however; soldiers of the Percherese Guard lined the shore and more arrived as each minute passed.

A flotilla of smaller craft carrying armed men bobbed silently in the bay itself. The men watched one of their senior officers board the foreign vessel, all silently wishing they had their Spur to lead them in what felt like a prelude to something infinitely more dangerous to their city.

The senior officer, also wishing Spur Lazar were handling this meeting instead of him, cleared his throat and announced himself to the two somberly dressed but nonetheless elegant men who received him.

"I am Captain Ghassal of the Shield." He gave a clipped bow of courtesy but said no more, his mind racing as to why a Galinsean ship—that much was obvious by the flags and the crests of the Crown of Galinsea—was in the Faranel. Close behind that was the question of how many ships of war were arriving behind it. Behind him he knew his men were going through the drills they had practiced over and over under Lazar's command, none of them at the time truly believing it would ever come to this. Attack had been promised for so long—for centuries—that the threat seemed no longer real and yet here it was standing before him. He swallowed hard and hoped the two men—who in all truth did not look like soldiers, more like dignitaries—did not notice his nervous gesture.

The elder of the two had white hair clipped back behind his head. He was clean-shaven, with a flinty gaze. His companion was still golden-haired but he, too, was whitening at the temples. They both looked to be in their sixth decade.

The elder spoke in a halting version of Percherese, his pronunciation squashing the light, almost musical language into something hard and guttural. "Captain Ghassal, we wish not to startle. I be Marius D'Argenny and he be Lorto Belsher." They bowed deeply.

"Galinseans?" the captain asked, still incredulous enough to offer the obvious question, but glad his voice was steady.

The men nodded. "We cannot speak no more language. Need interpreter," Marius explained with great care. Then he gestured with his arms to suggest that they were not an immediate threat. "Sailors," he added, pointing to the men. "No fighting man." Then he waved the Percherese soldiers to come aboard. Captain Ghassal understood this to mean that they were free to inspect the ship.

"Forgive my bluntness, brothers, but why are you here?"

Marius frowned. "Messengers. Interpreter, I beg. Zar must speak."

It didn't matter that they could no more understand his language than he could theirs. Ghassal reacted as if they would grasp his words with the greatest of ease. "Are you mad? Do you really believe I'm going to let you anywhere near the palace?"

Marius and Lorto put their hands up in confused submission. "Interpreter," Marius implored once again whilst his companion encouraged Ghassal's men to search everyone and the ship.

The captain looked around, exasperated. They could keep this up all night and still be no further by dawn. He considered the two men. It was obvious that, with so few sailors, they were not in a position to be of any threat. How would Spur Lazar have handled this? Lazar always encouraged his senior men to trust their instincts. *Your gut will tell you more than the naked eye*, he used to say. *Listen to it*. Captain Ghassal listened to what his instincts told him, and decided he could not risk the Crown's wrath should he send these messengers on their way without at least informing the Grand Vizier. They could, after all, be making a visit that might benefit both realms. He was a soldier, not a diplomat, and could not make political decisions. He would leave it up to the Grand Vizier to make the final choice on whether or not to involve the Zar—let the blame rest with the Tariq. Ghassal signaled for his own men to board the ship. "You will not mind if we take up your offer to search the vessel?"

It was obvious what he was saying; even though they did not

understand the words, they grasped their meaning, gesturing for the soldiers to freely search.

"Us?" It was the first time that Lorto had spoken as he pointed to himself and Marius.

Ghassal held up a hand. "You wait here," he said, pointing to the deck of the ship.

They understood and nodded their thanks.

He sent a runner to summon Grand Vizier Tariq in the hope that he might know someone who understood Galinsean.

A STORM WAS GATHERING within Lazar. The shock of the Zar's news had sunk in and he now felt numb. He knew that he was losing control. A whole year's worth of rage was coalescing into something hard and dangerous. He had to get out of the Zar's chambers before he self-destructed or did something regrettable.

He had hardly heard a word either Pez or Boaz was saying; he knew they were talking to him, at him, but he had turned inward, trying to wrest back control of the angry creature within. With a mighty effort he focused on the Zar, who was actually shaking him by the shoulders. As Lazar looked at him Boaz let go, as if he'd been seared.

"Lazar, please, say something."

The Spur shook his head to clear the flashes of light, the visions of Ana, the sensations of his back being stripped open and poison surging through his body, the memory of endless nights of fevered delirium and days of only near consciousness. Lies, treachery, betrayal. He thought of poor Jumo and then remembered Pez's sickening story of how Zafira had died impaled on her own temple's spire. And he thought of Ana facing her own death.

And amongst the images and the terror, he heard a stranger's voice, then two voices, then a dozen voices all calling to him, all saying the same thing. They whispered but he could not hear them above the roar of his own blood and the crowding noise, like thunder, that came with his memories.

"Lazar!" It was Pez stepping into view, slapping his face.

Release us, the voices whispered.

And then they were gone. Everything was silent, save the thump of his own heartbeat in his chest.

He looked about him. He was seated, must have stumbled to a chair at some point, and Pez was at eye level.

"Are you all right?" the dwarf asked tentatively.

Lazar could only nod. He rubbed his face, gathered his wits. This was not an auspicious beginning for his role as reinstated Spur.

"Can I get you something, Lazar?" Boaz asked, his voice heavy with concern. "I know you're upset. Perhaps some wine or even something stronger, a shot of terimla?"

"No. I shall be fine. Forgive me my behavior. The news is a true shock. I—"

Whatever he was going to say was interrupted by a frantic knock at the door.

Immediately Pez reached for the jamoosh that had been cast aside earlier and handed it to Lazar, who moved swiftly to cover himself.

"Wait," Boaz said, moving to the door. He opened it slightly and Pez and Lazar listened to him take a very brief message before he held up his hand. "Give me a moment, Bin." He closed the door and turned back to them. "There's something going on at the harbor and the Grand Vizier is apparently on his way to speak to me. It sounds urgent."

"I shall leave, Highness," Lazar said. "And go to my house, but I shall return in an hour or so, if you'll permit. I need to see Ana."

Boaz sighed. "She can see no one, my friend," and his voice was firm enough to brook no argument, despite Lazar's glower. "However, please do return. Salazin will take you through my private chambers so you can leave without being seen."

He signaled to the mute. Nothing further was said. Lazar and Pez removed themselves hurriedly behind Salazin.

GRAND VIZIER TARIQ WAS shown into the Zar's salon, and considering the buzz that Boaz could feel emanating even from his servants, the Vizier looked surprisingly unfazed.

"What is this all about, Tariq?"

"Majesty, please forgive us this interruption at such a late hour."

"I presume it is of vital importance to disturb me?"

"It is, Highness. Quite vital indeed. A Galinsean ship is presently anchored in the shallow waters just outside our harbor. On board a Marius D'Argenny and his companion, Lorto Belsher, await your approval for an audience. Neither speaks Percherese beyond a few words and no one speaks Galinsean other than you, Highness. I think we have no choice but to bring the two dignitaries to the palace."

Boaz felt his heart skip. A Galinsean ship! "Just one ship? What do they want?"

"Your guess is as good as mine, my Zar. Captain Ghassal believes them to be messengers. The ship has been thoroughly searched and the only oddity we turned up was a strange fellow who claims to be your former Spur's friend and once manservant."

"Jumo?" Boaz asked, hardly believing the coincidence.

"Yes, I believe that's what he called himself."

"Bring them before me."

As the Vizier departed to make arrangements, Boaz turned to Salazin and signed that he was to personally fetch the man who had been here earlier. And to return him quickly to the palace but through the back entrances, using the same seal of authority for any guards who questioned him.

BOAZ MET THE GALINSEAN representatives in his Throne Room, a vast and magnificent chamber with an impressively tiled ceiling of crimson and deepest blue. As this room was one of the highest points of the palace, soaring windows on either side provided a near-panoramic view of the city below and onto the bay where the torches, still burning on the foreign vessel, outlined its presence just outside the harbor.

A gentle lightening in the sky from ink to charcoal and a bright pink slash visible through the eastern bank of windows told Boaz that morning was almost upon them. His belly twisted with the knowledge that Ana would already have been woken for her dawn death. He imagined, as he waited for the Galinseans to be shown in, that she would probably be saying some prayers. She would refuse food or water. She would wear something simple, neutral, and she would no doubt look stunning all the same as she prepared to be consumed by the waters that ran into the Faranel.

He had cast aside sorrow over her death. It was a useless emotion considering her apparent determination to go to that dark place. And having listened to the Vizier's wise words, Boaz had realized that no matter how many times she might be saved, Ana would always find a new way to bring the wrath of the harem upon her shoulders. She did not fit here. Perhaps the drowning was a kindness to her—as she would no longer suffer, no longer have to struggle against Salmeo or Herezah, or find new ways to cope with her frustrations. He began to wish the news of her successful drowning would come.

Then he, too, could get on with finding new mates, siring heirs, and forgetting about the woman who surprised and delighted him so much. She had his heart but he knew he didn't have hers. So for this, too, he could let her go, could turn to the remainder of the harem for affection—even if it was contrived and came from women too scared to deny him or too cunning not to appreciate what it could earn them.

Real love was too painful, he decided. Better to be like his parents—making a great match in mind, in bodies, in what they could both achieve. Love was immaterial. Respect, pleasure in each other, and friendship were more enjoyable, surely, than the heartache of loving someone.

A gong sounded, bringing him out of his moody thoughts and back to the Throne Room, where the Galinseans were about to be presented. Despite its size, the room felt crowded. Soldiers, Elim, and Boaz's mute bodyguard were in maximum attendance—there was no question that the Zar of Percheron was well protected.

The two dignitaries were announced by the Grand Vizier and were flanked by a small company of Shield men, led by the Grand Vizier.

Boaz weighed up the two Galinsean men. As the Vizier had explained, they certainly did not look dangerous, and having recovered from the shock of seeing Lazar with his true light coloring, he could now see the likeness that must exist among all Galinseans. Apart from Lazar, these were the first men of the western realm he had seen.

Both men knelt without being asked or told. They touched hand to forehead, lips, and heart in the region's way of welcome and salutation. They spoke their thanks together in their halting Percherese.

Boaz responded stiffly with a welcome in Galinsean, and asked them to raise themselves, glad to note he got his tongue around the hard accent. As the men straightened he noticed quickly a look of stifled amusement on the face of the younger of the two.

Setting his jaw firm, again forming the words as accurately as he could, Boaz asked them their business. They did not smile this time but they looked puzzled.

In Percherese, the man known as Marius shrugged gently, "Forgive. No understand."

Boaz seethed. His Galinsean was hardly fluent but he thought he was capable of conversation—and certainly of making himself understood. He would not leave himself open to ridicule, especially with such a large audience.

"Fetch my tutor!" he ordered Tariq.

Everyone waited for an uncomfortable and protracted period whilst the sleepy man was dragged from his bed and summoned to the Throne Room. Soldiers brought him bowing and cringing into the room, disheveled and terrified.

"Don't be frightened, Rustaf. I want you to ask these men, please, in Galinsean, what their business is in our city."

Rustaf looked even more terrified, his eyes darting between the Zar and the foreigners.

Boaz nodded for him to proceed. Carefully, Rustaf spoke several words in Galinsean.

Again Marius answered, but this time in Galinsean, explaining something that Rustaf now looked baffled by.

"Well?" Boaz demanded.

"Majesty"—Rustaf quailed—"I do not understand their Galinsean. I can get odd words but no real meaning. From what he said, I think we're both speaking a foreign version of the language to each other."

"You mean I've been learning Galinsean for all these years and can't make myself understood?"

Rustaf bowed. "Highness. I have taught you only what I myself was taught. I fear perhaps our library has only the Old Galinsean. We do not speak the colloquial form, not even the high court form, perhaps. Please forgive me but we have no experience of conversing directly with Galinseans."

Boaz growled his displeasure and stood angrily. "Grand Vizier, did you not tell me that Jumo was on that ship?"

"Yes, my Zar. He is waiting outside."

"Bring him in."

SALAZIN KNOCKED AT THE door of Lazar's house and was surprised to have it answered by the owner himself. Inwardly rueful, he realized that the man had been officially dead for a year, so there would be no reason for him to have servants at the ready.

Lazar frowned. "What are you doing back here?" Then he shook his head, clearly berating himself for asking a deaf and dumb person a question. Opening the door farther, he called to Pez. "Salazin has returned."

Salazin's eyebrows lifted to see the dwarf waddling out to greet him—as far as he knew, Pez had been left at the palace when he had escorted Lazar back to his house earlier. It wasn't necessary to walk with the Spur all the way, but Salazin had wanted to see where he lived in case he needed to return one day.

Pez looked equally quizzically at him. "Razeen? What are you doing here?"

Salazin hesitated, his dark gaze darting toward the Spur.

"Razeen, Spur Lazar is one of us. He is one of Lyana's followers and he is, to put it graphically, up to his very arse in the same pursuit as us." Pez's expression softened at seeing the flicker of a grin in the mute's face. "I promise, you may speak freely before him."

Lazar looked all but offended. "Speak? I thought this man was a mute! And why are you calling him Razeen? The Zar introduced him as Salazin."

Pez sighed. "Long story, Lazar. Just listen. This must be important."

Razeen, known as Salazin in the palace, bowed to the Spur. "I have come to fetch you again for the Zar." His voice sounded scratchy from lack of use. He cleared his throat. "Two Galinsean dignitaries have arrived aboard a vessel that is anchored off our harbor. No one can understand them and their Percherese is sorely limited. The Vizier has organized to bring them to the palace in the hope that our Zar will be able to converse with them."

"Galinseans? Is it a war vessel?" Lazar looked stunned, the surprise of the mute speaking already forgotten in the wake of this alarming news.

"No, Spur, I don't believe so. I've gathered it is a ship of peace."

Lazar grunted. "No such thing in the Galinsean fleet. You can tell me your long story on the way back, Pez; let's go. There isn't much time before dawn."

"I've told you, you cannot interfere."

"And you think that will stop me, dwarf?"

The odd trio, one short, one masquerading as a mute, and the other fully covered in a jamoosh, ran out of the house, bound for the palace.

17

Elza raised a small handheld mirror to Ana's face. Ana didn't even bother to glance into it. "What does it matter," she said softly, "how I am clothed or my hair is dressed? All will be ruined shortly."

"Even in death you will be beautiful."

"Leave me, Elza," Ana said abruptly. "I am ready. I await my summons."

Once alone, she said a prayer to Lyana to watch over her father and siblings, to protect Pez in his secrecy, and to give Kett strength to face his death as she now faced hers. She begged forgiveness of her Goddess for Kett's suffering once again and also for not fulfilling what she was perhaps born to do. And surely if she were Lyana's incarnation—she would have more internal clues? Pez had had more than enough indication that he was a disciple of Lyana. But she? All the early doubts came into sharp focus for her in this quiet hour as she faced her death. If she was Lyana, then she was failing her followers before she'd even had a chance to do anything positive for their faith. What good was she as an embodiment of the Goddess?

Yes, there was that curiosity with Ellyana in the bazaar over the statue of Iridor, and then being able to communicate with Pez through a mind link, but there had to be a mistake. If she was Lyana, she would not be in this position. No. As much as Pez urged her to believe, Ana secretly held that it was Pez's desire rather than truth. He wanted her to be something special. Wanted her to be part of this strange battle he was part of. She, unfortunately for him, knew in her heart that she was nothing more than a goatherd's daughter who had consistently let down those who trusted and loved her. Death was a release from the responsibility of having to try again.

She spared a thought for Boaz, who must still be struggling with his decision. Ana knew her fate was best for him. He wanted something from her she could never give. Love was beyond them. Her heart was no longer hers to present to any but the man who had owned it for more than a year. And now finally her thoughts turned to Lazar and her mood found the darkness she needed where he was concerned. Ana, now aware that Lazar lived, allowed the betrayal that the knowledge brought to give her the courage to face this death with gladness.

He must hate her very much for causing the whipping that brought about this terrible lie, feigning his death, tricking all who relied upon him, and through his actions ridiculing the love she held for him. Again she reminded herself that it was but a one-sided love. He had never behaved in any manner other than formal and correct toward her; he had never sought anything from her and he had deliberately kept her at arm's length. The fault was hers, she berated herself. She wanted his love and so she had convinced herself that he felt the same way. It was delusion to have ever thought that he had taken such a punishment because he loved her. He was noble and honorable—that's why he took her flogging. Another Stone of Percheron—isn't that what everyone said of him? Cold, remote, incapable of love?

She tried to blot him from her mind, as now her tears were flowing freely. But her thoughts were treacherous. One minute they assured her he had no feelings for her, other than those of duty, and the next they were giving her the memory of him calling out her name as he suffered at the end of the Viper.

Try as she might, she could not deny that he had spoken it in agony. But there had been such passion, too, such yearning. And she also could not forget the way he looked at her just before the suffering had begun—his gaze searing through the veils that hid her own eyes as if searching for her lips to see her speak his name in response and in love.

Ana wept. She didn't need to be drowned to be killed. She was well and truly destroying herself on the harem's behalf. Now she no longer knew what to believe. Finally, as she steadied herself with the notion that death was within her reach—and thus escape from everything she despised—it mattered not how she viewed Lazar. In the end she allowed herself the small comfort that she had not misread the Spur. He had called out her name on the day of the flogging; that was how he had bid her farewell and he had done so with love. She would take that to the bottom of the river as her dying thought.

She heard a sound behind her and turned. Shadowed in the doorway was the unmistakable shape of the Grand Master Eunuch.

"Ah, sweet child, and so you finally shed those tears," he lisped. His swathes of ruffled silks made a rich sound as he stepped into the pit, light of toe and bringing with him the un-mistakable fragrance of violets. "It is near dawn, child, and time to go to your gods . . . or goddess, if you please." He giggled like one of the young girls in the harem at his supposed jest.

"Who will be in attendance?" she asked, drying her face with her hands hurriedly, not wanting Salmeo to see any further grief from her.

He tutted. "Surely you don't want an audience?"

"No. That's why I ask. I am hoping no one is there."

"We need witnesses, Ana, to sign your death statement."

"Who? Not the Zar?"

He smiled cruelly. "You flatter yourself, child. No, myself and the Valide will be doing the honors—if that makes any difference to you?"

"That is suitable," she said, and then said no more, leaving him to work out precisely what she meant by it.

"You look very beautiful, almost ethereal, and very fittingly so on this ghostly dawn. Wait until you see it, child."

"Why do you say that?"

"Oh, you'll see soon enough. The boatman and executioner await you, Ana, my dear. Do you need another moment to say a final prayer?"

"No. I'm ready."

"Good." He signaled to someone outside. A member of the Elim entered. "Bind her."

"Salmeo," Ana said.

"Yes?"

"Tell me how Kett is?"

"Oh, not nearly as brave as you, child. But I do have some good news for him. He will not be ganched as originally commanded by the Zar. He is to be drowned."

"How come?" she asked, secretly pleased.

"Something to do with dignataries arriving unannounced. The Zar does not want the palace gates to be crowded by eager onlookers at an execution. I have no further details, only an order from our Zar that Kett's sentence is to be changed to drowning."

"Why not drown us both together?" she asked fiercely.

"Perhaps," he said. "It's certainly a warm morning and I'm not sure I could face the discomfort of standing in the hot sun later and listening to Kett's dread wails." And he laughed. "Now come, child. I know those shackles are tricky to maneuver but I'm sure you'd rather walk to your place of death than be carried."

JUMO BOWED SOLEMNLY TO Boaz. As with Lazar, the man looked as if he'd aged since Boaz had last seen him. He found a sad smile for the loyal servant.

"Jumo, welcome back. I have some news to share later," he said cryptically, unable to announce it so publicly yet. "But for now I must ask you if you can help us at all with our Galinsean visitors that we cannot communicate ably with."

"They are here, Majesty, because of what I had tried very hard to share. That Lazar had died."

Boaz assumed as much. "I see. And did they understand you?"

Marius and Lorto watched the exchange with studied interest, frowning as they tried to grasp one word in five or six as the Percherese spoke their fast, fluid, and elegant language.

"I'm afraid they did. There were a lot of gestures and hand waving, pointing, and frustration. It took me a whole day of difficult explanation to get some semblance of the news across to them."

"Thank you. Can you explain, then, why they are here?"

Jumo looked at his Zar with an expression of disbelief. "To hear it from your mouth, Majesty, that you did execute the favorite son of Galinsea." He said this in innocence, unaware that the Zar did not already know the truth of Lazar's heritage.

A murmur went up around the room and the Zar glared, his eyes roving past soldiers and Elim alike. He couldn't blame them, however. This news that Lazar was a favorite of Galinsea was a shock. All but he still assumed the man was of Merlinea.

"And then what?"

Jumo looked appropriately embarrassed that he had to answer this. "The obvious, Majesty," he began, but his eyes shifted as he spoke—a mute had entered from behind.

Boaz noticed him, too, and signaled him to come forward. "Carry on, Jumo," he urged as the mute signed a well-disguised message to him.

Maliz, also watching these proceedings with great interest—albeit detached—as though he were participating in a piece of high drama, felt a spike of frustration that he couldn't make out what was being exchanged between the Zar and the mute. Salazin was being deliberately careful, which was odd—he'd have expected the mute to be deliberately careless so that he, the Vizier, could easily make out the conversation. He did not let that frustration show on his calm expression, however, as everyone heard Jumo finish what he'd begun.

"... considering the weight of offense, Majesty, I would hazard they will declare war."

Now a fresh murmuring erupted.

"They've come here masquerading as peacemakers but in truth to declare war?" Boaz asked, his tone incredulous. Neither of the visitors looked in the least bit fearful for their own lives, which could so easily be taken from them at a single command from the Zar. He gave a final signal to Salazin, who moved toward the door behind the Zar. "Silence," he called to those still reacting to the mention of war.

Jumo cleared his throat. "Highness, I cannot know for sure because I, too, am at the same disadvantage with language, but in light of who Lazar was," he said carefully, "I can appreciate their need to seek the truth. This is not a declaration of war yet. From what I can tell, these men from the Galinsean palace hierarchy have been sent on a mission to establish the facts."

"But how did they think they would with the language barrier?"

"That is my fault, Majesty. I conveyed somehow that you were fluent in Galinsean." Jumo looked suddenly mortified that he'd insulted the Zar.

Boaz rescued him. "Fret not, I have been taught a more ancient tongue of the Galinseans," he said generously. "It seems their language has long since evolved."

The Grand Vizier stepped forward, clearly tired of the talk and keen for some action. "Your Highness, how may we solve this issue? Frankly, if these men are here to declare war, I say we execute them now and send their ship into open waters, all crew dead and the vessel torched. Let that be our message to the Galinsean pigs who covet our realm."

"Nothing too inflammatory, then, Tariq? Diplomacy at its most subtle."

Maliz appeared unfazed by the sarcasm at his expense. "A declaration of war needs to be met head on, Zar Boaz."

The Zar's eyes narrowed. It was the first time in a year that he had felt himself out of step with his chief counselor. The man seemed eager for the realms to clash and he also appeared too casual about something so critical. It was almost as though he were enjoying everyone's angst—did it not matter to him? Surely the Vizier wanted to prevent war coming to peaceful Percheron? He didn't have time to ponder the Grand Vizier's strange reaction now, but he was not going to allow his realm to go to war simply because it felt threatened or needed to save face. Of course, no one but Pez could know he had the ultimate answer to their problem; he thanked his god again that Lazar had been returned from the dead and for his perfect timing in returning. "I am not a warmonger, Grand Vizier. Let me show you how I will resolve this issue—without it escalating into bloodshed."

Boaz raised a hand and silence fell heavily across the room as a door behind him opened and a tall, golden-haired man strode into the Throne Room. Boaz did not turn to greet the man or accept his low bow.

"Your Highness," the man said. Boaz kept his gaze on Jumo, taking secret delight in watching the former servant's eyes widen in shock and his mouth gape.

The Vizier looked quizzical, the soldiers hesitant, unsure of what this stranger's arrival meant. Pez danced in from another entrance, but even his antics could not sustain a lengthy distraction from Lazar, who had everyone's attention but looked uncomfortable with it as he approached the visitors at a nod from the Zar.

Jumo was now trembling in disbelief, though no one but the Zar noticed. Boaz smiled as the teary man reached for Lazar as he passed, as though Jumo needed to reassure himself through touch that he was real. A look from Lazar obviously communicated that their reunion must wait.

"Marius," Lazar said, holding out his hand. He looked and nodded at Lorto. "We have not met," he said to the younger man, "but welcome to Percheron, my home for the last sixteen years or so and to its Stone Palace."

The familiar sound of that voice was resonating within the minds of the uncertain soldiers; even the senior members of the Elim were shaking their heads with disbelief now. But more shocking to everyone in the room was that the old man, Marius D'Argenny, fell to his knees before Lazar.

"Lucien, Majesty." The diplomat kissed Lazar's feet in the Galinsean way of greeting royalty.

"Majesty?" Boaz repeated, on his feet now, perturbed.

Lazar bowed to Boaz and quickly spoke a few guttural words to the two now kneeling men, their heads touching the ground at his feet. "Zar Boaz, please forgive this untimely show." His voice was now clearly recognized by his soldiers, whose once solemn expressions were replaced with looks of relief mixed with disbelief.

"Shield!" Lazar spoke into the increasing noise. "This is your Spur commanding you to return to your barracks and posts. I shall speak with the men as one soon. Go now." His voice softened in acknowledgment of their obvious joy. "Please," he added. "All will be explained."

They hushed instantly at the command of their Spur, quietly filing out of the Throne Room; their presence was no longer required. Spur Lazar could single-handedly protect their ruler.

"Elim. You may return to your quarters, too," Boaz echoed, keen to clear the room and have a more private discussion. He wasn't exactly sure what was going on but he sensed that it would be best to expose as few people as possible to it.

The men in red followed the soldiers, leaving behind the bowed visitors, a shaken Jumo, the Grand Vizier, clearly baffled, silent Salazin, and Pez, who was walking around the rim of the room on his hands, making noises like a duck.

Boaz spoke calmly. "Tariq, in case you haven't guessed, may I reintroduce you to Lazar, who has returned to us from the dead and was reinstated an hour or so ago as our Spur."

If the Grand Vizier was surprised he didn't show it. "Ah, the late-night visitor. Spur Lazar, welcome back. That was something of a theatrical entrance, I must say, and my, how you have changed."

Lazar looked at the shrouded eyes of the Grand Vizier. "I could accuse you of similar change, Tariq. You look very well, very rejuvenated," the Spur replied.

Boaz interrupted whatever his Vizier was going to say in response. "Lazar, will you explain why these men are paying such homage, why they called you Majesty?"

Lazar glanced toward Jumo as Pez also ceased his duck noises. "Your Highness, may these men stand, please?"

Boaz nodded and Lazar spoke quickly in Galinsean. Both men moved slowly to their feet, looking at Lazar with a quiet awe that was not missed by the Zar and served to further frustrate him. "Well?" he prompted.

"Zar Boaz, this is very difficult for me to reveal to you. It is something I kept from your father . . . rightly at the time we met, I thought. But maybe it was wrong of me to perpetuate the secret for so many years."

Boaz frowned. "Secret? What secret?"

"My true identity, Highness."

Boaz was catching on. "Is Percheron in genuine danger?"

"It was."

"Your parents are not Merlinean. They are not even just straightforward Galinsean aristocracy, are they?" Boaz held his breath, his quick mind had guessed but he remained incredulous at what was about to be confirmed.

"No, my Zar. In this I have beguiled you and your father before you."

"Marius D'Argenny called you Lucien. Is this your true name?"

Lazar shrugged softly. "I took on my new persona many years ago. I was once Lucien. I am now Lazar."

Boaz felt soft flutters of panic within his belly but refused to let them take hold and fly. He reminded himself that he was the Chosen Son of Joreb; he would not let his father down. "And Lucien, I'm presuming, is one and the same son of the King of Galinsea."

"He is."

Boaz nodded, feeling the truth thump in his chest, send tendrils of fright through his gut. "How can this be?"

"It is a long story, Highness, as I warned earlier. But it is nothing to do with Percheron. Coming here was an accident—as you know, I was captured by Slaver Varen—not that I have regretted it. Well, perhaps recently . . ." He trailed off, sounding unsure.

Boaz was hardly listening. His mind was racing. "How bad is it, Lazar? I know my history but contemporary Galinsean politics is not my specialty. There are several sons in the royal family, am I right?"

Lazar nodded grimly. "I am one of three sons. I have a sister, too."

"But which son are you, Lazar?"

Now the Spur looked deeply abashed. "Firstborn, Highness."

Boaz closed his eyes momentarily to stem his rising alarm. "Galinsea believes we have executed the heir to its throne?"

"It seems so, by the presence of these dignitaries."

"Jumo, what in Zarab's name possessed you? Had I known precisely where and to whom you were headed, I would never have permitted it."

Jumo hung his head. "Having lost my master, Highness, and in the manner we lost him—through betrayal and treachery from within the palace—I no longer cared about anything. It seemed the right thing to do. I admit I wasn't thinking too clearly, in my grief. I had to get away from Percheron and I needed to somehow do more for my friend than I had." He stopped, embarrassed at such a long speech.

Boaz knew there was little point in arguing about what might have been. He returned his attention to his Spur. "Well, perhaps you could explain to them what actually occurred."

"Yes, Highness. Excuse me a moment."

The Zar and Vizier waited patiently as the Spur switched and spoke quickly in the guttural language of Percheron's traditional enemy. Questions were asked by the messengers and Lazar replied. Boaz could tell from the dignitaries' faces what they were learning as their expressions moved from interest to disdain, despair to dawning interest and finally puzzlement.

"What are they frowning at?" Boaz inquired.

Lazar looked uncomfortable again, flicking a glance toward Pez, who was miraculously quiet in the corner, smelling his shoes. "They wonder why my survival was kept a secret from you."

"Indeed."

"I have told them that it is as baffling to us as it is to them."

"You did tell them about Zafira? And that she has disappeared, so we cannot even ask her until she has been located?"

Boaz noticed how Lazar stiffened at the mention of Zafira; he caught how the Spur's gaze flicked briefly to the Grand Vizier in hesitation before he answered. "Not yet, Zar Boaz." It was a strange response, the Zar felt; hardly a comprehensive reply, with no explanation as to why he would withhold this information. Or why he seemed reluctant to speak freely.

"You knew the priestess?" Tariq interrupted whatever Boaz was about to say.

Lazar looked at the Grand Vizier with disdain, and deliberately gave Boaz the impression that the question seemed irrelevant to him. "I ran across her from time to time. In my line of work, you get to know most people in the city." He turned away.

Maliz persisted. "But how is she connected to you?"

"Yes, I'm sorry, Tariq, I'm only just realizing that you know none of this," Boaz broke in. "After the flogging Zafira cared for Lazar, but she told us—that is, Jumo and myself—that Lazar had died and that she had given him to the sea at his request."

"Why the priestess?" Tariq continued, his voice husky with keen interest.

Lazar shrugged. It was obvious to Boaz that the Spur didn't have a ready answer for Tariq's curious interrogation and appeared to be choosing his words with care. There was an undercurrent here that the Zar could not fathom, but he was sure Lazar was reluctant to explain more to the Grand Vizier.

"I took him to the temple," Jumo said into the silence. "Does it matter why now?" he asked, loading his question with disgust. "Lazar was dying. We needed somewhere peaceful, private. We went there in our misery. Is that wrong, Grand Vizier Tariq?"

Boaz watched his counselor instantly withdraw his curiosity, turn it around as if it were only a source of mild interest. "No, not at all. I just can't imagine why a man of Zarab would be taken to the place of the fallen goddess."

Again Tariq's odd answer gnawed at Boaz. Jumo was right, why did it matter where Lazar had been taken? What mattered were the lies that had followed. He took control of the conversation again. "Tariq, I want you to put your ear to the ground with all your networks and see if you can find out more about Zafira's disappearance." He noticed Lazar quickly hide a smirk. "You, too, Spur Lazar—use all the resources required to track her down. We cannot understand your situation fully until we have her explanation. The Galinseans deserve that."

As Lazar translated for the visitors, the Vizier asked, "And if we cannot locate her?"

"Well, we must find a new way to appease our aggressors."

"Zar Boaz?" Lazar cut in.

"Yes, Spur? Incidentally, is that how I should address you, or is there a formal title I should now accord you? Are you still our Spur or—"

"I am your Spur," Lazar said, cutting across the Zar's words.

Boaz paused, watching Lazar intently for any guile before he nodded. "All right, go on."

"This small delegation is not simply on a fact-finding tour. They require that a representative of the Percherese Crown travel to the capital and explain formally what has occurred . . ."

"Why?"

Lazar continued as if the Zar had not spoken. "With your assurance that I am alive."

Boaz sighed, aggrieved. "Can we not just send you in person, Lazar? I hate to lose you so soon after having you returned to us, but we are still presumably under the threat of war, until this is done. Am I right?"

"Yes, my Zar."

"However, your countrymen don't seem at all intimidated by being here. They obviously don't fear for their lives, so perhaps war is expected to be averted," Boaz noted.

"My father will carry out his threat if Marius and Lorto are not returned whole to Galinsea, together with your emissary."

"You are my emissary. Are you not proof enough?"

Lazar looked pained. "That's part of the long story, Highness. I cannot return to Galinsea with ease."

"But Jumo told us long ago you had talked about it only—"

"Talk is talk, Highness. I was considering taking a journey from Percheron—an extended one, yes—but whether I was going to return to Galinsea was questionable."

"Why? Is it dangerous for you to return there?"

"You could describe it that way. I have been formally banished."

"But you're the heir!" Boaz exclaimed, taking a step forward in his exasperation. "They've sent a delegation to learn of your fate. Zarab curse me, they're prepared to declare war over you."

"All true," Lazar replied, frowning uncomfortably. "But that doesn't mean they forgive, Highness."

Boaz pointed, realizing only belatedly that this was a habit of his father's when Joreb's ire was up. "Zarab save me, Lazar.

What could you do to your family that would have them pull in two such passionate directions?" he demanded, then added with incredulity, "They would slaughter a nation for you but not forgive you?"

Lazar remained calm in the face of the Zar's rising anger. "I'm afraid the King of Galinsea can be capricious, Highness. His Queen more so."

"I take it you mean potentially fatal?"

"Potentially. At the very least I would be thrown into the dungeons for the rest of my days. I am more useful here and my loyalties are to this Crown."

"Why, Lazar?"

It was as if a cloud passed through Lazar's thoughts, for Boaz saw his Spur's expression measurably darken as his eyes narrowed and he swallowed before answering his Zar. "I renounced the throne, Highness. The why of it seems irrelevant after so long."

Boaz shook his head. He briefly thought of the possibility of sending Ana, but she had no status and was now a condemned woman, about to die. Anyway, he didn't think her Galinsean was appropriate. "So I need an emissary. I can't send you and yet I have no one else, not even myself, who speaks Galinsean adequately to make themselves understood in that capricious court!"

It was only then that Boaz became aware of Pez dancing nearby, mimicking a woman's voice. He was talking nonsense but Boaz knew the dwarf's antics well enough to understand when his friend was conveying a message. Pez leaped onto the Zar's back, and although this startled everyone, the Percherese in the room all knew better than to react to anything the dwarf did, including this clownish behavior toward the royal.

"Go away, Pez, this is not the time," Boaz said, struggling to loosen the dwarf's grip.

"Trust me, she speaks contemporary courtly Galinsean fluently," Pez whispered before leaping down and moving away, breaking wind in time with each step, causing the Grand Vizier to snarl in disgust and the two visitors to look at each other uncomfortably.

"Forgive our palace clown," Boaz muttered, trying not to show that he was shaken by Pez's secret. Time was too short to dwell on it; Ana could already be dead. He composed himself. "Lazar, what about Ana? I understand that Ana can speak courtly Galinsean like she belongs in your palace."

Lazar didn't wait for permission. "Where?" he growled over the back of his shoulder, already running for the doors.

"The River Gate. Hurry! Second Bell marks the moment."

18

Salmeo was right. It was a curious morning, filled with foreboding. The Elim had prayed to Zarab as they escorted Ana behind the enormous eunuch to the region of the palace known as the River Gate. Ana, too, was entranced by the strange, eerie light this morning had brought.

She had never witnessed such a phenomenon and yet somewhere deep in her memories she knew—in the same strange way that she knew the names of the Stones of Percheron—that this was a rare eclipse when the moon shielded the sun, bringing an odd twilight to the day when it should be brightening to full morning.

The dark side of the moon seemed to mourn the proceedings and this interpretation was not lost on those gathered—Salmeo had to urge his Elim forward, to fight their fear of this sign from the heavens.

Ana smiled, convinced now that Lyana was soothing her,

showing Ana her command of all things natural. It was a genuine comfort and Ana took it to mean that Lyana would prevail in this battle. Zarab and his followers would not keep winning, would not continue destroying people's lives. A new era was dawning in Percheron, beginnning with Boaz but at a higher level with Lyana's triumph. Boaz would bring about the revolution in the palace that would filter through society and perhaps change Percherese life forever, whilst Lyana would restore the age of the priestess and harmony. Salmeo, Herezah, even Tariq, were primitive. Their time and traditions had passed. As these thoughts gave her courage, the sight of Kett gave her intense relief. He was here. They would die together, and quickly, Lyana in their hearts and peace in their minds.

LAZAR HAD NEVER RUN so hard in his life. He saw none of the people around the palace he encountered, didn't feel the stone walls he careened off or the toe he broke as he tripped. He ignored the burning in his lungs and the protest from his legs and the harsh breathing at his throat. Speed was all that mattered, speed alone would save Ana's life.

Coming behind him were Pez, whooping and screeching—a madman picking up on the lunacy around him—as well as the Zar, also moving swiftly but not so fast as to undermine his dignity. Jumo, who was not permitted freedom through the palace, was at Boaz's side, eager to break stride into a run. The Galinsean visitors had been left in the care of the Grand Vizier; they would be served refreshments as they waited, confused, in the Throne Room for the next update from the heir to their throne.

Lazar kept running. Damn the River Gate—the farthest point in the palace from the Throne Room. He knew once the Second Bell was sounded, Ana was as good as dead.

———

ANA STOOD, COMPOSED AND demure, in the gently rocking boat. Alongside her boat was a second, and in it, shaking with fear, was Kett and another Elim. Kett looked ghostly in the eerie light cast by the eclipse. Nearby, at the riverbank, on chairs brought especially for the occasion, sat the Valide and Salmeo. Standing yet farther away were the two Elim who had escorted Ana with Salmeo to her place of death. Not far from them, at a table sat a scribe, who served the harem. Witnesses aplenty.

Before her stood an enormous man. He was Elim, and one she had never seen before. Ana realized that the top of her head barely reached the middle of his chest; he must stand inches higher than even Spur Lazar, who was the tallest man she knew. His solemnity was tinged by dread, and Ana knew it was not only the executioner who was feeling disturbed by the strange twilight.

Fringing the black disk of the moon was a gossamer halo of sunlight. Again Ana was struck by the notion that this was Lyana talking to her, talking to them all, mocking the killers and uplifting Ana's spirits. Soon both her body and Kett's would be safe within their watery graves, whilst their spirits would rise to Lyana's bosom.

"Odalisque Ana, this is Faraz. He is the Elim responsible for executions within the harem," Salmeo explained as lightly as if he were introducing a guest for dinner.

She nodded at the huge man and he responded in kind, nervously glancing up toward the sun and moon, suddenly a single, glowing, sinister body in the heavens.

"Ana, you understand why you give your life today?" It was the Valide, attempting to draw out the agony for as long as possible, as usual, but even her voice sounded strained and she, too, uncharacteristically seemed nervous as she looked up to the skies.

Ana fixed the Valide with a long look. "I've worked it out, Valide, thank you."

"Perhaps you could explain it to us so we can bear witness that you did most certainly understand the charges brought against you. It is tradition." The Valide's voice was perfectly measured and polite.

"My naïveté led me to make some rash decisions, Valide," Ana said boldly. "I trusted people I should never have thought capable of honesty. I broke the law of the harem . . . again. Is that clear enough?"

"Be careful, Ana," Salmeo cautioned.

"Or what? You'll kill me?" She laughed aloud and it felt wonderful to see all his visible flesh quivering with rage.

Her triumph was short-lived. Herezah's cold voice cut through her amusement. "No, but I'm sure you would like to go to your death knowing that the family in the foothills you care about so much will not be punished for your misdemeanors. Your uncle's death should have been sufficient for your selfish pursuits. I hope that you will be content with two other deaths on your hands—those of Lazar and Kett."

Ana's resolve crumpled. She felt shaken at the threat, knew all her bravado had dissipated at a couple of cutting sentences from Herezah. "Can we just get this done with, I beg you? I have nothing further to add. Forgive my offense, Grand Master Salmeo. You may appreciate that I am trying to find the courage to die bravely."

Salmeo's scar lifted as he smiled, the gap in his teeth looking cavernous, now and then filled with the plump pink tongue that seemed to taste the air like a snake's. "I accept your apology, Odalisque Ana," he lisped, "and agree we should get 'this'—as you put it—under way, for this strangely dull morning is already warm and these dark silks are not breathing as well as they should."

Herezah made a tutting sound in sympathy. "You should have changed into the summery lightweight silks already, Salmeo," she admonished. "Odalisque Ana, you gave me your promise, your absolute word, that you would never attempt to escape from the harem again. Do you remember my warning?"

Ana hesitated, realizing now how brilliantly this pair had cornered their prey, then played with it before releasing it into that well-constructed false sense of freedom before pouncing again, this time fatally. She had to admit that they were superb manipulators. She recalled the conversation with Herezah well—how cleverly Herezah had led her through the discussion, extracting that promise for this very moment when she would hurl it back against her. Ana dropped her head, feeling completely dispirited. She wished Pez were there so she could at least hug someone good-bye. But, she realized bleakly, he was probably with Lazar. "Yes, I remember giving you that promise."

"Which you promptly broke that very evening."

"Yes, Valide."

"No one helped or encouraged you? This was your own decision?"

The scribe was busily recording the facts on his tablet of paper, trying not to look above at the halo of ethereal light surrounding the moon.

"All of my own doing," Ana echoed. "I coerced Kett into aiding me. He felt obliged."

"That won't save him, I'm afraid, Ana, but we appreciate your candor."

Salmeo looked to the scribe, who nodded. "We are ready, then. Step into the bags, please."

The Elim helped the bound Kett into the black velvet sack. To his credit, Kett was stoic, his eyes firmly on Ana. She was sorely reminded of a similar scene of despair not so long ago, during which they had drawn strength from each other.

"It will be quick, Odalisque Ana, fear not," Herezah said.

"The stones at the bottom of your sacks make it so," Salmeo added.

"I don't fear death, Valide," Ana said. "The thought of remaining a slave to the harem is far more daunting and a worse sentence than drowning—I'm sure you of all people understand."

Herezah smiled sardonically. "Well, I suppose you'll never know the difference between Valide and Odalisque, young Ana. I do, and the worlds are markedly apart. Sleep well in your watery grave." She nodded toward Salmeo.

To prevent Ana saying anything further to infuriate his mistress, Salmeo spoke and his tone brooked no interruption. "We await the toll of the Second Bell. You may tie them in."

The two men in the boats got busy pulling the bags up around their victims, at which point Kett began to jabber. Ana caught a glimpse of him before she herself was pushed deeper into the darkness of her death bag and it seemed as though her friend had fallen into a trance. Just then the solar eclipse passed; the moon shifted, and blinding, golden sunlight hit them all so ferociously that everyone shielded their eyes. As she stared at Kett, it seemed that he was bathed in his own tunnel of glorious light—and furthermore, he appeared to be fully a bird—a proud raven . . . the black bird of omen.

And then she was plunged into the velvet void as Faraz secured her bag with ties. She could hear Kett's muffled voice. He was jabbering in ancient Percherese, she realized with alarm, a language so different from the language spoken today that no one around them would understand him. It shocked her to hear him speak it. It possessed a harsher quality to it, more like Galinsean, and was delivered with none of the elegant intonation of the contemporary language. Kett spoke in a monotone that seemed to match the trance he had succumbed to. She could not explain how but she understood every word:

"I am Lyana's Raven, bird of omen, and bird of sorrows," he repeated over and again. To hear him quote Lyana frightened her more than she wanted to admit. Pez's warning that Kett might be a messenger rang in her ears.

She heard muffled complaining from Herezah and then chilling words from Salmeo: "Stick that knife of yours into him, executioner. We cannot bear the noise."

To her relief the Elim executioner refused. "Forgive me, Grand Master Salmeo, but tradition allows a prisoner to pray at any stage during his execution."

"That doesn't sound like prayers to me," Herezah moaned. "It's another language."

"Nevertheless," the executioner replied in a stunning show of stubbornness.

"Kett!" Ana shouted, and then, in the same ancient Percherese that was so annoying Herezah and Salmeo, she bid him farewell. "We shall meet again in Lyana's arms," she comforted, and felt hot tears stinging her face that Kett should die so lost and so confused.

"I am the Raven and you are the Mother," he suddenly said, frightening Ana to her marrow. "This is my omen. You must live, you must let the Goddess live, and you must help the creatures and the giants to live. Maliz has killed the priestess. Now you must find the Rebel . . . you must find the Rebel."

He kept repeating the final five words, and over his chant, she heard the Second Bell sound and the words "Drop them," ordered by Salmeo.

Ana felt herself picked up by the Elim executioner as though she were no weight at all and she heard him whisper a plea for forgiveness through the velvet before he grunted softly and dropped her over the side of the boat.

Cold hit her like a slap and then she was gasping as the river flooded into the bag and surrounded her as she sank to the depths. She had meant to gulp down the water to aid the drowning, but the shock of it finally happening prompted a primeval desire to hold her breath and live for just a few brief moments longer. Kett's ominous warning resounded in her mind as the stones dragged her deeper still and her lungs screamed for air.

19

Lazar heard the Second Bell and its tolling stopped him in his tracks. He bent down, hands on thighs as he sucked in air, and then he straightened with rage and shouted a mournful howl of despair. He could see the River Gate, could see where an Elim executioner peered down into the depths and where Salmeo and Herezah were turning toward his keening with expressions that were triumphant.

He was too late. Ana was gone.

He yelled again his anger but something akin to pain passed through his head and then the voices that he had heard once before came again. *Save her!* they urged, somehow familiar yet belonging to people he didn't know.

Who are you?

You must save her, they persisted, and then with fury driving their tone: *Go!*

Fear, he decided, was the final factor that gave him the impetus once again to hurl himself forward, even though he felt spent. Salmeo, approaching, his face frowning in confusion as to who this stranger running at them was, raised a hand. Lazar ignored him, launching himself headfirst into the river.

He prayed to Lyana to guide him through the waters. Fortunately this river came down directly from the mountains and was stunningly clear. Now, with the sunlight penetrating the water and the day bright again, he could make out the position of the boats. Lazar swam deeper and deeper, knowing he was running out of time.

He found one sack, and struggled with the ties. When he opened it at last he was horrified to see Kett's body float up, the young man's dead eyes staring sadly back at him. Lazar could not waste another second on Kett and looked around wildly, his body beginning to beg for breath as he spied the other sack crumpled on the riverbed. He reached for it, his fingers fumbling at the ties. Just as he felt his whole body give in to panic, somehow, miraculously, the ties came free on the bag. Lazar let the air in his mouth escape as Ana floated up into his arms, lifeless, her eyes closed, ethereal in death.

He would not accept it. Closing his mouth over hers, he gave her whatever little was left of the air in his lungs before he pushed up and away from the darkness toward Lyana's sunlight.

Lazar burst through the surface, gulping for sweet life; his lungs felt like twin furnaces but he sucked in air and, treading water, blew it into Ana's mouth again and again, weeping as he did so. Although it had been so many years ago, he could still remember the last time he cried, when as a young man something special had been taken from him. He would not permit it again. He sent a silent prayer to Lyana that if she returned this girl to life, he would never ask any more of the Goddess or her disciple. He would not follow through on his year's worth of suffering or his promise, made on the island when he was still battling to live, that if he ever saw Ana again he would find a way to show her his love.

Arms reached for them both but he had no sense of being hauled from the water, or being dragged onto the riverbank by the impossibly strong arms of Faraz. The executioner pushed the gasping Spur aside and pumped Ana's chest several times before he, too, went through the motions of breathing life from his own lungs into hers.

In his dazed state, watching the huge black man tenderly kiss Ana with life, Lazar became aware of Salmeo talking at him and Herezah giving orders from afar. But he ignored both. He watched the Zar's party arrive, Jumo hesitating at the gate whilst Pez showed no such fear, cartwheeling until he arrived at Ana's side.

"Let me," he whispered to the Elim, who sat aside, no doubt stunned by the urgency and authority in the dwarf's voice and likely shaken that the mad jester had spoken sense at all.

Lazar watched as Pez closed his eyes and laid his hands on Ana's chest, singing a vulgar song about goat's udders as he did so.

Herezah, taking no notice of the dwarf, pointed at Lazar. "And who is this stranger?" she demanded of her son as he arrived, ignoring all protocol in these unusual circumstances.

Boaz was not given a chance to answer, for Salmeo now joined in the fray with his own frustrations: "My Zar, Ana is dead. She has been executed as you sanctioned and as required by the harem. I—"

The Zar held a hand up to stop them both as Lazar took over

once again, pushing air into seemingly dead lungs and pumping Ana's chest to expel water and get the heart responding. "Well?" he asked the men fighting for her life.

"Who *is* this madman who leaps into the river and brings out an executed odalisque with not so much as a by-your-leave?" the Valide demanded, looking at the dripping stranger who continued to ignore them all. With no immediate answer from her son, who seemed more interested in Ana's body, she addressed the golden-haired stranger. "You! Who—"

Ana gave a small retch. Everyone around her became suddenly still and silent. She suddenly spasmed and vomited water, struggling to get that first easy breath. Lazar, holding her, relief flooding him, nonetheless became conscious of the pair of disbelieving and enraged stares focused on Ana. He wanted to hold her, feel her warmth, her life returning as her body warmed against his skin. He did not want to seem too intimate, even though he desperately wanted to kiss those lips, not just breathe life through them. But he must deny himself, keep his promise, for it seemed that Lyana had answered his plea.

Ana was breathing steadily again now, looking around, dazed, confused.

"Ana?" Boaz took charge as Lazar sat back, behind the young woman.

She took a long time to focus, unaware of who sat behind her, his head hung with relief. "Zar Boaz? Where—"

"Ana," he began, then cleared his throat. "This is a terrible thing we have done to you."

"Is Kett alive?"

"It doesn't appear so, Ana. I imagine he committed himself to the river as courageously as you did."

"Then why am I here, Highness?" Her voice was filled with despair. "Surely this is not your idea of a jest?"

He put his hands up in a warding gesture. "No! Ana, you were rescued because Percheron needs you."

Pez had sidled up and in a childish manner stroked her hair, humming a lullaby. Then he skipped away, glancing once at Lazar, who now silently pulled himself to his feet behind Ana.

His movement attracted the attention of the Valide. Their eyes met and in those few moments of what was surely numbing stupor, Lazar could see that she recognized who was standing before her, even though her mind was likely telling her that her eyes were lying.

"Lazar?" Herezah asked, bewilderment in her eyes now, reaching up to cover her open mouth behind her veil.

Ana turned slowly. Her lips formed his name, repeating Herezah's exclamation. This silent communication between them completely consumed him.

"Mother," Boaz began, but he was cut off by the Valide's laughter.

Lazar imagined her intensely agile mind must have crashed through a dozen scenarios as she tried to piece it together. "Every bit the Galinsean you tried to pretend you were not," she said, her tone cynical and cutting. "Hair dye. How simple, Lazar, and how truly cunning."

"Mother, we shall discuss this shortly. You require an explanation regarding the revival of a supposed doomed criminal and will have it, but right now I need the physicians to look at Odalisque Ana. Elim, if you please . . ."

Ana had not moved. Her body was rigid, her eyes filled with dread. Lazar had held her gaze, even though each moment it lingered it pierced his heart deeper until the wound seemed so great he felt sickened. There would be no speedy recovery from this injury. He knew exactly what she was thinking, understood her sense of betrayal, and whilst the Valide hurled her taunts, he had barely heard them. Even thought Ana was alive, he felt dead inside to see the pain of betrayal in her face. Lyana had granted him another sort of living death.

The Elim helped Ana to her feet and it was Faraz who gently insisted he carry her. When she was gone, Boaz spoke quickly, urgently.

"Mother, you should know that in the Throne Room, there impatiently await two Galinsean dignitaries who have the power to bring war on Percheron." He let that notion sink in before he continued, watching her angry eyes become wary now behind her veil. He knew that not even at her most imaginative could his mother have guessed that this was the reason for the Zar interrupting an execution. "I have no intention of giving them even a spark for their tinder and right now appeasing the enemy is far more important to me than appeasing your anger." As he paused she opened her mouth to speak, but Boaz shook his head, refusing her voice, continuing himself. "Lazar's presence has been explained and that explanation was due to me alone. He is the Spur of *my* Shield, and, as you know, he is answerable to no one but the Zar. When we have solved our immediate dilemma, and at my convenience, I will sit down and take you through the strange set of circumstances that have brought about today's excitement. Until then, Lazar and Ana are all I have between Percheron's peace or Galinsean war. Please excuse us."

Lazar, watching Boaz, knew he had just borne witness to the young Zar finally accepting the full responsibility of his

Crown. There was no doubting who sat on the throne of Percheron now.

In another situation, Lazar might have applauded loudly. On this occasion he simply bowed his head in courtesy to the Valide and followed his Zar as he turned to leave. Pez hurried behind, accidentally treading on the Valide's gown and her long veil, momentarily dragging back her head and ignoring her exclamation of outrage.

Salmeo remained sensibly silent.

20

B oaz was pleased to see that Tariq had played his role as dignitary to perfection, despite the language problem. He had arranged for a table to be dressed in an anteroom connected to the Throne Room, and servants had set up an enticing feast for the visitors. Seated on exquisite embroidered cushions, arranged on the floor, the two men had capitulated to the Vizier's urgings that they refresh themselves with some food whilst they waited.

It had actually not been long. As Boaz entered the chamber Marius and Lorto had just begun nibbling on the decadent array of brightly presented food. They struggled to their feet to bow, and Boaz, not usually prone to cynicism, was nevertheless uncertain whether the two visitors were bowing to the Zar of Percheron or the Crown Prince of Galinsea directly behind him.

"Ask them to make themselves comfortable again, Lazar,"

he asked, and listened as, in three briefly uttered words, the Spur had them both seated again.

Graciously, Boaz joined them on the floor. As a show of goodwill, he allowed a servant to wash his hands in a bowl scented with orange blossom before he dismissed all servants and reached for a small flatbread. Boaz was not hungry, not after what had just happened, but he knew that the breaking of bread together was one of the fastest ways to make strangers feel at ease. His history lessons had taught him that both Galinsea and Percheron followed the same tradition that generosity at the table—even to an enemy—was the highest form of hospitality and diplomacy. He dipped his bread into a thickly oil-slicked bowl of chickpea paste and ate, encouraging Lazar and the Galinseans to follow suit. "Make some small talk, Lazar—I don't care what you say but put them at their ease."

"They are at ease, Highness," Lazar assured him, before beginning a conversation that the Zar had no hope of following. Looking to Tariq, Boaz said softly, "We might yet save this situation, Grand Vizier. And our secret weapon is Odalisque Ana, can you believe."

The man shook his head. "I thought she was being executed, Highness."

Boaz sighed. "So did I, Tariq, so did I." Realizing that Lazar was addressing him, he turned his attention to the Spur, who concluded, " . . . about where we've been."

Boaz frowned.

"Excuse me, Highness, I've explained where we've been, and why we left so suddenly."

"Are they shocked?"

"A little."

"Barbaric Galinseans surprised by an execution?" the Grand Vizier asked.

Only Boaz, who knew Lazar well enough, noted the slight bristle at his deliberate barb.

"No, more intrigued that we would kill a girl for her ingenuity by using her bright mind instead of reprimanding her." He shrugged with mild apology. "Galinseans are pragmatists. They do not hold to tradition as closely as the Percherese."

"Have you explained anything further?"

"Not without your permission, Highness. Shall I do so now?"

"Go ahead. Let them know what we're planning in terms of the emissary. I presume they understand your reluctance?" he asked, and Lazar nodded. "Proceed. Tariq, come with me," he said, motioning toward the door. "Excuse me to them, Lazar, for just a moment. I need to brief Ana."

Lazar acknowledged his Zar but did not break from his discussion with their visitors.

Tariq followed Boaz outside. "You'd better brief me, too, Highness. I think I'm rather confused."

"Yes, I intend to. What I need right now is for you to organize for Ana to be brought before the visitors as soon as possible. She is being checked over by the doctors at present and I don't doubt she's in shock and not in a position to pay us the attention we require, but you need to impress upon her the importance of what I need her to do."

"Which is?"

"To travel to Galinsea as my emissary."

MALIZ ARRIVED AT THE harem, where he was met by the Elim.

"I'm here to escort Odalisque Ana, at His Majesty's request, to the Throne Room," he said to the eldest.

"I must fetch Grand Master Salmeo to speak with you."

Oh lovely, Maliz thought, *just what I need.* "Thank you."

The eunuch arrived shortly. "She is not ready," he said abruptly, giving the Grand Vizier no salutation.

"I shall wait."

"I can send her with an Elim escort, Tariq. You need not linger for such lowly duties."

"Nothing on behalf of my Zar is lowly. He expressly asked me to bring her."

"She is still with the physicians, and will be for some time yet, unless you want her coughing up river water all over the esteemed dignitaries."

"While I'm sure that wouldn't help our cause, apparently she is all we have."

"What is meant by this insult to the harem?" Salmeo spat, no longer able to maintain his calm facade. "This girl was to be executed. The harem deals with its own. What is the Zar thinking by interrupting our private and traditional proceedings?"

"Well, Salmeo, I'd suggest he's thinking of you. Should it come to war, you'll be amongst the first to be put to the sword. The Galinseans hate our traditions, you know, and the harem would be one of its major targets."

"I do not understand."

"I can see that. The harem has different meanings to different people, Salmeo. To you it is home, it is life, it is tradition—you know nothing else. To the Zar it is his most treasured investment, from where he will choose his heir. To the Valide it is her seat of power. To the people of Percheron it represents their heritage and an extension of all that is beautiful in their realm. It sets them apart from other kingdoms."

"And to those other kingdoms, it represents something else, no doubt," Salmeo interrupted.

Maliz didn't mind, he had nothing better to do just now until he could get some peace to ponder all that he had learned. "Ah, and now we come to it. You catch on fast, brother. To other kingdoms it is the symbol of Percherese wealth, decadence. It is, I don't doubt, envied, and thus a target of hate. It makes our Zar different from all the other kings who follow a monogamous marriage system, even though I imagine they lie with whomever they wish behind the palace walls. To destroy the harem is to destroy one of the key aspects of what makes Percheron so covetable, so exotic, so different."

"And tell me, Tariq, how does Ana fit into this campaign to save the harem, to save Percheron, as the Zar suggested?"

"I'm afraid I'm not at liberty to discuss matters of state so openly, Salmeo. I'm sure you understand, but suffice it to say that Ana will be taking on a new official capacity for the Zar."

"This is outrageous!"

"I suggest you take it up with Zar Boaz, Grand Master Eunuch. I am merely the escort today. How long before she is ready, do you think?"

"Wait here," Salmeo said, turning on his heel.

Maliz did as asked and took the time to replay in his head the conversation he had shared with the Spur about the old priestess. It was intriguing that the Spur, back from the dead, had been nursed to health by Zafira. Coincidence? Perhaps, but unlikely. Centuries of battling the Goddess had taught him that anyone even remotely connected to her was suspect. Was the Spur involved? Is that why his death had been contrived, his survival from the poison and his wounds kept a secret . . . but why? And then why would he come back . . . unless it was to be close to Lyana. But who was she? Maliz knew Lyana was close, possibly not arisen yet, though Iridor was. His only suspect was the dwarf, who was frustratingly proving to be every bit as mad as everyone assured the Vizier he was. The priestess had claimed that Salmeo was Iridor, but Maliz knew that had been a ruse. He'd spent too much time with Salmeo; he would know if the eunuch was Iridor.

So far he had Pez, Lazar, and this odalisque as potentially being involved but none were showing any of the usual signs of being close to the Goddess—the nervousness of her disciples was usually his first inkling that he was getting closer to Lyana, but Pez was impossible to read in his insanity, Lazar so remote it seemed he was passionate about nothing, and he hardly knew this girl. Tariq had met her on a couple of occasions but paid little attention. That she was beautiful and a troublemaker was as much as his memories could offer.

But Lyana was clever, Maliz admitted to himself. She had tried many guises over many cyclical battles. She had been an old woman once, other times she had given herself the most ordinary of looks and roles—one year a merchant's wife, another a harlot, once even a simple bread seller. He smiled remembering her most audacious attempt to confuse, when she had rebirthed herself as a lad. That had not worked very well—the female form was best.

As Maliz was thinking this, Salmeo emerged once again, this time with the girl, fully covered in the simplest of dark gowns and matching veils. The sea-green eyes appeared dulled, uninterested.

The Grand Vizier stood. "Odalisque Ana?"

She didn't respond. Salmeo murmured something to her.

"I am," she finally said, not looking at anyone or anything in particular.

"Is she all right?" Maliz asked testily.

"Well, she drowned once today, if that helps clarify things a little, Grand Vizier. Then she was revived, pulled back from the brink of death. The physicians say there is no outward sign of damage, but, as you can see, she is vague, to say the least."

"And this is who shall save Percheron. My, my . . ." Maliz decided he was going to enjoy watching this episode. This young woman could not be the reincarnation of Lyana. Had she been the woman he hunted, he would have felt it; would have felt every inch of his body respond to her magical presence. And her magic would have triggered his and released him from the prison of Tariq's mortality. Although he would ultimately die as the Vizier when this battle was done, Lyana's arrival gave him his full powers, feeding his fury, making his borrowed body invincible. He needed her to cross his path soon, for until such time he was vulnerable. Oh yes, none of his enemies realized that until Lyana's presence made itself physically felt, he was entrapped by the mortal man and could die as any mortal. It was his darkest secret and once again he thanked Zarab that Lyana had never known this. Her supporters always assumed he possessed his demon skills permanently. Maliz shuddered: it would be so easy for Iridor—whoever he was— to stick a knife into him or contrive a death by any number of means, and Tariq's body would die, taking with it the demon.

Maliz grinned, smug in the belief that they had never discovered this . . . and never would. Whoever Iridor was, he was no doubt treading very carefully, wary, believing that the demon could not be murdered in his sleep, poisoned during dinner, or simply met with some seeming accident. He would warn her other disciples, too, no doubt, that Maliz could not be killed by conventional means. In fact—

"Vizier Tariq, what are you smiling about?" Salmeo's lisping words cut through his thoughts.

"Ah, forgive me, Grand Master Eunuch. I was just thinking how sad it is that we hide our most treasured possession—great beauty—behind the veil. I have seen this girl; I know her magnificence. She would take our visitors' breath away."

"How little you understand the harem, Vizier Tariq, and how obvious that you have no wives of your own. Our women are never to be paraded before others. Their beauty is protected, to be enjoyed only by their husbands."

Maliz did not want to debate with the eunuch now. He was vexed that he'd been caught off guard momentarily anyway, and if he continued this conversation, that irritation might show itself. "Our Zar awaits, Salmeo. And no doubt he'll decide whether or not to allow this young woman's exceptional beauty to fall upon others. Odalisque Ana, if you please?"

"Elim will accompany you," Salmeo warned.

"As you see fit." Maliz turned once again to Ana. "Come with me, my dear. It seems you're suddenly the most important person in whole palace, next to the Zar," Maliz said, just loud enough for Salmeo to overhear, as he guided Ana away from the harem.

"Grand Vizier, forgive me, but I don't understand," Ana pleaded.

He believed her. Her eyes were so large and filled with confusion that he felt a strange thrill of sympathy for this young woman. This was not an emotion he was used to. He recalled Tariq's memory of her outstanding beauty, even as a fourteen-year-old, remembered the sweetly innocent body that didn't seem to match her oddly confident, direct manner that had so upset Tariq and Salmeo. "I can tell you some more—as much as I have been told. I know they're waiting for you, Odalisque Ana, but let us take the slower way to the Throne Room so I have a little time to explain."

"That's generous of you, Grand Vizier."

Maliz smiled. No one had ever accused him of that trait before. "How does it feel to return from the dead?" he asked conversationally.

She didn't pause before replying, as he had anticipated. "I feel angry."

"Why?" He hadn't expected that answer.

"Because I hate this place and everyone in it. My death was my ultimate escape."

There was true venom driving this statement, and he was pleasantly surprised by the passion in her tone. He began to appreciate what Boaz saw in this particular girl and he almost regretted telling the Zar that she was inconsequential. "That's a very sweeping statement, Odalisque Ana. Do you not crave life? How about everlasting life?"

She stared at him as they walked. "No, Grand Vizier. Life has not treated me kindly and there is nothing to look forward to with age. Dying young is appropriate."

The girl could be Lyana with that sentiment, he mused, but none of his senses were on alert. This was no goddess walking in disguise at his side. "Do you really hate everyone here?"

"I wouldn't have said it if I didn't mean it, Grand Vizier Tariq."

"I thought you were friendly with the dwarf," he probed.

"Pez has no sane process of thought. No one is friends with

him because it's impossible to understand him." He could tell she was being careful in answering this question and his ears pricked up. "I do, however, feel sorry for him. Pez is trapped in his mind as I am trapped in the harem."

"That's a clever analogy, Odalisque Ana. You spend a lot of time with the dwarf, I hear. Do you notice any moments of clarity with him, though? Could he be pretending, do you think?"

She stopped walking, the Elim behind her having to quickly halt. "Grand Vizier, why are you asking me this odd question?" and he could hear the soft tremor in her voice.

"Oh, nothing." He shrugged, intrigued now by her flustered response. Was she hiding something? "Simply baffled by him," he said mildly, encouraging her to continue by his side.

"But you've known him for many years, surely? How could I throw any more light on his sanity?"

Maliz was taken aback. She was certainly direct and very composed for someone of such a tender age. Definitely a match for the Zar. "I have known him for many years. For all his insanity, Pez has always made it very clear that he detests me."

She laughed. "Yes, he can be contrary to certain people."

"Who else does he dislike, would you say?"

Ana hesitated, then said carefully, "Grand Vizier, I don't think it is my place to comment."

"Well, let me offer some ideas," he said, airily. "There's myself, the Valide certainly, and without doubt, Salmeo. I've noticed personally that his hostility is carefully directed and often disguised as humor. But it is never directed at the Zar, never at you presumably, Ana, never at the Spur."

He watched her bristle at the mention of Lazar. He'd definitely hit a nerve there. He smiled inwardly. How delicious this was—secrets upon secrets. "Of course you know the Spur has also returned to us from the dead," he continued, giving up on the other thread of conversation for it was leading nowhere anyway.

"Yes," she replied, brisk and to the point.

"Ah, is he one of the people you hate?"

"I told you, I hate everyone."

"Including me?"

"Yes."

"How sad. I thought we were getting on rather well."

"That's not the same as liking someone, Grand Vizier."

"No, indeed. You have a good grip on diplomacy, Odalisque Ana, and that's why you'll make a fine emissary for our Zar."

"Grand Vizier," she said, her tone fractious, "you promised me an explanation."

Maliz was mindful of how little time they had. He would need to be brief. "I did. Very simply, a Galinsean ship is sitting in our harbor, having brought two Romean dignitaries. They bring a declaration of war."

"Here in the palace, threatening war?" she asked, incredulous.

"Not openly. But we have some sticky territory to maneuver through as we convince the Galinsean royalty that Spur Lazar is alive and well. Perhaps we can say the execution was a jest and apologize profusely about how the Galinseans don't share our sense of humor?"

She sneered at his sarcasm. He couldn't see her mouth but her eyes were incredibly expressive. Maliz found he was enjoying goading her, watching the spark of anger flare.

"But why is Spur Lazar so important?"

"Ah, and now you have hit the crux of the matter. I cannot explain this, but from what I gather, if he is dead so are we and thus we must convince them that blood flows strongly in his veins."

"How does this involve me?"

"My dear Ana, have you not realized that you are the only person who speaks Galinsean with such fluency?"

"The Zar does," she countered.

"And you know full well that it is not the same language that he speaks."

She nodded, abashed. "He speaks an ancient form of it."

"Which makes absolutely no sense to our Galinsean dignitaries."

Her frustration got the better of her. "Spur Lazar is alive! Lyana save me," she cursed. "Why can't he just go and present himself?"

Maliz stopped short. "Now why would you call down the help of the Goddess?"

"I"—she faltered—"a slip, Grand Vizier. I admit I support the role of the priestess. But I have never openly practiced," she assured him.

"That's right," he mused, "when you escaped the first time, they found you in the Sea Temple, didn't they?" He nodded for her. "Lyana's temple."

"Is that so wrong?"

"It's . . . unusual."

"Are you a hater of the Goddess, too, Grand Vizier?"

He liked the way she attacked when cornered. "I'm afraid so. I follow Zarab, child." He stored her "slip" away. Perhaps he shouldn't take his eye off Ana—or Pez, for that matter. She had been far too careful when discussing the dwarf, and her love for Lyana was rather damning. Still, she herself wasn't Lyana—that he was utterly certain of, and was strangely pleased about. Killing this feisty and beautiful woman would be a shame.

"My spiritual leanings are irrelevant, Grand Vizier—you were explaining to me why Spur Lazar could not sort out the situation by presenting himself."

"I can't explain that because I am not privy to the details. But the Zar seems to feel that that is not the best strategy." He had decided that Ana should learn the truth of Lazar's parentage from the lips of others. It would make for excellent entertainment, he was sure.

"And that leaves me—that's why I was plucked from the death waters," she finished.

"Correct. You speak fluent, current, and courtly Galinsean, as we all understand it. As I said earlier, you are now the single-most-important person in the whole of Percheron, save the Zar himself."

"No wonder Salmeo and the Valide are so disgusted." He laughed with genuine mirth at her comment and again she stared at him, trying to work him out. "Forgive my indiscretion, Grand Vizier."

"Nothing to forgive, my dear, I find them both slippery and conniving, to say the least." Now she looked shocked and he laughed again. "I suppose I shouldn't be admitting that to an odalisque." She shook her head, her eyes telling him she was puzzled by him, perhaps a little frightened. "Then we have both shared a secret that the other must protect. You have told me of your love for Lyana and I have told you of my hate for two very important people in the palace. Are we conspirators?"

The eyes behind the veil narrowed.

"You have nothing to fear from me, Odalisque Ana. Whatever you've heard about me—you should know that I am loyal to Zar Boaz. In fact, as you may have noticed, I have become very close to him. I don't care for what his mother might advise him, or for where the fat black eunuch might lead him." He watched his words take effect—a fragile bond suddenly linking them; he could see it reflected in those green eyes. "I will do whatever's necessary to protect the Zar and his personal interests rather than follow his grasping mother's agenda. We are fellow haters, Ana. Your secret is safe with me."

She hesitated only briefly. "Then so is yours, Grand Vizier," she replied.

"Good. What happened to the black eunuch boy, by the way?"

Her eyes misted and took on a faraway look. "The bird of sorrows is dead," she said sadly. "They managed to drown Kett."

Maliz froze. Forcing himself to move on before Ana noticed his start, he finally found his voice. "Kett, that's right. Why did you call him the bird of sorrows?" he asked, trying to cover the choked feeling in his throat.

Ana was still talking in a dreamy voice. "Oh, he called himself the Raven. It's funny, I always thought of him as a little black bird, scared by his own dark shadow sometimes and yet always courageous when he needed to be."

Maliz could feel his body trembling now. He was close, very close. He had won a small amount of Ana's trust and she had delivered something exquisitely important to him in a moment of carelessness. Ana might not be Lyana but she *was* involved in the struggle for the Goddess's supremacy. Perhaps her involvement was inadvertent or only minor but this girl was his first real clue to his prey. He could not keep her any longer from her duty—they had arrived at the Throne Room—but he must keep her close, find an opportunity to interrogate her further. "We are here, Ana. Zar Boaz is counting on you—in fact all of Percheron is counting on you, including your own family—to save us with your eloquence and diplomacy."

He knew the mention of family would add some extra clarity to her focus. Ana nodded. "I am ready, Grand Vizier."

He smiled warmly. "When we are not in formal situations, you must call me Tariq. Thank you for your discretion and trust. I will help you in your endeavors all I can." He had sensed where her loyalties now lay. "Perhaps I can get a message to your family, send them something? Money?"

Her eyes shone. "Why would you do such a thing?"

"Because I have no one to spoil and I'm glad you were rescued and we had this opportunity to get to know each other a little. You hold my secrets now. For keeping them between us—for your friendship—let me reward you in the way I know will count."

"We are not friends, Grand Vizier . . . not yet. Not money but a message, yes, or even news that they are well would mean everything to me."

"Consider it done, child." Before she could say more, he assured her, "I can find out where they are." He smiled like a kindly uncle. "Now, here we go . . . impress."

Ana nodded her silent thanks. Behind the shrouded eyes of Tariq, the demon Maliz smiled.

21

Ana's shock at seeing Lazar again—blond, bearded—almost unnerved her as she entered the chamber. She took the few moments as she knelt to her Zar to compose herself. In the fleeting second that their eyes met, she saw that Lazar looked as full of dread and discomfort as she felt. She could see the toll that his fight to survive had taken on him.

"Ah, gentlemen," Boaz began. "This is Odalisque Ana. Rise, Ana."

She did so, though she kept her eyes lowered. The Grand Vizier stood protectively alongside her. She could feel the weight of Lazar's stare, feel the heat of it sear past her veil and onto her skin, where it rested like a lingering kiss.

"Ana, you may remove your veil," Boaz said gently. "I want you to meet some esteemed guests of Percheron." It was also a command to raise her eyes. She did as her Zar bid and ignored the flare of pleasure in the strangers' eyes as they looked upon her fully. "This is Marius D'Argenny," Boaz said, his hand gesturing toward an older, silver-haired man with a stern face but lively eyes. "And this is Lorto Belsher. Neither speaks Percherese but I have told them you can speak a Galinsean that they will understand." She looked at the Zar and he gave her an embarrassed but encouraging smile. "You and I will talk privately shortly. Please go ahead, Ana."

She could feel Lazar's presence to her left as if he were a glowing brazier, radiating heat, and despite her anger and desire to be ice to him, she felt the pull of that warmth and the comfort it could offer. The thought of feeling his arms wrap around her, hearing him tell her he loved her, that he had never meant for her to suffer by his actions . . . the pull of him was so seductive, she felt herself sway slightly.

"Ana?" It was Boaz again, gentle but firm.

She rallied, forced herself to ignore the familiar yet strange man nearby, and she smiled for the visitors, before, in flawless, courtly Galinsean, she said, "We welcome your honorable presence in the city of Percheron," then bowed her head softly.

Both men smiled gently and explained the need for an emissary. A lengthy conversation ensued that only Ana and Lazar could follow. Boaz and his Vizier could do little more than settle sympathetic expressions on their faces and hope that Ana's words hit the right chord.

At some point Ana realized that Lazar had joined the discussion as well—offering her helpful insights into the ways of Galinsean royalty. She had paused, nodded, but still not looked at him, and only now turned fully to gaze upon the man at length—the man who dominated her thoughts, had been her reason for living, and indeed for dying. His golden hair suited him and suddenly no longer looked strange but right. The beard, however, hid the sculpture of his face and she longed to see it removed, imagined herself smoothing her hand across that firm jaw he ground so hard.

There was such sorrow reflected in his pale eyes that it nearly undid her. She felt a dry sob catch in her throat, but the occasion demanded she carry herself with dignity this day. Boaz needed it from her and it was the least she could do for the Zar, considering the way she had abused his trust. As well, her own family's safety burned in her mind. She did not want war to visit Percheron.

"Spur Lazar, pardon my ignorance, and, gentlemen, perhaps you'll forgive me for not appreciating the subtleties of the background to this situation, but I have to wonder why you three cannot simply return to the court of Galinsea. Lazar's presence would surely negate the need for war."

Marius gave her a soft smile but deferred to the Spur.

Lazar cleared his throat. "Yes, Odalisque Ana, that is the obvious path to follow . . . except I cannot."

Just to hear him speak her name again made her feel weak. She clenched her nails against the palm of one hand to steady herself. "May I ask why?"

"It is because I have been banished from that court," Lazar answered, his tone direct but his words less so; she sensed his discomfort.

"I see." She hesitated but then persisted: "Again, forgive my dullness here, gentlemen, but is it normal for Galinsea to go to war over someone they don't care about?"

"It is Lucien's status that is the problem, my dear," Marius replied.

"Lucien?" She looked at the old man quizzically.

"I am Lucien," Lazar cut in. She saw him take a slow breath as if working hard to control his emotions.

She stared at him for a long time. When she spoke again her voice was colder. "And, sirs, if you'll permit my question, who is Lucien to the Galinsean court?"

This time Lazar chose not to answer. Marius flicked a glance his way and then replied for him. "Odalisque Ana, I realize-people here are only just learning the truth of your Spur's background. I know how difficult this must be for him and for the Percherese Crown. But these are dire times and I have to placate an angry King. Before you, Odalisque Ana, stands Crown Prince Lucien, heir to the throne of Galinsea."

Ana's already unbalanced world rocked on a new axis. She felt dizzy at the revelation, but through the confusion everything about Lazar suddenly made sense to her. She understood his habit of secrecy, his closed-off emotions, his aloofness. None of that realization, however, helped relieve her sense of betrayal. He had deceived her, had deceived everyone.

"Royalty," she said, as if testing the word, then she gathered up her pain in the way she was becoming used to and put it aside. "Thank you. Now I understand why you need to involve a third party."

"You speak our language beautifully, Odalisque Ana," Lorto said.

She smiled, liking both the Galinseans for their sincerity. "Thank you, sir."

"In any other situation, you would be most acceptable," Marius was quick to add.

Lazar frowned, and Boaz, who had been watching the conversation carefully, obviously picked up that there was a problem. "What is it?" he interrupted. "Ana seems to be discoursing well with them."

"She is flawless; they like her very much," Lazar reassured him. "It seems we have hit a snag. I'm about to find out why, my Zar. Please indulge us a few moments longer." After Boaz nodded, he turned to Marius. "Why is Ana not suitable?"

"Majesty," the man began, apology in his tone, "Lorto and I can certainly vouch that we have seen you, conversed with you, and that you are well. The emissary is still required to explain Percheron's part in this. It is obvious something has occurred here for your friend and former servant to bring such damning news. You cannot expect the Galinsean Crown to simply accept that its heir has been executed by a foreign ruler."

Lazar's jaw began to work. Ana knew the sign that he was losing patience and addressed the Galinsean. "Marius, sir, tell me how we can make this go smoothly for Percheron. As you rightly say, Laz—forgive me, Crown Prince Lucien is alive," she said, trying not to load his title with her bitterness, "and Zar Boaz wishes to assure Galinsea that there was never an intention to execute your heir."

"We have no time for explanations, now," Lazar growled to his countrymen. "I brought the damage on myself. There is a quaint law in Percheron that allows its people to take punishment on behalf of others. Let's just say I exercised my rights in this realm."

"But Jumo conveyed that you were dead."

"He didn't know I was alive," Lazar countered, his exasperation rising. Then more gently, he added, "He also didn't know where I was. No one did—and, gentlemen, I include myself in that. I hardly knew I was alive. I had been poisoned by someone who did want me dead, but that person is a traitor to the Crown of Percheron. It was not sanctioned by Zar Boaz."

Ana wondered whether Lazar's brief and yet carefully worded explanation was as much for her benefit as it was for the Galinseans'. She inclined her head graciously to both her Zar and the dignitaries but spoke quickly in the foreign language. "I understand that time is of the essence, gentlemen. Perhaps blame can be laid later. For now, let us explain to our Zar why I cannot act as his emissary."

Marius nodded. "Forgive us, Odalisque Ana. As I said, you would be ideal, except that your status as a slave in Percheron may risk insulting the royal family of Galinsea. I would politely recommend that your Zar send his most senior counselor or more appropriately, a royal."

"Neither will be possible," Lazar cut in. "There are no true royals of Percheron, save the Zar himself. As for a senior counselor, the Grand Vizier has the highest status but he also is inappropriate." He glared at Ana, who was frowning at him in query at his latter point.

She held her silence, finally sighing softly and turning to her Zar. It was obvious to her that Lazar was not going to make this situation any easier.

Boaz had been concentrating hard on the foreign words flying about him as the four people who spoke and understood contemporary Galinsean conversed. Ana bowed in resignation. "Explain, Ana," he said.

"My Zar, forgive me," she began, thinking through the best way to present the Galinsean argument without giving offense. She already felt herself to be engaged in diplomatic juggling, with or without formal appointment as Percherese emissary to the Galinsean court. "I can certainly act as your emissary but my status is such that it will not make a strong enough impression on the royal family of Galinsea. I risk more damage to your Crown."

"I don't understand."

"I gather they need someone of high rank from Percheron. The Valide, the Grand Vizier . . . perhaps—"

"None of whom speak Galinsean!" Boaz cut across her, his exasperation spilling over. "How am I expected to keep both Percheron and Lazar safe? If I send him, they'll likely kill him. If I don't, they'll destroy us."

Silence descended on the room and rested heavily on everyone. It was Lazar who broke it. "I will go, Highness. My life has been forfeit for some time with my family and until not so long ago you accepted my death. Let me take my chances."

"Your death was never accepted, Lazar, never! I will not risk you, not again. Percheron needs you now more than ever. There has to be another way."

"There is," Lazar replied evenly.

All eyes shifted to the Spur, except Ana's, which remained studiously lowered, unable to look upon him without suffering. She could hear in his voice, however, that his idea did not sit comfortably with him.

"Share it!" Boaz commanded.

"May I see if it is acceptable with the Galinseans, Highness? I fear they're wondering what we're discussing and they sense your frustration. I don't think that we should estrange them at this delicate stage."

"Go ahead," Boaz urged him.

As Lazar spoke to the two men, Ana's eyes widened and then

her mouth opened slightly. "Spur Lazar, no!" She surprised everyone with her outburst and Lazar turned to glare momentarily at her. As he returned to explaining his proposition to the intrigued guests, Ana heard the Zar's soft voice close to her ear.

"Ana, you and I must speak alone later; there is much to clear between us, now that you—er, will be amongst us again."

She said nothing but inclined her head slightly in polite response to his wishes.

Marius nodded, said simply, "This would be acceptable to us."

Lazar, turning back to his ruler, found a grim smile. "They agree, Highness. The idea is acceptable to them."

SALMEO FELT UNPREPARED FOR this storm. For once, this was none of his making and it was rare for him to feel quite so helpless. The shock of Ana's revival had already sunk in and been accepted by him. The Grand Master Eunuch was nothing if not philosophical about life in the palace and would always work to find a way to turn every new situation to his advantage. He had calmed down, and sat now, slightly embarrassed, brushing imaginary lint from his robes as the Valide raged. She had held on to her anger, prompted by Ana's rescue and was seemingly unable to let go yet of her outrage at harem business being interrupted by palace protocol. Salmeo suspected the issue was more complex than simply Ana's survival—which was a shock for all involved. No, this was more; this was linked to coming face-to-face with a ghost in the shape of Spur Lazar. The Valide's fury and frustration were spiced by her confusion and disbelief at finding that the man she was so besotted by, the one she had thought dead for more than a year, was very much alive and still concerned with saving Odalisque Ana from her punishment.

He cleared his throat as Herezah continued spitting her despair. "Emissary! To the court of Galinsea, no less."

"It's baffling, Valide, I agree," Salmeo soothed.

She clenched her fists and groaned. "The sight of Lazar diving into that water and then coming up with her makes me sick to my stomach! How can he be back?"

"More to the point, Valide, how could she have not drowned?"

She ignored him. "They usurped my authority, Salmeo. It is not right that harem business is interrupted by outsiders."

"I know, but this was the Zar's wish. We are not in a position to openly contradict your son, Valide."

"I don't need the obvious stated, eunuch," she spat.

Salmeo disagreed but kept his counsel. Even though she was not raising her voice, this was the first time in her adulthood that he had seen her so flustered. Ana's survival, combined with Lazar's reemergence, had reduced the Valide to a shaking wreck. He had ordered her pomegranate tea to be infused with vinko to restore her calm. It was taking its time working, he noticed, another indication that the Valide's emotions were spinning well beyond her usual icy control. "Forgive me, Valide. I meant not to offend. I simply wanted to convey that the Zar had taken full charge of the proceedings—he even had the Vizier fetching Ana! What next? He was obviously not taking any chances."

"Why not send the Grand Vizier to Galinsea? He and Boaz are as close as brothers these days," she said, disgust lacing her tone.

"He does not speak Galinsean."

"Then Lazar, for Zarab's sake! The man's alive—isn't that what this is all about?"

He nodded, determined not to fuel her anger. He was already too close to getting burned. "I am as confused as you are, Valide. Please sip your tea. We can't have your voice hoarse for when you are presented to the Galinsean dignitaries."

"*If* I'm presented, Salmeo. It seems that Odalisque Ana is all that my son needs these days. Now she's his diplomatic representative at foreign courts!"

He could see her pulse pounding at her temple and began a soft tutting sound. "I suspect that is only because she can speak the language fluently, Valide, no other reason."

She opened her mouth, undoubtedly to hurl more abuse his way, but was halted when the bell sounded outside.

"Come!" Herezah ordered. Her personal attendant stepped inside. "Yes?"

"Valide, forgive my disturbance, but it is the Zar's secretary, Bin, with a message he must deliver personally."

"Well, he can wait, I'm busy," she growled back.

The slave looked terrified. "My sincerest apologies, Valide, but it is urgent, of the highest importance, and direct from the Zar's mouth, I am told to inform you."

Herezah scowled. "Send him in," she said, her hand waving in disdain.

Bin entered and bowed. "Valide, Grand Master Salmeo, please forgive my interruption."

"What is it?" Herezah said. "If you've come to invite me to supper with the Galinseans, they'll be waiting awhile. I need several hours for my toilet."

Bin bowed low again. "I do bring an invitation, Valide, but not for supper with the Zar."

"What then?" She sneered.

"He would like you to attend and witness his wedding."

22

Ana was hurriedly whisked from the Throne Room to be prepared for her marriage in the finest garments that could be assembled in such a short time. The Galinseans were shown to some accommodations where they could rest and freshen themselves.

Boaz asked Lazar to join himself and the Vizier in a private courtyard. Pez was nowhere to be seen.

Lazar had barely moments to spend with Jumo, who still wore an expression of incredulity as they walked along the palace corridors toward the Moon Courtyard.

"I can't believe it," the faithful servant said again. "And you look so different."

Lazar shook his head. "None of this need have happened if only I'd been asked."

"But they said you were unconscious, incapable of conversation, and then you died. What else could we believe? Even Pez was duped initially, I gather."

"He was. I owe you some explanation of what really happened, my friend, but right now we must make arrangements."

"Yes, I understand the urgency. I feel responsible. This war threat is because of my hasty actions."

"Don't, Jumo! You are the last person to be blamed for this mess. Ellyana is the villain. She and Zafira deliberately kept all information of my survival from you ... and worse, perpetrated the lie of my death. I'm so sorry."

Jumo grimaced. "I knew I was being manipulated at the time but I couldn't work out why. I still can't. What did Ellyana gain through her actions except chaos?"

"I think that's precisely what she was after. Or, more accurately, unpredictability. Be patient. I have some things to tell you but we must prepare to leave for Galinsea. The Zar awaits me."

"You're going?"

"I'm not letting Ana go alone."

"But she's not, she's—"

"She might as well be. No, I will be escorting her as far as the capital, if Boaz will permit it, and I can't see him refusing me. After she is delivered, I can melt into the city crowds, but at least I'll be there."

Jumo nodded. "All right. What do you want me to do?"

"Horses through the foothills, camels to take over from the edge of the Waste. Get fat old Belzo off his backside and doing what he does best: securing the Shield's supplies. We need to be self-sufficient—you know what a long journey it is."

"How many are going?"

"Marius and Lorto can return on their ship and hopefully

allay any eager Galinsean warships. Our party will be three, and no more if I can help it."

Jumo pulled an expression of uncertainty and Lazar knew his friend wanted to take more men. He also knew Jumo would hold his tongue on this, deferring to the Spur's knowledge of what might or might not further incite the Galinseans. Instead, Jumo asked, "Why the desert, Lazar? Surely ship is the best way?"

"It's too slow. We have to stop any invasion fleet before it leaves Galinsea. The desert is our only hope. Marius and Lorto will take their ship and hasten to their main flotilla. Thus they will prevent the Galinsean warships from moving any closer to Percheron and instead get word to my father via birds. By then, hopefully, we'll already be there and royal decree will go back to the warships ordering them to return to Romea."

"But you can't even enter the city of Romea apparently."

Lazar grimaced. "I know. I'm hoping to have a plan before we get there."

Jumo smiled. "Typical. Leave it to me."

Lazar gripped the man's shoulder. "Thank you, Jumo . . . especially for your patience."

The little man shrugged. "You're alive, that's all that matters to me. I'll leave you now. I have a lot to organize in a short time."

"Tell Belzo quality camels or I'll—"

"I know, I know . . . you'll kick his fat backside."

The two men grinned. Even though the trip already smelled so dangerous, it felt good to be preparing to travel together again.

"AH, LAZAR," BOAZ SAID, welcoming the Spur into his private courtyard, where he stood with Maliz. "Come, come."

Lazar glanced at the Grand Vizier, returned his gaze to the Zar. "Apologies for my tardiness, Highness. Arrangements needed to be made."

"My mind's a whirl—yours must be, too."

The Grand Vizier handed Lazar a cup of strong wine.

"I think we all need this," Boaz reflected. "Heartfelt thanks to you for coming up with an acceptable solution all around." He raised his glass to his Spur.

"It's radical, Highness," the Vizier said.

"Not really, Tariq. Quite normal, I would have thought, for me to choose a wife from my harem."

"I'm just imagining how it will reflect on you, Highness, that you've chosen a condemned prisoner who was actually in the process of being executed."

Lazar bristled. "The Galinseans know none of that, Vizier, and we can keep it that way. As far as they're concerned, this is a woman who speaks their language with grace and fluency and who is married to the Zar . . . that's a Queen in their eyes." He looked at the Zar. "You will make her Absolute Favorite, of course. Her status must be the highest there is."

"Of course," Boaz said. "I can only imagine the fury in the harem at how events have turned out," he said, smiling rue-fully, and then added: "I only wish I could have saved Kett in the chaos as well."

The Vizier looked thoughtful. "You misinterpret me, Spur. I think Ana—the little I've seen of her—is magnificent. We took some time together before she came to the Throne Room . . ." He watched Lazar's eyes narrow, saw the body tense. So, the Spur felt the same way toward Ana as she did toward him. Very interesting. Another relationship to watch. He smiled. "The Zar asked me to explain to her what was happening. I found her to be exquisite yet feisty, a good listener, and sharp, quick to assimilate information. She is precisely what is required for this role. I was actually referring not to the Galinseans but to those who stood to benefit by her death . . . those a little closer to home."

"You mean my mother and Salmeo," Boaz said.

Maliz didn't flinch. Oddly enough, he rather cared for Boaz and now Ana. Their lives were of infinitesimal importance compared to his own—both of them merely vehicles for a greater agenda—but still they had both managed to get under his skin somewhat, make him care—just a fraction—for their earthly pursuits. And so he preferred to be frank with Boaz, to guide him properly. He knew the Zar could handle constructive criticism if it was offered genuinely and at the right time. The Zar was no fool when it came to either the Valide or the eunuch. "Yes, of course I do. I'm not suggesting the Valide created the situation, but we'd all be lying to ourselves if we didn't see how she stands to gain by Odalisque Ana being out of the way."

Defense came from an unexpected quarter. "Whether it's Ana or some other wife, it will happen someday. The Valide understands the fragility of her own existence. She always has," Lazar replied.

"That's generous of you, Lazar," Boaz said. "My mother's mind works in fantastic ways sometimes. To be honest, there are moments when I despise her, but there are many more when I can only feel the highest admiration for her . She has survived and prevailed in an atmosphere of fear and suspicion. Unlike both of you, I've lived in the harem. Neither of you can begin to imagine what my mother has had to do to raise herself to the position she now has." Both men nodded thoughtfully. He continued. "I agree, Vizier, that my mother's position is protected as long as I don't take a wife. Ana was always a threat—as are all the women, as Lazar rightly argues—but the ironic part is that the Valide herself chose Ana. She always intended that Ana be Favorite."

"Just not so soon," Lazar added.

"That's right, not so soon. My mother's waited a long time to achieve her position and I for one can't blame her for wanting to hang on to it for a little longer."

"She won't lose her status, Majesty," Lazar began.

"No, but the beginning of the slide is there, isn't it? A wife is taken, an heir is born . . . it's only a matter of time."

"But, my Zar, you are still so young. You have many years before you hand over the throne to a son," Maliz commented.

"On the face of it, yes," Boaz said, frowning, "but things happen in life, Vizier, that none of us can foresee. If I'd said to you a couple of days ago that we would be trying to avert a genuine threat of war with Galinsea, you most likely would have laughed at me, called me paranoid. And yet here we are sending a sixteen-year-old girl into incredible danger to protect ourselves from that very invasion."

"What are you saying, Highness?" Lazar asked.

Boaz shrugged. "Nothing profound, simply pointing out the strangeness of fate. My father took a harmless fall from his horse—the same sort of fall he had taken many times before—but on that last occasion he was killed by it. The previous Zar died from accidental poisoning because he enjoyed bloatfish. None of us has such a firm grip on life that Zarab can't take it whenever he wishes. My mother has every right to feel angry at how things are turning out. Yes, she probably silently cheered

Ana's demise because I had announced my intention to choose her . . . it has taken her so long to attain her status and now it's being whittled away barely a year into her son's reign. But if I died by accident tomorrow, my mother would be finished and chaos would abound in the palace."

"Hurry up and sire a son on Ana, then, Highness, that's my advice to you." Maliz laced his tone with humor and Boaz grinned, but the demon had deliberately chosen his words to watch the reaction from the Spur. He got precisely what he expected.

Lazar cleared his throat. "Zar Boaz, we must leave immediately following the nuptials. I'm not sure there will be time after the ceremony for . . ."

"Oh, come now, Spur," Maliz drawled sardonically, "are you going to deny a man his wedding rights?"

"I . . ." Lazar looked flustered. "Zar Boaz, I—"

Maliz laughed inwardly. So, secret lovers within the palace. Forbidden, dangerous love . . . the best kind. "Well, if not a wedding night, at least a chance to consummate the marriage, make it real. Surely our ruse will sit more easily with our Galinsean dignitaries if they know the marriage is genuine."

Boaz was nodding—much to Lazar's dismay, Maliz noted. Maliz wanted to clap, he was enjoying himself so much.

"You're right, Tariq. If nothing else, it will give the appearance of authenticity. Good, that's settled," Boaz said, unable to disguise a distinct flush in his cheeks, "Ana will join me for a few hours after the ceremony. It is fitting. I do need to talk with her after all that has occurred."

Now the Vizier did grin openly. "Talk? Yes, indeed, Highness. I'm sure you will enjoy your conversation, but just let it be known that the marriage is consummated. All in the pursuit of diplomacy, Highness." He could feel Lazar seething nearby.

Boaz nodded again. "You may prepare to leave in the cool of the evening, Lazar."

Lazar nodded curtly. "As you wish, my Zar."

Maliz really had to stop himself from laughing out loud now. It seemed the Zar, for all his intelligence, couldn't even sense what seemed incredibly obvious . . . to him anyway. Maliz returned his focus to Lazar, enjoying playing the Spur as much as laughing secretly at Boaz. "Are we not led to believe that it is dangerous for you to enter Romea, Spur?"

"It is," Lazar answered. He wasn't doing a terribly good job of disguising his anger. "But I am the only one who can lead Ana there safely, successfully."

"Ah, so you get her to the city and then turn her loose alone? Surely she needs an entourage? We can't go to the Galinsean court like peasants, Zar Boaz?"

"Again, you're right, Tariq. Lazar, we need to think this through better. This is a royal visit. Granted, it's also a diplomatic visit, but my wife needs more protection than you're offering. As it is, you won't be able to go into Romea, so that leaves who? Jumo?"

Lazar was already shaking his head. "Zar Boaz, I must counsel you otherwise. Going across the desert is fraught with dangers. I cannot protect a large party."

"You cannot protect us anyway, Spur," Maliz chimed in, including himself in the party. His clever insertion was not missed by Lazar, who grimaced. "Surely this is such an important diplomatic mission it requires at least some of the usual pomp accorded such an event? We need to appear strong, confident, even if we are terrified out of our wits."

Lazar's eyes blazed with anger. Boaz was having none of it, though. "Lazar, I know this does not please you. Believe me, it does not please me either to have to send anyone to Galinsea, but Tariq is right. This mission is far too important for Ana to be cast into the enemy's den alone."

HE KNEW HE WAS beaten. And if good sense hadn't prevailed, he might have reached his fingers around the throat of the all-too-helpful Vizier, who seemed to be deliberately baiting him. This man was not Tariq—not by any stretch of the imagination. Lazar had no doubt now that Tariq was gone, replaced by the demon that Pez had warned him about. And Maliz had admitted to being alone with Ana—it was this fact that was driving Lazar's fury. She had been in such danger without realizing it. He had to speak with Pez.

"Who exactly would you suggest might make this party more acceptable, Majesty?" Lazar asked.

"That's a good question, I'll admit. Time is so short we don't have many options."

The Vizier piped up again. "I shall go, Highness, if you deem that suitable." Maliz didn't look at Lazar.

But Lazar reacted as if stung. "As head of security in Percheron, I would recommend that we need our head counsel—the Grand Vizier—close to the Zar."

"Well, I agree with both of you," Boaz said, shrugging. "Lazar's right. I feel you should always be close to the palace, Tariq. That said, you do have very high status and are closest counselor to the Crown. It would be a goodwill gesture to send you."

The Vizier nodded sagely, then frowned. "It occurs to me to suggest that you should also send Pez, as a gift, Highness.

Laughter is a great way to leap cultures, bridge our differences, and so on."

"Zar Boaz, I must protest," Lazar interrupted, frustration spilling over. "Really, I can't take a circus across the desert. I'm trying to stop a war!"

"So am I, Lazar," Boaz said, a fraction coldly, and the Spur knew he was no longer talking to a young man slightly in awe of him. The man in front of him was a Zar demanding respect from his Spur.

"Forgive me, Zar Boaz."

"Nothing to forgive," Boaz said, sensibly waving the moment aside. "We are all worried, and it may not appear so but I am fully sympathetic to your task of guiding people safely across the desert. It's frightening just to think of you taking that route. It's absolutely necessary, of course?"

"For speed, yes, Highness. By sea it would take two moons, which would not be fast enough to avert warriors hungry for booty. Marius and Lorto will stay the warships in open sea and send messages back to Romea. I'm hoping that by the time the birds arrive, Ana will have already argued her case with the King."

Boaz sighed, drained his cup. "Right, here is my decision. Lazar, you will escort Absolute Favorite Ana, together with Grand Vizier Tariq, and the Valide will go as Ana's escort . . ." He held up his hand, glaring, to prevent the furious outburst threatening to erupt from Lazar. "Ana needs the guidance of an older woman, and whatever else my mother is, she can be relied upon to be courtly. She is also incredibly perceptive when it comes to people. I want her there at that palace, especially as I realize you can hardly risk discovery. You will also take Pez—he will make good entertainment for our royal neighbors."

Lazar had to assume that Boaz's keen gaze was suggesting that he was sending the palace clown as help rather than hindrance. He pressed his lips together to prevent himself saying anything regrettable.

The Zar continued. "You will take a dozen of the Elim and four of my elite guard, the mutes, who will have the express task of guarding my wife. You can take as many or as few of your men as you wish, although I would prefer that you leave the city fully secured by the Shield in your absence. Zarab knows what might come at us in the meantime, especially if Marius and Lorto cannot head off all of those warships."

Lazar couldn't risk opening his mouth, such was his fury. Instead he maintained a stony silence. It was the Vizier who spoke up in response.

"Very good, my Zar. Please excuse me so I can make arrangements for gifts for our counterparts in Galinsea. Er, Spur Lazar, perhaps you can guide us in this?" He smiled and received a scowl in return. He continued: "The exchange of wedding presents will take place in three hours, Highness. I'm sorry it won't be the lavish affair it should be for your first wife, but I know you understand. We will do our best to impress with a wedding feast. May I suggest you rest until then. Spur Lazar, when do we leave?"

"At nightfall, as the Zar wishes," Lazar growled. "We can reach the foothills by midnight, sleep until an hour before dawn, and set out on the camels then." He hoped it sounded unappealing.

"Camels? Lovely," Maliz replied, a wry expression accompanying his words.

Lazar needed to escape. "Excuse me, Highness. I need to brief Jumo on the extra supplies we shall have to organize."

"Yes, go, by all means. Ensure that you take the royal tents. And, Lazar . . . ?"

Lazar looked back, the war inside him only barely sheathed.

"As unhappy as you are, I want you back here to witness my marriage to Odalisque Ana."

"I wouldn't miss it, Highness," Lazar said, and Maliz smiled.

23

The entire palace had swung into action. The kitchen had never worked more ferociously, although a feast for such a modest number of people was easy for the cooks to achieve. No Percherese wedding, rich or poor, peasant or royal, was complete without rice, tinted yellow with saffron. And in this instance, because it was the Zar, and the bride was his First Chosen, the golden rice would be scattered with precious jewels.

Animals were slaughtered, and although there was no time to roast them whole, alongside everything else that had to be prepared in time, the carcasses were carved up and simmered with vegetables. Soon the palace grounds were scented with the fragrance of cinnamon and cardamom, spicing the meat to be served with the golden rice. Beef was minced, spiced, formed into small individual mounds to be roasted over coals and served with flatbreads and yogurt laced with garlic and slivers of onion, together with fresh, ripe tomatoes. Anchovies were battered, ready to be deep-fried and served on beds of roka, the prized sweet green leaf that grows wild beneath the hills north of Percheron. The array of side dishes punctuated what would have to be a simple wedding feast, in truth, with magnificent splashes of color. Lightly cooked beans were dressed with lemon and garlic, artichokes stuffed with olive pilaf, vine leaves wrapped around small roasted vegetables flavored with fennel, dripping with tomato-scented oil. Sweetmeats vied for attention, glistening on platters, ready to be laid out on the feasting tables.

Simmered chicken breasts were beaten into strings to give texture to a rice dish that could be served savory or creamed and sugared for a sweet course. Meanwhile the hastily achieved showpiece was a camel, stuffed with sheep, which had in turn been stuffed with chicken that had a special fruity rice stuffing. Showpiece or not, it would have to be the final savory course to give the kitchens sufficient time to cook this spectacular dish reserved entirely for a royal wedding feast.

Vast trays of pastries were assembled. The favorite of the Zar was bar'shoula, dozens of layers of pastry so thin as to be almost transparent, with caramon nuts and dried figs held together by the region's sticky honey, then coated in a runny sugary icing. The pastry would be served with a small slab of Percheron's famous armak: clotted goat-milk cream shot through with ribbons of pomegranate syrup. The bar'shoula was dusted with gold for the royal occasion. For those who wanted to sample the famed icy sherbets of the Stone Palace, the kitchens were busy mixing the dark mulberry juice that had been sweetened and scented with rose petals into shaved ice. No Zar's feast would be complete without Percheron's frozen specialties.

Salmeo had just returned from the kitchens, where he had

personally delivered the cache of exquisite gems to be scattered over the golden rice. He had left behind a trustworthy Elim to watch over their use so that they didn't find their way into dishonest pockets. He had quickly moved himself past the disappointment of the failed execution. He was an opportunist at the best of times and from a young age had never lingered too long over any situation gone awry. There was always something to salvage from any circumstance, as long as you approached it positively. Already he was thinking ahead to the new court within the harem that would now have to be established to cater to an Absolute Favorite. Ana would need to be separated geographically from the Valide, as well as the other girls. She would now have her own retinue of slaves to serve her, as well as a personal assistant. As much as he found Ana a thorn in the soft belly of the harem, Salmeo found her spirit challenging as well. As much as he threw his lot in with Herezah, too much power to the Valide could undermine his control. Ana's presence would keep Herezah in check. If he played them against each other with his well-honed skills, he could be on top of things again. He would have to impose his own authority, of course, as soon as Ana came back to them from her diplomatic travels.

It was time now to make his way to a suite of rooms in the harem where he knew they were preparing Ana. She would have already been through the rigorous bathing ritual, and as he walked in, Elza and her helpers had Ana naked in their circle. They lofted soft-scented powder at her, dusting her entire body with a light mistlike covering of fine talcum that clung to the already applied oil of frankincense. The room was filled with the fragrance of the spice gently overlayed by honeysuckle, jasmine, gardenia—there were more scents, but he was so overwhelmed by the smell that he could not pick out the individual flowers that contributed to it.

"Are your hands readied, Ana?" he lisped, and she turned, her face a mask. He had anticipated anger—a scowl at least— but there was nothing. She appeared blank, but hatred emanated from her all the same.

Ana lifted her hands, palms downward, and showed him the intricate pattern of painted henna that stretched from her finger- tips to halfway down the length of her hand like short gloves. Her feet were stained with the henna bark also and dusted with gold so she glittered.

In a velvet pad, Salmeo carried the jewels she would wear to her wedding as well as the grit of diamonds that would be the final layer of dusting so her body sparkled for the Zar. The jew- els themselves were the same ones Herezah had worn when she had married Joreb, which Salmeo found fitting. These belonged to the harem rather than to Herezah, who possessed enough precious stones to look after a small harem of women herself. Joreb had always been generous, especially to his Absolute Favorite.

Salmeo knew the riches were meaningless to Ana but he en- joyed the slaves' exclamations at the beauty of the pieces when he unrolled the velvet.

"Emeralds only for this special day," he said, allowing the sun passing through the shutters to spark a fire through the magnificent jewels he held aloft. "To match your eyes, Ana. Why are they so sad?"

"Perhaps because I'm not dead."

Elza's face twisted in embarrassment at her charge's direct- ness but she remained silent, shooing away her helpers now that the Grand Master Eunuch had arrived.

Salmeo ran an appraising gaze over Ana's body. "Very, very nice," he lisped. "The drowning seems to have caused no long-term damage."

"None that you can see."

"Manners," Elza hissed as she hurried by Ana to pick up the baskets of dried, crushed petals that formed the talcum along with chalk.

"I have no reason to be polite to him," Ana said. Her voice continued to rise and Salmeo could see Elza tremble. "He has tried his hardest to destroy me, but like a bad smell I keep returning to spoil his days."

"Indeed you do, child," Salmeo said, his thick lips pulled into a pert grin. "However, it is not altogether as unpleasant as you think. But try not to goad me, Ana, remember when you return—"

"If I return."

He ignored her interruption. "When you return you will be all mine again, and while you may well be First Chosen and Absolute Favorite of the Zar, you will also be simply Ana, a member of this harem."

"You can no longer hurt or threaten me, Salmeo. I despise you. But you are nothing, the mere slime that gathers around any powerful person."

Though he should have been used to her insults by now, Salmeo found himself unexpectedly enraged by her boldness. "Is that so? I presume this attitude of yours means you've suddenly given up caring for your family, then."

He noticed she didn't flinch at his threat, and wondered what had changed. Her family had always been her weakness.

"You cannot threaten me with my family's welfare anymore. They have protection now."

"From the Zar?" He laughed. "He wouldn't even know who they are."

"But the Grand Vizier does, and should anything happen to my family that seems accidental or unusual, it will find you, Salmeo, because I have already warned Tariq of your threats."

"Tariq now, is it?" Salmeo carefully controlled the fire in his voice.

Ana nodded. "You share the same status, I gather. May I suggest you don't attract his ire—he has the Zar's respect, unlike you, and I imagine he's every bit as cunning as you or the Valide."

Although Salmeo inwardly fumed, he smiled softly, and put a fat finger against his lips. "Shh, be careful, Ana."

"I'm not scared of you or her anymore. I died today—a few more seconds beneath the waters and no one could have revived me. Nothing scares me anymore."

"You feel strong now, Ana, but I assure you, once you're back, it will be different. I can make others suffer. All the time you're away, you'll know they're crying because of you. Young Sascha, for instance—"

"You leave her alone!"

"And then there's the shy, pretty Lesan . . ."

"I swear—"

"What do you swear, child?" Salmeo encouraged. He watched her take a deep breath.

"Nothing," she said.

"Good. Treat me with respect, Ana, and perhaps we can start again with a nod toward your new status."

She stared angrily at him but said nothing.

"And be careful with Tariq. There is something rotten

there, something I can't fathom. He will not confer his favors lightly."

"You worry about your own relationship with him."

"Don't say I didn't warn you. Now turn, Ana, let me place these jewels around you. Elza, bring your silks, it is time to dress Ana for her marriage."

BOAZ ROSE, LOOKING AS elegant and eligible as his mother had ever seen him in dark, glimmering emerald robes over white silks. He stepped down from the dais and took her hand. She bowed, fluid and magnificent in her own multilayered silks of various colors. Though she knew she looked as stunning as usual, she had never gotten herself ready this fast before. When he raised her he kissed her hand. "Welcome, Mother."

"You honor me, Zar."

"As you should be," he replied.

Her eyes glittered with the anger she had had to bury over Ana's startling change in fortune. It was unbelievable—one moment a prisoner in the process of being executed, the next marrying into the Imperial Court of Percheron. It was not lost on Herezah that Ana now had equal ranking with herself within the harem. And she was careful not to show that this fact shattered her. "This is a surprise for us all."

"As much to me as well. As you're aware, I had formally chosen Ana. But it was an uninspired idea to make her my wife, and a very good one, which might just avert war."

The Valide turned to where she sensed the Spur stood. He, too, looked dazzling in all white, and even though he was paler than she recalled, his face looked more chiseled than she could remember. Despite her fury, she felt the familiar thrill shiver through her body at the sight of him. As usual, his expression was unreadable. From behind her veil she smirked. "And what do you think, Lazar?" she purred.

"It's what we all wanted, isn't it, Valide? From that very first day we all saw Ana, we knew she was perfect."

"Not so perfect, perhaps, now that we know how headstrong she is and how much she hates everyone here. Not to mention the lengths she'll go in order to impress that upon us."

"Still," Boaz interjected diplomatically, "it's the right thing to do and Ana can make the difference between bloodshed—our blood, that is—and peace. We must all keep this in mind. Forget what has gone before."

"Fret not, my Lion. I shall be a dutiful mother and will treat her as I would my own daughter," Herezah said, the cloying words sticking on her tongue.

"Thank you. I am grateful you say this, because I need you to act as her guardian." Herezah frowned, confused. "What I mean is you will be going to Galinsea as Ana's escort."

Herezah felt her perfect composure slip. "What?"

"Ana is representing us in the Galinsean palace. She needs a woman by her side, someone of your caliber to assist her. Take a couple of the slaves to see to both your needs."

"Boaz, really, I—"

"My mind is made up. Believe me, I've already had this fight with Lazar. But he is resigned to my decision and I trust you will not argue the point."

Herezah was incredulous. He had honored her with hon-eyed words, and now he was using that same sweetened tongue as a weapon, lowering her to the status of nursery maid. Before she could find words of protest, he had turned away at a signal from Bin.

"It seems we are under way," he said, distracted. "It's to be a brief ceremony, purely an exchange of gifts to seal the marriage."

Pez scampered in ahead of everyone, cartwheeling and whooping for joy. He was dressed head to toe in emerald and white to honor his Zar. Behind Pez came the Galinsean party—Marius and Lorto looked refreshed, as well as bemused by the dwarf's frivolity. They were accompanied by the Grand Vizier together with a host of Percherese dignitaries, all hastily assembled. Herezah grimaced behind her veil. It was not traditional for a Zar's marriage to be displayed publicly. It seemed vulgar to her that something so steeped in tradition and mystery was being paraded around almost as a piece of entertainment. Joreb would turn in his tomb—but then, although Joreb enjoyed tradition, he always encouraged his elder sons to think as daringly as their imaginations permitted. *We must move Percheron forward*, he used to tell the older boys on the rare occasions he gathered them together. *It's valid to keep an eye on the past, to respect what's gone before, but don't be left behind by not keeping your other eye on the future.*

It seemed to Herezah that her own son was taking a very forward-thinking approach. Already his short reign had seen so many of the old traditions discarded that she herself was beginning to feel somewhat antiquated in her views, and yet she'd always considered herself a relatively contemporary thinker.

Pez rolled nearby, pausing to shriek hysterically at Herezah, and this dragged her from her private thoughts back to the event before her. Coming through the doors now was Salmeo, looking very grand and exceptionally pleased with himself. He was holding the hand of Ana, who, dwarfed by his enormous stature, looked every bit the child at his side. Even though her hand was held by Salmeo, she walked as far from him as she could; there was little doubting how much she despised the eunuch. Above them, four Elim carried a silken canopy, embroidered with the finest gold thread. The canopy was a bright blue—Ana's choice—and that particular shade of aquamarine would now be her palace color, unusable by anyone else in the harem.

Ana was unveiled because she was in the presence of her Zar, and her arrival drew a hush of awed silence. As much as it galled Herezah, even she had to acknowledge that she had never seen a more glorious-looking woman. To think, just hours before, they had dragged her seemingly lifeless body from the river.

Ana sparkled—every inch of her glittered and glowed. Her garments had been carefully chosen to seductively reveal her diamond-encrusted shoulders and the golden-hued, flawless skin beneath. The palace seamstresses must have worked impossibly hard these past few hours, Herezah knew. The Valide jealously watched Ana kneel and then lay herself prostrate on the Throne Room's cool, magnificently tiled floor.

Herezah could not resist a searching gaze at Lazar, who, despite his own best efforts, looked ... what was the right word? ... forsaken. Something precious was being taken from him today, and when his own rigid stare slid from Ana to the Valide, Herezah understood that he realized she knew what he was giving up. She would not go so far as to call it love, but his desire for this young woman was certainly obvious to her. Something was dying inside Lazar, she could sense it, and it galled her more deeply than any other wound that she was not the one who was inflicting this pain on him. If only he could feel one tenth of the anguish, of the ache she'd felt for him, he might come close to understanding real envy.

From Lazar's forlorn appearance Herezah drew her ultimate

comfort, for this day that had gone so badly wrong for her. His suffering pleased her. Her son was marrying the girl she wanted dead, yes, but Lazar's impenetrable facade was being smashed, burned to rubble before her eyes.

She smiled at the Spur and both understood what her curving lips conveyed. He looked away, disgusted that she could read him as well as she had.

Into the hush, Salmeo spoke the traditional words. "Zar Boaz, King of Kings, Mightiest of the Mighties, may I present your First Chosen. The harem approves the marriage and we give you Odalisque Ana to be our sparkling jewel, a treasured possession. May she please you, my Zar, and bring you fine, healthy heirs. Brothers!" His final word was the signal for everyone to offer their good wishes to the Zar and his bride. Specially crafted lightweight wooden eggs were rolled toward the couple as Ana was lifted from the ground and then guided to stand directly before her husband. The wooden eggs were symbolic, meant to offer blessings for a fertile marriage, and in Percherese homes the custom was for the children of the two families being brought together to paint the eggs, with any design of their choosing. In the imperial palace it was also the custom for the eggs to be studded with tiny gems for the bride to collect as keepsakes. Some women, and always the First Chosen, swallowed one of the eggs, acknowledging their power to bestow fertility.

Ana chose a tiny egg encrusted with palest sapphires that seemed to reflect the color of the sea. It wasn't easy to swallow, of course, but when she opened her mouth as instructed, to prove it was empty of the egg, applause exploded into the room. The only person not clapping, Herezah noted, was Lazar.

Boaz cleared his throat and the room became silent. "Thank

you, brothers. I accept this woman to be my wife, my First Chosen and Absolute Favorite. She is to be known by that title from now on. We cast away Odalisque; she is now to be addressed as Zaradine Ana." He held out his hand and Ana stepped up one stair. She momentarily stood above all except the Zar himself. Boaz lowered his head and kissed her hand, drawing a box from his pocket. The box was carved, inlaid with pearl, and was too big for jewels. Once again Herezah was struck by the way her son was breaking from custom even at the most traditional point of his wedding ceremony, when the Zar would normally bestow a magnificent piece of jewelery on his First Chosen.

"This is for you," Boaz said, a smile stretching widely across his face. "Open it, Zaradine Ana."

With shaking hands she took the heavy box and did as she was asked, withdrawing exquisite miniatures, perfectly rendered in stone, of her favorite statues from Percheron: Beloch and Ezram, the twin giants; Crendel and Darso, the winged lions; Iridor, the owl; and Shakar, the feared dragon.

Ana opened her mouth in unfeigned delight. Herezah heard puzzled whispers around the room from those who could see the gift. Surely replicas of statues were meaningless to a beautiful woman?

"Do you like them?" Boaz asked quietly, but just loud enough for Herezah to overhear.

"I adore them, Zar Boaz," his new wife replied, and no one could mistake her pleasure.

"Let the feast begin!" Boaz announced, his own delight evident.

There was more bemused clapping and smiles before Salmeo called order for the final announcement. "Brothers, we ask you to follow the torches out into the courtyard, where the feast will be held. Our Zar and his new Zaradine will now consummate their marriage and we will provide proof shortly." His voice took on a conspiratorial tone and the men laughed. Even Marius and Lorto seemed to understand without the need for translation.

AS ANA TURNED TO follow Salmeo and her Zar, her gaze fell upon the Spur. There was no sense of triumph as she thought there might be within herself, and she saw only deep sorrow in the look he returned. He dipped his head to her in a crisp bow and took his leave. She was sure he would not be joining the festive celebrations over food. Her mind was a whirl and it was hard to know what to think, how to think. All she knew right at this moment was intense pain—for Kett mostly, but also for herself at being denied death, and for discovering that Lazar had lied. That he was alive and now she would be traveling with him. Worst of all, she knew, despite all her intentions, that she loved him harder at this painful moment than she thought possible. She hadn't forgotten her promise to Lyana either. It was an ironic turn of events. Lyana had granted her greatest prayer that Lazar somehow survive, even though death seemed so certain, and in return she had given her oath to the Goddess that she would not seek his affections. Lyana had been true and Ana intended to honor her pact with the Goddess. She hoped it would make it easier to keep her promise now that she had anger coursing through her veins, but it was matched equally by the familiar pain of desire. She would have to let them go to war within her and pray that anger won out. Right now the Zar would expect her to join him in his bed. She had not allowed herself to think about it until this moment, and as much as she liked Boaz, the thought revolted her. She had never seen him as a lover, more as a brother, but she had no choice. To keep those she loved safe—and she helplessly included Lazar in this small group—she had to see this through and be a dutiful Zaradine.

THE SIGNAL WAS GIVEN and Ana followed behind the men, carrying her box of statues, more precious to her than any jewels.

No one noticed the stillness of the Grand Vizier, who was still trying to understand the meaning of the Zar's gift to his Zaradine. Maliz was utterly convinced now that, although Ana was not the Goddess, she was his guide to the discovery of who Lyana was. How Boaz could be involved intrigued him—or was it just pure coincidence? Stranger things had happened in his lifetime, but he had learned to pay attention to everything, treat all potential clues as leads to the pathway he sought.

Ana and her box of statues—renderings of the very same creatures Maliz had personally turned to stone all those centuries ago—would lead him to that path.

24

Lazar did not join the festivities; instead he tried to put distance between himself and the Zar's private chambers, convincing himself that if he were physically removed he might also be able to remove the thought of Ana and Boaz from his mind. He found himself in a lonely orange grove on the fringe of the palace complex, mercifully empty of workers or servants. His head hurt from lack of sleep, but his heart hurt far more.

Pez found him brooding.

"You didn't hide it very well."

Lazar looked up from the ground, where he had been studying an ant's labors. "What do you mean?"

"Ana."

"That obvious?"

"Not to Boaz, thankfully."

"I thought I could handle it, Pez. I thought I was bigger, stronger, tougher."

"Than what?"

"Than love," Lazar replied wistfully.

Pez hefted himself onto the small stone bench seat next to Lazar. He was silent for a few moments. And then he sighed. "I hadn't realized how painful this is for you."

"If I didn't have to keep seeing her, it might be easier."

"This is true, but you have no choice now that war is coming. How do you think your parents will react to her?"

"I haven't known my parents in so many years it's hard to judge, but I can't think of a better candidate." Lazar sighed. "I would spare her it if I could, Pez, I hope you know that. But there is no guarantee that they would necessarily forgive me— or even listen to me—if I argued Percheron's case. Ana has as much chance as I do to gain their ear and they will spare her life—they have to, she is a diplomatic emissary. With me, they could do whatever they want—kill me, throw me into the dungeon. And I'd be no help to Boaz and Percheron in a stinking cell. I need to be able to fight this war if it's coming. I know how the Galinsean mind works."

Pez nodded. "Well, we shall all be there to give her confidence."

"You've heard, then?"

The dwarf grimaced. "Yes. In a way, I'm pleased—I'd rather keep my enemy close."

"It seems all my enemies are along for the ride."

"Herezah will certainly make it an interesting journey. I think we can count in days when she'll make her move on you."

Lazar groaned.

"It's probably a good thing. Keep your mind off Ana."

"I would not touch the wife of the Zar."

Pez shrugged. "That's good, then. Perhaps you can do us all a favor and keep his mother happy."

Lazar ignored the comment. "What about the Vizier? He's been goading me most of the afternoon."

"What do you think he knows?"

"I have no idea. He was certainly probing, trying to make connections."

"That's what Maliz is about. His whole reason for being is to find the clues that lead him to Lyana. He takes nothing for granted, leaves no stone unturned. There is no thread too weak for him to pull on. He will always follow each to its end."

"And I'm one of them?"

"Of course you are, but he doesn't know that. You are simply another person to be watched until you can be discounted as having no potential, no clues to Lyana's physical incarnation."

"Like what?"

"Some have already presented themselves. Kett, for instance—Maliz may or may not have made the connection."

"Kett's involved?"

"I'm sorry, Lazar. I haven't told you this. Kett named himself the Raven a long time ago to me."

"And who is the Raven?"

"The bird of sorrows. He lives a life of sadness, brings grave news, and if my memories serve me true, then he makes a prediction."

"A prediction of what?"

"Usually cryptic but traditionally related to the outcome of the battle. That's why we call him the bird of sorrows. It has never been good news for Lyana's followers. This time it may be different."

"Who does he tell?"

"It varies."

Lazar paused, thinking. "You think he gave his prediction to Ana."

"Possibly. They spent time together before he died. Perhaps that's what Ellyana meant about this time being different."

"I don't get you," Lazar said, frowning.

"Well, to my knowledge the Raven has never had access to Lyana before. He usually has to tell one of her supporters."

"And you think he's told Ana—"

"Lyana."

Lazar ignored the interruption. "You think he's given her some important information."

"I'm guessing. I have only the traditions of the past to go on, and as I keep telling you, this time is supposed to be different."

Something struck Lazar. "What happens when Maliz comes into contact with the woman he hunts?"

"Ah," Pez said, conspiratorially. He paused a moment. "Forgive me, I just had to check that no one was eavesdropping."

"Using the Lore?"

Pez nodded quickly before continuing. "Maliz hunts down anyone he suspects can lead him to the Goddess."

"And?"

"When he is finally aware of her, he comes into his true power."

"Only when he knows she has risen?"

"Yes, that's when his powers are all his to draw upon."

"So where has Maliz been all of this time before stealing Tariq's body?"

"He hides. Give himself to a body that requires very little of his powers to control. To tell the truth, he's powerless until he commits to a body."

"I don't understand."

Pez sighed. "Maliz lurks, for want of a better word, in a body he chooses deliberately because of its ability to hide him. For instance, someone old, someone very young perhaps, someone with an affliction. He lives within this body, virtually dormant. If it should die he can move to another body, but without Iridor's rising, he has no power to commit to a body."

"Take it over completely, you mean?"

"That's right. He can exist for decades, moving only should the host look like he's dying. But he can't use his full magic . . . just enough to make the body function and sustain itself. He is summoned when Iridor rises. He comes into greater powers at the rising of Lyana."

"Is it the same for Lyana?"

"Similar."

"And?"

"Well, traditionally he destroys her," Pez said irritably.

Lazar was frowning again. "He won't waste any time. He'll kill her on the spot?"

"If he can, yes. I believe in some cycles he's done just that. More often he has to struggle a little harder. She is evasive, and of course, she fights back."

"But if he has access to her, that is to say, he comes face-to-face with her, he has the power to destroy her?"

Pez misunderstood the question. "History shows that blow for blow, yes, he is stronger, but this time—"

Lazar shook his head. "Then Ana is not who you think she is."

Pez continued, talking over Lazar's soft realization, not registering what he had said. " . . . this time, being different, I have no idea how it will go. What did you just say?"

"I said, Ana is not the Goddess."

Pez frowned quizzically. "Why do you say that?"

"Pez," Lazar said gently, as if talking to a young child, "Boaz sent the Grand Vizier to fetch Ana from the harem only hours ago. They spent a considerable amount of time together because Boaz entrusted Tariq-Maliz, whatever you want to call him, to brief Ana on the plans regarding Galinsea. And what's worse, I sense she sees the Vizier as an ally."

Lazar watched his friend's face blanch, his lips part, but no sound came out. The Spur waited, knew it was a shock, understood that this news placed Pez in a situation of terrible limbo.

"Did he touch her?" the dwarf finally asked, his voice urgent.

"What difference does that make?"

"It's her touch that quickens his magic!"

Lazar looked baffled. "I don't know. I imagine he might have, considering how comfortable they seemed. He had ample opportunity to take her arm or guide her, even. They spent a lot of time talking. I'm not suggesting they're friends, but if you compare the body language of Ana and Salmeo to Ana and Tariq—"

"Maliz!" Pez spat.

Lazar nodded. " . . . it just seems more relaxed. If Ana was Lyana, she would be dead right now, not pleasuring the Zar." The words came out choked, angry.

"It can't be. This cannot be!"

"Hush, Pez," Lazar warned.

"You don't understand. Everything I've told you is right."

"I don't doubt—"

"No, listen! I felt her magic. It is not the Lore. It is something else. It has to be of the Goddess and . . ." Pez looked terrified. Lazar watched him search for more evidence. "You've said it yourself!" the dwarf suddenly said. "She knows too much about the ancients—she gave you the names of the giants, of the winged beasts; she can hear me over a mind link; she, too, said this time it would be different."

Lazar nodded but said nothing.

"She told you herself that she is an old soul. She has seen things in her dreams no goatherd's daughter would know of. You told me once she described Percheron's layout like the spread of a volcano's lava . . . as if marble had spewed out and slid down the hill to the water."

"I did." Again Lazar nodded, not wanting to crush Pez's attempt to justify his belief.

"She's never been out of the foothills! How could she know what a volcano looks like? How can she know who Beloch and Ezram are? How come Zafira believed that Ana is Lyana, as I do, and Zafira is now dead at the hands of Maliz? And don't deny that Ellyana thought Ana special." His words were tumbling over one another in his efforts to convince Lazar.

Lazar hated to contradict Pez's outburst. "Did she?"

"Ellyana gave her the statue of Iridor," Pez replied, his anger barely contained.

"But what does that confirm?"

Pez's face had turned so red with his passionate outpouring it looked as if he was going to explode at his friend's calmly negative approach.

Lazar continued softly: "It doesn't confirm or deny anything, my friend. Perhaps all who believe have been hoodwinked."

"Hoodwinked?" Pez's voice squeaked in his attempt to control his anguish; his expression was incredulous.

"Poor choice of words, Pez, forgive me. I'm simply suggesting that Ellyana, yourself, and Zafira have fixated on Ana because she *is* so unique, she *does* have a curious background, she certainly shows an affinity for Lyana, and—"

"Stop! We can settle this by finding out if he touched her."

"You said he hunts down every clue. Surely he would have tried; there is too much focus on Ana for him not to have his interest at least piqued by her. He was alone with her; he had ample opportunity. If he touched her, she should be dead." Lazar looked at Pez with deep sympathy. "She's not Lyana."

Now Pez looked as though he might weep.

"I'm sorry, Pez. Ana is simply a goatherd's daughter. You have to move past her, see her as nothing more than the Zar's wife."

Lazar meant it kindly but Pez reacted as if stung. "Instead of lecturing me, perhaps you should take some of your own advice!" He leaped from the seat and ran away on his short legs.

Lazar looked after him with sorrow, and understanding. The dwarf was right. He, too, must move on from Ana. She was no longer a forbidden odalisque—she was now the untouchable Zaradine, First Chosen and Absolute Favorite of the Zar. Any outsider who looked at her with desire would be punished with death.

Ana was now as good as dead to him, as Shara was—Shara, his first and only other love. After losing her, he'd sworn that he would never open his heart to another woman. He would take his pleasure, enjoy the transient release that lying with a woman offered, but he would return himself to stone—just like the sculptures of Percheron he admired so much. But he had broken his vow—had allowed Ana to touch his heart—and it had only brought more suffering. No female would ever penetrate his facade again and get beneath his skin. He stood, renewing his promise to himself and to Lyana to relinquish Ana.

"Ana is dead to me," he said softly, as if speaking the words sealed his oath.

A runner appeared, anxious and breathless. "Spur Lazar," he said, bowing.

"Yes?"

"The Grand Vizier has summoned everyone back to the Throne Room."

Lazar knew why and felt his stomach twist with despair and hated anticipation. "Lead the way," he ordered, knowing full well he could not escape this, no matter how much he wanted to walk out of the palace and just keep walking.

EVERYONE HE REMEMBERED FROM the wedding ceremony, save Herezah, had gathered in the Throne Room. He nodded at Marius, who smiled his response from across the room—obviously the feast had gone well despite the language divide. Salmeo was rocking on the balls of his slippered feet, wearing a smug expression. At the gesture of one of the mutes, the chief eunich quietly excused himself, presumably to return Ana to the harem and accompany the triumphant Zar back to his guests.

Lazar could barely disguise his contempt as he stared at the eunuch's massive back. His thoughts moved sharply from Ana, from the pain of this "marriage," to hatred for Salmeo. He couldn't prove it, but he knew, in his marrow, that Salmeo was the one responsible for the attempt on his life. Lazar had long ago dismissed Horz's involvement; he had not known the Elim well, but what he did know of him was unequivocal. He had originally thought it must have been Tariq's doing—the old Tariq—but his own security measures imposed within the palace would have prevented the Vizier having any access to the harem's apothecary or the weapons room. Then there was Herezah—she had all the reasons for being behind such an intrigue, but he could not see how she gained anything from his death, other than the satisfaction of separating him from Ana—but then the harem did that rather effectively. And for all of Herezah's faults she was a pragmatist; she would know how much Boaz would need to rely on his Spur. He also grimaced privately at the Valide's amorous interest in him—she definitely preferred him alive.

No, all of his suspicions this past year of convalescence rested firmly at the feet of the Grand Master Eunuch, who would have been incensed at the humiliation he had suffered for Ana's original escape, and who was vicious enough to order death to the person who had so painfully pointed out his failure. Salmeo was worse than a scorned woman. He was cruel and spiteful, and being in a position of power, he could have coerced any number of people below him to do his bidding. And Lazar was sure Salmeo would have covered his tracks very well, cowed each person in that line of dirty deeds with so much fear that no one would speak the truth.

A series of gongs sounded, pulling him back to the present.

Lazar sighed, knowing what was coming, and turned, as everyone else had, toward the great doors of the Throne Room, which now swung open. In floated the Grand Master Eunuch swathed in multicolored silks. He was beaming; the cavernous gap in his teeth was filled now and then by a bright pink tongue that seemed to taste the air. Aloft he held a silken sheet that was smeared unmistakably with blood. Not much, but enough to tell its own tale.

The clapping began, turning into a cheer and then a roar as a not-so-sheepish-looking Zar entered the chamber. Lazar had anticipated that Boaz would be embarrassed by the attention, but Boaz was neither smiling nor serious, and he didn't strike Lazar as triumphant or, by contrast, in any way reserved. Boaz simply looked regal. He carried himself tall and proud; now, in everyone's eyes, he could carry himself as a man.

This show of the bedsheets was customary, although it normally took place only between harem walls, more for fun than anything else and rarely showed any blood. But Lazar could understand why today this somewhat vulgar posturing was necessary. This public presentation was for the Galinseans. They would not know that the blood on the satin bed linen was likely false because the Grand Master Eunuch had already prepared each new wife-to-be in a manner that effectively took her virginity. Lazar shuddered. Nevertheless, whether or not the small bloodstain on the sheets was Ana's was inconsequential. The Zar had taken a wife and their royal marriage was now consummated. Ana might be traveling to the Galinsean capital as an emissary for the royal court of Percheron but now she was much more than a traditional envoy. Percheron, was sending one of its treasures, possibly the most precious of all its jewels—the woman who would bear the first potential heir to the Percherese throne. The Galinseans, as barbaric as they were believed to be, would have to take this woman's pleas seriously, for Percheron was risking its future by sending her.

That was the rationale behind the plan, anyway. The Spur knew it would work. As much as Lazar could pride himself on having suggested that the Zar marry Ana immediately, he took no pleasure in his achievement. In fact, he felt so empty he wasn't even sure he could hide his sour look at the stained silken sheet.

The blood of a virgin.

Ana's blood.

A virgin no more.

"Zaradine Ana," he murmured. The words rolled awkwardly, unhappily, off his tongue.

The cheering had not let up and Boaz was unsuccessfully trying to dampen the high spirits of those helping him celebrate not only the loss of his bride's virginity but also his own.

"Doesn't look too flushed for someone who has just mounted his first filly," someone muttered softly to Lazar.

Lazar controlled a start. How had the Grand Vizier managed to steal up so close to him?

Maliz continued: "Ah well, he's young . . . first time . . . probably all over in a blink." He smiled conspiratorially, laying a perfectly manicured hand on Lazar's arm.

The Spur flinched as if scalded. He hoped the grinding of his teeth didn't sound as loud to the Grand Vizier as it did in his own head. "I can't remember that far back, Tariq."

It was obvious to Lazar that Maliz noticed his overreaction, but the Grand Vizier's voice contained nothing more than his recently acquired sardonic tone. "Oh, come now, Spur Lazar. We all remember our first time."

"You can?" Lazar meant to sound flippant but the words came out with no humor at all.

"Of course, as though it were just moments ago. She was very young, very ripe. Delicious, as I recall . . . just like Ana."

The inflammatory words sounded like a test, as though the

man were waiting for him to make an error, admit something, reveal a secret. Lazar felt only revulsion. "Excuse me, Grand Vizier. I must offer my best to the Zar and make preparations for our journey."

"Yes, of course," the Vizier replied, infuriating Lazar with a knowing wink.

Lazar stalked away, unsettled by his own internal battle over Ana and unnerved by the Vizier's scrutiny. Knowing that beneath the newly charismatic facade lurked a demon added exponentially to his discomfort. It occurred to him, as he walked toward his Zar, that perhaps Maliz suspected that he knew something about who Tariq really was. Shaking his head, he chastised himself. He was being paranoid.

"Ah, Lazar," Boaz said, the warmth of his smile doing nothing to penetrate the iciness of his Spur's feelings.

"Congratulations, my Zar."

"Thank you. I'm not sure how to feel," Boaz admitted quietly. "I'm not yet seventeen summers and already married—sounds very serious and grown up, don't you think?"

"You are a Zar, the Mightiest of the Mighties . . . that is serious enough for any man of any age."

Boaz nodded his appreciation. "And she is so lovely," he added, a little too wistfully for Lazar's jangling nerves.

"Indeed. She was certainly more lovely tonight than she would have been bloated at the bottom of the river, fodder for the palace fish, Highness."

The Zar's eyes narrowed. "Are you all right, Lazar?"

Lazar reined in his bitterness. "I am, Majesty. Forgive me. None of us has had any sleep and I think I must pay attention to my recovery. I look robust, I know, but the poison took a heavy toll and I can get quite weary."

Both knew that, although the words were probably truthful, they were meant to distance himself from what he had actually meant. The real truth had been glimpsed but had quickly hidden itself. Lazar cursed silently, now adding severe irritation with himself for that transparency to his list of grievances.

Boaz became rigidly serious. "I feel like an enormous weight has been lifted off my shoulders since you returned, Lazar . . . was it only just hours ago?" He stepped down from his dais and embraced the Spur. "I'm so glad you're back. I need you."

"I know," Lazar replied, somewhat shocked by the public gesture and unsure how to respond.

"And I need you to keep Ana safe," Boaz added with a fresh intensity, his dark eyes glittering.

"Of course, my Zar, she is your wife, your—" Lazar broke off as Boaz shook his head.

"She is so much more to me. I will make special sacrifices for her. I couldn't offer her protection when she was the sole property of the harem. Now I can offer her all the protection in the world because she belongs to me . . . totally."

The words cut like a blade through flesh and muscle, through sinew and bone, straight to Lazar's soul. He took a steadying breath and replied solemnly, "I understand, Highness." Although he had no idea what Boaz meant by saying he would make sacrifices. What sacrifice did any Zar make for any women, wife or otherwise?

Boaz wasn't finished; determined to press his point, he moved still closer still to Lazar "I love her," he said fiercely. "There may have to be other women in my life but no one will share my heart other than Zaradine Ana. Her son, when she gives me one—and she will . . . her womb is possibly already quickening with my seed . . . is the only heir to this throne."

Lazar met Boaz's gaze. The intensity in the Zar's stare was almost unbearable.

Lazar had known Boaz since the day he was born. He had always liked him as a child and had liked him even more as a boy and then as a young man. He had pledged his faith to Boaz when Zar Joreb had revealed during a private conversation that none of his other sons came close to Boaz in suitability as a leader and had asked Lazar to pledge his faith to the Zar-to-be; it was easy to give oath to the ruler that he would lay down his life for Boaz if asked. He knew this boy turned man to be passionate, knew that he took all his endeavors seriously. Obviously getting married was no casual event, even though it had been done to save them from a dire situation. Lazar suddenly realized that Boaz might not have agreed to the marriage had he not been so smitten by the bride.

This realization hit him physically—as though someone had punched him hard in the belly without warning. Lazar had no time to brace for the breathless wave of pain that coursed through his body. He knew almost everything there was to know about Boaz, but he had never suspected that the new Zar was as in love with Ana as he himself was.

Lazar had been careful; Ana had had no sign that he worshipped the ground she stood upon, the very sunlight that glinted off her radiant golden hair. Jumo had touched Ana more than he. Lazar had deliberately avoided giving anything of himself, save his helpless heart . . . and she didn't even know that he had handed it over to her in those foothills, on that first night, when she had reached right to his core and claimed him as her own. He had given it willingly, with a sense of wonder, surprise, awe, and a depth of feeling he never thought he might reach again.

Ana had become his touchstone, his reason for taking a breath each day and then another and another. It was because of her that he had vowed to go on breathing, to go on fighting the disease that wanted him so badly, when it would have been so easy to surrender to it.

She had saved him because of his terrifying love for her. And here was another man claiming the same! And this man had no empty claim. Not only did she belong to him as wife but she now belonged to him in body. Boaz had taken her, joined their bodies into one, might even have already sired a child on her if the gods were paying attention.

Lazar felt dizzy. A surge of nausea overwhelmed him. The words *no one will share my heart other than Zaradine Ana* echoed around and around his mind, addled with angst, riddled with jealousy . . . the latter an emotion he had never experienced. He was the eldest in his family, the spoiled child, the boy who had never had to fear anyone or feel rivaled by anyone—the heir who'd been doted upon until he'd made his error, and even then it was his choice to leave Galinsea. Life had always been his to carve as he wished and he chose his own paths. In this timeless moment he knew he was being pushed from the chosen path. Another had the right of passage here, and save for a high act of treason, there was absolutely nothing that Lazar could do to prevent his own fall by the wayside as Boaz pushed past.

There was nothing Lazar could do. He bowed, outwardly honoring his Zar but inwardly feeling dizzy with despair. "You have my word, I will lay down my life for her to keep her safe," he managed to say.

When he looked up he was shocked again to see Boaz misty-eyed with emotion. "You already have once before. Thank you for offering again—this time to my wife, not to a common slave."

The words rang in Lazar's ears as a warning. All he could do was nod before muttering his excuses to go prepare for the journey.

AS HE WATCHED THE Spur's retreating back, Maliz stored away the memory of how Lazar had reacted when he had touched him. He had flinched as though he had been burned by a fire-brand. What had startled him so? There was no denying that the Spur was suspicious of him but Maliz believed that was because the Spur and Tariq had an historical disgust for each other. Maliz knew Tariq had despised Lazar for his looks, his stature, his popularity, his disdain for palace ways, all of which had seemed only to make Joreb hold the man in ever higher es-teem—they'd been little short of blood brothers in the early years, and Tariq had burned with jealousy that the counsel that was rightly his was being given by a soldier. And Maliz sus-pected that Lazar detested Tariq for his obsequiousness and constant desperation for acceptance and respect.

He would have to ponder this further and put Lazar beneath Salazin's watchful gaze. Maliz roused himself from his private thoughts with the recollection that he, too, would be a member of the party that departed Percheron city at nightfall. He, too, had preparations to make.

25

Ana was escorted back to the harem, where she was met by cheering and excitement from the girls, who had stayed up late to welcome her.

"They haven't yet grasped that she is their enemy," Herezah murmured to Salmeo when he joined her.

"Oh, but they will, Valide. Most are still barely out of childhood, excited by the novelty."

"How did she seem directly afterward?"

"No weeping, if that's what you mean, Valide."

He noticed how his news disappointed her. "Boaz finds it hard to hurt an insect," she retaliated, her words sour even. "So, tell me, how was she?"

Salmeo took a moment to consider his response. "Calm, dignified. There was definitely something between them."

"Be specific, Salmeo—what?"

"It's hard to say, Valide. I only delivered and collected Ana, so my time with them both was limited to barely moments. She appeared visibly nervous on the way to the Zar's chambers, but she struck me as sedate and entirely in control, with her usual sneer for me, when I reclaimed her."

"She doesn't appear flushed or too disheveled."

"No, but she did ask me for a few moments to tidy herself and I suspect one of the mutes helped."

"One of the mutes?"

Salmeo nodded. "That very serious one, who never smiles: Salazin's his name. When I was summoned, he met me, prevented me from entering the chamber, and then slipped into the suite himself. Bin met me and asked me to wait because the Zaradine had requested this time to dress herself, brush her hair." He shrugged. "Is something amiss?"

Herezah's frown eased. "No, I just remember my first time." She smirked. "Joreb made sure I could barely walk."

"As I recall, Valide, Zar Joreb kept you for many hours. Boaz lay with Ana for less than one."

"He's young, probably still a bit shy, unsure. The main thing is it's done. So how did they receive the bloodstained sheet in the Throne Room?" she asked, looking to where the girls were admiring that same satin sheet. It was the harem's turn to follow its traditional custom. She watched the girls take the four corners of the sheet, billowing it up into the air over Ana's head and dancing around her. A particular song about marriage, the spilling of blood, and fertility was sung with great enthusiasm.

"Oh, it was an inspired idea of yours, Valide, with excited applause and celebration—as you can imagine—and with quiet relief for those of us who realize what's at stake."

"And Boaz, how was he?"

"Looked rather pleased with himself, Valide," Salmeo lied,

knowing that this was what she wanted to hear, even though he was confused by the Zar's circumspect manner. This moment was surely tied to any young man's greatest sense of achievement, and although the Zar had carried himself with tremendous dignity, Salmeo felt the young man didn't display the usual expression of quiet triumph.

"Excellent," the Valide said, cutting across his thoughts. "As much as it galls me that she is the Zaradine and Absolute Favorite, we should be glad that things have fallen into place as they have."

This surprised the Grand Master Eunuch. "How so, Valide?" he asked politely, knowing that things had, in fact, gone utterly against their original intentions.

"Well, Salmeo, she is no longer in quite such an unpredictable position. Her duty is now directly to the Zar and I suspect our feisty Ana will not be as inclined to try her tricks to defy Boaz." Salmeo thought differently, felt that Ana obeyed rules only with herself, but he kept his own counsel. "But she remains very much under our control in the harem. I think if we take things slowly, carefully, we can begin to use Ana for our own ends."

Salmeo couldn't imagine that Ana would ever put a grain of faith in either of them again. He could not hide his surprise. "Ana's not gullible enough, Valide. She knows we manipulated her toward her own demise. I can't imagine how you will use her to your own ends."

"Can't you, Salmeo?" was Herezah's haughty reply. "That's because you lack imagination. Ana can always be controlled. We simply have to ascertain what she cares about."

"But, Valide—"

"Don't be disingenuous with me, eunuch. I know your

mind is as cunning as my own," she snarled in her soft, feline way. "There is no undoing what is done. She lives—it is not my choice but it is how things have turned out. We move on. Because of the Galinseans—Zarab save me!—Ana is now the wife and Absolute Favorite of my son. I cannot change this. But I can learn to live with it and see how best to work with her new status to achieve what I want."

He could only admire her. Her whole careful plot had drowned, sunk into oblivion like the young black eunuch. Salmeo knew that the pain of that failure would be intense for Herezah and yet her survival instincts always emerged to restore her resilience, fuel her creative spirit to begin plotting anew. "What do you want, Valide?" He was careful to keep his query innocent and utterly polite.

"Nothing more than you do, Salmeo. I simply want control of a regime that is rightly mine—and I shall have it. It may take longer than I had originally planned. Incidentally," she said, obviously finished with that discussion, "whose inspired idea was it to have Boaz and Ana married? Did the Zar come up with the clever plan?"

"From my understanding, it was the Spur's, Valide. I gather Lazar suggested it when all else seemed lost. Ana speaks the language fluently but no one would take her seriously enough as a concubine. She needs status to enter the Galinsean court."

"I see," Herezah said mildly, her perfectly shaped fingernail tapping against her teeth. "That does make it more interesting."

"How so, Valide?"

"Because it means our Spur, who is so clearly besotted by the one who is now my son's wife, is planning time alone with her out of the harem. Makes for good sport, don't you think, Salmeo?"

"But you'll be there, Valide, as chaperone," he warned.

"Exactly. And I cannot wait for him to make his move."

"How can you be so sure he will?"

She laughed, although it came out as a sneer. "Intuition. I've told you before, Salmeo, you may be more woman than man but you cannot think like one of us." With this insult, she left his side and glided elegantly toward the center of the room, where the excitement for Ana had at last quieted.

"Ana, my dear, how do you feel?"

Ana met the Valide's eyes with a fierce stare. "Empowered."

Salmeo was sure Herezah had anticipated a certain amount of defiance, but he wondered if she was ready for such immediate rivalry. She did not show her surprise, however, and continued in the same tone, as though Ana had not said anything confrontational. "You must be a little weary . . . and sore."

"I all but drowned today, Valide. My body is certainly tired."

She tinkled a laugh. "But you've lain with a Zar—surely you feel energized, triumphant?"

"Neither, Valide. I remain a prisoner of the harem. Until that status changes, triumph is not mine."

There was a shocked gasp from the girls as Ana so directly challenged the woman who scared them all.

"Indeed," said Herezah lazily, seemingly unflustered, but Salmeo knew her too well not to know that she would be inwardly fuming beneath her calm facade at such a public rebuke. "The Zar is young, he'll need lots of attention, unless, of course, he chooses others quickly."

"He is free to choose whomever he wishes, Valide. I'm sure you of all people understand this."

Salmeo noticed as a pulse began to throb at Herezah's temple. Ana was certainly hitting a nerve with her wintry defiance and it seemed she wasn't finished.

"I for one will not fret over it. He has taken my virginity now, as you can all see—perhaps he will enjoy more virgins before he returns me to his bed. Certainly he'll have a long wait for me, as I must make a journey to help Percheron avoid war. I'd be lying if I didn't say that this interests me far more than the vacant pastime of being a concubine with no other role in life than to pleasure a powerful man."

Every word of Ana's quiet but pointed speech was a bark of disdain directed toward the Valide, each sentence an accusation, a sneer for the life Herezah had carved for herself. Perhaps Ana didn't feel the gathering storm, or perhaps she did and pressed on regardless. Salmeo sensed the eruption moments before it occurred, hardly dared breathe as he waited to see if the Valide would lose her nerveless control in front of the entire harem.

Herezah struck fast, her slap across Ana's face claiming the shocked silence the Zaradine's words had created. Given the sharpness of its sound, it was surely a painful blow to its recipient. Ana's face snapped sideways from the force but she steadfastly remained on her feet and turned straight back to face the Valide again. Her green eyes glittered darkly above the smile she wore openly.

"Welcome to my new world, Valide," Ana uttered, loading her rival's title with scorn. "We are now equals. You will never again lay a hand on me or lure me into your dark schemes. You are at the end of your power, Herezah. I am just coming into mine. Both of us enjoy this status because of your son. I wonder which one of us he would choose if he had to?" Her smile widened, lifting the cheek with its livid hand mark.

The festive atmosphere had changed entirely to something

dangerous, threatening. Some of the younger girls began to weep. Herezah looked oddly bereft of any pithy response and Ana's left cheek was turning bright red—Herezah touched it now and nodded. There was something knowing in that gesture, Salmeo believed, and he moved as fast as his huge body would permit.

"Valide! Zaradine Ana! Enough." His voice had lost its usual high, breathy quality. Now it sounded lower, angry. "This behavior is unseemly for the harem." If he was shocked by Herezah's being baited into acting so completely out of character, he was more stunned by Ana's response. Her words had chilled him. It appeared that they were no longer dealing with a broken young woman, driven to the point of wanting to die. Before him Ana stood proud, defiant, and utterly confident in her own new status as wife of the Zar. There seemed not so much as a speck of fear reflected in those once wide, unsure eyes. Something had happened in that bedchamber with the Zar. It appeared that in taking her virginity, Boaz had given her something very precious in return. "Valide, we must get you prepared for travel. Zaradine Ana?"

"Yes," she said, turning her gaze for the first time in a long while from the Valide.

"You, too, must prepare for a long journey. I shall send some slaves."

"Do I return to my chamber?"

Salmeo almost laughed. Already Ana was, despite her carefully couched inquiry, suggesting that she should be based in her own wing of the harem—as was fitting for the Zaradine and Absolute Favorite.

He cleared his throat. "I know you can appreciate that there has been little time since this morning—"

"In preparing for a death and a wedding, you mean?" she said, her voice hard.

He nodded, determined not to be intimidated. "Precisely. There has been no time to set up your new accommodations. And there is no point, as you leave tonight anyway. I would appreciate it if you would return to your old chamber and guide the slaves in what to pack. You will need warm as well as light clothing. The desert is contrary at best." He gestured to Herezah. "Come, Valide. Girls, amuse yourselves." His last words he spoke brightly, although no one could take their eyes off Ana and the Valide, or break the cold silence that washed like a winter stream between them.

BOAZ SIGHED AT BIN. He was in no mood, not after the day's events. He thought again of Ana, wished he could be with her. "Yes, of course, show her in. Bring some apple tea."

The servant bowed, and closed the door, which opened again momentarily. The Valide swept into the chamber. "My Lion," she said, affection oozing from every pore.

"Salutations, Mother." He looked at her quizzically. "Shouldn't you be preparing for your journey?"

"Oh, I'm letting Salmeo handle all of that," she said dismissively. "I wanted to see you. Are you sure I should be going on this adventure?"

It was not like his mother to pass up any opportunity—and this was by far the most generous chance she'd had in her lifetime—to slough off the restrictions of the harem and taste a sense of freedom. "Very sure. My wife needs a female chaperone. I can't think of anyone more suitable or wise."

She ignored the compliment. " 'My wife.' How enchanting that sounds. How do you feel?"

Boaz felt instantly on alert. Her voice sounded too innocent, her tone too chatty, and there was normally nothing sickly
sweet about Herezah, yet here she was displaying the breathy
interest of a mother with nothing else on her mind but domestic
concerns. She was here on a mission and he would just have to
do the dance until she got to the point. He opted to be evasive,
which he knew would irritate her. He had learned this past year
of his reign that deliberately provoking the Valide tended to
bring her to her point rather fast. "About what, marriage?"

"Of course. What else could I mean?' She paused, then exclaimed, "Oh, I wasn't referring to you losing your virginity."
She tinkled a coquettish laugh.

He knew she lied. A knock at the door sounded. "Come,"
Boaz answered, distracted by his mother's odd behavior.

Bin ushered in a servant bearing a tray with the apple tea.
The man placed the tray on a nearby table at Bin's instruction
before both servants bowed and removed themselves.

"I feel delighted," Boaz continued. "She was always going
to be my first choice, but I'm sure you knew that. Surely you
were not surprised?"

"Only in the timing. It came so suddenly."

"Do you refer to the marriage or to the choosing, Mother?"

"Both, if I'm honest. May I pour?" Her voice was light, almost carefree, as if she were indifferent to his responses. He
knew differently. Boaz nodded, watched her elegant movements
as she prepared the porcelain cups of apple infusion, whose soft
scent now permeated the chamber, relaxing him.

"Then I'll be honest," he said pointedly but not unkindly.
He needed his mother working for him now and Ana needed
his mother's guidance whether she thought so or not. He took

the cup and sipped before placing it before him, giving himself time to think about how best to respond. "I chose Ana when I did because I was angry. The timing of your shopping trip to the grand bazaar was just too perfect—even for my normally generous tolerance levels."

"Oh, my darling boy, a mere coincidence. Had I known it would spark such a reaction—"

"Don't, Mother, please. Nothing in your life isn't planned and carefully thought through. I'm your son, remember. I know you better than almost anyone in this palace, save your fat eunuch, who covers your every movement."

"What are you implying?" Her tone was injured, though Boaz knew the hurt was feigned.

"Only that he would never contradict anything you do or say."

"That's his role, son. Grand Master Eunuch and Valide have traditionally worked closely."

"And plotted closely, too?"

Herezah's face was the picture of innocence. "What do you mean, Boaz? I'm really not understanding you. I come to see you, to congratulate you, and you turn on me like an angry dog."

"It's not like you to be quite so dull, Mother. It insults me that you think I am gullible enough to believe that you didn't plan your trip to the market in order to prevent me from seeing Ana. I know you didn't want me to marry her—" He raised a hand to stop her interrupting. "Yes, she is very suitable and I know you were the person who picked her originally, although perhaps Lazar might have that claim. But you have despised Ana since you first came to realize that she was not to be cowed by the harem—and that she posed a threat to your superiority."

"I think you've got me wrong," she said, lifting the cup to her lips. "I've always rather admired her."

"Possibly, but you're also jealous of her, Mother, although I am baffled by that. You are one of the most beautiful women the harem has ever seen. You have intelligence, elegance, status, and power. I find it altogether ludicrous that you have single-mindedly made the life of a young orphan so very miserable. You've forced her into taking extraordinary risks and on both occasions her life has been threatened. You nearly won today and I was powerless this morning. But I am no longer power-less—the threat of war overrides all rules . . . even those of the harem. So Ana may still belong to the harem but I have now be-stowed upon her equal status to yours. I'm presuming that this is what you came to see me about?"

Herezah took a deep breath and he knew she was weighing up her situation. She found no sympathy with him and he antic-ipated that she would likely change her approach. "I came only to offer my sincere congratulations to you, Boaz. I don't care much for Ana—it would be pointless for me to deny it—but I do admire her and I think she makes you a fine Zaradine. I just question her motives and indeed Lazar's."

This Boaz had not expected. "Lazar's? What in Zarab's name are you talking about?"

"Well, it's just that this trip gives them the cover they so crave. It legitimizes leaving the harem."

"Mother, you'd better quickly explain what you mean."

Once again Herezah gave an innocent, wide-eyed shrug. "Well, is it only me who knows that Lazar is in love with Ana?"

Boaz felt his throat tighten—he wasn't sure whether it was

from fright or anger, but he was convinced that the cause of that sensation and the sudden chill in the room was driven by jealousy. He struggled to retain his composure. "I'm not sure why you would say such a thing."

"Because it's true, Boaz," she said matter-of-factly. "Lazar might have sold Ana into the harem but I'd wager he began regretting that move within the first few hours of knowing the girl. And he's never stopped grieving over her loss. You, of course, don't know any of this, but Lazar did everything he could to win her a special day of freedom from the harem each moon."

Boaz blinked, as he always did when he was caught in a situation of deceit, and hoped his mother missed it. She must never know he had been a witness to Ana's Choosing Ceremony. "I heard some rumor to that effect."

"I see. And that doesn't trouble you?"

"Why should it?"

"That he would die for her—that we all thought he *did* die for her—doesn't surprise you?"

"He had no plans to die for her—he simply accepted her punishment, which was a whipping, not death. Like me, he railed against a rule that could impose such a harsh sentence on a young woman. I was unable to do anything more than commute the sentence to a lesser penalty. Lazar was far braver. He did the sort of thing my father admired him so much for, and it is why I feel the same way about our Spur. His poisoning was something entirely different. But to answer your question, no, I am not surprised that Lazar would take a flogging for Ana. If I could have, I think I would have, too."

Herezah seemed at last unsettled. "Oh, Boaz, please. She's a slave."

"So are you."

She wasn't quick enough to stifle her gasp, but she kept her silence as they stared at each other across porcelain cups, each taking the other's measure.

Boaz continued more softly; he hadn't wanted this to turn into a confrontation. "She's my wife. She is Zaradine and Absolute Favorite. Please don't overlook that, Mother, whilst you're away."

Her voice remained quiet but the tone was all granite. "Boaz, may I remind you that in the harem she is still answerable to the rules set by its internal hierarchy."

"Yes, I know. And I have no intention—not at this stage anyway—of changing that balance . . ." Boaz inwardly smiled as his mother blanched at his qualification. "But for the time being, Ana is out of the harem and traveling as diplomatic envoy for the Zar. In this regard she has exceedingly high importance and her status is equal to yours. You will not exert your formidable talent for derailing her when I need Ana using all of her emotion and eloquence in bargaining a peace for us."

"And Lazar?" Her words sounded like a demand.

"What about Lazar?" he roared, his patience spent.

"Well." Her expression told him she was unsure of her ground suddenly as she stammered slightly in the face of his obvious displeasure. "How do I handle that side of things?"

He regarded her with an expression of disbelief and no little disdain. "Do you really think Lazar is going to be handled— as you put it—by anyone? You're in *his* domain, Mother. He knows the desert better than anyone—he survived crossing it from west to east, as you might recall. He will not be looking to be advised by you, or indeed by anyone. When this caravan leaves, there is only one person in charge . . . and it's not you. Spur Lazar will make all the decisions."

"But you understand my meaning, son, I'm sure," Herezah said, and Boaz knew his mother, the clever chameleon, was trying a less confrontational approach.

"Are you asking me whether I give my authority for you to spy on Lazar and Ana? Are you asking whether I concede that I would be interested to find out if you can catch them in an indiscretion?"

"I'm asking you to take me seriously when I say that Lazar's interest in Ana is not all avuncular, as everyone seems to think!" She had not raised her voice but there was a fresh crispness to it, reminding him that she was his mother and was due respect.

"I shall say this once only. I trust Ana to be true. I trust Lazar with my life, her life, your life, and the lives of all the Percherese. Does that make it clear enough?"

Herezah's resolve to be diplomatic clearly snapped. "I will not be spoken to like this, Boaz."

"Someone has to speak this way, Mother, and I'm the only person of any real authority over you around here. You may control the harem through your clever ways, but contrary to your personal opinion, you do not control me. You haven't controlled me from the moment you kissed the emerald ring that graces my finger and hailed me as the Zar of Percheron. I know it must come as a shock to be taken from the harem, but you might as well get used to it now. You are being sent to Galinsea at my discretion as escort to my wife. That is all I ask you to do . . . guide her if she requires guidance, support her if she requires support, help choose her clothes if that's what's needed, but don't upset her by your cunning strategies. She is our only hope for peace—I cannot stress this enough. I trust you under-stand the delicate position in which we find ourselves?"

She matched the condescension in his tone when she said, "You say you trust Lazar. What do I do when he tries to steal private time with your precious wife?"

"To lie down with her . . . is that what you mean? Come on, Mother, be direct."

"What else does any man have on his mind where a beautiful woman is concerned?"

He sighed, none of the disdain gone from his stance. "Now this just makes me sad. I must ensure that the women of my harem enjoy a wide-ranging education. It's narrow thoughts like these that could set us back countless years. I want to be a Zar that people remember for his modern thinking and his dedication to change if it's a good thing for Percheron. If that's how you see men, then it blatantly shows me how damaging a place the harem truly is. Perhaps the Goddess was right, and we should return to the ancient ways of a matriarchal system, where women were treated with honor, respect, where their roles as priestesses were worshipped. Look what you've turned into, Mother. Do you really see yourself as being useful only as a vessel for a man?"

"You couldn't blame me if I did."

"No. But I can assure you that I'm not obsessed with the notion of bedding every girl in the harem, and from what I hear, Lazar's record of being with women is discreet, to say the least."

"And you know this how?"

"It doesn't matter, Mother. If Lazar were the lascivious sort, he would have fallen for the feminine wiles that you have so blatantly used on him in the past!"

He thought for one moment she might slap him, but instead she drew a long steadying breath to quell the fury he saw in her eyes.

"Please don't speak to me like that, Boaz. I'm due more respect from you."

"Mother, respect works both ways—remember how my father taught my brothers and me that?" She nodded angrily. "Well, do more than just pay lip service to your Zar. Respect me! Don't try to control me, don't try to anticipate my every move so you can be there first, don't destroy the small things that glitter in my life."

"Like Pez?" she offered sarcastically.

He stared her down. "Like Ana."

"You still haven't answered my question, Boaz, and I'm the one responsible for your new wife. What if Lazar makes an attempt on her?"

"He won't."

"Because he's honorable, you mean?" She sneered at the sentiment.

"Yes. Also because I will have spies of my own present."

She leaped angrily to the bait. "Ah, the Grand Vizier. Clever Tariq. How much higher inside you can he crawl, son?"

"You are quick to assume, Mother, and you would be wrong if you followed your assumption too closely. My spies will be watching you, too, so behave. I want you to go safely and be returned to me safely. You are my mother, my father's Absolute Favorite, and even though you might question it right now, I do love you. But you must know your place, Mother, and if I feel you trying to attach puppet strings to my back ever again, I will react accordingly. You have been well cautioned. Please heed my warnings about Ana, about Lazar, about your role in this critical event. And I suspect Grand Master Salmeo would appreciate your involvement in preparations for your departure—you have barely hours."

It was a dismissal and Boaz believed both of them knew this as surely as he sensed a shift in their already tenuous relationship.

AS HEREZAH SEETHED AT the angry dismissal but went through the polite motion of bowing to her Zar and then being shown out of his chamber, she understood she was no longer in a position to ever be the important woman in her son's life. She nodded to herself as she secured her veil and fell into step with her Elim escort, acknowledging that though Boaz was a Zar, with a choice of forty-two beauties, his love was given to one alone. That was dangerous.

She hated Ana, that much was obvious . . . but although she dared not even admit it to herself yet . . . she knew that deep in her heart she hated Boaz even more for his weakness regarding the girl from the foothills.

PEZ HAD LITTLE TO pack for the journey and couldn't concentrate anyway, such was his quiet despair over Lazar's revelation. His old friend was right; that was the painful truth of it. Unless by some miracle the Grand Vizier had not come into any physical contact with Ana, then, impossible though it was to stomach, Ana was not Lyana. He felt sick at the revelation and had been sitting in a corner of his chambers lost in sorrowful thoughts since he fled from Lazar.

If not Ana, then who? It had to be her! Magic pulsed through her body—he felt it. His mind had turned the ques-

tion over repeatedly. He had replayed every scrap of information he knew and he returned again and again to Ana. It was
where the finger stopped pointing. She and Lyana were joined.
And if he continued to believe this, then he had to believe that
by some grace of the Goddess, Maliz had not touched her, for
the demon would have known and he would have destroyed her
on the spot. He had to find out and be sure and there was no
time like the present. He threw the last remaining items he had
hurriedly pulled from his dressing room into a fabric bag and
left it outside his chamber door as required. Pez made a mental
note that he needed to speak with Razeen before he departed
and then, crossing his eyes, he made for the harem, deliberately
stumbling and bumping off the hallway walls.

No one troubled themselves with him, for by now the palace
was in a state of frenzied activity to get the royal caravan away
by nightfall. He bounced into the main divan suite and found it
filled with beautiful girls, none of them Ana.

"Ana?" he called, flapping his arms, pretending to fly around
the chamber.

"She's not here, Pez," one of the girls replied.

"Why do you bother with him?" another admonished.

"He understands sometimes." It was Sascha who was being
helpful. "Grand Master Salmeo has sent her to her chamber to
prepare."

He didn't respond; he simply flapped his way out of the
suite and made for the upstairs sleeping compartments, where
he found Ana with Elza and two of the Elim.

"Oh, not now, Pez," Elza sighed when she caught sight of
the dwarf apparently flying in, cross-eyed and burping.

Ana smiled softly at his antics in spite of her somber mood

but it didn't hide the nasty red welt on her face. Pez noticed it instantly. Stopping short, he managed to keep burping through his astonishment.

"Face, face!" he called, ignoring Elza's shooshing sounds. "Ana's hurt just like Kett."

It probably wasn't the best choice of words, he realized too late as he saw Ana's eyes cloud at the mention of her loyal friend. "Who's hurt pretty Ana?" he inquired gleefully of the Elim. "Was she screaming?"

"Get out, dwarf!" Elza said, exasperated, but one Elim came to Pez's rescue.

"We will report you if you speak with disrespect to him again," the warrior warned.

Elza grimaced. "He's upsetting her."

"He's also just made Zaradine Ana smile; perhaps you've forgotten."

"Oh, I have no time for this. How am I supposed to get a royal wife ready in such a short time?"

"You must do the best you can," the elder Elim said, and motioned to his companion. "We will wait outside for her baggage."

"They promised me help," the slave wailed to their backs.

"The 'they' you refer to intend to make it as difficult as possible, Elza," Ana counseled softly. "Did you really think they'd do much at all?"

"They should," Elza said matter-of-factly. "You have royal status now, Zaradine Ana."

"And nothing's changed for it, other than title," Ana replied gently, leaning down to kiss Pez on the head. "Are you coming with us?"

He nodded his reply, waiting for the slave woman to step into the dressing room to choose more gowns. "Who did this?" he mouthed silently, pointing to her face.

"It doesn't matter," she replied soundlessly as well. "I'm glad you're coming," she mouthed.

Pez pursed his lips, perplexed by her evasion.

"Ah, so you *can* be still and quiet, Pez," Elza said, bustling back in with a pile of silk garments in her arms. "Well, Zaradine Ana, at least you have no end of clothes to choose from. The Valide has been generous in this regard."

Ana sneered. "I need comfortable traveling clothes. We'll be on horseback and then camel, don't forget. I also need clothes to stay warm in."

"And clothes to stay cool in," Elza reminded her. "Zarab save me, but we need more time!" She flounced back into the dressing room.

Pez risked a whisper. "Ana, quick, this is important. Did the Grand Vizier touch you at all today?"

"Pardon?" She grinned helplessly at what sounded like a lewd question.

"I mean it. Did he at any time touch your arm or shoulder— any part of you—when he fetched you from the harem to take you to Boaz?" His gaze flicked to the dressing chamber, where he could hear Elza muttering about warm clothes. "Quickly, please!"

Ana appeared baffled but she frowned and gave his question the thought he pleaded for. After a few moments of consideration, whilst Pez felt tense to the core watching Elza and quietly praying that Ana would give a negative answer, she nodded. "Yes, as I recall, he took my arm, here"—she gestured—"and guided me through the gardens. He said we needed some time so we would take the longer way and then he could brief me properly."

Pez felt his last glimpse of hope shrivel. "You're quite sure?" he pleaded again, his voice choked with disappointment.

"Yes. I remember it clearly. Why?"

Elza reappeared and their conversation came to an abrupt close as Pez fell to the ground in a swoon. He broke wind as he landed and even Elza cracked a smile. "He's such a fool but it's nice to see you looking a bit brighter. How's that cheek?"

"I'll wear it with pride," Ana said mischievously.

Elza smiled wider. "You're wicked, Miss Ana. You'll have to be extra careful now around the Valide. She's revealed a lot today with her action."

Ana nodded and glanced toward Pez. He could hardly believe that Herezah had let her infamous control slip. There would be a reckoning, he was sure. But just now his mind was too confused to allow him any room to fret over the Valide's future actions.

Ana was not the Goddess incarnate.

So who was?

26

Ana was invited to travel with her Zar in a special karak for two carried by ten Elim. Boaz was determined to see the caravan off himself at the edge of the city, so it was a colorful, almost festive party of dignitaries and servants who snaked down the hill from the palace by torchlight, following the Zar's personal cavalcade. They were still celebrating their ruler's marriage, playing up the romance of the two virgins in their minds.

Inside the karak it was somber.

"I hope I won't let you down," Ana said, breaking the silence.

Boaz took her hand, and although it was dark in the karak, he stared into the eyes he knew were the color of the sea on a winter's evening. "You won't. You know you don't have to veil in here?"

Ana involuntarily reached for her cheek but stopped herself from touching it. "I know, I'm just trying to be respect-ful." There was not enough light to show the bruise that had developed but still she preferred Boaz to farewell her in a gentle frame of mind, rather than an angered one. His anger would only mean worse treatment for her once she was out of his im-mediate protection. She felt drained and not in the mood for any more confrontation anyway. As it was, the knowledge that Lazar would be waiting for them was making her feel intensely nervous. She shivered, another involuntary action.

"Are you all right?"

"Of course. I'm just thinking about what we must achieve."

"Fret not. They will be as enchanted as I was the first time I saw you. Use that effect you have on people, Ana, to its full devastating advantage." She sensed rather than saw his smile.

She nodded, unsure of how to respond to this. "Our agree-ment, Boaz—" she began, but he hushed her.

"Let's not talk about it."

She touched the soft bandage at his wrist. "Does it hurt?"

He laughed softly, pulling down his sleeve. "Not nearly as much as loving you does."

She leaned her head on his shoulder. "And I do love you, but . . ." Whatever she was going to say was cut off by Pez, who stuck his head in through the curtains, skipping to keep up with the moving karak. He balanced a lit candle in one hand, its flame dancing insanely in time with his skipping and throwing an unwelcome brightness into the karak.

"Forgive me," he said, careful not to be overheard, and sens-ing he had interrupted something. "I just wanted you to know we're close, my Zar." Pez wheeled away, braying like a donkey, but the pair was grateful for the warning, for a moment later they heard the Grand Vizier clear his throat immediately outside their karak as it rocked to a stop.

"Yes, Tariq?" Boaz said. From the other side of the silks, the Grand Vizier Tariq announced—a little unnecessarily now—that they had arrived. "Thank you. Give me a moment of privacy, please."

"Yes, my Zar." They heard the Vizier giving orders for everyone to wait a short while.

Inside, Boaz turned again to Ana. "What were you about to say?"

She shook her head. It didn't matter now.

"Well, may I embrace my wife farewell?"

"Seal our arrangement with a kiss?" She laced her words with levity. "I feel I have already let you down," she murmured.

He sighed once. "Ana. Just go in peace and know my heart is full. I will wait for your return and for you to be at the same peace. We shall take our marriage from there."

He was too generous. Her heart felt it might break from knowing how much pain he must be in. "You are easy to love. Kiss me, Boaz."

In the dark, he lifted her veil and for the second time that day let his lips convey all the love and desire he felt for her. Ana surprised herself by responding with equal ardor, knowing she needed to leave him something to cling to.

Gently he pulled away and smiled. "I'm going to remember this moment—this feeling—until you come home to me. We shall make a son together."

"And that would make you happy?"

Even in the dark she could see the glistening of his eyes,

filled with emotion. "It would. It would make me proud. It would secure the line."

"The others—"

"Are not you," he interrupted firmly. "I want *our* son to sit on this throne in years to come."

He was so intense that Ana had to look away, knowing that for all his declarations of love, for all his patience with her, his generosity, and especially for promising that any child of theirs would be safe, she felt every inch the traitor. For, as if she were attached to him by some invisible thread, Ana could still feel the pull of Lazar. She knew he was out there with all the others, patiently awaiting their Zar's emergence, indulging this wish for privacy but anxious to be gone. She could imagine his face—grimacing, as usual. The lines on either side of his mouth, so expressive even when he tried to hide how he was feeling, would be etched deeper, whilst his eyes would be flinty, glittering with disregard for the pomp and ceremony that now accompanied him.

None of her anger at his betrayal had dissipated, but sadly her desire to be close to him was equal to that rage. Its treacherous presence seemed to mock her efforts to be immune to Lazar as well as kind to Boaz, who, after all, had thrown her a lifeline. She hadn't thought she wanted to live, but as she had regained consciousness at the river's edge, one look at Lazar, at that face so filled with anguish over her, and she had known she wanted life more than death—even a life of constant sorrow, filled with reminders of what she had lost and what she could never have.

"I must go," she said, trying to cover the awkward silence prompted by her musing.

"Can you truly love me, Ana?"

She felt suddenly rigid with fear. Boaz was no fool; it felt as though he'd dropped in on her thoughts. "I just need time, Boaz."

"I understand, and I'm giving you that time—I think you can appreciate that I have already demonstrated my sincerity in this regard."

"You have. And I truly appreciate your leniency, my Zar."

"You must not abuse it, Ana."

The sudden warning shocked her. She felt breathless at the coldness in his voice. "What do you mean, Majesty?" She faltered, falling back on formality to hide her uncertainty.

"I mean simply this. The time I am extending you to grieve, to come to your own peace, to find it within yourself to be a reliable and settled member of the harem, is something I have surprised myself in giving you. My father would not have offered the same to my mother, or any of his wives, no matter how much he indulged them. And he would view this as a weakness in me."

"Is it?" she dared ask.

"You know it is. Where you are concerned there *is* only one boundary to my love. Stay within it, Ana, and you will know nothing but generosity and gentleness from me."

"And if I were to cross it?" She couldn't be sure what they were both alluding to and yet the question rushed from her lips as though she found the threat irresistible.

"No one will save you from the death I would impose on you."

This time Ana did lose her breath. There was not a mote of lightness in Boaz's words—he meant them as gravely as he spoke of his intense love for her. He was frightening in his black-and-white view of life. For all his intelligence and empathy, he viewed her with no shades of gray.

"What is that boundary, my Zar?"

He did not hesitate. "Fidelity. Stay true to me and you will never come to any harm again."

"You couldn't save me from your mother," she risked saying, referring to the Valide's cunning plan to prompt Ana's second attempt at escape.

"This I regret. I am aware of what happened today in the harem. Pez has informed me."

Her alarm was obvious. "Pez had no right—"

"Pez has every right. He and I were friends before he met you—we are lifelong friends. He is loyal to me and to you, Ana. He told me in order to protect you. Unfortunately the news reached me after I'd already had a rather stern talk with my mother."

"She came to see you?"

"After the incident, no doubt, hoping to cover her tracks. I've never seen my mother openly lose her temper—you must have said something truly fiery to provoke her. She will never dare strike you again."

"I claimed we were equals."

"On this journey, Ana, you may even bear a higher status in the minds of those you meet. As far as the palace generally is concerned, Zaradine and Valide are equal, perhaps my wife enjoying slightly more indulgence. Unfortunately, as far as the harem is concerned, the Valide has superiority. I cannot help this."

"But you can change it."

"Over years, perhaps yes. Not by the time you come back to me, however."

She knew there was no point in arguing this. Boaz was right. And then she considered all that had already changed for them.

Hadn't they both had to grow up these last few moons? Boaz was already acting every inch the powerful Zar and her behavior in the harem today had surely shocked all present, including herself. Even their odd bargain showed a new maturity—she must live up to her promise to her husband now.

"I will cope, my Zar. I will be a good Zaradine."

"No Zaradine, to my knowledge, has ever left the sanctuary of the harem." Again his words sounded like a warning; she felt a spike of tension between them.

"These are no ordinary circumstances or neither would I," she responded with equal care.

"There will be temptation, Ana. You need to heed what I have said." He was treading softly, she could see this, and yet he was determined to make a point.

Ana decided to be direct for him. "I will not try to escape, my Zar."

"I think we shall have to let history show us your faith here, Ana. Your track record suggests otherwise, but that is not what I'm referring to."

"You refer to my faithfulness," she murmured.

"Yes. Temptation will present itself."

It had been a long day and Ana's fatigue got the better of her. She became impatient with Boaz's couched words and innuendo, which felt suddenly sinister. "Who exactly do you think I might feel tempted by, Highness? The Grand Vizier perhaps, one of the Galinsean dignitaries? Or do you already suspect me of garnering attention from one of your mutes?" Even she could hear the edge in her voice, and regretted it.

He shrugged away her sarcasm. "I hope you'll never take that tone publicly," he said, his voice soft but firm.

"Forgive me. Dawn brought me a drowning and dusk has

closed on a marriage. By this coming dawn we begin a journey to a new realm, into a lot of uncertainty, and the avoidance of a war depends on my ability to charm our centuries-old rivals. These hours I've lived through have been daunting and I'm feeling a little weary, my Zar. I humbly apologize."

It was well phrased, with just enough emotion driving the words that he could feel her own sense of the unreal. He touched her bruised cheek affectionately. "I don't think any of us have given you sufficient credit for what you've had to live through today."

She wanted to shake away his hand but resisted, yet something in her could not let go of their earlier conversation with its darker undercurrent. She needed to know what he knew. "Who do you keep referring to, my Zar, as being a threat to my fidelity? Please be honest with me."

She saw the pain reflected in his eyes when he responded. "I refer to Spur Lazar."

Ana felt dizzy, wondered again if her husband could listen in to her thoughts. "I . . ." she stammered, flustered.

Mercifully he read her discomfort differently. "Don't fret, Ana. I know that you have done nothing to win any other man's admiration. All I'm suggesting is that other people seem to think Lazar regards you with something other than innocent care."

"Do you believe that?"

"I don't know what I think, Ana," and now he sounded plaintive, vulnerable. "I'm besotted with you, and that makes me jealous of any man, including the Grand Vizier, who will share any time with you."

"Boaz," she began, talking to him like a wife now, "I live in the harem. The only men I meet are half men, with the somewhat dubious exception of Pez. The man who spends most time with me is Salmeo, and the Grand Master Eunuch is so repulsive to me that I would rather make love to a monkey from your zoo than with him." Boaz barked an embarrassed laugh but nodded for her to continue. "I hadn't set eyes on the Spur before this morning, and that was because he rescued me from my watery grave." She decided it was pertinent to remind Boaz that for all his pledges of love, he had still permitted her execution.

"You must also remember I have thought him dead for all of this time. There has been neither opportunity nor desire on either of our parts. And so I believe this warning, from wherever it emanates, is nothing more than troublemaking, designed to make you feel unsure of me, of yourself, of the one man who is truly loyal to *you*—not your father, not Percheron, not because he has some other agenda. Lazar is loyal to you."

She hesitated briefly, then added, "This rumormongering can only have come from one source. One jealous source always looking to stir up trouble. I'm guessing your caution springs from something your mother has said. Would I be right?"

"And my own good sense that any red-blooded man would find you irresistible."

Relief flooded Ana's body as she realized that his suspicions were truly born of jealousy and hearsay; he had not looked into her soul somehow. "Well, on the occasions I have been with Spur Lazar, both publicly and privately, he has acted toward me with the usual coldness and distance he bestows on most. In fact I recall asking him why he disliked me so much. Spur Lazar has never let his gaze linger on me," she lied, feeling her face flush, "and he has certainly never laid so much as a finger on me—other than to bring me back to the harem when I escaped the first time and to drag me from the river's embrace." She was breathing hard, hoping a sense of indignation would cover her attempt at deception. Once again she blessed her luck that it was so dark.

"We shall never speak of this again," he said, accepting her response and her right to be vexed. "You're right; the Valide can provoke problems where none exist. It is her way—her method of survival from years of cunning in the harem."

"And her own infatuation with the Spur," Ana added.

He sighed. "Yes, there is that, too. Nevertheless, Ana, let me end this conversation by saying we are not discussing Spur Lazar or my mother but rather you. It is you who is being cautioned. It is your actions that will be watched and no doubt tested."

"I understand," she replied, not even sure she could look at Lazar in the next few moments without revealing to both him and the Zar how treacherous her body's inclinations truly were. She wanted to tell Boaz that her mind was willing but her heart was a traitor, that her desire to be dutiful could not match her body's desire to feel the touch of his Spur's skin against hers. However fleeting it was, she knew her body would risk the danger, risk the Zar's wrath, even if her good sense told her otherwise, and still it reminded her constantly that Lazar had betrayed her.

She kissed her husband one last time, and with the help of the mute known as Salazin, she stepped out of the karak, her traitorous eyes scanning the festive crowd, and instantly picking out the the man who dominated her thoughts.

He stood tall on a small rise that was slightly removed from the party. He was talking to Jumo and a few of his men. Beneath the soldiers their horses shifted and neighed, eager to be gone from the torches and crowd of people. And then, as if he could sense her presence, he looked up, and across the distance, he stared directly at her, into her eyes, into that perfidious soul of hers, no longer true to her but a slave to him. But something deeply sorrowful about the way he hung his head soon after they locked gazes gave her information far more revealing.

Ana knew then and there that whatever inclinations she was fighting, he was fighting them harder.

LAZAR DIDN'T NEED TO know she had climbed out of the karak. He sensed her presence instantly and broke away from his conversation with Jumo. His friend, ever sensitive to the mood swings of his former master, quickly picked up the thread of conversation with the other men to cover Lazar's sudden absence, even though he remained standing in the same position on the crest of the small rise.

The Spur's gaze locked on Ana's, and even though she was far away, he knew that for all of her posturing and his careful distance, nothing had changed. And that was dangerous. He lowered his head almost immediately. A part of him had secretly hoped that Ana did hate him, that she would and could never forgive him for the deception of his apparent death. He would have accepted her hatred as the price he had to pay for Lyana's grace in letting her live.

On the other side of the karak another figure, unmistakeably the tall young ruler, alighted to win his attention and surprised Lazar by searching him out immediately. Lazar was dismayed to see the young man's gaze flick immediately to Ana and then back to him. The Spur held his breath—surely, surely there was no suspicion? Despite the agony of his intense love for Ana, he knew he had never revealed it to anyone, not even to her. How could the Zar, of all people, have this thought in his mind, if he did have this thought at all?

He handed over the reins of his horse, muttered something to Jumo, and strode down the hill, ignoring the questions and inquiries thrown at him by various people until he reached the Zar's karak.

"Zar Boaz. You grace us with your presence."

Boaz smiled warmly and Lazar felt his shoulders relax slightly. "I thought it appropriate to see my wife off on this great journey, Lazar."

"Indeed, Highness." He looked over at Ana. "Zaradine Ana," and bowed his head slightly. "We have a sweet and docile filly for you to ride."

She said nothing but inclined her head and straightaway turned to Elza, who had bustled up to take charge. Elza was clearly enjoying the sudden notoriety of being the new Zaradine's personal slave, and her pleasure at the chance to escape the claustrophobia of the harem was also evident in her bright smile.

Lazar returned his attention to the Zar, all crisp efficiency. "We make for the foothills, Highness, and will camp there for a few hours. My intention is that we journey in the cool of the latest hours of darkness and the early hours of dawn until the sun gets more fierce."

"This is Samazen season, if I'm not mistaken?"

"Sadly you are not, my Zar. This is indeed the most dangerous time of the year to be anywhere near the desert."

"But it can't be helped," Boaz qualified.

Lazar nodded. "We have no choice. The desert is the fastest route. I will take every precaution."

"When can I expect news?"

"I will send Jumo back as soon as we know anything, but I imagine you won't hear much for a couple of moons, Majesty."

Boaz nodded. "You take with you precious cargo, Lazar."

"I will keep the Valide, the Grand Vizier, and Pez free from harm, Majesty—on this you have my word. As far as your wife goes, I will lay down my life for her as I would for you, my Zar, for she is now an extension of you."

At this Boaz fixed Lazar with an intense stare that the Spur met head on and did not waver from. There was a test in that long, searching look, and Lazar, despite his turbulent emotions, felt pity for the young ruler who was truly rising to his station and yet was obviously fragile where Ana was concerned. *I know the feeling*, Lazar thought, finding an uneasy smile. "I will bring her home to you safe and triumphant, my Zar."

And he saw something relax in Boaz as the young man said, "I know you will, Lazar, and for this I am in your debt once again." He reached for the Spur and pulled him close. "Bring her home, protect her from those who don't feel about her as you and I."

It was an odd choice of words, but despite the clumsy expression, Lazar understood perfectly what had passed between them. "As I stand here, Zar Boaz, you have my oath that come what may, Ana will live to bear you an heir." He was stunned himself by his equally inept answer, which smacked of something far deeper than either of them understood . . . and yet it seemed the right thing to say. Lazar couldn't explain it but it was as though he didn't choose the words, they chose themselves. Whatever or why ever they came, his words seemed to satisfy Boaz, who now grinned broadly and hugged him again.

"Perhaps she already has my heir in her belly," Boaz said brightly. "Go about your duties, Spur Lazar. I don't mean to hold you from them."

Lazar bowed, still baffled by what had passed unspoken

between him and his Zar—was Boaz openly acknowledging their shared love for Zaradine Ana? And his own curious response . . . how could he know she would give Boaz an heir? He shook his head, confused, and removed himself from the crowd of people as another karak began arriving, probably that of the Valide, he decided. He resisted the urge to cast a glance Ana's way and instead steadfastly fixed his eyes on Jumo and his mind on their departure, which would take place just as soon as they could get the women comfortable on the horses and settled.

The Samazen, he decided as he strode back up the rise, knowing she was watching him, was going to be the least of his problems.

AT JUMO'S WISE SUGGESTION, Lazar guided the party into the foothills in a northwesterly direction so that Ana would not feel the nearness of her family. Their small dwelling was close but not close enough that she would necessarily recognize the terrain as anything but indigenous to the foothills rather than to the region she grew up in. Jumo noticed that the Spur had doggedly resisted all contact with Ana on the slow climb into the hills, preferring instead to send Jumo on both occasions that he felt inclined to check with the royal party that all was well with their horses, the pace, their comfort.

Jumo returned now with the message that both of them had anticipated an hour earlier at least. "The Valide wishes to speak with you."

"And did she ask politely?"

"Something about not being of a mind to discuss her comfort with the Spur's slave." Jumo cleared his throat as if ridding himself of something distasteful.

"Gods rot that woman!" Lazar muttered. "I'm sorry, Jumo—"

"Don't be sorry. Her words, not yours, and I was glad to run the errand. It meant I could see Ana."

"More luck you," Lazar said.

"And save you the pain of it," Jumo qualified. "You know, Master . . ."

"Call me by my name in front of the Valide. Do not give her any ammunition. Let her see our familiarity."

"All right. I was going to say, where Ana is concerned, I'm afraid your face, legendary as it is for its blankness, is in fact rather easy to read."

"That bad?"

Jumo nodded. "If you don't want to give the Valide a weapon, don't even look at the girl."

"I haven't looked at her in thirteen moons!" he growled.

"And none of the heat has dissipated between the two of you."

"That's ridiculous, I—"

"What is? You both go out of your way to be so uncommunicative that it's obvious you're doing your utmost to look as though you have nothing to say to each other."

"We don't. Not anymore." Lazar scowled.

"Now I know that's a lie and so does the Valide. You've saved Ana's life twice now, Lazar. And knowing you as I do, I understand that you have not acted purely out of duty. Whether or not the Valide appreciates this is irrelevant. You need to act more naturally."

"Act naturally?" It was snarled with a mixture of incredulity and sarcasm.

Jumo ignored him and continued earnestly. This was important if they were all to survive. "Address her. Give her eye contact. Offer a few words—encouragement, inquiry, anything. Don't be afraid to be friendly. It's what they would anticipate . . . even though you're not friendly to most." He gave a soft smile to lighten the awkward yet necessary lecture, but Lazar had never looked more grim.

"That's just the point, I am afraid to be friendly."

"Why, Lazar?" Jumo pleaded. It seemed so simple to him, and Ana was so easy to get along with that surely the Spur could make it go lighter on all of them if he tried a bit harder. Jumo was startled when the sorrowful answer came.

"Because it will undo me, my friend. She is married now. She is Zaradine . . . more untouchable than she ever was."

Jumo had known Lazar for so long now, shared enough to know how his friend might react in any situation. But not this time. He had never heard Lazar sound so vulnerable, and it was frightening. Frightening that a man who had always seemed impervious not just to the wiles of women but to any true friendship beyond their own could now appear so fragile where this young woman, this forbidden woman, was concerned. He could only feel the deepest pity for his friend who he now knew was on the most dangerous of paths. No one, absolutely no one, could lay a hand on a Zaradine. It was one thing to covet an odalisque, a possession of the Zar but still merely a slave amidst a myriad of other slaves. But once elevated to wife, she instantly became something more precious, and to be Absolute Favorite and likely mother to the heir meant her face would almost certainly never be looked upon by another whole man again.

Ana had always done things differently, and even though this was not by her design, here she was now on a journey, not just leaving the harem—something Herezah, for instance, had never considered possible—but representing her Zar, her nation, in a desperate bid to avert war. Suddenly she had been elevated to a new status altogether—no longer just Zaradine, no longer just Absolute Favorite, no longer just woman, but diplomatic negotiator, a strategist possibly, who might just fashion the peace that Percheron wanted, needed. From today on, many men—strangers, foreigners, enemies—might look upon her face if need called for it.

All of that acknowledged, the truth was that in principle nothing had actually changed . . . and Lazar knew it. For all the uniqueness of this situation, this was still a royal wife—the Favorite—and to covet this one was to invite cruel death.

Jumo understood what Lazar was battling. It was etched deep into his friend's grief-stricken face. And Jumo wished, although he had suspected this forbidden love had deepened, that he hadn't assumed it would somehow be diluted over time, through their absence from each other.

He had convinced himself that if the two did not see each other for so long, Lazar's infatuation and what appeared to be Ana's childish attachment to the Spur might lose their potency. But Ana was not a child. She had been a young woman when they had discovered her, but she had the composure of one far older and obviously the maturity to match. No, their compulsion toward each other was stronger than ever and both were fighting it hard. Lazar's inspired suggestion that Boaz marry Ana for the sake of the nation was not just a desperate bid to secure her life and indeed possibly save Percheron, but also his skewed method of putting Ana so far out of his own reach that he could never do more than love her from a distance. And Jumo could see the price his friend was paying for that decision—undeniably the only decision he could make under the circumstances—and he also understood the debt would never be paid. Lazar would continue funding her security with his own pain—suffering seeming to be, for this man, a bottomless purse.

Jumo cleared his throat.

"I will try," Lazar replied finally, and the forlorn nature of his promise prompted Jumo to add something, anything, of a positive nature, before his friend turned his horse around to drop back to the royal party.

"I met your parents, Lazar. Perhaps you would like me to tell you about that meeting?"

It had the opposite effect than he'd hoped. More darkness deepened into the shadows of the Spur's face. "Perhaps," he replied, and Jumo understood he was simply being polite. After all, Lazar had not even asked after the King and Queen.

Lazar's companion sighed, looked toward the small valley ahead of them. "That's camp. The camels will be delivered in the next few hours. I'm glad you decided to bring fewer men than the Zar originally suggested."

Lazar nodded, said no more as he nudged his horse around and trotted unhappily back down the line of slow-moving people on horseback to the main party and to the woman who awaited him.

ATTIRED AS SHE WAS in a midnight-blue gown from head to toe, the dark eyes of the Valide flashed pure pleasure as his horse drew up next to hers.

"Valide, you wished to speak with me?"

"I do, Lazar. Why do you not travel with Zaradine Ana and

myself? Surely as our guide and our chaperone, your job is to stay close?"

He knew she was playing with him but he had promised himself he would not bite at any bait she dangled on this journey. He hoped his oath was not an empty one. "The danger, should it arise, Valide, is not here alongside you and Zaradine Ana but at the front of the column. You must forgive me but my job is actually to keep you safe by knowing precisely what is ahead of us."

"And what is ahead of us, Lazar? I see nothing but the dark shadows of thorny bushes and the black humps of dunes."

"And you would be right, Valide. But also, less than one league away is our stopping point for a few hours. Ahead is a small valley, safe as a resting place so we can take delivery of our camels and both of our esteemed women might take some sleep for a while." He looked across the Valide to where the silent Zaradine stared straight ahead into the night. He decided Jumo was right. He could at least try. "I imagine you must be fatigued, Zaradine Ana?" His voice was gentle and he couldn't have cared less what Herezah read into it.

He was surprised, though, that Ana answered him so readily. Her voice was steady, clear, when it came. "I was when I was at the palace, Spur Lazar."

"But no longer?" he dared, enjoying the fact that he had effectively cut Herezah out of the conversation momentarily.

"I didn't know if I would be able to stay upright on my horse, I was so exhausted, but curiously I feel refreshed to be out beneath the stars, infused with a fresh energy to be back in the foothills. I am close to my home, I believe?" The inquiry was there, he could not avoid it.

"We are in the same region, yes." He pointed. "Over there, in that direction, is where your home is." She sighed in answer and Lazar took that sad sound to mean that she had no home.

"So you will join us for supper, Lazar," Herezah said.

It was not a question but he responded as if it were. "Thank you, but I must decline. I have to ensure the camels—"

"The camels!" She laughed at him. "I'm sure amongst all these men someone else can receive and tie down the animals for a few hours, Spur. I believe you make excuses."

"Why would I do that?"

"You wish to distance yourself from us women. But we are in need of some company."

"You have the Grand Vizier—"

Again she interrupted him with a laugh. It was obvious she was enjoying this banter. Didn't she always, Lazar thought wearily to himself.

"I can engage the Grand Vizier in conversation anytime I choose—isn't that right, Tariq?"

The Grand Vizier, riding quietly on the far side of the Zaradine, dipped his head gently in a meaningless acknowledgment.

"But supper with the Spur is far more intriguing," Herezah continued. "After all, we haven't seen you for over twelve moons, Lazar. I'm sure Zaradine Ana will enjoy the opportunity to hear precisely what you've been up to all the time that we thought you were dead." She kept her voice breezy but her words cut like a sharp blade through him. It was all threat.

He bristled despite his promise to remain impervious to her baiting. "I'm sure Zaradine Ana's eventful day will demand that she rest, Valide. It would be irresponsible of me to ask her to squander precious sleeping hours in polite conversation over supper. We are not on a picnic, may I remind everyone. This is a journey fraught with unknown dangers and I'm afraid I must use my rank as Spur to insist that everyone, hungry or otherwise, take this chance to sleep. You will hate me when I send out the call to rouse yourselves in just a few hours. You can eat on the camels in the morning and you can feast when we break for camp tomorrow, but until then I will be busy with the activities entrusted to me by my Zar."

"Spur Lazar, I think you forget yourself. You are here to care for our needs—"

"That's exactly what I'm doing, Valide. Forgive me if my interpretation of care is different from yours, however. As Spur, I have duties. I am answerable to the Zar for your lives. I will do everything within my power to protect them . . . and that means ensuring this trip is not treated like some sort of festive event. Again, forgive my brusque words, Valide, but we are now in hostile territory."

"Hostile? This is still Percheron, Spur—"

"The desert kills, Valide. It is hostile to all creatures and does not differentiate between Percherese or Galinsean. It will destroy us as it chooses. I am here to ensure it is never given that chance. Please excuse me." He bowed his head to the Valide, then to the Zaradine, who did not look at him. "Tariq."

"How long before we arrive?" the Grand Vizier inquired.

"I shall stop the caravan very shortly and then I shall return to get the royal tent up and all of you settled."

Tariq nodded and Lazar took that as his opportunity to leave.

"OOH, THAT MAN IS so frustrating!" Herezah breathed.

"Only for you, Valide, it seems," Maliz observed. "Zaradine

Ana had little to say to him and I can see he has no time for me."

"It's true, our new Zaradine must be tired; after all she nearly drowned today. Tomorrow he will not be quite so slippery."

"Why do you pursue the Spur, Valide?" Ana asked, surprising Herezah by joining in. "It's obvious neither of you cares much for the other save what is necessary for formality."

"Don't question me, Ana! Please remember your place." Herezah bristled.

"As Absolute Favorite Wife to the Zar, Valide, or as the emissary who will try to negotiate a peace treaty for Percheron?"

"I forbid you to take that tone with me, Ana."

"You forbid me nothing, Valide." Herezah opened her mouth to retaliate but Ana did not give her a chance. "Out here, in the desert, we are equals. In fact, I think if I had to survive alone I might stand a better chance. I'm from these parts, Herezah, and I haven't forgotten the harshness of the wild or how to respect it. You have never felt its sinister touch and I suspect if you were alone you would capitulate at its first fiery breath of the day or its icy nighttime caress. You need the Spur, and not as an enemy."

Furious that the young woman had just addressed her by name, Herezah replied icily, "I don't need him as anything!"

"Anything other than a supper companion," Ana finished for her, "or perhaps a bedmate?"

Herezah felt the compulsion to strike this girl again, hit her so hard she might tumble from her horse, but she was too wily to succumb to that again. She knew Ana was playing her at her own game. The youngster was baiting her, willing her to strike, to let her son down, to bring shame on herself. She did no such thing. Instead she laughed.

"Oh my dear, you reveal too much of yourself. You are

fortunate for the veil and the cover of darkness, otherwise we might all see your burning cheeks. Do you really think no one sees through you? The Spur is not for you, child, no matter how much you covet him."

"I am a married woman, Valide."

"That's meaningless."

"Are you speaking from experience?"

Maliz coughed to hide his amusement at Ana's audacity.

"You overstep your status," Herezah warned, in the cold tone she was used to freezing people to the spot with.

To her rapidly increasing fury, the young Zaradine seemed impervious to the threat. "I warned you before: we are now equal. I'll respect your position in the harem provided you respect my new status. Out here, however, I abide by no one's rules but my own, Valide, and those of the Spur, who is leading this journey. As for suggesting that I am lusting for Lazar, I see no one panting around him like a dog in heat, save yourself."

At this Maliz clearly couldn't help himself. He broke into loud laughter. His outburst startled Herezah from her fury and prevented the Valide from breaking her promise and doing something ugly to Ana that she would regret. Instead she somehow managed to join the Grand Vizier in his amusement, after which she simply dropped her voice low, menacing, and murmured only for Ana's hearing: "There will be a reckoning for this once we return."

"If we return," Ana warned. Nothing further could be said; the Elim were forming an escort around them once again.

"We are stopping here for a few hours, Valide," the senior man said.

"Good," Herezah snapped. "I'm weary of this company and conversation. Please get our tents set up quickly."

27

The group of men, nomads, arrived with the camels at just past midnight. The camp was mostly silent; the Valide, Zaradine, and Grand Vizier were resting, if not asleep. The two women shared tented accommodation that could be considered grand—lavish by the visitors' awed stares—but Lazar knew that Percheron could have yielded something infinitely more breathtaking in terms of opulence had it been given sufficient time. The Grand Vizier slept in a smaller, gaudily colored tent that would normally be used by far lesser dignitaries. Still, he had said his good nights without complaint, and again Lazar was struck by the radical changes in the man. Tariq would have required accommodations that screamed richness and status, but Maliz couldn't seem to care less where he put his head down. Although in the past, Tariq had irritated Lazar as a meaningless, sycophantic drone, Maliz gave him a constant sense of unease. It was more than that, though. Maliz gave Lazar a feeling of dread, as though he were simply toying with everyone now, enjoying the angst within this party, not in any way involved or concerned. Coming along for the fun of it perhaps, even though his Zar expected it.

Pez materialized by Lazar's side. "Why are you staring at his tent?"

"I'm wondering why he's here. He could have easily made legitimate excuses. There must be a reason for him coming along that suits his own agenda."

"Ana, presumably," Pez replied without hesitation.

"We've been through this—"

"I know. And your claims damn my beliefs all the way to hell."

"And still you believe," Lazar finished for him.

"I do. I feel something in Ana. She resembles a plain mortal as little as I do. I don't have the answer, so don't tax me with the question, but I believe Ana is involved—as firmly as I believe you are."

"He cannot be here for Ana, though. Whatever you believe, he must have satisfied himself that she is not the Goddess incarnate."

"I agree. Perhaps that is the difference this time. Maybe Lyana is protected."

Lazar kept his patience. "Tell me. What occurs to him when Lyana comes into her power?"

At this the dwarf faltered. He knew Lazar was going to trap him again. "That, too, is confusing, Lazar, I admit. Traditionally, as soon as Maliz comes into contact with Lyana, he is endowed fully with all of his powers."

"Magic, you mean," Lazar qualified. He wanted none of Pez's cryptic answers.

"For want of a better word, yes."

"Are they noticeable?"

Pez smirked. "Does he break out in sores, or suddenly grow in stature, do you mean? No, Lazar, he is just equipped for the battle that will inevitably ensue between himself and Lyana."

"And traditionally they fight—hand to hand?"

Pez shrugged. "They use their powers against each other. She has always lost." He pursed his lips before adding, "But not this time."

"I reckon he's here for you. He's keeping an eye on the person who can lead him to the real Lyana."

Pez shook his head, determined to shore up his belief that Ana was still somehow the one. "Perhaps he's here for neither Ana nor myself. Why not you?"

Lazar laughed grimly. "We're going over stale ground, Pez." The dwarf nodded sadly. "Why can't I just go in there now and slit his throat?"

"I've explained this. He cannot die by ordinary means."

"Why not?"

"Lyana's presence gives him his powers."

Before Lazar could argue again that Ana was not Lyana and surely that made Maliz vulnerable, Jumo arrived with the news that the purveyors of camels were ready to do business.

"We have shared kerrosh. It is time," Jumo said.

Lazar nodded. "I have some animals to buy, Pez. Keep an eye on his tent. I don't care that it's guarded by Elim. Everyone's tired and might get sloppy. See that he doesn't make any attempt to enter the women's accommodations."

"I'll do one of my screams if he does."

Lazar gave him a sad smile before following Jumo down to

where the nomads sat patiently, cross-legged, warming themselves around a small fire that the soldiers had built.

"Are they speaking Percherese?" Lazar asked his friend.

"No. Use Khalid."

Lazar switched instantly into the language of the nomads, touching his hand to his forehead and breast as he welcomed the men and thanked them for bringing the animals.

They stood and responded in kind. This was purely formality. Their expressions were blank, their gazes guarded, as they watched the tall foreigner seat himself in similar cross-legged fashion.

Lazar got straight down to business now that the formalities were done with. "How many?"

"We were asked to bring twenty-five," the leader said.

Lazar nodded. "We'll need all of them. Are they watered?"

"Just a few hours ago. They will travel for many days without a need for drinking."

"Good."

"Where do you go, sir?"

"Across the desert."

The senior man whistled through his teeth, talked to his companions in a pidgin version of the language that not even Lazar could understand. He grasped every fourth word, though, and from their body language could tell they were not pleased at the notion that their camels might not be returned. He chose to interrupt their worried conversation.

"We will buy them outright."

"I cannot allow that. We have raised these camels from calves. They belong to the Khalid people."

Lazar knew better than to protest. As hostile as it was, the desert still supported several tribal families, wandering end-lessly from well to well to soothe the parched throats of man and beast. And their camels, in truth, meant more to them than one another. Camels gave them meat, milk, skins, transport, comfort, income. He'd always known that asking one tribe to sell off more than two dozen of its prized family members was an optimistic notion.

And he also knew by the man's objection that he was dealing with the right animals. Sometimes the wily tribes tried to sell unsuspecting travelers beasts who were used to traversing the stony plains. The soles of these animals were hard and shiny, unsuitable for the soft give of the sands. Jumo, of course, even with limited time to make his arrangements, would not have erred on this point, he reminded himself.

"I need these camels," he said softly to the man whose name, he had found out by listening to the men converse, was Salim.

"Then we will send some of our own men," the man replied. Lazar began to shake his head. The last thing he wanted was more people in the caravan. "Otherwise you cannot have our animals, not for any price."

Salim sounded very final. And Lazar was running out of pa-tience and time. He glanced toward Jumo, whose almost imper-ceptible nod urged the Spur to accept this deal. After all, what could it hurt to have some experienced desert travelers in their party?

It was probably fatigue that made him capitulate. "I accept your terms. How many men?"

"Four."

Lazar nodded. "All right. What price?"

And with those two words he set off furious negotiations. Lazar understood the way of the desert. The first price was simply the starting point from which he would now barter down as earnestly as they would argue the price back up. He ordered kerrosh, knew there would be another hour or more in this debate. Lazar would have happily paid their first price—unheard of, of course, but his men were tired and he was exhausted. Money was not an issue. The Zar had opened up the royal coffers and no karel would be spared in this journey. Boaz would scoff if he knew his Spur was wasting precious rest time in petty bargaining.

But this was the way of the desert folk. If you didn't follow the protocol, they would take offense.

As they finally agreed upon the hire price of men and camels, suddenly all the Khalid were standing, stretching, smiling, and nodding. Negotiations were over, and it was time for a final round of kerrosh.

Lazar worked hard at stifling a long yawn but lost the fight. Salim strolled over.

"I am Salim. You will appreciate my men. I can see from your tents that you escort important people."

"Bit hard to miss, isn't it?"

The Khalid smirked but not unkindly. "I would leave those tents behind if I were you, sir. Forgive my forwardness but the less attention you draw to yourselves in the Empty the better."

The Empty. It was the first time he'd heard the desert called that. Having crossed it once, he knew the title suited it. "Please call me Lazar. Should we expect trouble?"

Salim looked thoughtful. "Possibly. I'm presuming you're headed fully west?"

Lazar didn't want to tell Salim much more than he had to but the Khalid was obviously intelligent and had worked out much for himself. "Yes."

Again the man whistled softly. "With a royal? Has the sun boiled your brains?"

Lazar bristled but knew he must keep his temper even. He wanted those camels and he wanted to be gone in a few hours on their backs. "What do you know?"

Salim jutted his chin toward the tent. "The accommodations tell me plenty. The Elim guard tells me a lot more. You travel with precious cargo, Spur Lazar."

"And the fewer people who know, the better, Salim. What should I be fearing?"

"Apart from the scorching heat and frost at night, the lack of wells across to the west, and the Samazen?"

Lazar grit his teeth at the man's sarcasm. "And?"

"The western quarter of the Empty is not our region. Our people have no reason to travel those lands—I don't know of any tribes who move across the Forgotten Sands, as the west is known. But we hear things. Rumors of a fortress."

"What? In the desert?"

Salim shrugged. "All hearsay but I'm obliged to tell you if we lose our men and camels . . ." He trailed off, his tone sad.

"Why would you?"

Again he shrugged and it was beginning to annoy Lazar.

"What about this fortress? What rumors do you know?"

"That a madman had it built and has assembled his own army."

Lazar barked a laugh. "And you believe this? An army living in the desert."

"No ordinary army," Salim continued. "Men who care not for their lives on this plane."

Lazar was tiring of this conversation. "Salim, tell me what you know and be done. I appreciate your information and any guidance you can provide, but I wish no scaremongering of my men. We have an arduous journey ahead, fraught with all sorts of problems I don't wish to think about yet, and you are now adding to those problems."

"I know very little. Everything I have heard is based on information passed across the desert between the tribes. I have no idea if it is based on truth, nor do I know how exaggerated the information has become in each telling."

"Go on."

"No one knows why they're there—if they're there. I have no name for this madman people whisper about. Rumor says he is on a personal crusade, that he has over the past decade been persuading vulnerable, impressionable young men into his personal army."

"From where does he source these men?"

"People disappear all the time in the desert. The tribes know they will lose one or two men a year to its harshness. I think, if he exists, he is using this fact to prey on those people. He steals one or two from the tribes each year, watches them go through the motions of searching for their lost and then giving up, knowing the desert will claim lives." Salim put his hands up in a gesture of helplessness. "Who knows, he may even steal the people from the western cities, for all I know."

"Do you have any proof—anything real you can give me?"

At this, Salim's eyes narrowed and his lips tightened to a thin line. He nodded. "My youngest son, Ashar. He disappeared two years ago, when he was just fifteen summers. He was accompanying a party of two other Khalid. They were mapping out some new watering holes, as we have begun to open up some trading routes toward the west and—"

Lazar suddenly understood. "This is about your son! It has

nothing to do with our safety. Denying selling me the camels outright had nothing to do with tribal ways. You wanted to plant *your* men in *my* caravan. And all that talk about the royals—you don't care, you're using the royal party as cover." Lazar was past tired, past cranky, and was moving straight into fury.

Salim had the grace to look slightly sheepish. Again he gave the gesture of helplessness. "Have you a son of your own, Spur Lazar?"

"I have no children," Lazar growled, mindful of the small crowd, turning from their kerrosh and conversation to watch the two men arguing.

"Then you cannot begin to understand the lengths a father will go to in order to protect his child. Ashar is now seventeen—"

"If he's alive," Lazar said heartlessly.

The man nodded sadly. "Yes, if he's alive. I believe he is."

"And you want to use my caravan to find him."

"I don't believe this enclave is run by a madman. If it exists—and I believe it does—I think he is far from mad. Very sane in fact; very calculating, too. He would have the good sense to let a royal party pass unharmed through the lands he considers his. Stealing or killing royals would bring nothing but damnation onto him—and the might of the entire Percherese army."

"You can bet all your camels and children on that, Salim!"

The man did not rise to the bait. "As I say, I think he will let your caravan pass unharmed, but it will give me and my men the opportunity to get close enough not only to see whether the fortress exists but to get into it if necessary."

"You know you're the madman."

"Perhaps. But I love my son, Lazar, and no man steals him from me."

"You don't know that he's alive and you risk men and your own life on the chance that he is."

Salim studied him through dark, wise eyes. "One day I hope Zarab blesses you with a son. And then you will know the pain of parental love and the knowledge that, yes, you would die for that son on the off chance that your life might buy his."

Lazar shook his head in exasperation. "I want the camels."

"They are yours, but we come with them."

Lazar knew he was beaten. He raised a finger in the air in threatening fashion. "You and your men are under my command. Is that understood?"

"Perfectly."

"You go where I say. You do what I order."

"To a point. We shall break away from your caravan should we discover the fortress."

"Agreed."

They locked grim stares. Salim broke it by bowing his head to the Spur, hand on heart. "Thank you, sir. I will ready my men."

Lazar sighed. He was not going to get any sleep this night.

28

At Jumo's insistence, Lazar tried to get some sleep, but it eluded him despite the fact that his body was bone-shakingly tired. He dozed restlessly on a skin beneath a few goat-hair blankets. He knew he had only two hours before they would have to rise and get the caravan moving before the heat of the day set in. This was summer and it could kill within an hour if it so chose and if the unprepared decided to gamble with it.

He rolled away from the fire, and the men talking quietly around it. Feeling the frost near his face, Lazar acknowledged that a desert night could be just as deadly as the searing day.

Forcing his eyes closed, he found some fitful rest. Amongst his frequent stirrings, his dreams punished him. Voices called to him. They urged him to set them free but he had no idea where their prison was.

Unleash us on the land, Lazar. You will need us for the battle ahead.

Who are you?

Friends.

Where are you?

But there was no response and he realized he had jolted himself awake; he could hear Jumo's voice speaking quietly with Salim and his men. He drifted off again and this time if the voices talked, he didn't remember hearing them. This time his thoughts were with Ana, imagining how close she was and yet how very far from him. The words of Boaz returned to haunt him, that Ana's womb might already be quickening with his heir.

He squirmed, opened his eyes, and deliberately roused himself by turning back toward the fire. His gaze met Jumo's, which was full of reproach.

"You have another hour," his friend said.

"I can't sleep," Lazar replied honestly. "Let's start."

Jumo nodded, and the men began moving as one, quietly dispersing to see to their various tasks.

Salim approached as Lazar was disentangling his long legs from the blankets.

"The water you carry in those barrels will have to go into skins."

"They won't like it," Lazar said, his chin jutting toward the royal tent. But it was obvious he didn't disagree. "Go ahead. You have what you need?"

"Yes. That's the beauty of the goatskins; we can simply roll them up and carry them easily."

Lazar nodded. "Pick out three gentle beasts for our royal party."

Salim nodded. "And you?"

"Oh, the nastier the better for me," Lazar quipped. They

shared a smile of the desert, for most camels were cantankerous even in their most peaceful moments. The hobbled animals were already spitting and grumbling as their handlers began to get them up for the day.

"We'll give you Maharitz, then. She'll soon sort you out," Salim said, his normally blank face creased into a mischievous grin.

LAZAR STAYED WELL AWAY from the royal tent but he could hear its complaints. Herezah did not appreciate being woken whilst it was still dark, and she was berating the unfortunate Elim given the task. Not a word of complaint from Ana, of course, and Maliz was already dressed for the desert in simple light robes and a fashez, the turban that men favored when traveling in the sands. Lazar was impressed as he watched the man stretching outside his humble enough tent. He felt a stab of something akin to sorrow. It seemed a pity; the demon was a far better Vizier—a far better man, in fact—than his host had ever been. Despite his fear of what lurked beneath the shell of Tariq, Lazar rather admired the no-nonsense, direct, and charismatic way in which the Grand Vizier carried himself these days. In a different situation perhaps the two of them might have found common ground . . . friendship even.

He shook his head free of such fanciful thoughts and reminded himself that Maliz was a demon, not a man, and that he would destroy Percheron and any number of its people, if necessary, to achieve his own aims.

A smaller figure emerged beside the Grand Vizier from the royal tent and Lazar immediately looked away. He was not quite fast enough, however; he felt his breath sucked from him with a fresh gust of pain. Ana had sensibly chosen the light-colored, unadorned robes of the desert for their journey. She was still veiled, however, and that helped to keep her distant, even though she was standing only fifty paces from him. He stole a glance and grimaced at the easy conversation that had instantly been struck up between the Zaradine and Grand Vizier. Ana was even laughing gently as she, too, stretched in the heavy atmosphere of the dewy night.

A soft lightening to the east nudged at Lazar's thoughts—he must get the caravan moving. This cool was a false prelude to what the desert sun would bring once she was allowed to banish the moon and claim the skies.

Salim ambled over. "We are ready, Spur."

"Good. I will need to speak with the royals and they will need help mounting their beasts when the time comes," he reminded him.

The man nodded and without needing to say a word seemed to be able to give orders to his men with gestures or expressions. They were all well rehearsed in journeys such as these and obviously required no verbal reminders of what they should do.

Lazar steadied himself and strode across to where Herezah was still ranting behind the drapes of the tent. "Good morning, Zaradine Ana," he said as cheerily as he could, his heart hammering as she turned her gaze fully on him. He could not see her eyes as clearly as he would have liked in the low light but it was not necessary, their color was etched brightly in his mind. "I won't ask if you slept well," he continued with an effort at levity, including Maliz now with a nod. "Grand Vizier."

"Feel free to ask, Spur," came the sardonic reply. "Zaradine Ana was just telling me that this was her deepest, most pleasurable sleep in thirteen moons. I certainly slept like a babe at the breast."

Lazar could believe it. Gone was the stoop of the Tariq of old; and the man standing before him belied his age of well past threescore years.

"You look fit indeed, Tariq," he replied. "I am glad you found some rest, Zaradine," he added, unable to turn away from her just yet. The ache in his chest did not lessen when her eyes crinkled at their edges and he knew she smiled the smile that he held dear in his memory. He did not need the veil removed to know its brightness and warmth.

"I thought I'd become soft in my time in the harem, Spur, but I suppose one's heart never forgets what is closest to it. Memories of sleeping on a red blanket on the hard earth, beneath the stars of the foothills, are not lost to me and will remain my happiest."

To the Grand Vizier it must have sounded like the wistful memory of sleeping in her father's home in the foothills and he smiled indulgently. "Then you are blessed, Zaradine Ana, to experience such pleasure again."

Lazar didn't hear him. To him Ana's words provoked a distraction that left him so deeply wounded he could not have come up with a reply if she had expected one. Ana was not referring to her father's hut; she was recalling the nights spent traveling amongst the foothills after leaving her family dwelling, during which she slept in the company of two men—Lazar and Jumo. They had taken their time with the journey; even in her naïveté, Ana had known it didn't take so many days to reach the city. During this time Lazar had given her his own red blanket to sleep on. She had commented at some point that such a hot color did not suit the Spur's cool approach to life. And Jumo had quipped that a man's desert blanket is the truest reflection of his spirit. Even Lazar had cracked a wry smile at that.

Now all he could do was bow gently toward her, his throat closing with the emotion he was choking back.

"So, we leave now?" The Grand Vizier interrupted his thoughts.

Lazar coughed. "Er, yes, that's what I'm here to tell you—" Before he could finish, the tent flap was thrown back and the Valide stomped out.

"What time do you call this?" she demanded of everyone in her fury but especially the Spur. She looked glorious in her anger and dishevelment.

But her beauty was winter to Ana's beauty, which was all things summery—and that coldness had never held any allure for the Spur. "This time, Valide," he said politely, "is what I call traveling time."

"It's night, for Zarab's sake!"

"It's the early hours of the morning before dawn, Valide. It is cool and safe for us to begin our journey before the heat of the day. The sun will be fierce in a few hours. I explained this."

"You explained little. You leave your servant to do all your bidding."

"Jumo is not my servant, nor is he yours. He is my friend."

"He is irrelevant, as is his status! I refuse to leave my tent until I have washed and breakfasted and it's light enough for me to see which clothes I shall wear. Do you understand me, Spur?"

Lazar sensed the smirk on Tariq's face. He knew the Grand Vizier was enjoying watching the standoff, seeing how the Spur would handle the Valide's bullying tactics.

He bit back his own anger but his voice had lost the gentleness that had imbued it when he addressed the Zaradine. Now it was as hard and cool as the marble of the Stone Palace. "Valide, in the desert there is no status. I am sorry to enlighten you that your position in the palace carries only the weight that I allow. I permit that you are shown formal respect but you will not interrupt the resolution of what is—I think you're forgetting—a diplomatic crisis." He held up a finger. "First, there will be no washing in the desert from here on in. Today I will allow you a small bowl of water, as this is our first morning and water is still plentiful. It won't be, starting tomorrow. We shall have only what we can carry, and that is needed for our sustenance, not our personal pleasure."

Another finger went up. "Second, if you can eat some flat-bread as you walk, that's called breakfast, and I am happy for you to do so. If you prefer not to, you will have to wait until we mount the camels when you can nibble on your bread with one hand and drink from a skin with the other." His voice became harder still. "And if that wounds your sense of etiquette, Valide, my personal apologies, but I shall have to ask you to wait until we have stopped for the day before you feast fully." She opened her mouth to let fly with a new tirade but he stopped her with his third finger going up alongside its companions. "And third," he said with a finality in his voice, "may I suggest that you adorn yourself as sensibly as the Zaradine and the Grand Vizier have chosen to do for this day's travel. You will regret it otherwise. But it is, I might add, your choice."

He now turned to face all three of his royal party. "Gentle beasts have been chosen for you. The men are waiting over by the camels. Please cover your heads now, for the sands will begin their fun." He gave no further eye contact to the Valide, instead turning to address the waiting Elim.

"Take the tents down immediately—I'll give you only minutes to get it all packed away and onto the beasts." He bowed to his guests and strode away.

But Herezah unwisely stalked him, stabbing at him with her manicured finger. "How dare you speak to me like that, Lazar. You are my servant, you—"

Lazar swung around. "In the desert I am King, Valide; I am your god, your master, your ruler. You will do as I say in order to stay alive. My job for my Zar is to get you and the royal party safely to Galinsea to broker a peace between our two realms. And then I am charged to bring you back to Percheron safely. I am *not* your servant, and something you should perhaps realize, Valide, is that I never have been. You are the slave, bought by a harem to pleasure a Zar. I chose my role for Percheron, you were sold into it."

Her voice, when it came, was a whisper. "Oh, there will be a reckoning for this when we get back to the palace, Lazar. You are never going to survive this indiscretion."

He leaned close. "Remember who you speak to, Herezah . . . I am the heir to the enemy throne and I can keep you captive in Galinsea if I so choose." Of course his threat was empty but she didn't know that. He turned away from her and this time she let him walk away.

Only they shared the exchange, only they knew the threat they had made to each other. And only Lazar knew how suddenly terrified Herezah must have felt as her realization hit of where she was, without a single ally. No Salmeo to do her bidding, a Grand Vizier who no longer fussed around her, no royal son to protect her with his status. Around her was controlled hostility everywhere she turned.

"Lazar!" she yelled to his retreating back.

He didn't turn, kept walking away from her, but held five fingers in the air so she knew that was the number of minutes she had before he would move the caravan out.

She returned angrily to her tent, already being expertly brought down at one end.

"Please, Valide," a senior Elim urged, "please let us help you dress."

Lazar had left her no choice but to meekly enter her half-crumpled tent and put on the colorless, lightweight robes that were already laid out.

Behind her, and out of earshot, the Grand Vizier and the Zaradine shared a conspiratorial smile.

"I think this journey is going to be very good for our Valide," Maliz whispered to his companion. "And highly entertaining for us."

THE CARAVAN OF TWO dozen camels set off not long after, Lazar asking everyone to lead their beasts for the first couple of hours.

"When the sun is out fully," he explained, "we mount up, to conserve your energy. We will stop moving when the sun is at its fiercest and then move again at the end of the day and into evening." And that was all he said before the slow-moving beasts took their first steps into the wilderness. Herezah and Ana walked with Tariq, with Elim leading their camels as well as their own.

No one spoke. There was not much to say after the fiery confrontation earlier. Everyone probably believed Herezah was sulking but whether she was or—more likely—was deep in her agile thoughts, she remained sensibly quiet behind her veil. Ana seemed to be enjoying the early-morning silence, which was broken only by the call of wild birds of prey. Maliz looked un-moved by the desolate vista sprawling before them. Jumo dropped back to offer some advice to the royal party.

Up ahead, Pez and Lazar moved slightly apart from the oth-ers, the dwarf skipping, pointing at the sky.

"What have you seen?" Lazar asked.

"A great deal of sand. Nothing stirs, apart from the odd scorpion or lizard. No problems as far as I can see, although I had to be very careful and will have to continue being watch-ful." Lazar gave him a quizzical look. "You can hear the fal-con up above?" Lazar nodded. "There were others and they'd like nothing more than to bring down a large snowy owl on the wing," Pez explained testily.

The Spur looked toward the horizon, where the sun sat on its rim: a great fiery ball, promising a furnace not too much later in the day. He looked up and saw a lone falcon, a fearsome hunter that could stalk and kill a desert bustard despite its prey's poison liquid, as easily as it could a pigeon. And then he looked across the golden wilderness as the last clumps of patchy grass lost their fight and capitulated fully to the parched sands of the Great Waste. He had survived this once before and he intended to do so again, but he felt a twist of fear in his gut. He was re-sponsible now for so many other lives.

"This is madness, Pez," he murmured.

"We have no choice. If fighting a battle of our faith is not hard enough, we now face war with our fellowman." He shook his head with disgust.

"And it's all my fault," Lazar muttered. "I could have averted this."

"How? By going yourself?"

"Of course! My reluctance to go alone means we are all

under threat and this perilous journey guarantees nothing." He sounded helpless.

"Lazar, tell me what your father would do if you did appear before him."

"There would be no war with Percheron."

"And?"

"I would be put to death."

"I see," Pez said thoughtfully. He paused and then spoke again, firmly this time. "Can you unequivocally guarantee that there would be no war with our realm?"

It was the Spur's turn to pause and consider. He took his time, so long in fact that Pez could have been forgiven for thinking he'd forgotten a question had been posed.

"I cannot give that guarantee."

"Why?" There was satisfaction in the dwarf's tone.

"Because of all the kings of Galinsea who have resisted the temptation to invade Percheron for its riches, I believe in my heart that my father is the weakest with regard to its seductions."

"So, in taking full blame and presenting yourself at the palace at Galinsea we risk not only losing you to the grave but we still run equal risk of war, even after having given our lives to chance in the desert."

"I regret that you paint an accurate picture."

"Then stop blaming yourself. You are doing the right thing, taking the best option by keeping yourself alive to lead our men if required whilst also escorting the one person who might just be able to broker the peace we need."

"What if my father wants war anyway? This is the best excuse he's ever had."

"I think that has already occurred to all of us, Lazar," Pez counseled gently. "Boaz would have worked this out from the very first moment he met the Galinsean dignitaries. As Zar, he has to leave no stone unturned to keep his people in peace. Your idea to marry him to Ana was inspired. If anyone can charm a king, Ana can."

Lazar sneered. "If you knew my father, you'd know that he is not prey to the usual foibles of a man."

"I think I do know your father," Pez said, and winked at his friend. "I think the man I call friend well reflects his bloodline."

"Ah, well," Lazar said very softly, almost a sigh. "This is probably true to some extent."

"What happened between you two?" It was obvious that Pez didn't expect a reply, or more likely anticipated being told to mind his own business, because surprise registered on his face and his skipping halted momentarily when he was answered.

"I loved a woman that my parents did not approve of. Keep skipping, Pez."

"Not from the right family?" the dwarf asked, hopping now.

"You could say that," Lazar said, giving a sorry smile. "She was . . ." He trailed off.

"Special?"

Lazar nodded.

"I presume she is no longer alive for you to be unable to so much as speak her name," Pez said gently.

"Yes, she is dead."

"Killed by your parents?" Pez asked, his tone filled with disbelief.

"I like to see them as murderers, but a more generous, perhaps more realistic, person might say that they helped contrive a situation that would prompt her death."

"She killed herself?"

Lazar nodded sadly. "It was the only way she felt she could prevent our family being torn apart. I was the son, the heir, and my father would not have her as the next Queen."

"Her death achieved nothing, then."

"Nothing toward healing the rift in our family, no. And nothing toward ensuring that the present heir to Galinsea take the throne. But she offered me my freedom through her act, and her bravery gave me the courage to not ignore that gift. I did not look back once I fled Galinsea. I did not want kingship, did not want to preside over a nation that preferred to steal art—or raze it—rather than create its own. Most Galinseans are heathens when it comes to art or poetry, music and dance."

"I'm sure you are too harsh, Lazar. Did it not occur to you that you could be a King who changed his people's attitudes?"

"I was eighteen when I fled Galinsea."

Pez took Lazar's hand. "And Boaz is seventeen and running his realm."

Lazar looked abashed. "He is a better man than me."

"And now you speak rubbish like a true Galinsean! When will you accept that you were born to lead? You can't help yourself; you have kingship qualities in your blood—you cannot escape your line."

"I have."

"And yet here we go, heading back to Galinsea from where you hail, from where you fled, from where you think you can hide."

"You're right," Lazar admitted. "I can no longer hide."

"That's right. It won't stop here. Your parents will find you."

"I know. I have been thinking that once this is over—if we can avert war—maybe I'll leave Percheron."

"Run away again? We need you, Lazar. Boaz needs you, and more importantly, Percheron itself needs you—not just because you are its Spur, but I'll risk boring you again by reminding you that we are caught up in a different battle as well."

"That one has to wait."

"It will take its own course as and when it chooses."

"As and when you know who the Goddess is," Lazar reminded him.

Pez ignored his gibe and left the topic of Galinsea alone for the time being. "Have you noticed how friendly he is to her?"

Lazar didn't need to ask to whom Pez was referring. "Yes." He sighed. "She is falling for his charms." He noticed the dwarf balk. "Oh, I don't mean he is seducing her for her flesh. No, he is winning her as a friend, something Ana so badly needs. I can't blame her for being attracted to his charismatic ways. If we didn't know better, perhaps we might fall for them, too."

"I can't tell you how dangerous this situation will become if Maliz gets her under some sort of influence."

"She is *not* Lyana. Her very presence here, alive and well, should assure you of that."

"It doesn't!" Pez snapped. "Ellyana said it would be different this time. And it is. Ana is involved. Her very name suggests she is."

"Now you're grasping at the proverbial camel's hair, Pez, and you don't have a good grip."

"If you don't trust me, at least humor me. Have I ever led you down a wrong path? Please, if just for my own sanity, go along with this. Allow that I might be right, that he is preying on her." Pez cartwheeled and Lazar patiently walked alongside, waiting for the dwarf to return to his skipping beside him.

"For what?" he continued when Pez had rejoined him. "What can he gain?"

"If she is not Lyana, as you claim, then I have to presume he believes that she knows who Lyana is, or that she can lead us to the real Goddess."

That stopped Lazar in his tracks. "I hadn't considered that."

"Well, do so now. And keep walking. He watches our every move."

"Hush," Lazar warned as Salim approached.

Pez was already humming a nonsense song and picking his nose.

"We should mount up now," the Khalid suggested.

Lazar nodded and held a hand up to slow the column to a halt. Pez moved forward, striding on his short legs, adding a skip every few steps.

Lazar could feel the sweat seeping into the back of his shirt. As he walked toward the royals over the soft flurry of the sands, he wrapped the desert turban around his face so that only his light eyes could be seen.

He bowed. "Valide, Zaradine. We ride from here for the next two hours."

"I have never ridden a camel before," Herezah said, still sulky.

"I will show you, Valide. Come, I will get you mounted." He flicked a glance toward Ana and saw the soft hurt flash in her gaze. "Zaradine Ana, Salim here will help you onto your beast. Tariq . . ."

"I can manage, thank you, Spur," the Grand Vizier said,

and shooed away any help. "You looked as though you were in deep conversation with Pez, but the Zaradine here says that Pez was just talking his usual nonsense, that you apparently humor him."

"Zaradine Ana has been quick to notice much about the palace and to understand its ways. She appreciates the value of Pez's humor. Yes, he is mad, but sometimes his very madness can bring a strange sort of clarity to those around him. Laughter is a great tonic."

"I didn't notice you laughing, Spur," the Grand Vizier said, more slyly now.

"You were obviously not paying enough attention, Tariq. Pez was teaching me one of his nonsense songs. He is wonderful at taking my mind off the tedium of our journey."

"Was it the song about the butterfly and the ass?" Ana interjected.

"No, though he did sing that one to me yesterday, Zaradine. Today it was actually the one about smashed pomegranates."

"Oh yes, I know that one. It's funny, even though it's so silly."

"Quite," Lazar said, giving her a soft smile. "I do humor Pez, Grand Vizier, and it would be helpful if you would, too. He has his place and his part to play for the palace, but he is also fragile and I'd rather not deal with him in one of his strange moods if I can help it."

"I shall do my best, Spur."

Lazar nodded his thanks and hoped Ana would notice how he included her as he swept his gaze by her and back to Herezah. "Shall we go, Valide?" he said, knowing she would have felt a small stab of triumph at his sudden show of humility toward her. His good sense had overridden his anger and he had vowed during these hours of walking not to lose his temper with her again. She would find ways to punish Ana instead of him and besides he needed everyone calm and ready for the ordeal of the desert.

Jumo waited by the Valide's camel with her handler. "This is Masha," he said, "and we are assured she will not try any tricks."

"Good," Herezah replied, looking dubiously at the kneeling animal, who was chewing indifferently, awaiting her burden.

"We won't ride like the Khalid, Valide," Lazar said politely. "We will seat you at the back of the camel's hump on top of a saddle that is laden with blankets."

"You're not trying to sell me on the idea that this is going to be comfortable, are you, Spur Lazar?" she replied, a little more like the sarcastic Herezah of old.

"I wouldn't dare. But you will get used to her swinging gait quickly. My best advice is that you simply allow your body to drift with hers. Don't fight it, just go with it and by this evening you will move in tandem with her."

Herezah pointed. "That man—that tribal man over there— he is kneeling on his saddle."

Lazar shook his head in some awe. "I know. It's their way. They can go at full gallop like that and never lose their balance. I always swore I'd learn how to do that."

"Is this why you suggested I wear the pants and robes of the desert, Lazar?" she said, a tease in her voice now.

"It is," he joked in his deadpan way. "You will be more comfortable for riding and I promise you, Valide, you are far cooler in these robes than you would be in the formal wear to which you are accustomed."

"I swear I wouldn't be comfortable in this heat even if I were naked!"

Lazar noticed Jumo stifle a grin. Herezah was back to her flirtatious best.

She could hardly miss his grimace. "I was making a jest, Lazar. Have you ever understood the concept of smiling at somene's jest, even just to be polite?"

"Yes, Valide. As you can see, I'm not very good at it."

"Indeed." She rested her hand on his shoulder and gave an appreciative smile at touching him. As she stepped close to the camel she seemed to lose her footing and Lazar had to step up close to steady her, his hands instinctively clasping her waist. Her hands more knowingly clasped around his neck. "Thank you," she breathed. "These are certainly slippery creatures to climb aboard."

Jumo gave Lazar a look of soft exasperation, for Masha had not so much as blinked whilst Herezah was attempting to mount her. Lazar pretended he did not notice Herezah's ruse and allowed her hands to linger around his neck as he ensured that she was seated properly on the saddle.

"As I said," he began, releasing himself from her embrace, "it's not exactly comfortable, but you should not be too sore if you don't resist the swaying."

"I shall remember that," Herezah said, and he knew she was not referring to his advice so much as his touch. "That's the sort of tip we give new girls in the harem." She pretended to stifle a playful smile.

Lazar kept his expression deliberately blank in response and turned to check that the other royal guests were on their camels. He could hardly fail to see the look of injury that Ana threw at him. Clearly, she hadn't failed to notice Herezah's pantomime.

"Come," Jumo said, well able to read the undercurrent swirling around them. "The sun has no patience."

29

The first seven days passed in a monotonous routine as everyone settled into rising before dawn and walking for a few hours until the sun noticed them and threw down her fury. They would then ride for another four hours, hardly wasting words, focused on nothing other than the sway of their camels and making it through the next hour when the skins of water would be handed around. The camels did not drink any water during this time but Lazar knew from Salim's urgings that on this eighth day they must make it to a well or the animals would simply stop. Everyone, including the royals, had given up eating until the cool of the evening—no one even bothered with the morning flatbread anymore.

Salim complained that if his men had been allowed to bring a saluki, the dog could have coursed for the desert hare and they might have enjoyed fresh meat. Fortunately he had shared this gripe only with Lazar, who kept it to himself. He didn't need anyone fantasizing about fresh roasted meat when all they had was thin dried strips of goat that had been packed at the palace.

Still, it, together with the flatbread they cooked each evening, oil, dried fruits, and nuts kept them alive. He knew everyone's stomach was grinding as they began to adjust to this lean new diet and soon he imagined the gauntness that struck all desert travelers would begin to appear amongst the ranks of this party. His body was already wasted enough and he was sensible enough to take Jumo's advice seriously that he should eat more.

"We can always kill one of the camels in the future." Jumo had urged at the outset.

Salim had come up with a solution this morning when they had woken groggily to the screech of several falcons swooping above.

"If we could catch ourselves a bird, he could hunt hare and bustard, just as easily as a saluki."

"How?" Lazar asked, intrigued.

"If we find the well today, we will have to rest the caravan and take that time to hunt a bird."

Lazar nodded, more out of fascination at the idea of trapping and taming a falcon than out of agreement. "This well—you're sure it's about two hours from here?"

Salim shook his head. "There is no surety in the Empty, my friend."

"Then—"

"But we have knowledge that a well should be two hours due west of here," Salim finished.

Lazar accepted this—what else could he do but get the caravan moving in its westerly direction and hope the Khalid's "knowledge," as Salim put it, was true?

An unspoken truce had fashioned itself around the Spur and

the Valide, and most in the party, including the Elim, were feeling less tension on the journey as a result. Lazar didn't trust Herezah's easy manner, of course—he had known her long enough to appreciate the masterful pragmatism she could demonstrate when cornered. Herezah had no doubt taken stock, realized that she had no supporters amongst this company, and decided that locking horns with the only person who was obliged to protect her was sheer madness. Lazar knew the Elim were entrusted with her care and safety, but she had punished them long enough that he was sure if it came to a choice between saving Ana or the Valide, they would choose the girl. The Spur was different. He was bound by oath allegiance to his Zar, her son. He was not so sure which way he would go if forced to make that same choice.

HEREZAH'S GOOD SENSE HAD prevailed during this last week and she had bitten back her own fury, swallowed her pride, and allowed this uneasy peace between herself and the Spur to build. It certainly made for a less tempestuous time and she noticed that Lazar was dropping back from the head of the caravan more frequently now to talk with the royal party. He seemed ever so slightly more relaxed—that is, she thought grimly, if a stern expression and distinct lack of humor could be considered relaxed.

She noticed he paid Ana no special attention and seemed to enjoy the Grand Vizier's company, although once again, how did one tell if Lazar was enjoying anything? He certainly talked more to Tariq than to either of the two women. Ana was saying little enough anyway. The girl had become all but mute these past few days, withdrawing entirely into herself.

"What is wrong with you, child?" Herezah finally inquired. "Why don't you speak?"

"Forgive me, Valide. I have kept to myself because I haven't been feeling well."

"What sort of unwell?" Tariq inquired gently. "Do you need more water? I can—"

"No, I'm not overly thirsty," Ana replied. "I just feel slightly nauseous."

Herezah shared a sly glance with the Grand Vizier and knew they were wondering the same thing—whether Ana might already be pregnant.

"Don't worry on my account," Ana continued. "I'm perfectly capable of the journey, just not in the mood for conversation."

"That's all right, Zaradine Ana," Maliz said, touching her arm. "Just keep us informed. We're here to protect you."

Ana gave him a small smile of thanks from behind her veil and returned to her silence. They rode on for another hour until Jumo dropped back this time, smiling widely and with information that was obviously good news.

"We have found the well. We shall stop here for the rest of the day, water the camels, and replenish our own stores."

"I thought these beasts didn't require watering," Herezah said.

Even Maliz laughed at her statement. "Do you mean *ever*, Valide?" he said, bowing to show he meant no disrespect, simply some levity. "Camels can go for long periods without water—in this case I think we've been traveling, what is it, seven full days?" Jumo nodded. "We will no doubt plot our journey by the availability of wells. The beasts need to drink for many hours to refresh themselves, but then they will be able to go another six days or so."

Herezah didn't reply but didn't look abashed either. Camels were meaningless, smelly beasts of burden as far as she was concerned, and so long as one didn't die beneath her, that was all she needed to know about them. "So we camp here?"

"Yes, Valide. The Spur, myself, and some of the Khalid are going hunting after the watering but the Elim will remain to guard you."

"Hunting?" Herezah said, her eyebrows arching with surprise. "What?"

"Falcons," Jumo replied, unable to conceal his excitement.

"Oh, I should like to see that," the Grand Vizier said. "Include me in the party."

"I shall let the Spur know your wish, Grand Vizier."

THE ATMOSPHERE AROUND THE camp was almost festive as the tents went up far earlier than usual, and everyone could sense the Khalids' relief that they had found the promised well. It had been unused for a long time and was half buried, but nothing that three men digging hard for an hour couldn't unearth. Before long the water was surging again, goatskins were being replenished, and the camels were happily restoring themselves. Men's laughter could be heard and conversation was flowing in tandem with the water.

Lazar sipped the bitter nectar from the earth and grinned for the first time in ages. "Sherem!" he said to Salim.

"Sherem!" the Khalid echoed, offering up good health to all.

Pez turned cartwheels for everyone and the Khalid laughed and clapped. They had already worked out that the dwarf was insane but it troubled them not; they seemed to like the little man who entertained them with his acrobatics and obvious problem with flatulence, which curiously enough affected him only when the royal party was near.

"And now we hunt the falcon," Salim said to Lazar. "Come."

Jumo had already mentioned to Lazar that the Vizier was keen to observe the hunt, and though Lazar had greeted this news with a grimace, he could hardly refuse, so the Grand Vizier, together with Lazar, Jumo, a babbling Pez, and four of the Khalid, set off, having taken their leave of the women and the rest of the party.

They moved slowly on foot, for the sun was scorching the sands this day. Nothing moved except them, not even a scorpion or snake. And then they heard it, the high-pitched shriek of the two falcons that had seemed to be following them the past few days.

Lazar mentioned this to Salim, who agreed. "These birds are patient. They wait, they watch, they are opportunists who never know when something might move that they can hunt and eat."

"So what do we lure them with?"

Salim touched his nose in a knowing way. "Watch," he said, and pointed to one of his men, who dragged from a sack at his waist a plump pigeon.

Everyone's mouth went slack. "He's had that with him the whole way?" Lazar asked incredulously.

Pez waddled up and stroked the pigeon's head, licking his lips in an obscene way.

"Very lucky none of us discovered that stowaway until now," the Vizier commented, for once agreeing with the dwarf. "I love roasted pigeon."

"What now?" Lazar asked.

"We make a hide. Only one man can do this, so you will have to simply watch from a distance. It requires patience, so if any of you don't think you can make it through an hour or more of absolute stillness beneath this sun, you should return to the camp now."

Lazar nodded. "We understand." He looked around at the party and translated. No one blinked. "I think everyone here wants to remain. We'll need some shade, though."

Three of the Khalid unraveled sand-colored fabric that had been tied around their waists.

"This is what we use," Salim said as the lengths were given to the Percherese. "From the sky, if we remain still and upwind, the falcon will not know we are here."

The Khalid showed the uninitiated how to set up their shade, even how to sit. And then the Percherese watched with great interest as the men of the desert set about digging a shallow hole into the sand to create the hide with yet more of the fabric on top. Once that was completed, Salim came over to remind his audience of the need for silence and stillness. As he climbed into the hole, Pez began to sing softly and Lazar quieted him with a gentle touch to the dwarf's shoulder.

"Why is he here?" Maliz asked, his tone still good-humored, and yet there was a sense of irritation beneath the inquiry.

"For the same reason you are, Grand Vizier."

"He's told you he wanted to witness this, did he?"

"In his way, yes. I have known Pez for almost two decades, as you have, and I understand him through his eccentricities."

The Grand Vizier did not look convinced and was about to say so when he was interrupted.

"Hush," Jumo murmured. "They are ready. Do you see, they have tied a length of all but invisible string to the leg of the pigeon, its other end to a stone. The falcons are still here, hovering, circling. They are peregrine—shahin—and highly prized."

"Do they not use the hawk?" Maliz whispered, captivated by the unfolding scene.

"They prefer the shahin for their speed, courage, and tenacity. A shahin does not give up."

"So why would they ever use a hawk? I've seen them used on the gravel plains."

"My understanding," Jumo whispered as Lazar wondered when Tariq had ever visited the gravel plains two hundred miles north of Percheron, "is that the hawk—or hurr, as the desert tribes call it—has better eyesight and is more suited to that region."

Maliz nodded, satisfied, seemingly unaware of questions silently flying around him.

Lazar believed the demon had made his first real mistake in his effort to conceal his two identities. Lazar knew for a fact that Tariq had not done much traveling beyond the city's borders and also that the Vizier—as he'd spent most of his life at the palace—would have sneered at anything connected with the desert.

"The Khalid will launch her now," Jumo whispered.

"You know a great deal about this, my friend," Lazar murmured. "I'm impressed."

Jumo shrugged. "We hawked as youngsters but we were told stories about the desert tribes of the Great Waste and their shahin. I feel privileged to share this."

Lazar smiled inwardly. Jumo suddenly looked like a boy again in his obvious excitement.

"Here she goes," Jumo warned. And at his words, the pigeon was thrown aloft. With a great flapping of wings she steadied in the air and then began to ascend, the string unraveling behind her.

The falcons noticed her immediately, for a pigeon is hardly silent in its bustling effort to rise. One flew behind her, banked, and then dipped its wing, shaping itself into an arrow that would swoop through a killing arc. The men watched, enthralled, as the pigeon, still ascending and unaware of the danger, was hit at full force and killed in the air before both birds toppled back to the sands.

Salim cautiously appeared and stealthily made his way to the stone to which the string was still attached. Up ahead the bird of prey was tearing at feathers and flesh.

Jumo spoke softly as Pez, seemingly disinterested, unraveled a long thread from his robes, smiling at its endless length. "The falcon always faces upwind so it cannot pick up the scent of the man," Jumo explained. "It is also gorging now, not paying as much attention to its surrounds as it might otherwise. It is vulnerable in these moments only. Watch."

The string was ever so slowly reeled back in and the falcon came closer and closer until it was barely a stride away from where Salim was secreted in the hide. The hunting bird seemed to be so engrossed in its kill that it didn't even sense the reaching arms and only realized it was caught when the Khalid began shouting and cheering.

The group returned to camp triumphantly and everyone watched with fascination as Salim threaded a piece of cotton through each of the bird's lower lids and tied the ends at the top of its head, drawing the lids up so the falcon was blinded.

"How long does it take to train him?" Herezah asked, fascinated.

"Depending on her intelligence, she can be ready in a week."

Sounds of surprise came from the audience.

"That fast?" Lazar asked, incredulous.

Salim nodded. "I promise you, meat in a week."

That night, everyone slept well and happy at the thought of fresh meat—everyone, that is, except one: Ana did not eat birds.

PEZ FELT UNUSUALLY RESTLESS. He lay on his back, hands behind his head, and looked with awe at the canopy of stars winking in concert. Pez knew it was impossible but it felt to him as if a storm was brewing. He had always been sensitive to weather changes –as a child, he would start acting oddly, become agitated, unable to concentrate or be still, hours before thunder and lightning occurred. That's how he felt now, and even though he had—in private, at least—grown out of the immature behavior of running in circles or making a lot of noise when a lightning storm was coming, he had never lost the sensation of inward turmoil.

It had not happened that often over the years, if he was honest. Living in Percheron meant temperate weather most of the year, but from time to time a storm would hit, bringing with it the fire in the sky that so excited him and yet also gave him a sense of doom ... the sinister thunder rolls in the distance always suggested to him that something ominous was coming.

There was no lightning and certainly no thunder now—just a supremely clear and starry night that was frigidly cold despite the heat of the low fire the Percherese slept close to. The Khalid preferred to sleep alongside their camels, using the warmth of the beasts to heat them. Pez could see that even Lazar was snoozing—no doubt lightly—but the rhythmic rise and fall of the man's chest suggested he was asleep. He sat up and smiled to himself. He might be one of the few people, ever, to see Lazar relaxed in slumber. In repose, Lazar looked younger, the flames of the fire smoothing out the lines of his face and the hollows in his cheeks that had so deepened with his illness. In truth, this journey, despite all of its danger, was helping Lazar to recover better than any potion or quiet existence on an island ever could. Lazar was a man of action. Pez nodded—yes, the journey itself would do him immense good, but he still appreciated the untroubled, no longer grave countenance that the quiet suspension of sleep brought to Lazar. He almost wished he could wake Ana and show her how friendly Lazar could look . . . so long as he wasn't awake.

He silently stirred himself and climbed to his feet to stretch. The thought of Ana prompted him to get up and climb out of the warmth of his blankets—he had no idea why. Now that he was up he thought he might as well move.

Glancing at Lazar, he noticed that his friend's eyes were suddenly wide open.

"Ah," he whispered. "And there I was thinking how peaceful you looked."

No one else stirred. Jumo was snoring and the royal tents were still. None of the Khalid moved.

"I was—you woke me."

"I was silent," Pez hissed.

"You're like one of the Zar's elephants moving around." And the edge of his mouth creased in a grin but was gone as swiftly as it had arrived. "What are you doing anyway?"

"Going to relieve myself."

Lazar nodded, closed his eyes, and rolled over. "Don't go far," he murmured.

Pez hadn't known he was going anywhere until this moment. Pulling his blanket around his shoulders, uncaring of its dragging along the sands, he made for the closest dune that was still well away from the main camp.

He turned to look back. In the tiny circle of light that the small fire threw out, everyone appeared fast asleep. He cursed his luck that he wasn't sleeping as well, especially as he had felt tired enough to be one of the first to snuggle beneath his blankets, singing a lullaby to himself about cranberry sherbet. Pez slipped into the black void behind the dune and decided he might as well relieve himself now that he was there. As the stream of hot liquid brought the familiar sound of all things normal and his bladder thanked him for this unexpected comfort, a voice spoke to him. Both bladder and its flow froze with fear.

"Pez, thank you for coming."

"Who—"

She materialized beside him, her own glow giving him just sufficient light to recognize her.

"Ellyana."

"Are you done?" she asked, smiling so kindly that he didn't even register any embarrassment as he covered himself.

"How did you—"

"Always so many questions. Come, we have things to discuss."

"Come where? If I'm gone for more than a few moments, Lazar will—"

"He will not know. Trust me."

She led him deeper into the desert toward a nearby dune,

which, when he arrived closer, he realized held some sort of rocky cave at its base.

"Why didn't we see this when we made camp?"

"You don't have to whisper, Pez. No one can hear us." She smiled. "The sands hide and the sands reveal, as they choose. There are plenty of rocky outcrops and cave systems in the desert but most are covered by the sands."

"What are you doing here?" He had lost his initial shock and decided to be direct. Ellyana had a talent for being vague.

"I wanted to see you."

"Why not the others?"

"Well, to begin with, I suspect Jumo wishes to stick a blade into me."

He frowned. "You may be right."

"Although I also suspect that deep down he'd admit that he'd go through the same pain and ordeal if it meant life for Lazar."

"I suspect he would. Jumo is loyal to the death."

"Yes, he is. Poor Jumo," she said, looking at the sky, her tone wistful.

"What does that mean?"

She shrugged. "He is a good man."

"What do you want, Ellyana?"

"I need you to do something for me."

"Your tasks have a way of turning nasty. You know about Zafira, presumably?" There was no friendship in his tone now as he recalled the devastating moment when he discovered his old friend, impaled on her own temple's spire. All for the sake of her faith and the demon who hunted his followers.

"That was the work of Maliz."

"Your hands have her blood on them, too, Ellyana. You

put her into that danger. She had nothing to fight him with, no wings, no magic, probably no idea he was even coming for her."

"Zafira went to her death willingly, Pez. She was brave, she was old, and she was ready to sacrifice herself for Lyana."

"Lyana! I'm sick of hearing her name! She is not Ana. You have led me wrong. You have lied and cajoled and gotten us all to do your bidding, but I'm no longer your servant, Ellyana." In his anger and frustration he startled himself as he realized that he might begin to weep.

She noticed it, too. "This is a cause worth weeping over, Pez. Your memories as Iridor will tell you that lives have been lost in many ways and on so many occasions that for their sake alone—for their endeavors and their bravery—we must fight on. We have no choice, my friend. You are Iridor and you have a reason for being."

Pez hung his head. "She calls him friend now."

"I know," she replied, her voice tender again. "But she is safe for now."

"How? How can he spend time with her and touch her and not know?"

"I warned that this time it would be different," she replied, more cautiously now, he noticed. Pez had learned that when Ellyana took this approach, she was usually not telling the full truth, using her talent to divert him.

"Why can't you just be honest and tell us what you know?" he demanded.

"Because you must trust. The less each knows, the better . . . and Pez, I am but a servant, like you. Don't presume that I have all the answers."

"But you never give us any answers, only questions."

"I am not your enemy."

"Sometimes it feels as if you are," he grumbled.

"Please, Pez, trust me."

"What do you want me to do?"

She whispered something to him then. His eyes widened and his mouth opened in disbelief.

"I cannot," he murmured. "I will not."

"You must!" she insisted. "For her sake, you must. It is her protection."

He began to look around wildly, desperate for someone to save him, ridiculously hopeful that Lazar would step around the dune now and demand to know what was going on.

"Pez, you are Iridor. You are the messenger, the go-between, the only conduit we have." She tried to give him something but he let it slip to the sand.

"I cannot," he repeated.

Ellyana picked up what he had dropped and pressed it into his gnarled hands. "You must," she urged. "Trust me," she beseeched, and her expression was one of such supplication that all that was Iridor within him responded and he clutched her gift to his breast, tears leaking down his misshapen face.

"Go now, my precious one. This time we fight the battle with stealth and cunning."

"And we shall win," he said, trying not to make it a question but a mantra to cling to.

"We will win," she assured.

He watched Ellyana fade into the darkness of the night desert until he was alone, suddenly cold again. He looked at what he clutched near his heart and felt a stab of fear at what he had been charged to do.

Pez didn't know how long he stayed in that position or when

he finally decided to pick his way back to the camp, but as he pushed himself deeper into his blankets Lazar spoke.

"That was quick," he mumbled. "Now sleep, Pez."

The little man wriggled closer to the fire, but no amount of heat was going to smother the chill he felt in his heart at Elly-ana's bidding.

30

The next week passed in a slow cycle of repetitive days. Herezah no longer complained and was one of the first to rise, dress carefully in her desert robes, and be ready to travel. She now ate walking, on camel back, or whenever she was hungry—she no longer demanded ceremony, although Lazar had to admit she maintained a great elegance in all that she did, even here in the desert. He allowed each member of the royal party one bowl of water every three days to wash and appreciated how hard this was for someone like Herezah, who had known daily bathing rituals since she was a little girl. But the Valide did not complain. It seemed the release from the harem that this journey afforded her had offered her a glimpse at how life could be without plotting and cunning, without always looking ahead to where the next iota of power could be gained over the people she was forced to share her life with.

Lazar understood. The desert was a great equalizer. As

he had told her, there was no status out here. Survival meant everyone helping one another, respecting one another, sharing ... all concepts the Valide had forgotten or gradually had had squeezed out of her in the selfish, single-minded existence of the harem.

Ana was quiet and eating little. Lazar asked Herezah how the Zaradine was faring and she simply waved her hand and told him not to worry.

"All new wives become broody and introverted. She'll get over it."

"She's not eating much."

"Are you keeping such a close eye, Lazar?" she asked, eyebrow arched. She meant it in jest but of course Lazar wasn't used to genuine lightheartedness from the Valide. He was accustomed to her fluctuating between viciousness and lustfulness—there had never been an in-between.

"She is the reason for this perilous journey, Valide," he answered gravely. "Of course I'm keeping a close eye on her." In fact it was Pez who had told him that Ana was not eating much, for the dwarf liked to be around the cookpot for the evening meal and the group allowed him to stir the broth or cook the flatbread—a simple enough task, even for an idiot. He shared the duties with the mute called Salazin, who was in charge of supervising the preparation and presentation of all the royal food. Pez liked to dish the food out, too, and he always bowed rather comically to the Zaradine before handing her a bowl and bread, urging her to eat, watching her take her first ladleful or bite, but somehow managed to spill the Valide's broth on the rare occasion one was cooked, or drop the Grand Vizier's bread in the sand.

"Well, you have no reason to fret. She has complained of

an upset belly but I have given her something for that. It will ease."

"Perhaps she will brighten with some fresh meat."

"I think we all will. This diet is excellent for preserving one's figure but it makes me feel weak. I need blood now and then, Lazar," she said, eyeing him directly.

Lazar left it at that, for the conversation was going in a direction he didn't like, but he intended to keep his own watch over the Zaradine. She appeared to have faded these past couple of days. She no longer watched him, and he didn't believe she had spoken more than a few words to anyone recently. If she was sickening, Lazar needed to know.

He asked the Valide and even the Grand Vizier, but if either had suspicions, neither of them shared their thoughts as to why the Zaradine was so suddenly off color.

ON THIS EVENING THEY were sitting around the usual three campfires. The Khalid sat around their own conversing in their curious language that sounded as though they were always arguing with one another. Lazar, Jumo, and Pez tended to range between either the Khalid's fire and that of the royal party. The Elim kept themselves entirely separate around their own fire, although never far from their two female royals.

Tonight Lazar and Jumo sat with the royals. Pez was dancing a jig for the Elim, who sang for him. The royal party watched the Khalid, particularly Salim with his falcon.

"Have they named him?" Herezah asked.

"It's a female falcon. She's simply called Shahin," Jumo answered.

"Why do they stroke her all the time? I don't think that man has been separated from the bird since he trapped it. He even sleeps with it tied to a post near his face."

Jumo nodded. "That's right, Valide. When they are training a bird to the lure, the person who is taming it must give it every moment. He talks to her, touches her all the time, keeps her close. The bird gets used to the particular man but also the talk of men, the movements of men, so she will not be startled by us. They will brand her soon on the beak with Salim's mark and she will then be fully his—companion, provider, friend."

"So the falcon can definitely hunt?" Herezah asked, her eyes glittering in anticipation.

"She is magnificent on the wing."

Both Herezah and the Grand Vizier sighed. "It will certainly be nice to taste some fresh meat again," Maliz admitted. The flatbread diet was wearing on everyone now. The cheese and fruit were dished out sparingly and had become such a treat that Herezah admitted she couldn't imagine what it would be like to sit down to a palace meal again with all of its decadence and sophistication.

"How much longer, Lazar?" she said to the Spur, who was deep in thought, his hollowed face even more handsome in its gauntness. His guarded expression looked more vulnerable now and the chin he no longer kept rigorously shaven had a thin close growth of hair. He was beginning to look like one of those priests they'd heard about who did special penance by living in the desert for weeks on end.

But then Lazar always looked as though he were doing penance. Nevertheless, when he raised his eyes to her to answer, she felt the familiar thrill of being close to him and his attention given to her. In the past she would take that attention whether it was accompanied with his usual gruffness or just his disdain. Since she had realized she had no allies and was making an effort to cooperate, she had noticed a slackening of that cool aloofness he maintained. She had discovered he was even capable of conversation and had been stunned a few days back when he had joined herself, Ana, and the Grand Vizier and spent an hour talking about desert life, even reminiscing about his first experience with it and making his escape toward Percheron.

It had been so tempting to ask why he had needed to flee Galinsea, but the truth was that Herezah was, for a rare time, enjoying the simple pleasure of conversation and the even greater pleasure of seeing Lazar relaxed in her company—even smiling, praise Zarab—so much that she was not prepared to risk the moment in curiosity. She knew what would have happened. He would have thrown down the shutters of his mind, his face taking on that sober, blank expression as though chiseled in stone, and he would have made some excuse to leave them. And so she had promised herself to do nothing but listen and revel in his refreshingly easy manner for however long Zarab granted it last.

Lazar replied after several moments of calculation. "If we continue at this pace, which is relatively good, I imagine at the new moon."

"Twenty-two more days of this?"

"I'm afraid so," he answered her.

She shrugged but noticed the surprise flit across his face at her complacency. Perhaps the desert was doing her a power of good.

"Zaradine Ana, are you keeping up your water intake?" Lazar continued gently.

She nodded wanly. "Yes, of course. You gave us strict instructions."

"You are very quiet."

"I am fine, Spur, thank you."

"Perhaps we can offer you some dates. The sugar will help."

"I couldn't eat anything more," she said softly.

Looks passed around the fire. She hadn't eaten anything of substance, barely nibbled at her bread.

"I think we should all get some sleep," Lazar advised. "We will get up a little earlier than usual tomorrow as we'll need to give some time in the cooler hours of the day to hunting the desert bustard."

"They're definitely here?" Herezah's eyes gleamed; she was determined to eat well tomorrow evening.

Jumo answered. "Yes, we have seen them and they are relatively plentiful in this region."

"Sweet dreams, all, then," the Grand Vizier said, rising and stretching. "Come, Zaradine, let me escort you to your tent."

Lazar scowled, but he covered his expression quickly and offered to walk Herezah back to the tent. With an expression of surprised delight she took his arm. Nevertheless he kept his eyes facing rigidly forward on the back of the Grand Vizier, who now put his arm around Ana's small figure as they strolled back to the accommodation.

SHAHIN WAS BEAUTIFUL, LAZAR decided, and so proud as she rode on the arm of Salim.

"She is tame now," Salim told him. "She will always enjoy a man as her companion now."

"Is she not attached to just one man? You?"

"Only to begin with. We sell our birds all the time, and so long as they are treated well, they will cleave to a new owner. But this one is special. There is an intensity to this falcon I have not seen in a long time. And she learns so fast. She is valuable."

"So you will not be selling her?"

"Never."

Jumo and one of the Khalid riders arrived excited.

"They're just over the rise—at least four of them," Jumo said.

Lazar actually smiled. He had never seen Jumo so animated and could understand that his friend was reliving a boyhood memory with this hunt. He wondered why they had never hunted with birds before, the two of them. Perhaps they'd do so when they returned to Percheron.

"If we had dogs it would be easier. Dogs and falcons are invincible when they work together," Salim moaned.

Lazar hadn't realized that the salukis and shahin would normally work in partnership. "Can she kill enough for us?"

"Oh yes, but the bustard is a fearsome prey. It fights hard to its death and it also squirts an oily muck at its predator. It will take many days before we can fully clean a falcon of the mess on her feathers. That's why we usually use dogs and more than one bird."

"How many can Shahin take alone?"

Salim shrugged. "A good one can probably kill up to eight or nine, but she will take six or seven on the wing to half that on the ground."

"So we have to get the bustards moving?"

"Yes, my friend, that's your job."

And so with guidance from the other Khalid men, Lazar and Jumo, with Pez flapping his arms and hobbling alongside mimicking the bustards, flushed the fat desert birds from their hollows in the sand.

It was several hours of mighty battles for Shahin. Sometimes the fight with her prey would rage over forty yards. Salim was right; the bustard was a warrior. Oil was splotched darkly over the golden ground in its attempts to thwart its attacker. But Shahin was wily and had obviously hunted this prey on many occasions when she was wild, for she nimbly avoided being coated. She was not so successful in avoiding blows from its wings, and on her third kill was stunned by one of these blows. Salim finished off the dying bustard, breaking its neck, for he was worried about his falcon. She came around, though, and within a short while was taking her fourth bustard, attacking initially on the wing and then killing it fully on the sands.

"A beautiful sight," Jumo murmured as they watched the two birds tussle in the air and then plummet behind a particularly large dune.

"Ah, if we had the dogs, this would be so much easier." Salim sighed.

"I'll get it . . . and her," Jumo said in high excitement, sprinting off toward the dune.

"Have you ever seen him like that?" Pez asked, out of earshot of the others, as he looked at Lazar's uncharacteristically open and grinning expression.

"Not in all the time I've known him," Lazar said, scratching his head. "We're definitely going to do this again, Jumo and I. We shall train our own birds and hunt regularly once this is all done."

"And grow old together—you make a fine pair," Pez said, with only a hint of sarcasm.

"You know what I mean. This is fun. Jumo and I spend so

much time in our dutiful pursuits for the throne that we forget to stop sometimes and just do things like this." Lazar waved at where Jumo was just scrambling over the dune, his arms cartwheeling as he reached the summit. "Simple sport, utterly carefree." He laughed as his friend turned and waved before disappearing at a full run down the other side.

Pez touched his arm. "Keep that promise. It is very good for your disposition, too," he said, winking. "I don't think I've ever seen you so relaxed."

Lazar's smile faded. "You know, Pez, I've never felt quite as carefree as I do at this moment. I know it's not true but right now I feel as though I have no responsibilities, no duty to anyone, no politics or diplomacy to consider . . . nothing but freedom and enjoying being amongst a companionable group. I feel closer to Salim in this short time we've known each other than I have to anyone in Percheron in almost two decades, save yourself and Jumo."

"That's because you let Salim in. You're so controlled all the time, Lazar. So deliberately distant that no one can be your friend. You only like the rare underdogs. You let me in because I was a freak and allowed you to discover my secret; and you let Jumo in because he was different, not one of the Percherese. Salim is Khalid—that makes him different, exotic, and, of course, he speaks another language, so that makes him entirely inaccessible to the rest of the party except yourself and Jumo. And then there's Ana—"

"Don't, Pez. It's hard enough. I need no reminding."

The dwarf sighed. "I'm sorry. Enjoy your light mood. Without the Vizier around, thank Lyana he felt obliged to keep Ana company, we can all be carefree," and he began to mimic soaring like Shahin. "I'm going to find Jumo and our wonderful falcon," he called behind his back, flapping his arms and struggling up the sand dune.

The other men were already excitedly running up the dune to catch Jumo, with Pez in hot pursuit, pretending to chase them down as Shahin had done her latest kill. Lazar paused alone in the sands to savor this moment of pleasure.

He heard a shout go up in the distance—it was Pez, he thought—and assumed the celebrations were in full swing. They would be eating bustard tonight and perhaps Ana might brighten as well. Lazar ran up the dune, his long legs sinking into the soft golden sand, and he was still inwardly grinning when he reached the top. There he was faced with a sight more chilling than he could ever have imagined.

His mood evaporated in an instant as he stared death coldly in the face.

31

Back at the camp Ana was vomiting. She had eaten little for her first meal of the day but even that tiny amount was now staining the sands well beyond the royal tent.

"Well, if her womb has quickened—and it sounds promising—we may have begun securing your son's throne, Valide." Maliz secretly wished he'd gone with the hunting party but he hadn't been able to resist Ana's pleas when, frightened by her worsening state, she had begged him to stay.

"I suppose I should be pleased." Herezah sighed, fanning herself to stir the hot air beneath their canopy. "I just wish it wasn't hers."

"Why do you hate her so? She is good for your son."

"No, she's not, Tariq. He is besotted with her. Boaz needs more wives if he is to truly secure his throne."

"And you think he won't because of Ana."

"Boaz has developed such a fascination for this girl that I

don't notice him taking any interest in any of the other beautiful young women we have assembled for him. This is dangerous."

Maliz understood more than Herezah wanted him to. He accepted her reasoning, knew what she said was right, but he also knew Herezah's main concern was how much power might be given to Ana if she remained Boaz's only mate. It was not so far beyond the realm of imagination that she could rise to be not only Zaradine and Absolute Favorite but also potentially Valide within ten moons.

"Dangerous for whom, Valide?"

"For all of us, Grand Vizier. Surely you're not naive enough to believe that one woman for the Zar is how the new regime will shape itself. It is wrong. Joreb will curse his choice of successor."

"Joreb chose well, Valide. He chose well with his Favorite and he chose well with her son."

Herezah eyed the Grand Vizier and felt momentarily lost for words. "You know, Tariq, you could have said those same words to me two years ago and I would simply have sneered at you for the sniveling, self-important, and oily character that you once were. Now I take them as the compliment you intended."

"I'm glad of this. It is sincerely meant, Valide, but then I speak only the truth."

"You never did before."

"Before what?" he asked, amused.

"Before Joreb died, before Boaz took the throne and you went through some sort of change, emerging from your chrysalis, to give us this new sober, intelligent, charismatic Vizier."

"Charismatic?" he echoed, and smiled seductively.

"I swear you're a different man, Tariq. You didn't buy some

special magic, did you, along with that magical potion you told me of that keeps you suddenly young and virile?"

"Virile?" Now he sounded disbelieving.

"Don't be coy, I see you looking at women now."

"Why wouldn't I? Surrounded by such beauty."

"Tariq, I have known you all of my life and not once have you looked at me in the way you look at me now. I see how you look at Ana, I see how you appreciate all women from slave to dignitaries' wives whenever they're permitted to attend formal functions. It is perfectly normal, I agree, it's just that before Joreb died, you were all but sexless."

Maliz clapped his hands and openly laughed. "Let's just say I hid it well, Valide. There was no room for my true personality at the palace under Joreb. The sycophant suited him."

"He hated you."

"But I suited you, always ready to play the willing servant," he added, seemingly unfazed by her candidness.

"What changed you?"

"Boaz can benefit from me being honest."

She felt he was speaking in riddles, giving her no clear answers, but pressed on. "What are your intentions with Boaz?"

He became more serious, intense. "You have nothing to fear from me, Valide. Be assured of this. My interests lie elsewhere than in power and money. I do not want to be the puppeteer, simply a reliable adviser."

"Then you truly have changed," she said, genuinely surprised. "Your whole life with Joreb was spent in petty power struggles with Salmeo, gaining little ground or respect for yourself out of any situation."

"Yes, and I didn't enjoy it, Valide, but I served a purpose and I served Joreb loyally through it all."

She acknowledged the truth of what he said with a nod. "And now?"

"Still happy to serve."

"Without seeking power or reward?"

"Reward comes in all shapes and sizes and all colors, Valide." Again the shaded answer, she thought. "With Boaz as Zar, we all have the opportunity to help him shape Percheron into the single most powerful realm of the region. We are easily the richest but now we need to add strength with ships, and our army. We must learn to secure our boundaries at the desert and we now have an opportunity to forge a formal peace with Galinsea that might secure the Percherese from that threat for centuries. And we will all benefit in the ways we desire, I'm sure."

"You make it sound easy."

"It can be if people like yourself stop chasing your own little plans and simply support the Zar. You want for nothing as Valide and I know Boaz admires you tremendously—would appreciate your input frequently—but you trouble him with your desire to use him toward your own ends. If you don't mind me being frank, Valide, you should have no ends of your own. You are a woman. You cannot rule . . . not ever. But you can have a different sort of power if you'll only relent. Give up your own mission—whatever that was or is—and give yourself over entirely to Boaz's needs. I think you'll be surprised at how much he will reward you for that kind of support."

Herezah tapped her front teeth with a fingernail that no longer shone as she liked.

Maliz continued. "Your association with Salmeo—and the depths to which it has stooped," he added, knowing she understood his meaning without him verbalizing it, "will not serve you well in the long run. Salmeo is dangerous and he himself stands on shaky ground. He has taken incredible risks because he probably believes he has your protection. I'm sure you know that Boaz has no time for him and is ever suspicious of him. If he could have accused the Grand Master Eunuch properly for the attempt on the Spur's life, Salmeo would no longer be drawing breath."

"It was proven as Horz. The man admitted it," Herezah replied.

"And you know that Horz being a murderer is as likely as me becoming a young man again." He smiled, a wicked glint in his eye. He had already decided that when this battle with Lyana was done and he had destroyed her once again, he would be choosing the body of a young man to inhabit, no matter what the cost to his energies. He was weary of creeping around in the bodies of old men and women, living in squalor to await the next cycle. No, this time he planned to enjoy the time of peace in luxury with a body that allowed him the freedom to take full advantage of such decadence. He was going to especially enjoy the pleasures of women.

He had, in fact, already decided on his next victim. It was too irresistible now that he'd allowed himself to become so involved with the power struggles in the palace. Who better than Boaz? Then he could not only sleep with any number of the beautiful creatures in the harem but he could finally taste the delicacy that was Ana. He would be gentle with Boaz as he died. He genuinely liked the young man and rather pitied that he must perish, but he coveted the Zar's body and his position more than he was affected by any reservation of conscience. His smile widened at the thought of giving lots of heirs to Percheron.

"Fret not, Valide, I will promise you something."

"What is that?"

"Many wives for your son and plenty of heirs—in fact I think I can promise you that Boaz will lie with virtually every woman in your precious harem. What's more, I'll even let you choose the heir."

"You will!" she echoed, incredulous.

He chuckled, cleared his throat, feigning embarrassment. "What I meant to say is, I feel very sure that Boaz will be guided by you in his choice of heir."

"How can you guarantee me that?" she demanded, bafflement in her face.

"Just trust me, Valide. You know Boaz already does. Throw your considerable intelligence and wiles behind your son. Forget everything else—join me, help me build his power base. We can make him the most invincible Zar that has ever ruled Percheron—and then everything you desire, save you actually ruling, will come to you."

"You want me to trust you?"

He nodded. "Start with Ana," he said. "She is probably carrying your grandchild. And she and that child begin your future."

Herezah hesitated but only briefly. "All right, Grand Vizier, you have my word. When this task is done, I shall give you my trust and we shall see how well you can keep a promise."

Maliz pulled a smile across Tariq's face. This was all so easy.

AS LAZAR CRESTED THE dune, he felt the blood drain from his veins. He was sure it was all pooling in his ankles, for his legs felt too heavy to move and his body felt suddenly clammy, despite the dry, intense heat.

Below him a thick silence reigned. Men looked up at him

with stunned expressions of helplessness and the one who looked the most desolate of all was Jumo, already sunk to his thighs but holding Shahin carefully aloft.

"Quicksand?" Lazar croaked, incredulous.

Everyone nodded sorrowfully, even though the question needed no answer, and then the silence became suffocating, as Lazar picked his way carefully to stand alongside Pez.

Tingles of fear soared through his spine, stiffening his neck and drying out his mouth. Before Lazar could assess the situation or offer empty placations, Jumo spoke up.

"Sorry, Master." He shrugged, making Shahin ruffle her feathers. "I should never have struggled. They say you can float on quicksand if you don't move too much. I forgot that advice in my panic." He switched to Khalid. "I'm going to throw Shahin. She will come to you, won't she, Salim?"

The Khalid mumbled that she would and they watched as Jumo, ever practical, launched the falcon, sinking still further for his efforts. She flew directly to Salim's outstretched arm and he stroked her, squeezing back his own emotion.

"Salim," Lazar barked, finding his voice. "What can we do?"

"Nothing, Spur," the Khalid murmured. "Your man is lost to us."

"Don't say that! Do we have fabric?" he asked, pointing to the men's waists, remembering the material they had fashioned canopies from. "Anything we can fashion a rope from?"

"We brought nothing," Salim said, pulling at his robe to convey to the Spur that they had only the clothes they stood in.

"Then we use our clothes!" Lazar roared, pulling at his robes furiously. He was stripped to a loin cloth in moments.

"Lazar! Lazar!" Jumo called frantically, desperate to still his friend, win his attention.

Pez grabbed his arm. "Listen to him, Lazar." Salim frowned, hearing the dwarf speak sense for the first time.

Lazar stopped his frantic activity, turning ashen-faced to his companion of so long. Around him the Khalid murmured softly at seeing the Spur's damaged back, but Lazar heard nothing. He looked into the sad face of Jumo, who now spoke to him in soothing tones.

"It is too late, my friend. Look, I am already in past my waist. You cannot pull me out—unless we had the camels, of course," he said, "but they are too far away. Instead of false hopes and your rushing off to fetch those beasts in vain, I'd rather go calmly now with your face the last I see before I go to my god."

PEZ WATCHD WITH AGONY as Lazar fell to his knees. "Jumo . . ." His voice was so broken that Pez had to look away.

The dwarf turned his gaze to Salim, and the Khalid understood, quietly summoning his men with a small gesture. One by one they filed past, each touching his hand to head, lips, and heart, whispering, "May Lyana take you quietly to her breast." Pez couldn't believe what he was hearing; the desert people had not relinquished their faith in the Goddess, not out here in the Great Waste, where no one came to censure their spiritual devotion.

Salim was the last to offer his farewell to Jumo and then he turned to the dwarf and gave a small, sad smile. "It seems we have both exchanged a secret, brother," he said, in halting Percherese.

"Indeed," Pez murmured in flawless Khalid. "Yours is safe with me."

Salim nodded, risked laying a hand on the Spur's bare, trembling shoulder, and squeezed gently, wincing at the sight of Lazar's back—a maze of scar tissue—before he quietly moved away and over the dune, leaving the three friends and their new companion, death, to make their peace.

Jumo had sunk almost to his chest. "Forgive me for bringing this pain to you, Lazar."

Lazar was openly weeping now, although he made not a sound. "What can I do?" he begged in a distraught whisper.

"Let me go," the brave man from the north beseeched. "And know you have been loved by another who has never had a better friend."

"Pez!" Lazar looked around wildly. "The Lore. Surely you can—"

Pez shook his head. "No," he said sadly.

"You have magic. Lift him free."

"I cannot."

"Then keep him alive long enough for me to fetch the camels. I will hurry," he said, frantically leaping to his feet. "We might have a chance."

Pez knew irreparable damage would be wreaked on his friendship with the Spur with his next words if he was truthful, so he lied, hating himself for the deception. "The Lore does not work that way."

"What do you mean? It's magic! Look, man, he's to his breast. Please, I beg you." He fell again to the sand. Lazar looked a broken man, tears streaming down his face, on his knees, all but naked, his arms open in supplication.

It was only the memory of Ellyana's visit that kept Pez strong and resolute. He did not falter, added more weight to his lie. "I have to be touching him for the Lore to work," he snarled. And something inside him broke as he watched Lazar wilt, his hands cupping his weeping face, his body racked with grief.

"Lazar." It was Jumo, his voice still firm, filled with courage. "There is no time now. Listen to me. We never did speak of your parents. You must go on now. You must hurry and get to Galinsea. They are serious about this war and it has nothing to do with sacking Percheron for its riches. It is about you and you alone. And it is about revenge. No language barrier could prevent their understanding of my tidings. They wept at my news that you were dead—I wept with them. It is over, Lazar, whatever happened between you and them all those years ago. They believe they've lost a son to their enemy. The heir to their Crown. Go to Galinsea and tell them they did not."

With much effort Lazar dragged his head up and looked at his friend. Pez had never seen him so haggard. Not even at the flogging had he looked so completely broken emotionally. During the flogging he'd fought back. Fought back with grim silence and by somehow holding on to life. Right now he looked ready to give up all of his spirit and let grief kill him in the sands beneath the blazing sun.

"They want forgiveness?" Lazar asked Jumo incredulously, his voice tight as a drum.

Jumo shook his head sadly. "As far as they know, you are dead; forgiveness cannot be sought or given. They want Percheron to pay and they'll take that debt in blood, unless you and Ana prevent it." The murderous sludge was inching toward his neck—it would not be long now. "I am ready to die, Lazar," he said into the thick silence. "Do not let my passing stop your mission, or the Percherese will die, down to the last child. Your father didn't need to tell me that, I could see it in his eyes. It was only your mother's urging that convinced him to send the delegation, to give Percheron a chance to prepare itself."

Jumo was fully buried to his neck now and Pez was amazed at how calmly the man allowed himself to sink. There was not so much as a flicker of panic in his eyes. Here was a man resigned to his fate, accepting his lot and using his last moments to build the courage of his great friend to accept as well and to go on with life. Pez felt the pricks of tears at his own eyes and knew he, too, would never recover from this sad scene. Jumo displayed such courage and grace and the best Pez could do was to lie to him. He hated himself. He could have saved Jumo, could have kept him somehow elevated in the quicksand long enough for camels to be brought and for him to be pulled free of death. But he could not risk openly using the Lore, not with Maliz so close, not with the demon paying him such close scrutiny. Before, he had escaped discovery because Maliz had stumbled across the Lore and not known what he was touching or to whom it belonged. And Pez had covered his tracks well. But out here, the coincidence would be too great. If Maliz detected magic it was obvious he would put it all together amongst only a handful of people in the desert. There was only Lazar and Pez to be suspicious of and Pez knew that Maliz had probably decided that Lazar was no threat—he was certainly not Iridor. And so in his fear that Iridor would be destroyed before he even fully discovered Lyana, he kept his Lore to himself and refused to risk using it so openly. Maliz would surely come rushing back with the rescue party and everyone would demand to know how Jumo had been kept from sinking. No, no! Too many questions, too much revealed . . . too much danger to the cause that was Lyana.

"I'm so sorry, Lazar," Pez whispered as Jumo for the first time began to struggle to keep his chin high.

"Jumo," Lazar croaked. "I have loved you better than any."

"Don't waste those words on me, my friend. Give them to Ana." The mire began to close around the back of Jumo's head, now turned to the scorching sun. "Lyana take me," he cried to his Goddess, "I am ready." And then somehow he pushed himself beneath the swallowing sands, no longer prepared to wait for death's wet kiss.

"Jumo!" Lazar roared as he leaped to his feet. "Jumo!" He continued screaming until his voice was hoarse and there was not so much as a mark upon the surface of the quicksand to show where his friend had been.

Lazar, his throat raw, his eyes red and angry, and his cheeks wet from helpless, useless tears, slipped once more to the hot sands in a silence thick with grief. After several long minutes had passed, by which time Pez could see Lazar's naked skin burning, the dwarf rallied himself from his dark thoughts and pulled himself up the dune to fetch the others who were waiting on the other side in their own grim silence.

"He will need help," he said.

Whether Lazar was aware of the tenderness shown to him that sorrowful day, Pez could not tell, but the Khalid gently picked him up from the burning sand and having sensed he would not permit himself to be dressed, they made no fuss, simply wrapped his robe around his scarred back.

"Walk, Spur," Salim whispered, "he died with courage. Hold yourself proudly for him."

They were the right words to say, it seemed, for Lazar finally straightened. He took a moment to press his hands to his face, wiping away all trace of tears. Pez privately grieved that the carefree and wonder-filled expression that Lazar had worn that morning had been banished and the granitelike countenance had returned. Pez wondered whether Lazar would ever let that sense of lightness enter his world again. He feared the Spur would remember moments of lightness only as dangerous and heartbreaking: the Galinsean love, Ana of course, and now the hunt—on each occasion he had opened himself up to pleasure and each time he had been left broken, having lost someone precious.

No, Pez didn't think Lazar would return from this loss fully and he felt the bile gathering in this throat that he had permitted it to happen. He could have saved Lazar this pain, saved a life . . . two lives, in fact, if he counted Lazar's, which would forever suffer by this experience.

One of the Khalid picked up the dead bustard and, with a soft murmuring of a prayer, tossed it into the quicksand where Jumo had been swallowed.

"That meat is tainted," Salim said in explanation.

No one said anything more. The group, with hung heads, moved out silently from the now innocent-looking patch of desert where death had come to claim a life, leaving no mark that the man had ever existed, and walked with a heavy tread back to camp.

"AH, MEAT!" HEREZAH EXCLAIMED at the first sight of the men returning.

Ana, who had rallied these past hours and even gotten a blush back into her cheeks, noticed immediately that all was not right. "Something's wrong," she said. "Look at Lazar."

He wasn't difficult to pick out at the best of times, but half naked it was all the easier.

"Zarab save us!" Herezah said, startled.

"They got the birds, I can see, so the hunt's been successful," the Grand Vizier said, frowning. "But you're right, Zaradine, there's nothing triumphant about this arrival."

"There's one less of them," Ana said suddenly, having had the wherewithal to count the party.

"Probably one of the tribal men has run off," Herezah said, distracted by the sight of Lazar and the promise of a good meal tonight.

Ana joined the Grand Vizier, who had stood. She squinted. "I think it's Jumo. I can't see him." Her fears were confirmed as the men drew closer, sorrowfully entering the outskirts of the camp, where the camels sat patiently.

Lazar strode past the royals but gave a swift glance to Ana, who saw the pain reflected in his eyes and lost her breath anticipating what was coming. Salim could speak only a smattering of Percherese. He tried to explain but it was hopeless. Pez could hardly translate in present company.

"What is going on here?" the Grand Master demanded.

Pez arrived flapping his make-believe wings but now stood still. "The sands swallowed Jumo," he sang, "the Spur has no appetite, and the fat birds fell from the sky." He began to dance before flapping off.

The royal party looked back at the dazed group of men before them and one of the Khalid began to mimic sinking, struggling for breath.

"Drowning?" Herezah asked. "How do you drown in a desert?"

"Oh, this is ridiculous. Where is the Spur?" the Grand Vizier said. He walked to where Lazar was busying himself, grimly pulling back on his robes and tying back his hair. "Spur Lazar, we gather something has happened to your friend, Jumo. Would you settle our confusion, please?" His voice was low, kindly.

"Certainly," Lazar said matter-of-factly, but there was a tone of danger in his voice now that even the Grand Vizier would be able to recognize as the sign of a man on the very edge of his emotions. "Jumo is dead. Quicksand. There was nothing we could do."

"Spur, I can't imagine——" The Grand Vizier reached out his hand to convey his condolences but Lazar stepped backward.

"I prefer to be alone." It was all the courtesy he could show at this time. "Forgive me." He pulled on his turban and walked away, Pez crawling on all fours beside him.

The Grand Vizier did not hear Lazar's comment to the dwarf but Pez suddenly stopped, stood up, and watched the tall man stride away.

THE FRESH MEAT THEY had all looked forward to tasted bitter in their mouths. Only Maliz, it seemed, took real pleasure in the roasted bustard. Even Herezah had the grace to dine quietly and sparingly in her tent, though Salim had urged all to eat the food that the gods had provided and that Shahin had risked her life to give them.

Through gestures he managed to convey this and the Vizier took up the torch for him, insisting everyone in the royal party and all the Elim partake of this rare opportunity for freshly cooked food.

"We have a long journey ahead," he counseled, "with no idea of when fresh meat will come our way again."

They ate in moody silence. Pez was nowhere to be seen and Maliz presumed he might be with the Spur, but judging from the body language of both earlier, he was reluctant to assume that the dwarf was welcome at Lazar's side. He wondered what had happened between them.

Herezah emerged and Maliz was surprised to see her thank the Khalid for their gift of meat. The men of the desert bowed to her. The desert did strange things to one, Maliz decided, and then he watched, intrigued, as she cut herself another piece of the roasted bird and reached for some of the cooling flatbread.

"You have a good appetite, I'm pleased to see, Valide," he said, unable to mask all the sarcasm from his voice.

"I eat but little, Tariq, as you should know. This is for Lazar."

He smirked. "Good luck."

"The point is, Grand Vizier, we cannot have our guide and protector dropping dead from starvation. I'm hoping to appeal to his practical side, at least persuade him to eat for his health, if not pleasure."

"You'd do better, then, to let the Zaradine take that food to him."

Herezah bristled. "You think her persuasive powers are greater than mine?"

He regarded her with a soft look of vexation. "Are you truly interested in his health, Valide, or would you also appreciate his company?" He stayed the inevitable rush of insults coming his way by raising a hand. "Forgive me. I simply mean that perhaps they can encourage each other through this maudlin time. They are both miserable and neither is eating. We need both strong and healthy—they are our most important companions. The Spur as our guide into Galinsea and the Zaradine for the deal she must broker."

Herezah did not respond, but she walked back to her tent and looked inside. A quiet exchange took place and Ana stepped out this time, pale and watchful.

"Come, Ana, you have a task to achieve," Herezah said, and

led the girl away from the camp to where they knew the Spur brooded.

THEY FOUND HIM WITH his head between his knees, long arms encircling all, as if by closing himself off to the rest of the world, he could avoid its pain. He heard their soft footfall and raised his head. Herezah saw Ana wince to see the grief in his face.

"Please." He began shaking his head.

"Lazar, you must eat something. The desert is unforgiving, I'm discovering," Herezah began softly, conversationally. "It makes no distinction. I gather it will happily kill the healthy without mercy, although it prefers the malnourished, I'm sure."

He nodded, but said nothing, although his expression showed a quirk of surprise. She knew what it was—he had never heard gentleness in her voice. Perhaps the Vizier was right, she thought—perhaps the desert does make strangers of us.

She pressed on. "The journey ahead is perilous enough—you've warned us of that so many times—without our adding to the danger through lack of food or care for ourselves." Herezah pushed Ana forward as she continued arguing her case. "Please, eat something. I don't care whether you don't taste it or even want it. But we all care that you remain strong and see us through this trial. You need this meat."

The Spur turned his gaze fully onto Herezah now and she felt the familiar weakness that his regard could always provoke. She was used to it being loaded with disdain and felt suddenly unsettled that on this night nothing but vulnerability was reflected in his eyes.

"Imagine what a fine counselor you could be to Boaz if only you'd . . ." He didn't finish.

"Yes," she said, a little more brightly, "the Grand Vizier urges the same. If I didn't know better I'd think you two were in cahoots." She tried to laugh but it came out a choked sound. "But none of you men has lived in the harem. You don't know how it shapes everything about its inhabitants, how it turns you from a happy and carefree eight-year-old into someone who is forced to scheme in order to protect yourself. No man can know the fear of bringing a son into this world when you know from his very first cry that he will probably be slaughtered—except you don't know when—and that all that stands between him and the blade is what lies between your own legs and how well you wield that weapon."

She was breathing hard, was surprised by the effort it took to reveal her true emotion to this man . . . the only man she had ever wanted for her own—the one she hated more than any other because he wouldn't capitulate to her.

Lazar looked at the ground and Herezah had to wonder whether he felt a prickle of shame as she continued: "No man can know what it is to fight every day of your life to secure your own and your child's longevity. This fight means shutting yourself off to *everything* from friendship to pity. Compassion, care, sympathy—they are all emotions I have not been able to risk, Lazar, and after a lifetime of having to be strong and ruthless, of keeping all weakness at bay, you forget how to even touch again on those emotions." She unveiled herself and he saw the movement, raised his head to look at her. "I have only this," she said, pointing to her face, "to win favor, and this," she said, pointing to her head now, "to use that favor to its best effect. I won, Lazar, because of my face, my body, my wits. My son was not slaughtered. My son is Zar."

He watched her for several moments before he replied, Ana's

presence hardly registering with him at this moment. "Then your work is done, Herezah. You have succeeded in your life's mission. Boaz is safe. You are safe. It is time to tear down the barriers and be the person you might have been had you not been attached to the palace."

"I might say the same to you," she replied swiftly, "except we are creatures of habit, you and I; we are too old perhaps to change what we've become."

"It is never too late," he murmured.

"I shall try, then, if you will," she challenged. "I am genuinely sorry for the loss of your companion. I didn't know him until this journey, but when I bothered to notice, he seemed pleasant, intelligent company. And anyone who calls you friend clearly is something special, seeing as how you let virtually no one into your life. So do the right thing by this man. Begin by eating something."

Herezah nodded at Ana, who moved to hold the plate out to him and spoke for the first time. It struck the Valide that her soft tones touched Lazar as tenderly as if she had used her hands. "Don't let Jumo's life be given in vain, Lazar. From what I can gather, he was chasing down this food so we could all eat well this night. Honor him: eat."

WHERE HEREZAH'S WORDS HAD lifted his spirits somewhat, Ana's words injured him. The Zaradine's easy tenderness, her ability to touch deeply on all that troubled him, seemed to rub salt into the wound that was Jumo's death. He wanted to reach out and bury his head in her hair, hold her close. He despised that she belonged to the Zar.

He reached for the plate instead. "I will eat, Zaradine, for Jumo's sake, and in his memory, if you will, too."

It was the capitulation he knew they had been hoping for. Both women instantly moved to sit beside him.

Lazar had to admire Herezah for risking rebuke as she laid her cool fingers lightly on his bare arm. "Thank you," she said, then removed her hand swiftly.

Lazar had not flinched away from Herezah's touch—it was his quiet acknowledgment to the Valide that he understood and admired the courage it must have taken for her to lay out her emotions in such bareness, to him of all people. However, as she spoke more brightly, looking out into the distance rather than at him, to cover the fleeting awkwardness, Lazar took the plate from Ana and he deliberately allowing his hand to brush hers. In that moment he felt the connection, saw it in her eyes, sensed it in the soft caress she returned to his palm.

Later that night he mourned Jumo deeply, and that only intensified his sorrows over Ana, over the touch that told him she was his, had always been. The hurt over his two favorite people blended and his grief that he could never be with either again intensified his sadness. He grieved again at the thought that they could never be together. He needed to be alone with his thoughts, to clear them. He must accept that Jumo was gone from his life and he must lay his desires for Ana to rest once and for all. Love equaled pain, and he had no more room in his heart for it. Loneliness could never get worse, a solitary life was quantifiable and once accepted, became routine, manageable, and even comfortable . . . familiar as a comfy old chair or a favorite shirt.

As everyone was settling down to sleep, he drifted away from the main group, unnoticed, and in the cover of darkness moved stealthily from the camp. He needed to walk, to feel the cold of the desert night, to let it chill him and cool the flames of desire that Ana's simple touch had fanned.

It occurred to him in the dark that he was in danger of walking straight into quicksand as Jumo had, and that made him slow his urgent stride and make for a dune rather than the flat earth. The sand slipped beneath his feet, still warm in its depths, but he pushed on until he crested the dune, and there he lay, hands cushioning his head as he stared up at the bright crescent moon that had just emerged from a shadowy cloud. From an early age he had sought the moon for solace, but now it mocked him. *Still alone, Lazar?* it asked. *No parents, no friends, no lover?* He lost himself in sad thoughts of a life that felt unfulfilled, even though as few as fifteen moons ago he might have believed his life full and happy. Fifteen moons ago he had not met Ana and he had had a companion called Jumo. Fifteen moons ago nobody knew his identity and voices did not speak to him in his mind.

He did not hear the soft scramble of someone climbing the dune, but he did recognize the figure when it reached his eye level. He sat up, alarmed.

"What's wrong? What are *you* doing here?"

"I had to speak with you . . . alone."

"How . . ." He was lost for words.

"No one knows I'm gone. I told Pez—I think he understood. He's not happy, of course, but he will warn me should the need arise."

"Ana, I—"

"May I sit beside you?"

He nodded, then thought better of it. "Perhaps we had better sit on the other side," he suggested.

He knew she smiled behind her veil. "Yes, we are illuminated here on the top of the dune, aren't we?"

Lazar did not return the smile. Instead a tension, emanating from him like a tautly strung bow, stretched to the one person he'd least expected to find himself alone with. His throat felt too dry to talk and he cleared it nervously. "How do you feel?"

"Happy now that I'm here."

"Yes, the desert can offer comfort. The harem has been very cruel to you."

"I'm not referring to the harem," she said, releasing the veil and pulling away her head cover so that her golden hair could feel the touch of the night's soft, chill breeze. Some of the silken strands blew away from her face and he could see her profile in all of its ethereal beauty beneath the moonlight. "I mean here . . . with you."

He had to look away from temptation. "It's too dangerous, Ana. I cannot risk you—"

"What can they do? Tell me off? Tell Boaz? Kill me?" She laughed softly without humor. "They've tried it all before and I fear none of it. I am their only hope apparently and I do this for one reason alone. You should know now that I care nothing for Percheron, I care nothing for my own life, I really don't care if war comes, save for the anxiety I have for my father, brother, and sisters. I was meant to be dead by now, and in truth, death suited my needs, for it would have brought closure to a life filled only by misery."

He remained silent, guarded, wishing he could turn back time, wishing he had never visited that hut in the foothills. He was the reason for her misery.

She continued softly now, none of the passion gone from her voice but the fire of her words settled to a more gentle glow. Her eyes were not turned toward his but out into the darkness where shadows of dunes hunched like ancient creatures. "My only reason for not objecting to this marriage and this journey was that it meant I could see you, share your life for just a little longer. We have never spoken truthfully, you and I. It is time we did, before it is too late and our mission is done and I am either dead in Galinsea or returned to a living death in the harem. I am sure that we will not be allowed to see each other again once this is done with."

He tried to sound unfazed, even though he was intimidated by her forthrightness and unsure of how to respond. "I don't see why not. They have no reason to forbid—"

"They have every reason. Herezah would no more trust me alone with you than she would herself. And Boaz kno—"

The mention of the Valide made him bristle. "I admired the Valide's candor earlier this evening but that's where my admiration ends. Let me assure you that I can trust myself alone with her, Ana. Whatever she might try, nothing would come of it," he said sourly.

"She would find a way, Lazar. She always finds a way. She admitted as much this evening. And I know this from bitter experience."

He remained silent.

She qualified her earlier statement. "She would seek out some way to compromise you."

"Herezah has nothing that can surprise me."

"No? I imagine her next move will be to alert you to the fact that I might be carrying her grandchild?"

Shocked, Lazar was unable to form any words for several long moments. Finally she turned her gaze from the distance to focus fully on him, and even in the dark he could see the sparkle of her eyes. She waited for him to speak.

It all fell into place for him now. "That's why you've been feeling so sick. Is it true?"

She shrugged. "I do not know, yet," she replied carefully, "but I hear them whispering. She and Tariq have already convinced themselves that I am pregnant with the next heir. They have almost convinced me."

Lazar felt dizzy with dismay. So many thoughts swirled around his mind, mainly selfish, angry ones, directed at Boaz for having tasted the pleasure of Ana's body. But he fought those back into the recesses of his already scarred heart, where he could lock them deeply away, and focused instead on the practical worries. "We should not have you and the child endangered in the desert," he blustered.

"Everyone seems quite happy to endanger me. My child, if there is one, is hardly a problem and should not change anything. The baby is safe as long as I am, whether I am in the desert or imprisoned in the harem. The only suffering is borne by me and there is no impact on anyone else, least of all the child. I am the tired one, the one who is constantly feeling sick. If we brokered this peace, then it matters not whether I am with child or without. The baby would be killed anyway if war came to Percheron—don't try and tell me otherwise." She glared at him.

"No, you're right," he admitted. "You and the baby would be two of the first dealt with. No heir to Percheron would be permitted to survive."

"Then he's in danger whether I'm here in the desert or cocooned in my prison at the palace."

"He?"

She hugged her knees to her chest. "Herezah thinks of her grandchild as a he."

"When will you know if you are pregnant?"

She shrugged. "My bleeds are unreliable at best. Another moon perhaps."

"How did you get past Herezah anyway?"

"Pez. He gave her a sleeping draft."

Lazar gave a very halfhearted tweak of a smile. "Crafty." Then he sighed, wishing he wasn't being tested like this with Ana so close and the unique opportunity of being alone. Again he chose safe ground. "What did you want to talk to me about?"

"I wanted to share my sorrow for the loss of Jumo, but not with an audience, and one that in all truth doesn't really care. He was always so kind to me. I loved Jumo."

"That makes two of us," he said miserably. "It was a terrible way to die."

"Is there a good way?" she asked, echoing his gloom.

"In battle perhaps, or whilst one sleeps. I would take either."

She smiled sadly. "I also wanted to have this chance to talk about us."

He felt the catch in his throat again, swallowed back the fear that she was moving them onto less secure ground. This was how Jumo must have felt, panicking, sinking further into the mire. He grappled for a hold on something solid, something real, something irrefutable. "There is no us, Ana," he said, his voice betraying how hard it was for him to remain this distant, this controlled. "You are the Zaradine, now potentially the carrier of the heir to the throne of Percheron. I am your servant. There is no us. There never was."

"You're not very good at lying, are you, Lazar? You're far better at the gruff, angry truth."

"I do not lie."

"Then why did you touch me so surreptitiously this evening, if not to steal a part of me for yourself? Why did you touch me fifteen moons ago when I was first being presented to the Valide, if not to hold on to me for just a little longer? Did you think I didn't feel that fleeting kiss of our skins through the sheath I was forced to wear? Did you think that because I was so young I didn't have blood pounding through my veins or the desires of any young woman?"

"I . . . I . . ."

Lazar could tell she was not going to let him off the hook now that she had him squirming at the end of her line. "Why did you come in search of me when I escaped? Was it all about duty or was it about getting to me first, seeing me again? You could have led me from the temple—I was capable of walking—and yet you carried me. Was that sheer generosity of spirit or did you want to feel me against your body?" He hung his head and still she persisted. "At least Boaz declares his love, you just sneak around it. You prolonged our time together in the market on the first evening we came into Percheron and on the morning of my discovery. You fought for my freedom during the Choosing Ceremony, and later, after I'd not only relinquished it but brought the full might of the harem's censure upon me, you fought for me again, this time with your own life. You took my punishment. You died for me, or so I was told. You think you hide your feelings but you are transparent to me, Lazar. You always have been, even though you act in a way to confuse me."

"I betrayed you." He was desperately grasping at straws, hoping to incite her rage, to turn her from him, but especially to prevent her from speaking more truth, and showing him so clearly for the duplicitous person he was.

She touched his long hair, a tear escaping down her cheek as he closed his eyes for fear that he might just reach for her and never be able to let go. "I know now that the betrayal you speak of was not of your own making. Zafira and Ellyana created the deception, not you. I can see how sick you've been. Sick enough to no longer have the strength to dye your hair and stop running from the person you are. A Galinsean Prince." She shook her head, seemingly still unable to fully digest the truth. "This hair color suits you more."

"This is dangerous. We can't . . ." He stammered, unable to finish his sentence for the rush of longing that engulfed him, rendering him helpless beneath her fingers as they moved to caress his soft beard.

"We might never have another chance," she said, shocking him further with her reckless, suddenly mature approach. He tried to tell himself that she was shy, reluctant, that the loneliness of her life and despair over Jumo's death had provoked her into seeking him out—the one person who might understand and share her grief. He told himself he must not take advantage of her in this state. But the truth was that he knew Ana had always been precocious and wise beyond her years. And she was not shy, far from it. She had registered his desire from the first moment they had met and although she might not have fueled it, she had certainly accepted and welcomed it in her quiet, guarded way.

"When you were flogged for me, do you know you told me you loved me?" she breathed near his ear, sending fresh currents of fear and lust racing through him.

"I was dying," he groaned in a last ditch attempt at denial.

"No, you were honest. It was the one occasion I have seen your emotions bared, your expression so free of disguise. You knew you were as good as dead, that it didn't matter anymore. And you released the truth of what was in your mind."

He tried once more. "I don't remember."

She pulled his chin around, forcing him to face her. "I remember it clearly. I clung to it for all these moons as my touchstone. I kept my veil, spattered with your blood, as a way of keeping you alive for me. Before you succumbed, I told you I loved you back, Lazar. And unlike you, I never lie to those I love." She leaned close and touched her soft lips to his.

Lazar, Spur of Percheron, mustered all the courage he had left inside and pushed her back. It took all of his willpower, for he wanted her so badly he knew he could not fend her off again. "Please, don't do this," he beseeched. It was more of a warning.

Ana shook her head sadly. "It is done," she whispered, and this time when she leaned toward him, he did not resist. He had nothing left with which to ward her off, no more weapons with which to fight her, no more armor with which to shield himself.

And so he yielded.

He pulled her close and returned her kiss with such passion that starry explosions winked and blinked behind his closed eyelids, his hands cupping her face in an effort to own her. And then, as the moon once again slipped behind the clouds, Lazar surrendered wholly to her warmth, which banished the cold whipping at their bared bodies, and to her brightness, which burned like a golden fire within him. He knew no other thought but Ana for what felt an eternity; he familiarized himself with every inch of her young, velvetlike skin. As he kissed the curve of her waist he mumbled, "This bit belongs to me," making her laugh throatily, and with surprise. He had not heard Ana laugh like that before and would never know that neither had she. It was the sound of sunshine and calm seas, of blue skies and heavy-scented blossom; it was happiness, fulfillment, satisfaction, all in one. He told her this and she accused him of sounding like one of Pez's nonsense rhymes. And as, finally, their lovemaking subsided into a languorous, sensuous quiet that wrapped itself around their entangled limbs, she stroked his damaged back and he lulled her off to sleep humming a Galinsean lullaby.

Lazar, however, did not sleep. He wrapped her nakedness with his robe and silently begged the night's frost to kill him, for if he could not have this moment again, he would sooner die. His melodramatic thoughts eased as time passed slowly and he chose instead to memorize the curves and planes of her face, so childlike in repose. She breathed softly, a wisp of her hair rising and falling with those breaths, and he gently touched her belly in aching jealousy, wondering whether it did indeed carry the heir to the Percheron throne.

She stirred at his touch, stretched slowly, sensually, and smiled at him. "How long have I slept?"

"Long enough here," he murmured reluctantly. "You must go back to the royal tent."

She began to object but he placed his finger over her mouth. "We have put Pez at risk enough."

She nodded and sat up. "I hadn't thought that I'd put him in danger. You're right, Tariq sleeps lightly."

"And Mal—er, Tariq, he—"

"You wanted to say Maliz, am I right? Do you believe this tale that I am Lyana?"

He shrugged. "I don't know what to believe, Ana. Pez believes it."

"Earnestly," she said sadly. "But I think he's going to be disappointed."

Lazar nodded. "So do I. If you were who he thinks you are, the demon would have already made his move."

She looked startled by his directness. "The Grand Vizier kill me?" She shook her head. "And how do you know that Tariq is Maliz anyway?"

"Ah, well, I think in this respect Pez has some argument. I have known Tariq for more than a decade. This is not the Tariq of fifteen moons ago. This is entirely a different man, who looks the same and has the same tone of voice but doesn't use the same words or even mannerisms that Tariq did."

"So you believe in Maliz? In his existence, I mean?"

He nodded. "Yes, and as firmly as I believe in Iridor's existence—and I have seen Pez as himself and as the owl. The magic is real."

She frowned. "Maliz did touch me."

"Which is why I don't believe you are Lyana. Poor Pez."

"He keeps telling me that you are involved, too."

He grimaced. "I don't see how. I think once he discovers the real Lyana, he'll forget about us."

"Who can she be?"

"If she exists at all," he warned.

"Ellyana is real. She obviously believes Lyana rises."

"Yes, none of it makes sense," he admitted. He sighed as he unfurled his arm from around her. "Time will tell."

"Lazar."

"Yes?" he replied, distracted by pulling her robe over her shoulders, keen to get them both dressed and out of danger of discovery.

"I have loved you since you came down that incline to our hut and laid claim to me."

"Ana. You are so young, you have—"

"Don't. Tell me the truth. There are no witnesses, just us."

He stood, robed himself, and then pulled her to her feet, taking the long pause as some precious time to formulate the words he had wanted to say to her since that same moment when his very breathing had been arrested at the sight of her. He also remembered Jumo's dying words—owed it to his beloved friend to honor that request.

"I have known what I thought was love only once before. It brought me nothing but grief. But what I feel for you I now realize is true love because it never stops hurting. It hurt to first meet you, first fall in love with you. It hurt so much more to love you from a distance, but now that I have loved you physically, I know the pain will never soften and blur as it did with Shara." He kissed her hand. "But if this is all we can have, then I accept and take the pain and I thank all the gods of the world for giving me this time with you. Yes, I love you, Ana. I always have and I will continue to do so from a distance until I take my last breath. You never need to doubt me."

He allowed her to throw herself once again into his arms and they remained in that embrace, fighting back their tears, for several minutes before he disentangled himself. "What we have had, no one will ever take from us. I wish I'd had more courage to resist you so that neither of us need feel such loss, but I will never regret these hours and I thank you for giving me such a gift."

Before she could speak again, he pushed her toward the camp. "Now go, I beg you. Return as silently as you came."

"And you?"

"Soon, I promise."

He watched her retreat down the dune, waited until he lost her in the darkness before he turned his back on her and wept. He had lied to her. He was not grateful; the fleeting gift of herself was a curse and it would haunt him forever with an unrelenting taunt of what he had once tasted but would never taste again.

As his tears dried, he became aware of another presence, a presence in his mind. The voices were back, calling strongly to him now. He heard them more clearly at this moment than he had ever heard them previously. Until now they had sounded distant, unintelligible, as if muffled. Now, as Ana left him, they rumbled clearly in his mind.

Release us, Lazar, they called to him.

In his ire, in his frustrated understanding that Ana had given herself to him once and once only, in his fury at losing Jumo in such helpless circumstances, he lashed out: *Tell me who you are or leave me alone!*

He hadn't expected a response, and when it came he wished he had never posed the angry question.

I am Beloch.

I am Ezram.

I am Crendel.

I am Darso.

I am . . . the list continued, all names of the mythical creatures of the Stone City of Percheron that he had always admired.

MALIZ STIRRED. HE HAD never been a deep sleeper, but these hot days and cool desert nights, as well as all the fresh air and constant activity, were combining to ensure he slept far more soundly than he could ever remember. Still, something had disturbed him, and as he lay in his small, suffocating tent, he considered what could have woken him. There were no sounds outside, save the gentle spit and crackle of the fire. It would be out by morning and no doubt Lazar would be sending people all over to scour for anything combustible. He had already warned that they might have to live from then on without warmth at night or any heated food. The Spur had urged the Elim to cook up stocks of flatbread in case the lack of fire material became reality. Maliz shook his head clear of the mundane—he was really beginning to think like a man, he berated himself—and focused on what had disrupted his sleep. He had been enjoying these cool desert nights of slumber but had also learned long ago to trust his instincts. If there had been no sharp noise to awaken him, what had shaken him from pleasant dreams? And now that he thought about it, he had not come to from his unconscious state gradually. He had been woken abruptly. He had simply opened his eyes in shock as if reacting to a loud noise or a nudge.

He knew it was useless trying to probe. Imprisoned so completely within Tariq, he had almost none of his magics to call upon. He almost wished he could inhabit some old wretch again, one of those temporary, disposable hosts he used in his dormancy—simply to have the freedom to range outside of his body, just once even. How frustrating that he had committed to the Grand Vizier and so had to rely on wit and cunning . . . and touch, until Lyana herself had risen and provided his power.

And that's where this thought dwelled. Lyana. Had something occurred with her that had somehow fractured the status quo of the present spiritual world? She could not have risen or he would have instantly felt his magic quicken within him. And yet something niggled, something he couldn't latch on to, as if it hovered at the periphery of his vision. He sat up, shaking himself fully from the dozy sense of comfort beneath his blanket, and tried to pay attention to what was ranging through his mind.

Lyana. He tracked back through past centuries. Her rising had always triggered the same response—a violent one—an arrival of his magic that made him suck in air as though gasping for his last breath or as if someone had punched him hard in the belly. But Lyana's rising had not woken him or he would be feeling the effects and the orgasmic sensation of his powers coming fully to him. And yet this disturbance had the hallmarks of Lyana. It was abrupt, it had not announced itself, and now it remained hidden. He desperately wanted to believe it signaled her rising but he remained impotent, so it couldn't be.

Now he did hear a soft footfall outside. Quickly he pulled back his tent flap, all of his frustration poured into the action.

Ana jumped. "Oh, you scared me, Grand Vizier."

He frowned. "What are you doing, Zaradine?"

"Relieving myself," she said airily, her expression suggesting it was none of his business. "I had hoped not to disturb anyone. I'm sorry I woke you."

He considered. "Did you make a noise?"

She frowned in thought.

Maliz carefully modulated his tone, made his voice friendly. "It's just that something did wake me, and I was just trying to work out what it was."

She gave a sheepish shrug, all but her eyes hidden behind her veil. "Forgive me, I did trip over your tent rope on my way to that dune." She pointed to the near distance. "I'm so sorry."

He waved his hand toward her. "It is nothing to forgive."

He yawned. "I was just enjoying a nice dream, I think, and was sad to be pulled from it."

She giggled softly. "Can you remember your dreams? I rarely can."

"I remember everything, Zaradine. In this one I was a god, with immense power, and I had just persuaded a horde of beautiful nymphs to visit my mountain palace in the sky."

In the dying glow of the fire, he noticed her eyes widen slightly at his words. Possibly she was shocked by the image he described, or was it the mention that he was a god? He noticed the hesitation before the smooth answer. "And now you tease me, Grand Vizier."

He smiled indulgently and for good measure touched her arm. Nothing, as before! This girl was definitely not Lyana. "I do. Actually, I was an old man, chasing after a rather lovely young creature who was understandably running from me with all her might."

He saw her eyes reflect soft amusement now. "I think you're far more charming and attractive than you give yourself credit for Grand Vizier. There are plenty of women, I'm sure, who find you irresistible."

But only one interests me, my young Ana, he thought. *And you are not her . . . but you will interest me when I become Boaz.* "Oh, I do hope so, Zaradine, and once this mission is done with and we are returned to Percheron, I might try to find them."

She nodded her approval and then disappeared silently into her own tent.

Maliz had to wonder whether his instincts had sent him a ruse. And whether in chasing off after Pez, he had actually left behind the real trail in Percheron, where Iridor existed and could lead him to the hated Goddess. He grimaced. Lyana was cunning this time. But he would find her and he would take his time killing her. His mind moved again to Ana. No. Not her. But if not Ana, who?

NOT FAR AWAY, YET distant enough not to disturb the sleepers, Pez was retching violently but with no idea why. His grief over Jumo aside, he had not partaken of any of the meat. The nausea had suddenly come upon him—no warning, just a violent surge through his body before a darkening of the sand where he stood.

What was it? What could have disturbed his body so? His head throbbed and he sat down to lean against the dune.

"Pez," a voice whispered.

He leaped up, startled but still dizzy from his exertions. "Ellyana," he murmured, "don't creep up on me like that."

"I cannot use magic to reach you or he will sense it. He is very alert just now."

Pez knew to whom she referred. But didn't know how she would know the demon's state of mind. He stole a glance around the dune to check that Ellyana could not be seen from the campsite. "I am unwell."

"I can see that," she said softly. "It is not what you think." She could see his heavy brow frowning in the moonlight. "You are not ill. It's because you are Iridor."

"I don't understand," he groaned quietly.

"You will. I am here to tell you that our previous agreement regarding Ana is no longer necessary."

He ignored his aching head to stare at Ellyana, not that he could make out her features in the darkness. "Why?"

"Just do as I say, Pez." She turned to leave.

"Wait," he growled in a low voice. "Is she Lyana?"

He thought he might have caught a ghost of a smile across her face but there simply wasn't enough light with the moon intermittently shrouded by clouds. "Have patience, Pez. All will be revealed."

"Why won't you tell me?" Pez persisted.

"For your protection," she murmured, angry now. "Just let Ana be. Iridor knows. Search yourself, and you will find the answers you hunt."

Pez looked to the sands, and shook his head with repressed frustration. When he looked back up, Ellyana had disappeared. So had his headache. He felt suddenly fine—the smothering pain had gone as fast as it had come, and the nausea was nothing more than a memory. He glanced over and noticed the dark patch of sand. He hadn't imagined it; he had been sick.

None of it felt natural, and Ellyana's curious arrival, timed perfectly to coincide with his disturbance, told him his nausea and headache were somehow linked to the Goddess. Something had happened . . . but what?

32

It had been two days since he had lost Jumo, and although leaving the region of the quicksand and his death had helped to clear the morbid atmosphere that had pervaded everyone's waking thoughts, it had done nothing to improve Lazar's grim countenance. If anything, the latter had seemed to worsen into a dulled, impervious expression. Pez knew everyone assumed it was grief. But he suspected it was terror at Lazar's dark thoughts of longing for the Zar's wife.

Lazar, in his withdrawn state, hadn't realized that Ana had begun vomiting most of the meager bread and fruit she tried to eat in her bid to keep her side of their agreement, or that Salim was becoming decidedly nervous as they entered a part of the desert known simply to the tribes as the Empty. It took Pez and a hissing, angry exchange on this second night after Jumo's death to finally get Lazar to take notice of anything more than his camel or the horizon.

Pez found Lazar in the black of night sitting alone on the top of a dune well away from the campfires.

"I need to talk to you," he said, anticipating hostility. They had not spoken directly to each other since Lazar had banished him from his side after Jumo's death.

He received precisely the animosity he expected. "I have nothing to talk about," Lazar replied coldly.

"Do you mean in general or with me specifically?" Pez asked, prepared to go along with the fight that was certainly due between them.

"Both."

"Lazar, I think something's happening that we don't know about. Whether or not you want to talk to me, I'm the one who has to make you understsand. For all intents and purposes, you're not aware of much at all just now."

"Go away, Pez."

"I will not."

"I don't wish to discuss Iridor, Lyana, this battle, or Maliz. In fact I don't wish to discuss anything. I want to be left alone."

"This has nothing to do with any of that, Spur. This solely concerns your job for your Zar."

"What is it?" Lazar said through gritted teeth.

"It's Salim. He's not saying much, but the language of his body and the tension he is creating amongst his own is saying plenty."

"Such as?"

"I'm not sure, but we're all feeling it. That's why I've brought it to you. There's an uneasiness."

"I'll need more than that to go on."

Pez shrugged in the dark. "It's hard to say. Salim seems overly watchful, nervous. He keeps looking this way and that.

I swear he looked over his shoulder earlier today. It's certainly giving me a sense of unrest and I know the others feel similarly, from eavesdropping on their conversations."

"Have you spoken to the Khalid?"

"How can I? The Grand Vizier has nothing to focus his attention on at the moment except me, I feel."

"Don't flatter yourself."

"Listen, Lazar, pay attention to what I'm saying. I think something dangerous is afoot."

"Does your big nose twitch from the Lore and tell you this, or do you have any facts to give me?"

Pez knew Lazar was being deliberately provocative, determined to goad him into the fight the Spur clearly wanted. He wouldn't bite, not yet. "Salim senses trouble but he's not telling us anything. You need to talk to him."

"Why should I? Simply because you feel something in the air?"

"Lazar, it's more than that."

"Well, I don't feel anything," Lazar said dismissively, obviously hoping to end their conversation.

"That's because you are in an Empty all of your own, Lazar," Pez snapped, his temper no longer in check. "You arrogant fool. Prince or not, you are all Galinsean. Don't ever say I didn't try!"

Lazar surged to his feet. "You dare talk to me like that!" he warned, turning now to stare angrily at the dwarf.

"I think I'm the only one who isn't scared of you, or that look that I can't see in the dark but I know is on your face. If you want to hit me, break my jaw again, do it. I can heal myself again if I have to."

"You seem quite at ease with using the Lore on yourself, or for Ana." Lazar sneered, dropping his voice low now.

"Ah, so now we come to it. I understand what this is all about. This is not about Jumo. This is about me refusing you. Even after I helped Ana to have some time with you when I thought you both deserved it." Whatever else he thought about that moonlit night he left unsaid.

Lazar sighed and in that sound Pez heard the gratitude the Spur clearly felt . "Go find another playmate, Pez," he urged. "I don't wish to talk about this."

"No, but then you never do. You run away from anything and everything that pricks at your emotions or requires you to open yourself up to others. What have I done, Lazar?"

"It's what you haven't done," Lazar replied, almost a whisper, deep sorrow in his voice.

Pez knew his recent lies would follow him for the rest of his life. He was glad Lazar could not see his face or the despondent expression written on it. "I explained to you already, I needed to touch him. How was I supposed to do that without perishing myself?"

"Well, even in my panic at that moment I could imagine you turning yourself into the owl and hovering over Jumo's head if you had to. You could have touched him easily that way."

Pez had not thought of that, curiously enough, and now, feeling even more hollow—if that was possible—he grasped at a fresh deception. "I . . . I cannot use the Lore when I am Iridor."

"I think you're lying, Pez."

"I am not—"

"I'll tell you why I think you're lying and why you chose not to save the life of someone utterly loyal to Percheron, and very close to me. No one should die like that, swallowed by the earth, slowly drowning in a dark mass in front of an audience that couldn't . . . or in this instance, wouldn't help."

Pez felt his belly clench, praying inwardly that Lazar had not seen through him. "Listen to me, I could not use the Lore—"

Lazar continued as though Pez had not spoken. His voice was calm but edged with ice now. No one could hear or see them. "I think you lied to me and to Jumo and you continue to lie to me and even yourself because you chose a dream over reality. What do we really know of Lyana? And yet for her you allowed one of the best men to have ever walked at your side to die an agonizing death of suffocation. Jumo showed more courage in death than you have ever shown in life, Pez." Reluctant, angry tears were rolling down his face as he pointed at the dwarf who could not see the tears but could make out his accusing finger. "In your stifling fear of Maliz, you killed my closest friend." Pez's expression turned from dismay to despair, his large head moving from side to side in denial. "You might as well have, Pez. You could have saved him but you chose not to, and I only worked out why on the way back to camp. You couldn't risk Maliz sensing your magic, could you? Jumo died to keep you safe from the demon." Lazar's reasoning was right; he had hit on the truth but the accusation was unfair and Pez hoped he knew that, too. But Lazar didn't care, obviously. He clearly wanted someone else to suffer this pain of loss alongside him. Pez understood that most of the others were carrying on as though Jumo were already something of the past, a distant memory soon to be forgotten, and of no real importance.

He watched Lazar bend over and retch, giving back to the desert the small amount of meat that had been stolen from it a few days previous. And as he did so he heard Lazar swear that he would never eat any bird again. He would join Ana in her idiosyncrasy of not eating a creature that flies. His reason was different, of course, Pez realized—Lazar's best friend had died chasing down the meat of the sky.

Pez was breathless from the pain of Lazar's words. They stung because for the most part they were true, but he refuted the accusation that he actually killed Jumo; he just hadn't felt in a position to save him. It was too dangerous for him, for Ana, for Lazar even . . . for all of them who were connected with the rising of Iridor and the ultimate battle ahead. None understood how their very lives hung on a fragile thread of secrecy. He could almost hate Lazar in this moment for making him feel so responsible for Jumo's demise.

He had to force himself to take a deep, steadying breath. "Yes, there may be some truth in what you say, Lazar. But I didn't withhold my magic to save myself. In this you are unjust, for my life as Iridor is forfeit. I made that most difficult choice without much more than a second in order to save your life and especially Ana's. Over the centuries Maliz has chosen a variety of ways to destroy Lyana once he's had her at his mercy. I thank my Goddess that I have never had to witness it but I have learned about it all the same. He once physically tore her limb from limb, until she lay scattered in pieces; another time he disemboweled her but kept her alive for an hour or more—and I can't tell you what a slow, agonizing death that was for her. Jumo's, if you'll forgive me, was swift by comparison."

"Stop."

"Then there was the time he ate her. Roasted her alive over hot coals and carved her up to consume at his leisure. She took a long time to die that day, too, as I understand. My personal favorite, though, was learning how he slowly bled her to death.

Each day he would drain some more. It took her many days of suffering, witnessing her own demise as he drank the blood he drained from her."

"I said stop," Lazar commanded.

"Another time—I think it's the occasion Maliz enjoyed the most—he raped her over and over. And when he was spent, he forced other helpless individuals to line up and rape her until she died. Again she suffered with courage—it took her a day and half of endless rutting, her arms and legs pinned out by stakes in the ground, to capitulate."

"Stop, I said!" Lazar roared, knowing his shout could be heard for miles. Pez, against his own desires, but for the sake of appearances, began to do a jig, hoping that the audience from afar would assume his endless chatter and movement had so infuriated Lazar in his despair that he had reacted with anger. "Please, I beg you," Lazar whispered.

"You need to understand what we are dealing with here. He takes pleasure in injury, pain, suffering. He never lets her die easily—he prolongs her agony, enjoys her slow death. He will do this to Ana, and I know him so well, I believe he will keep you alive and make you watch. You see, I think our Grand Vizier has worked out your weakness, Lazar, and whether or not you believe that Ana is Lyana, is irrelevant—just as a simple woman she makes you vulnerable. He has seen this and he will make you pay the price for that helplessness. He will dream up something even more spectacular knowing he has an audience and you will share her every groan, her every plea to die, and he will do this to you purely for his own amusement. This is why I had to choose. There was no surety that I could have saved Jumo but there was a guarantee that I would not reveal myself and thus endanger Ana and yourself. Believe me, I have not lived easily with myself these past two days and nights. If it had only been my life to jeopardize, Lazar, I would have risked it gladly for Jumo, but there were too many lives at stake. The price was too high."

"Would the Lore have saved him?" Lazar demanded.

Pez shook his head with a sense of hopelessness. "I cannot say. I could have tried, that's all, and perhaps we would have won, but Maliz would have worked it out. Apart from sensing the magic, not just he but others would have had to wonder how we kept Jumo aloft long enough in the quicksand for the camels. There was too much risk."

Lazar hung his head. "We cannot bring him back."

"We cannot. I made a decision for the greater good. I stand by it. I'm sorry if you deem it wrong, but Ana is safe for the time being and soon I will prove to you why we have suffered this loss, why her life is so important to us."

"If she continues to survive."

"She will survive, I promise." The certainty in the dwarf's voice made Lazar turn toward him sharply.

"How can you be so sure?"

"Instinct," Pez said, too quickly, and Lazar heard the catch in this throat, as if Pez had realized he was wrong to have shared his thoughts openly. They had argued enough, though; there was no point in opening a fresh wound. "Will you forgive me?"

"We cannot bring him back," Lazar repeated.

"That is not an answer to my question. We have been great friends over the years. We trust each other. I don't want to lose that."

Lazar stared out toward the moon, which was shrouded by clouds this night and shivered against the chill. "Prove me wrong, Pez. That's all I ask of you. I doubt Lyana, I doubt Iridor . . . prove me wrong and let my friend's death count for something."

Pez nodded. "I will do that, my friend—may I still call you that?"

"Of course, Pez, I—" Lazar's sentence was cut off as he was knocked sideways by a powerful shove.

HE FELT PRESSURE AT the top of his arm, and in the darkness of night he couldn't see much, but when he clutched at where he felt the sensation, he was aware of pain and of a sticky wetness on his palm, and impossible, though it seemed, an arrow sticking out of his arm.

"Pez," he began, incredulous, now wavering on his knees.

"I am gone to fetch your sword," the dwarf said. "Get that arrow from you. We are under attack."

Lazar ignored the pain, growled as he broke the arrow as far down the shaft as he could, and got himself quickly to his knees to scan the surrounding dunes. *I can't see anything,* he thought anxiously, praying that Pez would change into Iridor and make a reconnaissance flight to locate the enemy with his sharp owl night sight.

He waited for what felt an interminable length of time, his frustration increasing with each passing second. Finally he heard scrabbling nearby and tensed, prepared to throw himself down the dune. Without a weapon he was useless to his group and completely vulnerable.

"It's me," sounded a familiar voice. Pez crawled up on his belly, two swords somehow in tow. "Don't ask me how I did that."

Lazar took the swords and automatically weighted both, swinging them in the air. "Tell me."

"A small army, you could say. There is no indication who they are or why they've attacked us. The Elim are making a good fight of it, but they are dying. There is no rallying point— they need you. It's each man for himself, though all are fighting to keep the royal tent unbreached."

"Salim?"

"The Khalid have fled, I think, although they could be dead. I didn't have time to check."

"Stay out of sight. You're no use to us in the fray and I'd rather you kept alive."

"I'll watch and keep you briefed."

"Don't risk too much?"

"This time I can save many lives with my magic—I am obliged to take the risk because you and Ana are involved. I hope Maliz is too occupied to be sensing Iridor."

"Thank you," Lazar said, and although it hadn't been mentioned, Pez knew that was thanks for the time with Ana. As he watched the Spur run nimbly and silently down the dune, he felt a momentary guilt that he hadn't asked after Lazar's arm, but then Lazar didn't seem to care much anyway that blood was flowing down to his wrist; thank goodness the arrowhead was still buried, preventing the open wound from spouting too much blood at this stage. He also needed to think about how Lazar was suddenly talking to him through a mind link. This was new and assured him that Lazar was involved in Lyana's struggle. Pez cast a silent prayer to Lyana to protect Ana and Lazar and then he changed into Iridor to try to scout for a particular member of the Elim, one he hoped would not lose his life here this night.

LAZAR HIT THE BOTTOM of the dune at a full run and with such force that his sheer momentum, together with wheeling swords, killed five men before they even realized they were being attacked. He was shocked at how many men were in their camp and he had no idea who was foe or friend in the dark; he had to hope anyone from their own group would scream quickly or somehow recognize him before he dealt a killing blow.

After a momentary pause to take in the stupefying scene—many of the Elim were already dead, only a few were courageously fighting on, holding the royal tent secure—he settled himself in to the serious business of maiming. Lazar had never been a fan of slaughter. He held true to his creed that the single most important task in any battle is not to kill but to disable your enemies so that they can no longer kill you. He was only one man but he had the twin benefits of surprise and coming from the rear, which he used to best advantage now as he set about his subtle art of slashing through Achilles tendons, hacking off sword arms, chopping at knees or hands. Fighting with two swords was his specialty—it was a Galinsean skill, and he had been one of his nation's leading talents. Since he was old enough to support his own weight, his father had thrust a practice sword into each hand, and so Lucien had learned from a tender age to wield a sword equally well with either hand. As he grew older he understood and mastered the art of separating himself mentally into two fighting sides, each working independently of the other. It was no mean skill.

If any had been capable of taking time away from his own fight to watch him now, he would have been awed as Lazar dispatched twenty-five men, single-handedly, in what seemed merely moments. In fact someone was observing him. A man on a camel, shrouded in black, so like a shadow that if not for the beast, Lazar would not have seen him.

THE MAN IN BLACK robes silently applauded. He'd never seen such a magnificent display of ferocity. Such single-mindedness, such devotion to the cause. This fighter was a man to admire.

A rough count told him thirty of his men now lay mortally wounded or incapacitated. He worried not for any of them. Their lives had been given years ago; this was the culmination of their faith, when they proved their devotion. On the warrior's side, they were down to one brave Elim, holding off several of the watcher's men, but he could not last, for there was a line of others ready to take any of his enemies' place as soon as they fell.

Perhaps these two were worth saving.

"Shaba!" The command was heard and the fighters, all shrouded in dark robes, only their eyes visible, obeyed that instruction and immediately froze.

SALAZIN, BLEEDING FROM SEVERAL slashes, was breathing hard and looked to Lazar now for his lead. Lazar had barely broken a sweat but none of the intensity of his fighting rage had left him. He had eyes only for the leader on the camel. "Who are you?" he demanded.

The man responded in perfect Percherese. "I think I'm your savior."

Lazar ignored the facetious response. "Why have you attacked us?"

"Why not? You enter my land without permission, steal

my fowl—although I understand a debt was paid, as is right, and—"

"Your land? This is desert!"

"My desert," the stranger replied, unruffled. "The Empty belongs to me."

"Where? What do you own in this wilderness," Lazar asked, "that you are permitted to slaughter for it?"

"That is my business."

"No warning, no messengers?"

"You should not be here. You entered the region of my fortress and you—"

"Fortress!" Lazar's anger turned to cold rage. "For what have you killed these innocent travelers?" he yelled, incensed that only one of the Elim remained alive.

"Trespass," the shrouded one replied. In the burning torchlight, Lazar looked lost for a response. "And the fact that I hate the Percherese," the man added. "I'm hoping your Zar is behind that tent flap. It would give me great pleasure to kill him, especially as I understand he is childless."

Lazar felt his blood turn to ice. Over his dead body only would this murderer take what stood behind that tent flap. "I am Lazar, Spur of Percheron, I—"

"I know who you are. Bring out the royals," the stranger commanded.

Salazin, the remaining Elim, raised his sword. It was useless. Lazar made a gesture to the mute that in any language meant: *stay your hand*. They were hopelessly outnumbered; he would have to risk that this madman had no interest in lesser royals. It was a big risk—these were men, after all, and the people about to be presented were women. Fair game.

Maliz, Herezah, and Ana were dragged out of the tent. Lazar looked to Herezah and shook his head slightly. He knew he could count on her to understand. More torches were lit so their enemies could see their captives more clearly.

"Ah, no young Zar. Who are these people?"

He addressed the royal party but Lazar answered. "Vizier Tariq is making a diplomatic journey to Galinsea. He brings with him his wife and daughter." To her credit Herezah didn't flinch, although Lazar knew what insult he had just given. He silently thanked her with his eyes for understanding and cooperating. She bowed her head, as did Ana.

"I don't know much about you, Tariq, but for some reason I thought the Percherese Grand Vizier was unmarried and childless."

Maliz bowed. "Sir, so did I." Lazar felt his insides do a flip. So the coward finally emerges. "Until my beautiful Farim came to me."

"Farim?" the stranger queried.

"My new wife." Maliz gave a soft conspiratorial sigh. "I lay with this woman when I was a younger man. I did not know that my seed had quickened her womb and she had given birth to our beautiful Ana here. Farim came to me when Ana was turning fifteen and told me the truth. She needed help securing a good husband, a good life, for our daughter. She had never asked for my assistance before. I had forgotten about her entirely, in truth. But Farim is persuasive and far more handsome in these older years than the gangly young creature I recall having bedded. And Ana is a beauty; I could not resist her needs."

"How do you know that she is your child? You took the word of a woman you had not known for so many years."

Maliz shrugged. "Would you not if this pair were presented

to you, sir? I am old, I am wealthy, I have nothing in my life. Farim and Ana have given me reason to wake up and bless my stars. Whether Ana is of my seed or not, it is irrelevant. These women are mine now."

"Very admirable," the man said, his head to one side. "Bring the girl closer."

Lazar had silently reveled in the Grand Vizier's supremely crafted lies but now his heart lurched as Ana moved to stand in front of the stranger. With no warning the man ripped away her veil.

"You need never cover yourself for any man," he growled. "Choose it only if you do so for your own modesty or faith." He pulled her farther aside, lifting a warning finger to Lazar and to the Vizier.

"Come, child."

"Where do you take her?" Lazar demanded, fear coursing through him.

"I wish to speak privately with this girl who stares at me so defiantly."

Lazar could only watch helplessly as Ana was drawn away.

HE WITHDREW ANA TO behind his camel and then closer to some dunes before he spoke directly to her. "Any other Percherese woman would have screamed, or covered her face with her hands if I'd done that to them."

"I am not any other Percherese woman, sir. I follow no man's rules."

He removed his own face covering, but in the dark she could not make out his features. "If you follow no man, who do you follow?"

"Only my god, sir."

"Zarab is not a worthy—"

"I spit on Zarab, sir," she said for his hearing only, and she felt rather than saw the tension she provoked within him. "I follow Lyana alone. And if that curses me in your eyes, I am not afraid of you."

He brought his hands together in a gesture akin to prayer, rested his fingertips against his mouth as he considered her. "Lyana. Do you believe she will come again?"

"I believe she is rising, sir. She will be amongst us very shortly."

He gave a deep chuckle. "You intrigue me, Ana."

"And what of the others . . . my parents, the Spur?" She carefully omitted Pez, for she had not seen him. Hopefully he might raise some alarm, perhaps persuade the Khalid to rally and fight.

"They do not intrigue me."

"You're going to kill them?"

He cocked his head to one side again. "The Spur is an extraordinary fighter. He certainly has a keen interest in you."

"What do you mean?" she stammered, caught off guard.

It amused him. "I mean he has unwittingly revealed himself to me. Throughout the Grand Vizier's monologue, the Spur's eyes never left you."

"That's not true," she whispered.

"How would you know? Your head was bowed. He briefly gave attention to your mother but his concern is for you alone. Does he love you, Ana?"

"I . . . I hardly know him," she answered, flustered, frightened for Lazar.

"Well, because you mean something to that proud man, whose fighting prowess I can only admire, I shall give them a sporting chance. And I shall give him a choice."

"What choice?"

"Heart over duty. Which do you think he'll choose?"

She shook her head. "I don't understand."

"Let me give you a demonstration, then," he whispered close to her ear. "I'm thinking the very proud and honorable Spur of Percheron will choose duty . . . very sad, because I think you would like otherwise. Come, child, watch."

ANA AND HER CAPTOR reemerged, much to Lazar's relief, but the pause that followed felt too sinister for him to trust this stranger, who had already killed on a whim. The metallic smell of blood clung like a death shroud about him, warning of more to come. The first streaks of dawn were slashing across the wide desert sky; though it was barely light, he could now finally pick out the ghostly eyes of their oppressor; the rest of his face was hidden behind his desert turban.

"Brothers, sisters, a decision has been reached. It is because of this beautiful creature who stands beside me that I have decided to spare your lives . . ." Herezah sighed in visible relief at his words, and Maliz's shoulders relaxed. " . . . for the time being," the stranger continued. "What happens next is entirely up to your Spur."

Now all of them looked baffled. Lazar tensed and noticed Salazin firming his grip on his sword. The stranger was certainly not done with them.

"You have two fighters with you," the man explained to Maliz and Herezah. "Both formidable, especially your Spur. He is surely worth ten of mine." He rapidly spoke in his own tongue. They watched as a dozen of his warriors stood to attention and walked to stand in a line not far from the royal tents. Lazar didn't need to be told what would happen next. He dropped his angry gaze to the ground, marshaling his strength, turning his fury into focus, readying himself for battle and the inevitable grief that he knew was coming.

The man said something else to his men, and as one, they responded in an affirmative-sounding cheer.

Returning his attention to the captives, the stranger explained, "On my signal, my men will hunt you down and kill you as they choose. What stands between each of you and death is this man over here"—he pointed to Salazin—"and your Spur, who has a rather nasty decision to make." He chuckled.

"Wait!" Maliz cried out. "This is barbaric."

"Then we are brothers-in-arms, Vizier. I have never found that your precious Zars over the years, or the god you pray to, have shown any mercy."

"To whom?" Maliz beseeched.

"I'm sure you'll work it out, Vizier, when the hour is upon you. And it's coming; that, I promise you."

Maliz began to jabber. "What are we expected to do, unarmed, without mounts?"

"Run, I think, would be my first suggestion. My second would be that you leave right now." Lazar could tell he did not jest; there was no longer any amusement in his voice.

Maliz looked at Herezah and she in turn looked to Lazar. They both looked terrified. Salazin was the first to move, silently ushering the pair, pushing them into a trot. Herezah tripped on a tent rope, stumbling slightly, but Salazin grabbed her, kept her upright, pushed her forward. Maliz didn't bother to wait for the Valide; he was already running as fast as his legs would allow. Lazar gritted his teeth, felt sure he would run through the cowardly Vizier with his blade if he got the chance. He looked back at the man who taunted them.

"Give me Ana," he demanded.

"No, Spur. She is mine. As I said, I find her intriguing. You may rest assured that her life alone is safe, although you now have the power to secure the Vizier's . . . and the Valide's." At Lazar's start, he chuckled again. "Did you think I would fall for those lies? They were nicely done, too, and if not for my reliable information, I might have believed them. But no, I know who that man is and I know that his companion is the Zar's mother and I know that beside me stands his new Zaradine and Absolute Favorite. I also know that you and she have a . . . special understanding, shall we say."

"I'm warning you, whoever you are. Do not lay a finger on Ana."

The stranger laughed. "You are not in a position to threaten me, Lazar. I still have twenty men ready to cut you down, and as good as you are with both of those blades, you will not catch me. But you can try. I know you want to." He shouted a command and Lazar looked in horror as the men who were lined up yelled some sort of war cry and began their pursuit of the desperately retreating trio.

"Here is my camel, saddled and ready," the man offered. "Take it, and hunt my men down as they hunt your people. You have a duty, Spur, to your Zar. His wife is safe—I give you my absolute word—but his mother is not. She is at risk of a horrible death, for my men have not had a woman in a long time."

Lazar felt the grip of panic around his insides. The despair of choice.

"Heart or duty, Spur? Choose."

Lazar looked out toward where Herezah had fallen over. Her pursuers were still some distance away and Salazin had turned to help her, sword raised. He would no doubt fight to his death to keep her safe for a few minutes more. But the men would be upon them soon. He returned a sad gaze to Ana.

"Ah, duty calls," the man said, laughing delightedly. "Say farewell to Ana, Spur. It's unlikely the two of you will ever see each other again."

"Ana," Lazar said, ignoring his tormentor. "I shall come for you."

Howling laughter followed his promise but Lazar met it with the disdain it deserved. He bowed to the woman he loved. "Wait for me," he impressed upon her, and before the man could taunt him further, he addressed him. "She is with child. The heir to Percheron. Do not harm her."

"I will not harm Ana, but I cannot say the same for the child."

"Heed my warning, stranger: I will come for you and I will have your blood."

The man ignored the warning, "Hurry, Lazar, they are almost upon the Valide," he warned.

Lazar ran and leaped upon the camel that had been cajoled to its knees. The handler let go of the rope that held the beast and it instantly pushed itself to its feet.

"What is your name?" Lazar demanded.

"I am Arafanz, of the Razaqin. May you and your kind never forget it."

Lazar urged the camel forward, then gave a final glance to Ana, whilst a slap on the animal's rump from the handler spurred it into an almost instant gallop. Lazar gave a blood-curdling howl, loading it with all of his hate, every ounce of fury he had ever felt. The camel, trained for battle, ran the men down easily, and from his vantage, Lazar no longer gave any quarter. He beheaded his foes, one after another, until four of them together managed to bring the camel down, at which point he leaped nimbly from the dying beast before it crushed him. Without breaking pace, Lazar continued to fight in a haze of bloodlust he had never felt before.

The remaining warriors kept backing their victims farther and farther from their camp. Herezah was hurt; she was limping and Lazar could see that she had been cut, blood blooming at various sites on her body. The men had deduced that attacking the Spur was useless—he was too good for all of them—so they concentrated their efforts on tormenting the helpless woman, hoping to draw Lazar into their midst and best him that way. Salazin, realizing their intent, dragged Herezah from the fray.

The warriors fought bravely, ferociously. If Lazar had had the opportunity, he would have marveled at their willingness to die. As it was, he had never encountered such lack of care for life and so he dispatched them as efficiently as he could. They were no match for his whirling swords. Salazin returned to the fight and, with one swing of his curved scimitar, took off a man's head, as Lazar finished off the final two with a series of concerted blows.

He bent over to breathe, unable to speak. It was too soon after his illness for this sort of exertion. Sucking in air, he used the time to gather his wits, to regain his calm. In the distance he could see that the camp was deserted and understood that Arafanz would have disappeared with Ana the moment he himself charged across the sands to fight.

"How is the Valide?" he asked, straightening.

"She needs the help of physics." Salazin's voice sounded gritty from lack of use and from his own exertions.

Lazar nodded, the direness of the situation sinking in. He needed to get the Valide back to Percheron. Without their royal emissary, the journey to Galinsea was now lost, and he could hardly go on alone, even if he'd wanted to, and leave the Valide.

No, his duty called. He could hear Arafanz's laughter still echoing in his mind. How well the man had played him.

"Where is Tariq?" he asked.

"Cowering somewhere," Salazin replied in a hiss.

"Find him. I will take the Valide."

The last of the mute guard nodded and jogged off in search of the Grand Vizier. Lazar trudged to where the Valide lay panting in the distance, bleeding in the sand. Dawn had broken fully, and although it was still cool, it would not remain so for long. He hoped she had not heard his murmured conversation with the "mute."

"Put your arms around my neck, Herezah," he said, and surprised himself with the gentleness in his voice. She opened her eyes, looked at him with an unsure frown. He lifted her easily and settled her into his arms. "I'm taking you home, Valide. Please stay alive, for all our sakes."

Herezah didn't smile but even injury had not cowed her biting wit. "And waste the chance to be this close to you for the first time in my life, Lazar? You jest." She breathed shallowly, her face pale. "No, I will not die. I think I will savor every moment." He would not look at her but he realized she knew he battled his emotions, understood that it must have taken every ounce of his strength to run toward her and not Ana. "Thank you, Lazar," she said quietly.

He had nothing more to say, although inwardly he set his promise in stone, carving it mentally on his heart, burning it into his flesh. He would return for Ana.

EPILOGUE

Pez had watched it all unfold with increasing horror. He could not hear what was being said, but it didn't take much expertise to work out what was happening once the man in black robes brought Ana back from behind the camel.

He had seen the intruders line up, had watched the heated exchange between Maliz and his captor, and then felt frustrated, helpless, when suddenly the Grand Vizier, Herezah, and Salazin had set off running. He knew what would come next.

Rightly enough, Lazar was wavering between giving chase and staying with Ana, who remained encircled by the stranger's arm in an embrace that looked all too proprietary. Pez knew he was keeping Ana; that explained Lazar's reluctance to leave. He wanted to save her but presumably she didn't need saving as such. The man looked relaxed—he would not hurt her. But he would hurt the others and that's where Lazar's duty lay. He was compelled to save the lives of the Grand Vizier and, especially, the Valide. She in particular was his responsibility. Ana was not under threat, Pez guessed.

And then he watched with shared despair as Lazar jumped onto the camel and gave chase. He would kill all the attackers, of that Pez was sure, but he could not be in two places at once. And Pez was also sure, as the stranger urged Ana onto another camel, that Lazar could not know where she was being taken. And in the vast desert, how would he ever find her again?

Ellyana had given him no clues, curse her, but she persisted in making him believe that Ana was vital to Lyana's rising. She had given him instructions so horrible that he had not wanted to carry them out; he had resisted, argued, but she had calmly impressed upon him that without this deed, all could be lost. And so he had enlisted the help of Salazin and together they had followed her bidding, hating it even as they went about their secret task. And then that night, Ellyana had reversed her instructions. It baffled Pez. But it still did not divert him from his duty as Iridor.

His duty remained with Ana—he was none the wiser as to whether she was the physical embodiment of the Mother Goddess, or just another pawn. But he could not take the chance. He would follow her captor; Iridor would be Lazar's eyes.

He cast a final glance toward the Spur in the distance, watched him cutting down the enemy expertly from behind, his camel reaching them with ease.

He had no time to reach Lazar to tell him what he was doing, and he would not risk a link through the Lore that could alert Maliz, or worse, alarm or distract Lazar. Already the black-robed men and Ana were well into the distance, moving fast.

The shifting sands would cover their tracks quickly enough, and without a beast of his own, Lazar could never give chase.

Pez transformed into Iridor. Then he flew. Harder, faster, than ever before, giving chase to an unknown enemy into the Empty Quarter of the Great Waste.

Courtesy of the author

FIONA MCINTOSH was born and raised in Sussex in the UK, but spent her early childhood commuting with her family between England and West Africa. She left a PR career in London to travel, and found herself in Australia, where she fell in love with the country, its people, and one person in particular. She has since roamed the world working for her own travel publishing company, which she ran with her husband until she took up writing full time. McIntosh lives with her family in South Australia.

You can find out more information about Fiona or chat with her on her bulletin board via her website: www.fionamcintosh.com.